NO. 17 CURIOSITY LANE

CHRISTIE BARLOW

One More Chapter
a division of HarperCollins*Publishers* Ltd
1 London Bridge Street
London SE1 9GF
www.harpercollins.co.uk

HarperCollins*Publishers*
Macken House, 39/40 Mayor Street Upper,
Dublin 1, D01 C9W8, Ireland

This paperback edition 2026
1
First published in Great Britain in ebook format
by HarperCollins*Publishers* 2026
Copyright © Christie Barlow 2026
Christie Barlow asserts the moral right to
be identified as the author of this work
A catalogue record of this book is available from the British Library

ISBN: 978-0-00-870809-2

This novel is entirely a work of fiction. The names, characters and incidents portrayed in it are the work of the author's imagination. Any resemblance to actual persons, living or dead, events or localities is entirely coincidental.

Printed and bound in the UK using 100% Renewable Electricity
by CPI Group (UK) Ltd

All rights reserved. No part of this publication may be reproduced, stored in a retrieval system, or transmitted, in any form or by any means, electronic, mechanical, photocopying, recording or otherwise, without the prior permission of the publishers.

Without limiting the exclusive rights of any author, contributor or the publisher of this publication, any unauthorised use of this publication to train generative artificial intelligence (AI) technologies is expressly prohibited. HarperCollins also exercise their rights under Article 4(3) of the Digital Single Market Directive 2019/790 and expressly reserve this publication from the text and data mining exception.

Christie Barlow is the number one international bestselling author of twenty-five romantic comedies including the iconic Love Heart Lane Series, *A Postcard from Puffin Island* and *The Story Shop*. She lives in a ramshackle cottage in a quaint village in the heart of Staffordshire with her two dogs.

Her writing career came as a lovely surprise when Christie decided to write a book to teach her children a valuable life lesson and show them that they are capable of achieving their dreams.

Christie writes about love, life, friendships and the importance of community spirit. She loves to hear from her readers and you can get in touch via X, Facebook and Instagram.

facebook.com/ChristieJBarlow
x.com/ChristieJBarlow
bookbub.com/authors/christie-barlow
instagram.com/christie_barlow

Also by Christie Barlow

The Love Heart Lane Series
Love Heart Lane
Foxglove Farm
Clover Cottage
Starcross Manor
The Lake House
Primrose Park
Heartcross Castle
The New Doctor at Peony Practice
New Beginnings at the Old Bakehouse
The Hidden Secrets of Bumblebee Cottage
A Summer Surprise at the Little Blue Boathouse
A Winter Wedding at Starcross Manor
The Library on Love Heart Lane
The Vintage Flower Van on Love Heart Lane

The Puffin Island Series
A Postcard from Puffin Island
The Lighthouse Daughters of Puffin Island
The Story Shop
The Café on the Coast
No. 17 Curiosity Lane

Standalones
Kitty's Countryside Dream
The Cosy Canal Boat Dream
A Home at Honeysuckle Farm

For Debbie Cook ('Debs')
30 December 1954 – 31 March 2025

In loving memory of a true warrior.

Debs faced life's hardest battles with extraordinary courage, grace and unwavering strength. She was brave, dignified and endlessly inspiring – the kind of woman whose light continues long after she's gone.

It is an honour to dedicate this book to her. Debs was a devoted reader of my stories, and knowing that my words brought her even a moment of joy, comfort or escape means more than I can ever truly express.

With love and deep respect, always.

Christie x

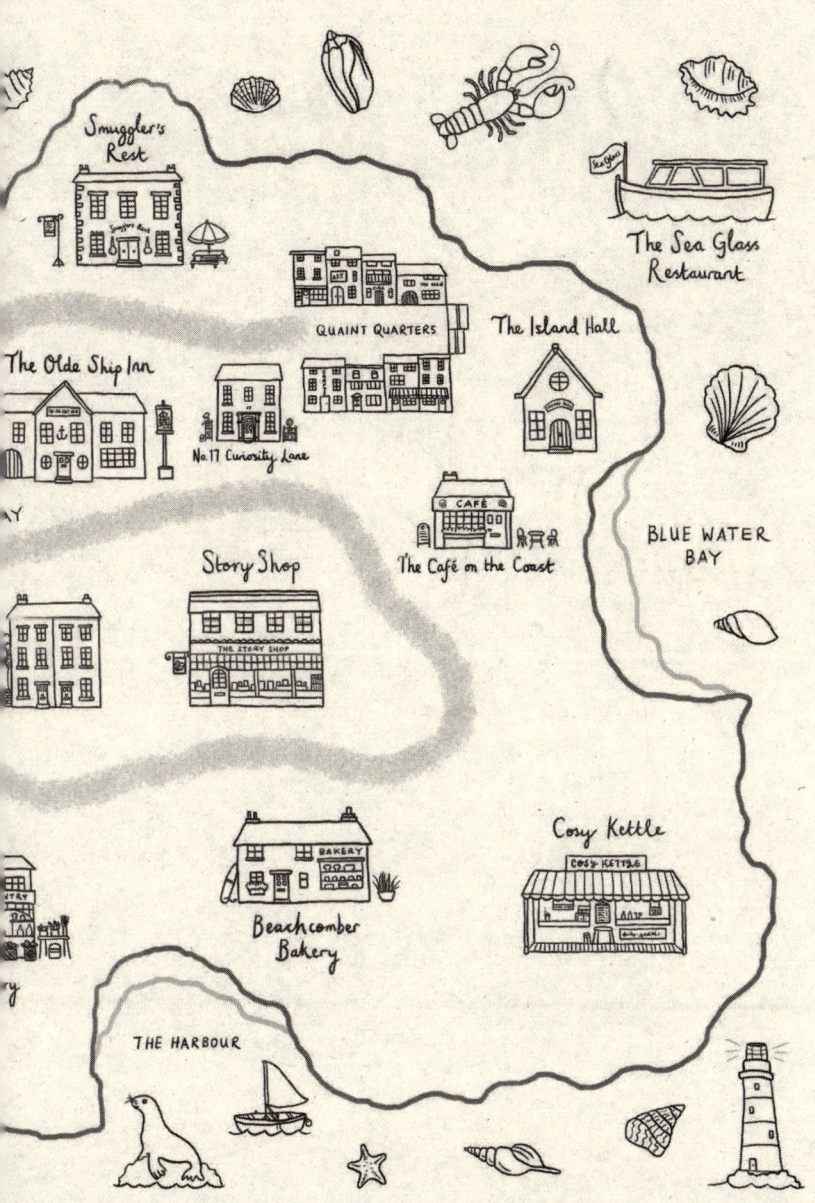

Prologue

Matilda Hartley knew she was dying. She had known for some time now, alerted by the weariness in her bones, the breathlessness that came too easily and the way the world around her had begun to slip into a gentle haze. But at eighty-five, she could not complain. Life had been long, rich and, in many ways, full. Yet she knew there were some wounds that had never healed.

For the past sixty years, Matilda had lived on Anchor Way, where she ran her beloved antique shop, No. 17 Curiosity Lane. Today, she had made her final visit to Edgar Carmichael, the local solicitor, whose office sat just next door to the shop. Edgar had been both her solicitor and her friend for six decades, and he was a man she trusted completely. This morning, he had simply nodded as she signed her name on the final will and testament, the document that would ensure the shop she had poured her heart and soul into wouldn't end up in the wrong hands. She had left everything to Fern Talbot. Her sister's grandchild.

Fern likely had no idea Matilda even existed. They'd been strangers all their lives, with Matilda estranged from her family for what felt like for ever. Still, Fern had been going through life unaware that, somewhere in the background, an old woman had been quietly watching over her all along.

Matilda had long ago accepted that there would never be any family reconciliation, and now her sister had passed away, there was no chance. But Fern was different. Hopefully, she had not been poisoned by the events of the past, and didn't know anything about the lies. Hopefully, her innocence would help her to uncover the truth.

Matilda traced a finger along the edge of the vinyl record she held in her hands. The label bore a name that everyone knew, a name that should have been hers. Beside it sat the music box, its ornate carvings delicate yet sturdy, a relic of a secret so long buried that only two men alive still knew its weight. She exhaled. The past had done its best to bury her, but now, with the end in sight, she wasn't about to go quietly. Sixty-five years ago, she'd gone to her family looking for help, hoping for some kind of justice. Instead, they'd looked at her with cold eyes and shut the door. They didn't believe her. Worse still, her sister turned on her, whispering that she was merely jealous, and losing her mind.

She had lost everything that day.

Her family. Her reputation. Her name.

Yet, decades later, she still held the key to the truth. But time was running out.

Matilda looked around the shop and stared at all the oddities and artefacts she had gathered over a lifetime. She had spent years crafting this place into a sanctuary for lost things and forgotten stories. Perhaps, if fate willed it, Fern would find the truth Matilda had so carefully buried in the shop, knowing it was the only thing that could change history.

Chapter One

Fern Talbot shut the lid of her laptop before stretching her arms above her head and then rolling her shoulders. Another workday done. Her inbox was still overflowing with interview requests and press releases, but for now, they could wait. Music journalism was her passion, but even she needed a break from industry gossip and album reviews at six p.m. on a Friday.

Swinging her legs off the couch, she padded across the polished wooden floor of her Fulham apartment, the rumble of the London traffic a distant backdrop through the open window. Her home was everything she'd ever wanted; chic yet cosy, filled with sleek furniture, framed vinyl covers, and a record player that sat beside a neatly stacked collection of albums. The top-floor flat offered a sliver of a view of the iconic London skyline through its large sash windows, and was an urban haven that suited her perfectly.

Hearing the letterbox clang, she bent down to collect the post from the doormat. A fan of digital convenience, she rarely received anything important by mail. The usual assortment greeted her: a pizza menu, a flyer for a yoga retreat, and yet another reminder about retirement planning, something she was determined to ignore for at least another few decades. But nestled among the junk was something different. A thick, cream-coloured envelope embossed with a solicitor's stamp.

She turned it over in her hands. The name printed on the front ... Edgar Carmichael & Associates – meant nothing to her, nor did the address beneath it: Puffin Island. She had never even heard of the place. Intrigued, she slid her finger under the flap and tore it open. The paper inside was thick and smooth, the kind that suggested some kind of importance. The enclosed letter was as formal as it was bewildering.

Dear Ms. Talbot,

We regret to inform you of the passing of your great-aunt, Matilda Hartley. As the sole beneficiary of her estate, you have inherited her business, No. 17 Curiosity Lane, Puffin Island...

A great-aunt? She didn't have a great-aunt. At least, not one she was aware of. Fern had never met a Matilda Hartley in her life. She barely had any family left; her parents were gone, her grandparents long since passed, and no one had ever mentioned a Matilda Hartley. Her own story had always been a quiet one. She had been adopted as a baby by older parents who'd longed for children but had been forced to give up hope of a biological child and instead seek other avenues to fulfil their dream of being parents. Her mother was fifty at the time, her father nearly seventy, but they were young at heart and energetic, throwing themselves into raising her. But time marched on and things changed. By the time Fern turned ten, her father was gone, and when she was twenty-two, she lost her mother, too. And there had never been talk of distant cousins or great-aunts with antique shops.

Yet, according to the letter, this Matilda was her great-aunt. And for reasons unknown, she had left Fern an antique shop of all things. She had never once set foot in an antique shop unless you counted the time she'd bought a vintage Rolling Stones T-shirt at a flea market in Camden.

Fern blinked. Then she read the letter again, this time aloud, as if the words might make more sense if spoken.

'No. 17 Curiosity Lane?' she muttered. 'What in the actual…'

Perplexed, she grabbed her laptop and googled 'Puffin Island'.

Immediately, images and a description popped up.

Puffin Island gives a distinct and spectacular character to the Northumberland coastline just off the town of Sea's End.

She clicked on the images. Independent shops lined a charismatic old high street called Lighthouse Lane, and more bespoke shops were dotted along the picture-postcard harbour beside a pretty lighthouse. There were rainbow cottages, an art gallery, a book shop, a café and, apparently, one antique shop that now belonged to her.

And then she saw it. A photo of No. 17 Curiosity Lane. Fern zoomed in to take a closer look. From the outside it looked like a relic of a bygone era. Its exterior, no doubt once charming, showed signs of wear and neglect, the large windows at the front framed by peeling, chipped wood, revealing cluttered windowsills inside. The sign, 'No. 17 Curiosity Lane' in vintage lettering hung askew, the faded 'Matilda Hartley' beneath the name barely legible. Fern could imagine the sign creaking in the coastal breeze, scarcely clinging to its last days of grandeur.

Outside the shop was a trestle table cluttered with old things: books, trinkets, cups and saucers… It all looked horrifying to Fern. It was not a world she was familiar with.

'What am I supposed to do with an antique shop?' she muttered to herself, pacing her minimalist kitchen. Her entire world was built around music: reviewing albums, interviewing bands, chasing the next big thing. Her life was backstage passes and exclusive listening parties, not dusty old furniture and porcelain figurines. She shuddered just thinking about it.

She pulled up her emails and fired off a quick message to the solicitor, requesting clarification. Maybe there had been a mistake. Maybe there was another Fern Talbot out there, one who actually cared about brass candlesticks and Victorian tea sets.

She wasn't expecting a reply at this time on a Friday night, but by the time she had finished drafting an article about a rising indie band, the reply had come through.

No mistake. You are the named beneficiary. The shop and all its contents are legally yours.

Fern still couldn't quite believe it. 'Bloody hell, why me? A shop full of junk to clear out and a dilapidated building to sell.'

It was absurd. Completely and utterly ridiculous. But there was no avoiding it. She needed to go to Puffin Island, sift through whatever mess this mysterious great-aunt had left behind and offload the place as quickly as possible. Then she could get back to real life – the one that didn't involve dusty antiques or crumbling shopfronts.

Her phone buzzed.

It was Ella.

Ella had been her friend since the very first day of primary school, when they both had freckles across their noses, knee-high white socks and rucksacks that were far too big for their small shoulders. They'd been placed in the same class, two nervous five-year-olds sitting side by side, eyeing each other cautiously until disaster struck.

During break time, Ella had struggled to open her juice box, her small fingers fumbling with the straw. In a moment of unfortunate determination, she squeezed too hard, sending a stream of orange juice straight down the front of Fern's pristine uniform. There had been a split second of horror, Ella's eyes widening, Fern's mouth dropping open, before Fern, instead of bursting into tears, had simply grinned. And in a moment of pure five-year-old logic, she had deliberately squeezed her own juice box right back at Ella.

By the time the teacher arrived to break up the 'juice war', the two girls were howling with laughter, their uniforms sticky, their friendship cemented.

From that day on, they were inseparable. They went through primary and high school side by side, surviving disastrous haircuts, impossible maths exams and terrible dates, and now, by some stroke of fate – or perhaps the sheer strength of their long-standing friendship – they worked at the same music magazine and lived in the same London apartment block, just a few doors apart.

Ella was the holy trinity of Fern's social life, part agony aunt, the sharer of her cocktails, and the voice of reason she occasionally ignored.

ELLA
You're coming tonight, right?

Fern swiped open the message just as a second one came through.

ELLA
You cannot bail on me! LUST THEORY are in town!

Ah. That explained the urgency. Every time the band rolled through London, Fern and Ella were front and centre. It was tradition. Drinks, music, a little too much fun and, more often than not, an over-friendly liaison for Fern with Jax Devlin, the band's lead singer.

Jax was everything a rock star should be – leather jackets, wild curls and a voice that could melt anyone within a fifty-mile radius. Charisma dripped off him like expensive aftershave, and he knew exactly how to use it. He was trouble. Glorious, thrilling, predictable trouble.

Fern's gaze flicked between Ella's texts and the letter clutched in her other hand.

The sensible thing, the easy thing, would be to go out, drink overpriced cocktails and wake up tomorrow with a headache and the scent of Jax's aftershave lingering on her skin.

Instead, she typed a reply.

FERN
Something's come up this weekend. I'm taking annual leave for a week. There's been an unexpected death in my family. I'll update you soon. Sorry!

She hit send before she could change her mind then sent her boss an email. She knew he would understand, and if anything urgent came up she could work remotely.

After the email was sent, Fern checked the train app, noting that the earliest departure from London to Northumberland was at eight a.m. She would need to change trains at Newcastle at 11.15 a.m., before boarding a connecting service to Alnwick at 11.45 a.m. From there, a final local train to Sea's End would depart at 12.30 p.m., arriving just before 1.15 p.m.

The journey would take just over five hours, not including the time it would take to cross the causeway to Puffin Island, assuming the tide was on her side.

Walking into her bedroom, she pulled out a suitcase from under her bed, unzipped it and opened her wardrobe doors. 'What does one even pack for an island full of antiques?' she mused, half to herself, half to the void. Definitely not the leather jacket she wore to gigs or the towering heels she'd perfected the art of running in. With a sigh, she packed the usual necessities then tossed in some jeans, a couple of sweaters and – grudgingly – a pair of practical boots. Her laptop followed, because there was no way she was abandoning work completely, even if it meant writing from the middle of nowhere.

She hesitated as she reached for her notebook, the one where she scribbled unfinished thoughts about the state of the music industry, half-written reviews and, occasionally, lyrics she would never admit to writing. Tucking it into the side pocket, she zipped up the case and exhaled. Tomorrow, she'd be on her way to Puffin Island, a place she'd never been, to deal with an inheritance she'd never wanted, left by a woman she'd never known.

Whatever she found there, she was certain of one thing: it wouldn't change a thing. She'd sell the shop, wrap up any loose ends and be back in London before anyone even noticed she was gone.

She was packed and she was ready. Or as ready as she could ever be.

Chapter Two

Fern shot upright, heart pounding as the shrill chime of her alarm shattered the blissful silence. Disoriented, she slapped her hand around the bedside table, knocking over a lamp, and what she really hoped wasn't last night's half-finished cup of tea, before finally locating her phone. It was six a.m. On a Saturday. A time she usually only encountered when stumbling out of a Soho club, heels in hand, with regret setting in for the midnight tequila shots.

She flopped back against the pillows with a groan. This was unnatural. Criminal, even. But then, through the sleepy fog, the reason for her ungodly wake-up call broke through. The train. Puffin Island. No. 17 Curiosity Lane. Matilda Hartley's shop. Correction: Fern's shop.

With a noise somewhere between a sigh and a battle cry, she forced herself out of bed and shuffled towards the bathroom. A quick shower blasted away the worst of her grogginess, the scent of citrus shampoo snapping her into something resembling alertness. As she massaged foam into her scalp, the reality of the day settled in. She still wasn't entirely sure what she was walking into, but one thing was certain – she was about to find out.

Thirty minutes later, dressed in dark jeans and a fitted trench coat, Fern slipped out of her flat into the warm London morning. She quickened her pace towards Fulham Broadway, dodging a man wielding an oversized laptop bag like a medieval weapon and a woman powerwalking with the determination of someone late for a very important meeting or a very good breakfast.

Euston Station, eight a.m. train, coffee. In that order.

Descending the steps, she joined the pack of Londoners who had long since accepted that personal space was a myth. She couldn't understand why the tube was as busy as a weekday rush hour on a Saturday morning, but the proliferation of Lycra suggested there was some sort of race or marathon happening this morning. She reached the platform just as the train arrived, the doors slid open and Fern braced herself. It was the usual morning sardine-tin scenario, but she was a seasoned commuter. Sucking in a breath (not too deep, as there was always the risk of inhaling someone else's deodorant or body odour), she wedged herself inside, clutching her suitcase like a life raft.

The train jolted forward, and she swayed in time with the crowd, riding the wave of bodies like an unwilling participant in a very slow-motion mosh pit. A man's newspaper smacked her shoulder, someone's coffee threatened to tip onto her trench coat, and an apologetic stranger's backpack was now essentially her new dance partner.

She made the change from the District to the Victoria line at

No. 17 Curiosity Lane

Victoria and then began the journey north through central London.

With each stop, she inched closer to the door, mentally preparing for her grand exit. As the platform at Euston loomed into view, she angled her suitcase like a battering ram and went for it. The trick was to move with confidence, but not so aggressively that she ended up in an accidental game of human dominoes.

Freedom. Cool air. Space to breathe. She'd made it.

All she needed now was caffeine. Then she could make a mad dash for the next leg of her journey.

She took a deep breath, glancing at the departures board, glad to see that the next train was on time. She assumed – hoped, really – that it couldn't possibly be as claustrophobic as the tube had been. With that small reassurance, she grabbed a coffee from the station kiosk and collapsed onto a bench.

Once the train pulled in, Fern hopped on quickly, but still found herself weaving through carriage after carriage, dodging suitcases and apologising as she squeezed past standing passengers. Finally, in the very end carriage, she spotted an empty seat next to a man with a guitar propped up against his leg. His blond curls were a little out of control, as if they had a mind of their own, and a faint shadow of stubble sharpened the angles of his jaw. Dressed in jeans, a white T-shirt and denim jacket, he somehow carried off the double-denim look with effortless ease. His well-worn Adidas trainers, scuffed and softened by years of use, hinted at a man who valued comfort over trends. Then there was his smile, as he caught her eye and moved his guitar to make more room for her.

The second she took in his aroma, she hesitated before sitting down. His aftershave was unexpected, something woody, warm, with a hint of spice, like cedar and amber, with the faintest trace of citrus lingering beneath. It wasn't overpowering, but instead strangely inviting. She slid into the seat beside him, after lifting her suitcase on to the luggage rack. A sideways glance confirmed he was watching her, the corner of his mouth twitching like he was holding back a grin. Caught, she quickly looked away, only to find herself smirking as well.

Twenty minutes into the journey, the stranger spoke. 'Hey,' he said, his voice carrying an easy confidence. 'Long trip ahead?'

Usually, she avoided conversation on public transport at all costs, but something about him made it difficult not to engage.

'Yes,' she replied, surprising herself by matching his energy. 'Involving a tube, a train, then a bus across a causeway.'

'Puffin Island?' he guessed.

She raised a brow. 'Are you psychic?'

'The causeway gave it away,' he said with a grin. 'Beautiful place.'

'I've never been before, and I won't be staying long. I'm just there for some family business. Not exactly a holiday.'

He nodded thoughtfully. 'Still, not a bad place for whatever family business you've got going on. I'm Daniel.'

'Fern. It's a family business I knew nothing about. Apparently, I've just inherited a junk shop.'

'That sounds rubbish.' He smiled, holding up his hands. 'Sorry, bad joke.'

She playfully rolled her eyes as her gaze drifted towards his guitar. 'So, do you play?' she asked. 'Are you in a band?'

He chuckled. 'Not quite. I play for me, but busk sometimes.'

'That's cool,' she said, tilting her head. 'How long have you been playing?'

'Not long, actually. A couple of years.' He ran a hand over the guitar case. 'My boss taught me. She was into music and made me play so she could sing.' His voice softened, and for the first time since she'd sat down, his smile faltered. 'She's just passed away.'

'I'm so sorry,' Fern said gently. 'I didn't mean to…'

'It's okay.' He gave a small, sad smile. 'She had a good life.'

For a moment, they sat in silence, the hum of the train filling the space between them. Then, at the exact same moment, they both opened their mouths to speak.

They stopped, stared at each other, then laughed.

There was a twinkle in his eye, and Fern was taken by surprise, feeling a flutter in her stomach.

'You go first…' they chorused in unison.

Then laughed again.

Before either of them could continue, the train ground to a halt, but there wasn't a station in sight.

A murmur of confusion rippled through the carriage as people glanced through the windows. They were in the middle of nowhere. Then an announcement sounded through the carriage.

'We are experiencing a power failure. Engineers are on their way, but we anticipate a significant delay. Please remain on board. We apologise for the inconvenience and will keep you updated.'

A collective groan filled the carriage. Fern's stomach sank. Of course, the universe would throw this at her today. She exhaled, shifting slightly in her seat as the train remained stubbornly still. She glanced at Daniel, who seemed entirely unbothered by the delay.

'Well, that's just perfect,' she muttered, folding her arms.

Daniel shot her a grin. 'Look at it this way, we've been gifted more time to chat. Fate's doing us a favour.'

She arched an eyebrow. 'You think being stranded on a train is romantic?'

'Absolutely. A forced proximity trope in real life.'

She couldn't stop the smile on her face and glanced towards his left hand – no ring – but someone as good-looking as him was bound to have a girlfriend.

Just at that second there was a loud rumble. Embarrassed, Fern glanced at her stomach. She had only grabbed a coffee at the station and was hungrier than she'd realised.

Daniel smiled and opened his rucksack, pulling out a neatly wrapped sandwich. 'Should have been for my lunch, but it sounds like you need breakfast and I can't have someone going hungry on my watch.' He gave her a warm smile that made her stomach flip more than the hunger pains.

He offered her half the sandwich. 'Cheese salad. Homemade.'

She hesitated for only a second before accepting it. 'Thanks. That's … really nice of you. Only if you're sure though.'

'I'm sure.'

Taking a bite of the sandwich, she nearly groaned with delight. 'This is really good. A sandwich always tastes better when someone else makes it.'

He smiled at her and gestured to her mouth, and she quickly wiped the mayonnaise from her lip.

When they'd finished the sandwich, he retrieved a KitKat

from his bag, unwrapped it and snapped it in two. Without a word, he handed her a piece.

Fern took it with a small smile, their fingers brushing briefly.

The old woman opposite them let out a wistful sigh. 'It's so lovely to see such kindness. I met my husband on a train,' she continued, a gleam in her eye. 'Euston to Lichfield Trent Valley. I was twenty-four, and so was he. We laughed the whole way. Neither of us wanted to get off. So he didn't.' She smiled; a soft smile, full of memory. 'He stayed with me the whole journey. Then the rest of my life.'

Fern pressed a hand to her heart. 'That's so beautiful.'

A beat of silence passed. Then…

'But that's not…'

'We're not…'

They spoke at the same time, their words tumbling over each other. The old woman simply patted her handbag with a knowing smile. Fern's heart was doing something entirely ridiculous to her chest as they both stopped speaking and gave each other a smile.

'Hear that? We're a picture of romance,' teased Daniel.

Fern played along with a mock-serious nod. 'Clearly, we're meant to be.'

The young boy accompanying the woman, pointed at Daniel's guitar case. 'Can you play for us?'

'My grandson,' the woman shared.

Daniel grinned. 'I could. But do you want to try?'

The boy's eyes widened. 'Really?'

'Of course.' Daniel guided him through a few simple chords, patient and encouraging. The boy's excitement was contagious, drawing smiles from the other passengers.

Someone clapped along as Daniel took the guitar and translated the chords into an easy melody.

Fern found herself watching him closely. He was charismatic in a way that felt effortless, his easy-going nature making strangers feel like old friends. How had she never met anyone like him before?

Just then, her phone buzzed in her pocket. She pulled it out to find a text from Ella.

> **ELLA**
> You missed a great night last night, only just getting home!

Next came a succession of photographs, and there he was, Jax Devlin. The photos showed him backstage with a cigarette in one hand and a bottle of beer in the other, surrounded as usual by a bunch of girls. She wondered which one he'd taken home.

Fern sighed, locking her phone and shoving it back into her pocket. She shouldn't care – she didn't care … or at least that's what she kept telling herself. Jax Devlin was nothing more than a bad habit, a comfortable, predictable disaster she kept returning to because the alternative was stepping into the unknown.

But as she watched Daniel strumming the guitar, charming an entire train carriage with nothing but a few chords and a smile, she realised just how tired she was. Tired of late-night texts and early-morning regrets. Tired of men who only knew how to love themselves.

Daniel glanced up then, catching her staring. 'What?' he asked, brow quirked in amusement.

'Nothing,' she said quickly, holding his gaze, and for the

first time in a long time, she wondered if maybe, just maybe, there was more to life than chasing a thrill that always left her feeling empty.

It was three hours before the train finally jolted forwards. Daniel was still entertaining the carriage, guiding the young boy through a simple rhythm while the other passengers tapped along. Fern hadn't stopped smiling, because whilst being stuck on an unmoving train for three hours would usually have frustrated her, she was very much relaxed and having a good time. Watching Daniel made her want to know more about him.

But then, with a sudden shift in momentum, the train began to slow. The overhead tannoy crackled to life, a voice saying, 'Next stop, Brackenholt.'

Daniel's hands stilled on the guitar. His brow furrowed, a flicker of confusion crossing his face before his eyes widened in horror as he looked out of the window.

'Shit.' He shot up so fast he nearly knocked over his rucksack. 'This is my stop!'

Fern blinked. 'Wait, what?'

But there was no time. He was already grabbing his things in a frantic scramble, shoving the guitar back into its case and slinging his rucksack over one shoulder.

The train gave a final shudder as it came to a complete stop. Daniel turned to Fern, a mixture of regret and urgency flashing across his face.

'I ... uh...' He hesitated and, in that half-second, something hung between them. Something unspoken. Something neither of them had expected.

The doors hissed open. Daniel took a step towards them but was still looking at Fern.

Fern sat frozen, willing herself to say something, anything. But what?

And then the moment slipped away. Daniel shot her one last crooked smile, a glint of something unreadable in his eyes, before dashing towards the doors. He jumped off the train just before a whistle sounded and the doors slid shut. He was gone.

Fern sat there, heart racing, a hollow sort of ache settling in her chest.

She'd never got his number.

She hadn't even asked.

The train lurched forward once more, carrying her away from a man who, against all odds, had made her feel something real for the first time in a long time.

The old woman sighed wistfully. 'That's how the best love stories start, you know. Unexpected. Unfinished.'

Fern shook her head. 'This isn't a love story.'

The old woman simply smiled. 'We'll see.'

Chapter Three

Feeling a pang of disappointment as the train carriage emptied, Fern sank back into her seat. Daniel was gone and now all she had to look forward to with each passing mile was the chaos of No. 17 Curiosity Lane. There was only one more stop, Sea's End, when the coast finally came into view. The vast, endless stretch of sea contrasted sharply with her view back in London. Instead of towering buildings and crowded streets, the horizon seemed infinite, the water glimmering in shades of turquoise and silver, breaking against the rocks in a rhythmic, soothing pattern. Fern's gaze swept across the dramatic coastline. It was beautiful, a wild beauty she didn't often see.

Two minutes later the train pulled into the quaint station at Sea's End, picture-perfect and exuding warmth and charm. The station was small but vibrant, with bright hanging baskets overflowing with petunias and geraniums in a riot of pinks, purples and reds, swaying gently in the breeze. The whitewashed station building, with its cheerful yellow trim, stood against the backdrop of a sparkling blue sky, accented by the sound of waves crashing in the distance. The platform was dotted with benches, all freshly painted, and a couple of friendly station staff waved as the train slowed to a stop. Gulls flew overhead, their calls mixing with the scent of the sea that filled the air. All she needed to do now was catch a bus across the causeway, and though she was three hours later than planned, she held on to the hope that the tide hadn't turned yet, and she could still make it to the island.

She made her way to the bus stop just outside the train station entrance, where a small group of disgruntled passengers had gathered. After a couple of minutes, the verdict was clear: the bus had broken down. The next one wouldn't be there for hours, and by that time the causeway would be submerged under the rising tide. And Fern? She'd be stuck in the town.

Her fingers moved automatically, pulling out her phone to check for an Uber. A couple of hopeful taps and … nothing. No cars. No drivers.

She turned to a woman standing nearby. 'There don't seem to be any Ubers in the area?'

'Ubers haven't found their way here yet,' came the reply.

'Really? No Ubers?'

'The causeway is walkable, if you don't mind the unpredictable terrain, the encroaching tide or the ever-present chance of being pooed on by the gulls.' The woman cackled with laughter.

This wasn't how Fern had imagined her arrival, but she had no choice, she would have to embark on a potentially soul-crushing odyssey across the causeway. She set off, her suitcase bouncing painfully over the rough ground as she trudged forward, the causeway stretching endlessly before her.

When she finally stepped onto Puffin Island, Fern stopped and stared. The Google photos didn't do this place justice. It was Instagram-perfect, the beautiful rainbow cottages and pretty shops she'd seen online stretching along the cobbled high street with a stream running at the side.

'Hello, you look a little lost. Can I help you at all?'

Fern blinked and looked up to see a woman standing in the doorway of a quaint little bookshop, her expression warm.

'Could you tell me how to get to Anchor Way?'

'Straight down to the bottom of Lighthouse Lane, then turn left. You can't miss it.' The woman smiled.

'And is there a B&B around here?' Fern had just realised she'd never even thought about accommodation, and with the train having been over three hours late, she hadn't much time to find a bed for the night.

The woman pointed in the same direction. 'Once you've turned left, it's just a short walk. Staying long?'

'Not too long,' Fern said vaguely, unsure of what she was walking into.

'I'm Amelia, the owner of The Story Shop. If you need anything, you'll find me right in here.' She pointed over her shoulder as she gave a welcoming smile. 'I'm always around.'

Fern offered a grateful nod. Amelia's easy smile made her feel like she'd stepped into another world. A welcoming one.

She hesitated for a moment, then said, 'I'm Fern. What's Puffin Island like?'

Amelia's face softened. 'A wonderful place with just the best kind of community. Everyone looks out for each other.'

'Do you live here?' Fern asked, curious to know more about the little island.

Amelia pointed to the upper floor of the bookshop, where a row of windows overlooked the bay. 'Right up there. Best view on the island, especially on a day like today.'

Fern followed her gaze, imagining waking up to the sight of the sea stretching endlessly into the horizon. Even the idea of it – the salt in the air, the quiet lull of waves, the leisurely walks on the sand with a coffee in hand – was a stark contrast to her life in London.

Amelia's friendly welcome made Fern feel unexpectedly at ease. In London, the only person who would greet her with such a smile was Ella. 'It looks a wonderful place to live.' She turned to leave, but then the words slipped out. 'By any chance, did you know a woman by the name of Matilda Hartley?'

'Oh, yes. She passed away recently. Owned No. 17 Curiosity Lane, a wonderful little antique shop, full of the strangest things.' She paused, then leaned against the doorframe of The Story Shop and grabbed a folded local newspaper from a nearby stack. 'Here you go. There's a write-up about her. Lovely tribute, really. No one's quite sure what's going to happen to the shop, though.' She hesitated, lowering her voice conspiratorially. 'There's a rumour going around that she had some sort of relative that's on their way from London. I'm not sure how they're going to fit in here, as they're no doubt the sort who drinks overpriced lattes, wears designer coats and will probably see inheriting the shop as a massive inconvenience.'

Fern bit back a grin and saw a flash of panic go across Amelia's face.

'Oh no,' Amelia said, briefly closing her eyes. 'Please don't tell me you're that relative.'

Fern gave a sheepish shrug. 'I am. But to be fair, I am a little stuck up, drink overpriced lattes and love a good designer coat.'

'Sorry,' Amelia apologised immediately, scrunching up her face in embarrassment.

'Honestly, don't worry about it. I know nothing about this place or my great-aunt Matilda.'

'She was one of a kind and she will be missed. You'll be able to read all about her on page five.' Amelia gestured towards the newspaper.

They stepped inside The Story Shop to shield the newspaper from the breeze and Fern opened it up.

Legendary Antique Dealer Matilda Hartley Passes at 85

Puffin Island has lost one of its most cherished figures with the passing of Matilda Hartley, the eccentric and beloved proprietor of No. 17 Curiosity Lane. Her tiny shop, brimming with forgotten treasures, was a haven for collectors and wanderers alike.

Her passing at the age of 85 leaves a void in the heart of Puffin Island. The world seems a little dimmer without her bold presence, but her legacy lives on in the countless treasures she preserved and the stories she safeguarded...

Fern found she felt a little sad, which was daft, given that she was reading about a relative she hadn't even known she had. There was much more to the article but Fern was keen to see the shop for herself, so she looked up at Amelia and asked, 'Can I keep this?'

'Of course, and I'm sorry about what I said before.'

'Don't worry about it. I may have been travelling since eight a.m. this morning but I do have a little sense of humour left.' She smiled to herself. That was primarily down to Daniel. If he hadn't made her train journey so enjoyable, she'd undoubtedly be in a right bad mood by now! She waved goodbye to Amelia and walked down the lane. After she located No. 17 Curiosity Lane, she was heading straight to the B&B in search of a bed for the night.

And there it was, right in front of her – No. 17 Curiosity Lane.

It looked exactly like the pictures online. It was in need of paint and repair, but the old stone building had a fairy-tale charm, with ivy creeping up its walls and the crooked wooden sign swaying gently above the door. Fern stood outside, suitcase at her side, staring at it with a dazed sort of disbelief. She still couldn't wrap her head around the fact she'd inherited an antique shop. An actual, real-life, full-of-old-stuff antique shop.

She was about to chalk this up as yet another bizarre twist in her life when something caught her eye, a light flickering inside the shop.

Her heart pounded. Was someone inside? A squatter? A ghost with a taste for ambient lighting? Steeling herself, she gripped the handle and pushed the door open. It creaked, releasing a thick, nostalgic aroma comprising dust, polished wood, old books and that distinct air of things with stories to tell.

Then she saw him. She couldn't quite believe her eyes.

Leaning back on the chair behind the cash desk, one leg resting over the desk itself, chewing on a pencil, looking entirely at home, was *him*. The gorgeous man from the train. The one who smelled out of this world. The one who had handed over half his sandwich with a grin, shared his KitKat without hesitation and let a starry-eyed little boy strum his guitar like it was the most natural thing in the world.

Daniel.

Her heart was now pounding for all the right reasons.

What were the chances? Slim. Non-existent. She had spent the rest of that train journey quietly wishing she'd asked for his number, convinced she'd never see him again. Yet here he was, grinning at her like the universe had decided to play matchmaker after all.

Fern couldn't stop the smile spreading across her face.

He took his leg off the desk and leaned on the counter, arms folded, eyes twinkling with mischief. 'Well, well. If it isn't my favourite train companion. What are the chances?'

Her laugh bubbled up before she could stop it. 'I cannot believe this.'

'Neither can I,' he admitted, his lopsided grin doing something ridiculous to her stomach. 'But I'm thrilled about it.'

She shook her head, giddy. 'This is surreal.'

'Or,' he said, 'it's fate.'

The way he said it – so easy, so sure – made her pulse race.

She tilted her head playfully. 'What exactly are you doing in *my* shop?'

'Your shop?' He raised an eyebrow, grinning wider.

'It was left to me by my great-aunt Matilda … whom I actually didn't know existed until twenty-four hours ago.'

'I think you'll find it's *our* shop.'

Her eyes widened. 'Explain. Quickly.'

He clapped his hands together. 'Right. So, funny story…'

Chapter Four

Daniel gestured to a nearby chair. 'You might want to take a seat. Brace yourself.'

Fern sat down. She was still riding the high of seeing him again, but she hadn't had him down as the kind of man who loved dusty antiques, so his appearance in the shop left her feeling completely confused. He seemed the type you'd be more likely to find at a music festival, sprawled out on the grass, not hiding away in an old curiosity shop.

'All right,' she said, raising an eyebrow. 'Explain.'

Daniel leaned against the counter, arms crossed. 'Matilda and I were friends. I was her apprentice.'

Fern blinked. 'Apprentice?'

'Yeah! Like a Jedi, but for antiques.' He grinned. 'She found me at an auction house a couple of years ago, aggressively bidding on a teapot I didn't even want purely to annoy some posh bloke who'd called me "boy".'

Fern smothered a laugh. 'Of course you did.'

'Matilda *loved* my spirit,' he continued. 'Said I had "a keen eye for mischief", which apparently is a desirable trait in the world of antique dealing.'

Fern pinched the bridge of her nose. 'So, what? She just *gave* you a job?'

'Yes.'

'And you love antiques?' Fern glanced around. 'You don't look like the antique type to me.'

'What does an antique type look like?'

'I don't know, just … not you. Aren't you too young to be into antiques?'

'Are you stereotyping antique lovers?' He narrowed his eyes.

'Not at all, I just imagine antique dealers to be like those you see on TV programmes – older and more weathered.'

'You can't believe everything you see on TV.' He winked. 'Anyway, as I was saying … just before Matilda passed away, she told me I could live in the flat upstairs and she made me promise that I wouldn't let anything happen to this place. I asked her what that meant and all she said was that someone would be coming soon, and I might need to talk them around into seeing the beauty within these walls. That must be you.'

Fern stared at him. 'So what you're saying is, I haven't just inherited a shop full of dusty trinkets, but also *you*? A sitting tenant?'

Daniel flashed a lopsided grin. 'And a damn *good* one, if I do say so myself. I don't make too much noise, I take the bins out, and I only borrow the good biscuits in times of emergency.'

She laughed. 'Right, so I can count on you not to pinch the chocolate Hobnobs?' She paused, then grimaced. 'Please tell me this place doesn't come with any animals as well.'

Daniel pointed to the top of the piano, where sat a very still, very *not alive* cat. 'Only dead ones. Matilda's cat was called Lucky, but she wasn't very lucky,' he said with a wince. 'It was all very unfortunate ... a lorry—'

Fern held up a hand. '*Stop.*'

Daniel nodded solemnly. 'Matilda had her stuffed. She said it would be good for morale.'

Fern exhaled, dragging a hand through her hair. Matilda hadn't just left her an antique shop, she'd also left her a chaotic, ridiculously charming lodger and a *stuffed cat*.

Daniel clapped his hands together. 'So! I guess this means we're now business partners slash housemates! While you bask in the glory of your unexpected inheritance, I'll make tea. That's what people do when faced with life-altering news, isn't it?'

Fern watched as he disappeared through a doorway at the back of the room, leaving her alone with No. 17 Curiosity Lane in all its eccentric glory. She turned slowly, taking it all in. The place was mad. Floor-to-ceiling clutter. A grandfather clock that ticked with a tired clunk. Lampshades made of things that should *not* be lampshades. A doll in a glass cabinet that may or may not have just blinked.

She let out a shaky breath. Inherited. She'd inherited this. From a woman she'd never even heard of.

A great-aunt. A shop. A flat above it.

Her first instinct was to sell, obviously. Get it valued, flog the lot and maybe go on a ridiculously overpriced holiday. But now there was charming Daniel to consider, currently clattering about making tea in the home where he lived. He had no idea that she'd planned to throw the whole place on

Rightmove and have done with it. Which would mean tossing him out on the street.

She walked over to the desk and ran her fingers across the battered wood, the layers of varnish worn away by time and stories she would never know.

The place was *mad*.

It was like an antique shop had collided with a Victorian curiosity cabinet and then been sprinkled with a generous dose of *what on earth is that?* Shelves heaved under the weight of peculiar objects like brass telescopes, pocket watches frozen in time, and an alarming number of porcelain figurines with judgmental expressions. Gilded mirrors reflected the glow of a dozen mismatched lamps, their light pooling over old books stacked in precarious towers.

And somehow, in the middle of it all … was *Daniel*. The man from the train. Potentially the man of her dreams. And definitely the man whose world she was about to destroy.

Just at that moment she heard something rattle … and it wasn't coming from the kitchen. Fern froze but her eyes flicked to a tall, glass-fronted cabinet filled with dolls, all of them staring at her with a sort of eerie lifelessness that made her stomach tighten.

And then, just as she took a step closer, one of them – a frilly-dressed thing with faded pink cheeks – squeaked out, '*Mama?*'

She clutched her chest, her heart slamming against her ribs as she staggered back. 'What the—?!' she yelled.

Daniel's voice drifted from the back room. 'Oh yeah, don't mind Audrey! She does that sometimes.'

Fern glared at the doll, which sat there innocently, as if it hadn't just tipped her soul into the depths of hell. She was about to turn away when something hissed at her.

She spun around.

A stuffed cobra, coiled and fanged, stared at her from a shelf, its beady glass eyes catching the light.

'Nope. Nope, nope, nope.' She backed away, only to bump into a grandfather clock, which chimed loudly.

She jumped, letting out another strangled yelp, just in time for a wardrobe on the far side of the shop to burst open.

A gorilla lunged out.

Fern shrieked.

She tripped over a footstool, crashing into a pile of embroidered cushions as the gorilla wobbled, flailed, then toppled over onto the floor with a solid *thud*.

Silence.

Daniel reappeared, holding a tray with two teacups. He took one look at her wide eyes, then at the stuffed gorilla sprawled on the floor.

'Oh,' he said casually. 'You've found Gerald, then?'

Fern pointed an accusatory finger. 'What is *Gerald*?!'

'A gorilla,' Daniel said, laughing. 'You get used to him. I think he's been stuffed in there for quite a few years.'

Fern dragged herself upright, inhaling deeply through her nose. 'This shop is *cursed*.'

Daniel chuckled, handing her a teacup. 'Maybe. Here, the tea will fix everything.'

She eyed it warily. The cup was cracked. So was the saucer. 'Do I even *want* to ask?'

Daniel beamed. 'They're antique, and would you believe this is the very teapot I won at that auction? The one I *heroically* saved from the clutches of a posh bloke who wanted it purely to match his scone set?'

Fern stared at him.

Daniel raised his own cup in a toast. 'You, my dear reluctant shop owner, are drinking from a vessel of pure triumph.'

Fern cracked a smile. She didn't want to, but Daniel made her smile. He was funny, and despite the fact that she was tired, hungry and still vaguely traumatised by Audrey the demonic doll and Gerald the airborne gorilla, she couldn't stop taking a sideward glance at him. She'd never met anyone with such good looks *and* a sense of humour. In London, they only ever seemed to come with one or the other.

'What have I inherited?' she murmured again, shaking her head.

Daniel grinned. 'A shop full of stories and things, a flat with a very reasonable sitting tenant, and best of all … a lifetime supply of unexpected chaos.'

Fern rolled her eyes, but there was still a smile tugging at her lips.

'Wait till you see upstairs.'

This was going to be interesting.

Chapter Five

'Right then,' Daniel announced, clapping his hands. 'Time for the grand tour of Matilda's Museum of Madness.'

Fern had just finished her tea – miraculously unpoisoned by whatever ancient dust particles lived in that teapot – when Daniel encouraged her to follow him towards the back of the shop. 'Kitchen…'

Fern poked her head around the door. It was small, with a table and a couple of chairs against the back door.

'The living room,' he said as they stepped into the room next to the kitchen. Fern immediately noticed the curtains. One red. One green. One a mystery colour.

Fern pressed her fingers to her temples. 'I feel like I'm on drugs. Who chose this colour scheme?'

Daniel smirked. 'Welcome to Matilda's world. Come on, you'll *love* what's upstairs. It's the best part.' He gestured for her to follow him up the rickety-looking stairs.

The moment she set foot on the first step, the stairs let out a noise – not just a creak but a full-bodied, theatrical, whale-in-distress *wail*.

Fern jumped back, hand flying to her chest. 'Did the stairs just scream at me?'

Daniel patted the banister fondly. 'Ah, yes. That, my friend, is the acoustics of a house with character. Just keep moving, and try not to step on the fourth one unless you fancy an impromptu slide.'

Her eyes narrowed. 'What do you mean?'

Daniel merely gave her a *you'll see* smile.

Fern took another few steps, and as her foot connected with the fourth stair, the whole thing sank.

With a yelp, she lurched forward, arms flailing, trying to grab hold of anything to stop herself from falling face-first into the abyss of creaky doom. The closest thing to grab was Daniel and she crashed straight into him. He caught her instantly, hands gripping her waist, and the sudden impact thrust them both back a step, leaving her in his arms.

For a heartbeat, neither of them moved.

She was pressed against his chest, her fingers gripping the fabric of his shirt. His hands, warm and steady, lingered at her waist and when she looked up, her breath caught.

They were close.

Like, *ridiculously close*.

Lips only centimetres apart, his breath warm against hers.

His gaze flickered down to her lips for the briefest second. Then he grinned. 'If you wanted me to sweep you into my arms, you could've just asked.'

Fern gave him a playful shove. 'Oh, shut up.'

He laughed, releasing her, and she straightened, her face feeling flushed.

'I'd suggest you try to remember to avoid the fourth stair unless you're angling to fall for me again.' She shooed him on. When they reached the top of the stairs, she blinked twice. The landing looked like it belonged in ten different time periods at once. The wallpaper was a clashing mix of faded florals and geometric Art Deco swirls. The ceiling boasted a brass chandelier missing half its crystals, and the floor was covered by at least three different rugs, none of which matched.

He swung open a door to reveal the bedroom. The first thing she saw? The moose head. It loomed above the four-poster bed, with its enormous glass eyes staring straight into her soul.

'Oh my God,' she gasped. 'How do you sleep with that looking at you?'

'Usually with both eyes closed.' He grinned. 'Let me introduce you to Maurice! He's been here longer than me. Great listener, this one.'

Fern dragged her horrified gaze around the room.

The bed anchored the room and was ornate and wooden, the kind of gothic four-poster that suggested those who dared to sleep in it might mysteriously perish in the night. And worst of all? It was the *only* bed.

Fern turned to Daniel. 'Is there another bedroom?'

'Nope.' He smiled widely. 'This is the only one. But it's *very* spacious. Loads of room,' he said, gesturing grandly.

'You are not suggesting we...' Her mouth fell open as she struggled to find the words.

'Come now, we're hardly strangers! We own the same shop and—'

'Er, I hate to burst your bubble,' she interrupted, 'but I'm Matilda's sole beneficiary and so the sole owner of all of this. And as much as you're gorgeous…' She faltered as her thoughts turned in a very inappropriate direction, but then shook her head. She couldn't go there now! '…There is no way I'm sleeping with you. Or with a moose watching over me!'

Before he could reply, she yanked open another door to what turned out to be the bathroom, and shrieked. (This shop was not doing her vocal cords any favours.)

'What is *that*?' she asked, staring at the bathtub, which was currently occupied by a creepy Victorian-age mannequin.

Daniel stuck his head around the door, looking completely unfazed. 'That's Eleanor!'

Fern's eye twitched. 'Why is there a mannequin in the bathtub?'

'Matilda used to have her in the shop to model clothes, but they became very attached and so Matilda moved her up here. She said they were like best friends, and Eleanor kept the place from feeling lonely at night. I just haven't yet got round to moving her.'

Fern clutched the doorframe, taking deep breaths.

'I need a drink,' she muttered.

Daniel clapped his hands together. 'Brilliant! There's a pub down the road. We'll celebrate your newly inherited business and home, and you can tell me all about how excited you are to be my new housemate.'

'I won't be here long enough to be your housemate, and I'll have to give the pub a miss. I'm off to grab a bed at the local B&B.'

'You won't find anything as good as this place.'

'I'll take my chances.'

As she followed Daniel down the stairs, dodging the *traitorous* fourth step, she caught herself smiling. Because, somehow, against all odds, Daniel had made this place feel almost magical, and she didn't hate it as much as she'd wanted to.

Chapter Six

Fern stepped out of No. 17 Curiosity Lane and headed down the lane pulling her suitcase behind her. As it rattled along the uneven cobblestones, she inhaled a lungful of crisp, sea-salted air. It was very welcome compared to the scent of old books and antique dust, which were definitely not her usual vibe. She had spent her career flitting between backstage lounges, five-star suites and first-class flights, sipping champagne that cost more than some people's rent. She wasn't proud of it, but she could admit that she was a snob, and she would never in a million years dream about sleeping in a shared bed with a stranger in a flat that looked like a cross between a haunted museum and a taxidermist's fever dream. Having standards didn't make her a bad person, it just meant she knew what she liked, and she definitely didn't like the idea of sharing a lumpy bed with a stranger, with a moose's head looming over her. Even if that stranger happened to be ridiculously good-looking.

Daniel was firmly on her mind. He had the kind of charm

that made him seem like he belonged on magazine covers, not behind the counter of a dusty antique shop. He should have been striding down a New York catwalk, not fixing wobbly shelves and rearranging creepy porcelain dolls. It didn't make sense to her. Why would someone like him choose to live and work in a place like that?

As she walked along the path with the distant sound of waves rolling against the shore, she let herself imagine an alternative reality. One where, perhaps, she wouldn't mind sharing a bed with Daniel, though in a hotel suite with Egyptian cotton sheets and a champagne room-service menu, of course. But there? In that flat? Absolutely not. With a shake of her head, she pressed on towards the B&B. Some things were non-negotiable.

The Puffin Island B&B was a quaint two-storey building with ivy-clad walls and a bright, welcoming red door. A small brass sign beside said door read: The Driftwood Lodge B&B. This was exactly what Fern needed: a quiet, sensible, normal place to stay. Then she saw the sign.

NO VACANCIES.

She froze, suitcase handle clenched in her fist. Oh, come on. Maybe it was a mistake. Maybe the sign was decorative, meant to make the place feel exclusive. Yes, that had to be it.

Not one to be easily deterred, she pushed open the door and stepped inside. The interior was as charming as the exterior, with wooden beams, floral wallpaper and an assortment of knick-knacks that made the place feel lived in and cosy. There was also the comforting sight of quaint armchairs, and an elderly Labrador snoring near the reception desk. Behind the desk stood a woman who immediately smiled. She was kind-looking with bobbed hair, glasses perched on her nose, and a cardigan that suggested she'd perfected the art of cosy living. 'Hi there, I'm Lena, can I help you?'

Fern strode across the reception area, forcing a bright, hopeful smile. 'Hi! Please tell me that sign outside is a mistake.'

Lena gave her a sympathetic look. 'I'm sorry but it's not. We're fully booked.'

The hope in Fern's chest died a swift and tragic death. 'Fully booked?'

Lena nodded. 'It's the annual Cosy Crime Enthusiasts' Convention this weekend. Every room's taken.'

Fern stared at her, waiting for some kind of punchline. When none came, she exhaled slowly. 'You're telling me I have nowhere to sleep because of amateur detectives?'

Lena, bless her, looked genuinely apologetic. 'It's a very dedicated crowd. They come dressed as their favourite sleuths, and spend the weekend solving fictional murders and debating the best way to poison someone without getting caught. Harmless fun … mostly.'

Fern blinked. 'Mostly?'

Lena hesitated. 'There was a small incident last year involving a very realistic crime scene and an actual police response, but I'm sure they've learned their lesson.'

Fern laughed but she was still disappointed there was no room at the inn because of murder mystery enthusiasts. 'Not even a tiny room? A cot? A broom cupboard?'

With a smile, Lena shook her head. 'I'd offer you my own sofa if I could, but someone has already claimed it.'

Fern deflated. 'Just my luck.'

'I know the hotel on the island is also full, but I have a list of other B&Bs over in Sea's End you could try? You're more than welcome to grab yourself a drink and use the living room to make a few calls.'

'Thank you, that's very kind.'

Fern spent the next hour calling every B&B and hotel within reach. Nothing. No last-minute miracle. No backup plan. She was going to have to go back to No. 17 Curiosity Lane with her tail between her legs. She thanked Lena for her help and headed back outside, the now familiar sound of her suitcase rattling against the cobbles providing a soundtrack as she slowly made her way back to the shop.

As she stepped through the door, something unexpected hit her – the rich, savoury scent of garlic, herbs and something undoubtedly delicious. Leaving her suitcase by the stairs she followed the aroma through the shop, pausing in the kitchen doorway.

In the corner of the kitchen, a small wooden table had been set for two. Two steaming plates of pasta. Two wine glasses. A bottle of white wine chilling in an ice bucket. And there, standing by the table, was Daniel.

'Took you long enough,' he said.

Fern blinked. He had done this for her?

'I had a feeling you'd be back,' he continued, pulling out a chair. 'Also figured you might be hungry. You've had a long day, and no doubt only eaten that half sandwich and KitKat on the train. You must be starving.'

She hadn't expected this and barely knew what to say. She settled on 'This looks amazing.'

'You wouldn't get this treatment at the B&B,' he said smugly. 'Take a seat.'

She sat down and her stomach betrayed her for the second time that day, growling loudly.

Daniel smiled as he poured them each a glass of wine then placed a salad on the table. 'Tuck in.'

She didn't need telling twice. Fern picked up her fork and took a bite. The pasta was silky with a sauce that was rich and perfectly seasoned. 'This is so good.' She glanced at him. 'You make the best sandwiches, you cook the best pasta and you play the guitar? I'm impressed.'

'I take it the B&B was full of crime enthusiasts?'

'Yes.'

'I'll thank them later.'

She grinned. 'You make sure you do.' She held his gaze longer than necessary, savouring the moment of awareness. She really enjoyed flirting with Daniel, but the reality of sharing a bed with a complete stranger was something else entirely, and worries about what she was going to do were still looming in the back of her mind.

After they'd finished the food, she helped to wash up, her mind turning over her options. Finally, she had to admit there was only one choice. She took one last fortifying sip of wine then looked Daniel in the eye. 'Okay. Ground rules. Technically, I own this place—'

'Hasn't taken you long to assert authority, has it?' He grinned, taking any sting out of his words.

'Can I ask you to sleep on the sofa?'

'Of course. That was actually my plan. I even put clean sheets on the bed whilst you were gone. I suppose if I get lonely down here, I can always talk to Gerald.'

'You can.'

'Now that that's settled, tell me, what has your day been

like as the new owner of an antique shop?' he asked, sitting back at the table.

'On the whole … it's been interesting, but I'm absolutely shattered and need my bed.' She pointed to the stairs.

'Fair enough,' he said, grabbing her suitcase and carrying it up the stairs to deposit it in the bedroom.

'Sweet dreams, city girl,' he said, giving her a little salute before closing the door.

There was a beat of silence before a loud moo floated in through the window, causing her to jump.

'Daniel!' she shrieked.

The door creaked open again, and there he was with a lopsided grin.

'I've changed my mind. I don't want to sleep on my own,' she said quickly, before she could talk herself out of it.

'If you insist,' he said, stepping into the room.

'You have to stay on your own side of the bed.'

Daniel smiled. 'Anything you say, city girl.'

'What is that noise?' she asked, as the moo sounded out again. 'It sounds like cows.'

'It's the puffins! Welcome to Puffin Island!'

Fern turned to find the moose's glass eyes staring right at her.

She prayed she was going to survive the night.

Chapter Seven

Dressed for bed, Fern stood in the middle of the bedroom, arms crossed, assessing the house of horror she had agreed to spend the night in. The moose head loomed above the bed like a judgmental overseer, its beady glass eyes catching the dim glow of the bedside lamp. The different-coloured ancient curtains fluttered slightly in the draught from the ill-fitting window. And then there was the bed itself. Despite Daniel claiming it was spacious, it was actually narrow, lumpy and utterly unsuitable for two people who barely knew each other.

'You look like you're trying to summon the courage of a condemned prisoner,' Daniel observed. 'I'm not that bad.'

'That is debatable.' Fern eyed the lumpy pillows sceptically. 'Pretty sure these pillows are stuffed with antique dust mites.'

Daniel let out a laugh before disappearing into the bathroom. The sound of running water filled the room, but Fern didn't take her eyes off the chaos that surrounded her. How had this happened? This morning she was in her stylish

London flat, surrounded by sleek furniture and pristine everything. Now she was in a building surrounded by antique horrors and a moose that looked like it was plotting something sinister.

Exhausted, she flopped onto the bed. Just as she'd thought, it was uncomfortable and smelled faintly of something old, though that wasn't surprising, considering the entire shop was a museum in, and of, itself. The sound of an electric toothbrush caught her attention, and she rolled her eyes towards the bathroom door, not expecting to see Daniel in just a towel, casually going about his business. Her eyes fell on his toned shoulders as they flexed with the motion of his arm. She blinked. It took her a second to process what she was seeing. Daniel didn't exactly look like someone who spent their days lifting dumbbells or doing squats. Yet here he was, impressively built.

Her stomach did a little flip. Butterflies. She actually had butterflies. She groaned inwardly, feeling ridiculous. She'd known the second she saw him on the train there was something about him, a kind of chemistry, but she reminded herself that indulging that thought could lead to a whole new level of complicated. Despite the good-looking lodger, she was here to get the shop sold and get back to London as soon as possible.

He walked out of the bathroom, now wearing pyjama bottoms, and she briefly closed her eyes, feeling him slip underneath the covers. The bed dipped alarmingly under his weight and in a moment of sheer survival instinct, Fern reached for the extra pillows and wedged them firmly between them.

'What are you doing?'

'Building a wall,' she said, stuffing another pillow into place. 'This is a diplomatic boundary. You stay on your side.'

Daniel grinned. 'Are you actually being serious?'

'Deadly.' She fluffed the last pillow and lay back, satisfied with her makeshift fortress. 'You could be a mass murderer for all I know.'

'If I was do you think a pillow wall is going to stop me?'

'Any precaution will help.'

He rolled onto his side and switched off the lamp. 'Good night.'

'Good night, Daniel.'

Fern closed her eyes, willing herself to go to sleep. She was shattered, but she was also wide awake, aware of every little noise as the room creaked around them. Somewhere in the depths of the antique shop below, a clock chimed ominously. The wooden beams groaned above them. A floorboard creaked outside the door. She swore she could hear the mannequin shifting in the bathroom, adjusting its stance in the darkness.

'Daniel?' she whispered.

A grunt came from the other side of the pillow wall.

'Do you hear that?'

Silence. Then a very deliberate 'No.'

Fern swallowed. 'I think there's something in the room.'

'There isn't, I promise.'

She leaned over the pillow wall and lightly tugged his arm. 'I'm serious.'

'So am I. Go to sleep.'

She tried, she really did, but then something rustled. Her pulse raced and she looked up to see the moose head's shadow elongate as the curtains billowed. She let out an unholy shriek and launched herself across the bed, straight into Daniel, the pillow wall collapsing between them.

'Fern!' he gasped, startled awake. 'What are you doing?'

'There was … there was something…'

He gently held her by the shoulders. 'It's just the wind. It sometimes gets a little breezy living by the sea.'

She was practically on top of him, breathing heavily, her heart pounding against his chest.

'Are you sure?'

'Positive.' His voice was low, amused. 'Would you like me to check for ghosts?'

'Don't joke.'

His hands on her arms were warm, steady, and she became abruptly aware of just how close they were, their noses nearly brushing in the dark. His scent – something woodsy and clean – filled her senses. She swallowed nervously.

Slowly, deliberately, she peeled herself away, returning to her side of the bed. She tried to rebuild the pillow wall, but Daniel just sighed, plucked one from the pile, and tucked it under his head.

'Try and go to sleep, Fern.'

She lay back down, staring at the ceiling. It took a long time for her heartbeat to settle, but somewhere in the early hours of the morning, she finally drifted into a restless sleep. She dreamed of winding corridors, of antique clocks ticking out of sync, of Daniel standing in the doorway of the shop.

Then she woke up. Warm. Comfortable. Safe.

She opened her eyes, blinking against the weak morning light streaming through the mismatched curtains. Something was…

Oh, God.

She froze. Her arms were wrapped around him. Her forehead was resting against his chest. One leg had somehow tangled with his, and his arm … when had that draped around her waist?

Slowly, she shifted back, but the movement made Daniel stir. He mumbled something incoherent and pulled her slightly closer before realising…

His eyes snapped open. Their gazes met.

Silence.

Then…

'Don't say a word,' she ordered.

'I'm saying nothing,' he replied, amused, as she disentangled herself and made a run for the safety of the bathroom.

An hour later, Fern stood leaning on the kitchen counter watching Daniel fry eggs. The air smelled of coffee and toast, and for a fleeting moment, she let herself enjoy the warmth of the scene, the normality of it. She couldn't remember the last time she had cooked breakfast with anyone. Every time she had ended up in Jax Devlin's arms, she had been kicked out of the hotel room in the early hours without even the cab fare home, just so the paparazzi didn't get a photo. She was thankful to have dodged the embarrassment of being caught, and her face plastered all over the tabloids, but there was always a lingering sting of knowing she was probably just another of the many – many – secrets he refused to acknowledge in daylight.

Here, at the back of No. 17 Curiosity Lane, things couldn't

be more different. There was no pretence, no carefully curated façade. Just the two of them, bustling around the cramped kitchen, nudging each other out of the way with playful elbow jabs and lots of conversation, with the sound of the antique radio playing feel-good tunes.

'Pass me the butter, would you?' Daniel asked, glancing over his shoulder.

Fern reached for it, but her fingers closed around empty air as he snatched it first. 'Too slow,' he teased, grinning as he held it just out of reach.

'Very mature. What are we, seven years old?' She shook her head, suppressing a smile as she grabbed the butter from his hand then began to spread it over thick slices of toast. The butter melted instantly, pooling into golden pockets. She took a sneaky sideward glance at him, realising it felt like she had known him for years.

'I know you're watching me.'

'I'm not,' she protested as she placed the toast on two mismatched plates.

Daniel slid the eggs on top then handed her a plate. 'Look at us,' he mused, sitting down at the table. 'We're like a proper domestic couple,' he said with a twinkle in his eye.

'Aren't we just,' she replied, cutting the corner of the toast and dipping it in the egg before taking a bite, all the while watching him.

Daniel's hair was doing its best impression of a bird's nest, sticking up at wild angles like it had staged a rebellion against gravity. His stubble was just the right amount of scruff to make him look good, and he wore a well-loved Blondie T-shirt, the graphic cracked and faded from years of devoted wear. They ate in companionable silence, the occasional clink of cutlery the only sound filling the space between them.

Every now and then, Daniel took a slow sip of his coffee, looking so completely at ease. There was no hurry to his movements, no performance; it was just him existing. Jax had never been like that. With Jax, everything had been about image, about carefully orchestrated moments, about control. As Daniel reached over to steal the last bit of her toast, grinning as she swatted his hand away, she thought, maybe, just maybe, there was a better life out there for her without Jax.

She wondered what it would be like to be in a relationship with Daniel, but pushed that thought from her mind. She needed to have a serious chat with him and this seemed like as good a time as any, so she took the plunge.

'We need to talk.'

'That phrase never leads to good things.'

'I'm going to call the estate agent today, get this place valued, and then I'm putting the shop up for sale.'

She had Daniel's full attention now. 'No, you can't.'

'Excuse me?'

'You can't sell this shop. Matilda wouldn't want that.'

'She's no longer here, and I don't really want or need an antique shop.'

'This is my home, my job. I'm not going anywhere.'

Fern sighed, rubbing her temples. 'Daniel, this isn't your decision.'

'Actually, it kind of is.' He put down his knife and fork. 'I live here, I work here and I know this place inside out. You have no idea what you're getting rid of.' He held her gaze, and there was something about the way he looked at her, his hazel eyes steady and unwavering, that made her pause.

'Please don't make any hasty decisions.'

'Daniel, I don't want an antique shop on an island I didn't even know existed a day or so ago. My life is in London. The best I can offer is to give you first refusal.'

He shook his head. 'I can't afford to buy it. Look, let the idea of it all sink in first, before you decide what to do with it. Please.'

'I don't even know the first thing about antiques,' she declared.

'Then work in the shop with me today and I'll teach you.'

'What?' She gawped at him.

'You can't make any sort of decision until you've had hands-on experience. You'll learn and you'll fall in love, I promise. We open in ten minutes.'

Fern stood in the shop staring at the little sign that read CLOSED. Sunlight streamed through the dusty windows, illuminating the haphazard collection of oddities within – the brass telescopes, mismatched china sets, ancient globes and a disturbing number of porcelain dolls.

'Go on,' Daniel encouraged, sipping his coffee like he had all the time in the world, 'turn it over.'

'This is ridiculous,' she muttered, but she reached out and flipped the sign to OPEN.

'There we go. Your first official act as the new owner, and because it's your first day, you get the comfy chair.'

Fern turned, eyeing the 'comfy chair'. It was an ancient, overstuffed monstrosity with a floral pattern, its arms sagging, its cushions suspiciously lumpy. 'That thing looks like it's possessed.'

Daniel grinned. 'Exactly. Enjoy.'

As she sat down the chair let out a groan of protest, its springs creaking beneath her weight.

And then ... nothing happened. No customers. No curious browsers. Just silence.

She sat in absolute stillness, staring at the front door. The occasional sound of a clock ticking or the creak of a contracting floorboard were the only things breaking the monotony. Fern drummed her fingers on the armrest. 'Does it ever get busier?'

Daniel stretched, leaning back against the counter. 'Not really. But when a real treasure hunter walks through that door, your life will change.'

She exhaled. 'I don't think I've ever been so bored,' she muttered.

Suddenly, the bell over the shop door gave a feeble jingle, and Fern jolted upright as an elderly man stepped inside the shop. He was tall, with the most elaborate moustache she'd ever seen, and silver hair swept back in waves. His tweed coat was immaculately pressed and hinted at old money, but his warm, inquisitive eyes softened the image. He held a sturdy wooden cane, though he didn't seem to rely on it much.

Daniel, who had been lounging behind the counter, straightened instantly. 'Here we go,' he mouthed at Fern. 'Your very first customer.' He widened his eyes and tilted his head slightly, silently urging her to say something.

'Can I help you at all?' asked Fern.

'I'm just looking,' the man replied as he browsed through a pile of music books, then turned his attention to the piano that was standing upright in the far corner. He propped his cane against it, sat on the stool and lifted the lid. His fingers slid over the keys and immediately Fern was impressed. This was a man who knew how to play.

'You play well,' said Fern, standing up and stepping towards the piano.

'I do, but not for a long time.'

'She's a bit of a gem, that piano,' Daniel said, joining them and resting a hand affectionately on the lid. 'Needs a good tune, mind you, but she's got a story.'

Fern turned to look at him with interest.

'This belonged to Matilda, the former owner of this shop,' Daniel continued. 'She passed away recently but she used to play it nearly every day. Sometimes classical, sometimes ragtime, even the odd jazz standard when she was feeling playful.'

The elderly man nodded appreciatively.

'She studied at the London School of Music,' Daniel added. 'Talented doesn't even begin to cover it. This piano'—he tapped the frame lightly—'is early twentieth century. Solid walnut casing, original ivories. She kept it in impeccable shape, up until the last year or so, anyway.'

The old man didn't speak for a moment. Then, softly, he played a few more notes, letting them linger in the still air of the shop. 'It's a mighty fine piano.' He seemed lost in thought for a moment.

Daniel smiled. 'It is.'

Fern looked at Daniel. 'Matilda studied music?'

'She did,' replied Daniel before turning back towards the man. 'Would you be interested in purchasing the piano?'

The man shook his head. 'Not on this occasion, but it's extremely impressive,' he replied, standing up and grabbing his cane before moving towards an antique gramophone and browsing through old music memorabilia.

As they watched him, Daniel leaned in and whispered, 'How did you not know that Matilda studied music?'

'Like I told you, I didn't even know she existed until forty-eight hours ago.'

Daniel widened his eyes. 'You know nothing about Matilda?'

'Nothing whatsoever,' she admitted.

The man turned towards them. 'I don't suppose you have any music boxes?' He swept a glance around the shop.

Daniel shook his head. 'I've never seen one and I've worked here a while.'

The man nodded as he waved his cane in the air and turned and walked back through the door.

'Tell me more about Matilda. It's crazy that I write about musicians for a living, and I've ended up inheriting a shop once owned by a talented musician.'

'You write about musicians? That sounds an amazing job. Your next feature could be about how you found a man on the train whose guitar playing dazzled you, and you lived happily ever after.'

Fern rolled her eyes. 'Back to Matilda.'

'Spoilsport. I believe she was an incredible composer back in her time.' Daniel picked up an acoustic guitar that had been propped beside the counter, settling it upon his lap.

Fern, still processing everything, watched as he absentmindedly strummed a few chords. The sound was warm and rich, filling the shop with an easy rhythm. He wasn't just playing nonsense, there was a melody there, something familiar yet unknown.

Curious, she stepped closer. 'What are you playing?'

Daniel glanced up at her, his fingers still moving over the strings. 'A song Matilda taught me.'

'She taught you?'

'Yeah. She had all these melodies in her head. She'd hum them while working in the shop. I picked up a few.' He played a chord, letting the note linger, then gave her a teasing smile as he strummed a jaunty little riff.

'Can you write a song about me? Go on, sing something.'

'All right, you asked for it. Here goes nothing.'

He strummed a lively, upbeat rhythm, and then began to sing,

'Well, here comes Fern from the big city lights,

'With a suitcase full of dreams and a head full of heights.'

He strummed a few more chords and carried on.

'You claimed you were scared of the moose's head, but let's be real…

'You just wanted to cuddle, to see how I'd feel!'

Fern threw back her head and laughed. 'You are mad!'

He struck a final chord, a playful grin spreading across his face. 'Don't even pretend you didn't love it!' he teased, his voice warm and light as he leaned the guitar against the desk.

'That was so ridiculous, Daniel!' she said, shaking her head. 'I was scared of the dark and all that mooing.'

'That's your story and you're sticking to it? But on a serious note, I think we'd make a good team running this shop.'

'Daniel, I'm a music journalist. I'm not cut out to run an antiques shop on Puffin Island. This is all just junk and there are no customers. From what I've seen there's no way this place is making money.' Immediately, she saw the smile slip from his face. 'I know you don't want to accept it, but I'm here to clear out all this junk as quickly as possible and get back to London.' Her voice was firm but not without a hint of hesitation. She hated upsetting him.

Daniel met her gaze. 'This was Matilda's life's work. You can't just get rid of it all. She's collected most of these pieces herself. Each item in this shop tells a story.'

Fern could see the look of dismay on Daniel's face. She tried to smooth things over while still making clear that the shop would be sold. 'This place … it's had its time. Matilda would never have wanted it to become a burden. Yes, she loved it, but things change. I mean, how much money can this place make? Is it really a business? No one's bought anything today, and you're living in a … haunted house,' Fern said, gesturing around the shop. 'I mean, it's not even a place you can bring girls back to. It can't be doing much for your love life.'

'Matilda wanted this shop to go on.'

'You can't make me feel guilty.'

'I'm sorry, I don't mean to, she just…'

'She just what?'

'She knew her life was coming to an end, and she told me never to let this shop go as it would be my fortune and my future.'

'Then why did she not leave the shop to you? Why would she leave it to me, someone she had never met?'

He shrugged. 'She gave me the tenancy agreement, and she promised everything would work out.'

'How long is the agreement for?'

'A lifetime.'

Fern blinked. A lifetime? That was ... not the sort of arrangement you could just brush off with a polite eviction notice and a scented candle. 'You surely don't want to live here for a lifetime?'

Her mind buzzed. Should she speak to the solicitor? There had to be paperwork, clauses, footnotes, *something* about this. Matilda had left her a business and a flat, but also, apparently, a full-grown man with a lifetime lease.

Was that even legal? Could you *inherit* a sitting tenant? What happened if you wanted to sell? Could you just turf someone out who'd been promised security by the person who left you the whole circus in the first place?

Her stomach churned. This wasn't just an inheritance anymore. It was a minefield.

Yet here was Daniel, utterly relaxed, as if this situation was completely normal.

'It's all I have, and I will be forever grateful that Matilda looked out for me. The shop's a mess, sure, but it's got character. You can't just erase all that. It just needs a good tidy-up.'

Fern raised an eyebrow. 'Well, I'm not exactly in love with "character" in the form of creepy old clocks and moth-eaten tapestries. This place is practically a museum and that smell...' She laughed – but Daniel wasn't laughing.

A silence fell between them. Fern could feel the tension. She hadn't expected him to feel so strongly, but she knew at some point there would need to be another difficult conversation as her job and home were both in London.

'I'm going to take a breather,' he said and pointed to the front door. She watched in silence as he wandered onto the lane, and when the cuckoo clock chimed loudly, she nearly jumped out of her skin.

This shop, and the memories of Matilda, seemed more important to him than she'd realised. She looked all around. What exactly was she going to do?

Chapter Eight

The afternoon passed slowly. Fern had spent the last three hours perched behind the shop desk watching the dust particles dance in the afternoon sun and resisting the urge to lay down her head and admit defeat. Not one customer. Not even a window shopper. She shifted in the uncomfortable, lumpy chair and sighed. If this was what island life had to offer, she was doomed. A bell chimed in the distance, probably from the bakery down the street, taunting her with its promise of human activity. Why hadn't she just shut up shop this afternoon and gone to find the local estate agents? She could have had the For Sale sign flapping in the wind by the end of the week. Daniel hadn't reappeared. He'd taken his guitar with him and Fern thought he was probably busking somewhere, making more money in ten minutes than this shop probably did in a week.

She drummed her fingers on the wooden counter, then out of sheer desperation decided to at least pretend to be productive. Pulling open the drawer of the antique oak desk beside her, Fern was immediately engulfed in a cloud of dust. She coughed, waving the air clear, and peered inside. A single object sat in the drawer, a thick, battered accounts book, its corners dog-eared, the spine barely holding together. She hesitated, then picked it up and flipped to the most recent entry.

Her stomach dropped.

The last recorded sale was weeks ago. Fern blinked and doubled-checked the date, but she hadn't misread it. The last item sold – she squinted at the scrawled handwriting – was a porcelain ballerina figurine, for £18.50.

All Fern could think was: how the hell was Daniel even taking a wage from this place? She skimmed through the previous months, expecting to see at least some sign of a thriving business. But there was absolutely nothing. The numbers were sporadic at best. A dusty book here, an old brass key there. One month showed a total income of £62.

Fern shook her head in disbelief. This wasn't just a struggling shop, it was a non-existent business. She leaned back in the chair. She classed herself as quite an intelligent person, with oodles of common sense, so she couldn't fathom why Daniel was so certain that this rundown, neglected shop was something worth fighting for. Did he not realise how hopeless this was?

The bell above the shop door suddenly jingled, snapping her out of her thoughts.

She looked up eagerly; finally, a customer! But it wasn't a customer. It was Daniel. He waved a white carrier bag in her direction like a white flag and placed it on the desk in front of her.

'Still here then? I was half expecting to come back to a skip outside and a shop half empty.'

'Now there's an idea,' replied Fern. 'Especially after seeing this.' She pushed the accounts book towards him. 'The last recorded sale was weeks ago. For eighteen quid. Tell me, how exactly are you paying yourself? Or do you run on fresh air and optimism?'

'Well, technically, I'm not paying myself,' he admitted. 'Matilda never did, either. Not in the conventional sense.'

Fern frowned. 'What does that even mean?'

Daniel leaned against the counter. 'It means that this place was never about making money. Matilda ran it because she loved it. Because she believed objects carried stories, and those stories deserved to be found by the right people.' He tapped the book with one finger. 'If you're looking for a thriving business model, you won't find it in there.'

Fern crossed her arms. 'So she just gave stuff away for free and neither of you took a wage? What am I missing here?'

Daniel grinned. 'Sometimes she'd trade. Sometimes she'd wait for the right person to walk in. She told me this shop was a goldmine, you just had to believe in it.'

Fern rubbed her temples. 'Believe in what? Miracles? That is not how businesses work.'

He shrugged. 'It worked for Matilda.'

'Did it?'

'I get it,' he said, quieter now. 'You think this place is a lost cause, and maybe it is. But Matilda left it to you because you're family, and she hoped you'd do the right thing.'

'Matilda didn't even know me. This whole situation is bizarre.'

'Please give it a go, and don't do anything hasty,' he said, then smiled. 'I mean, some girls could only dream of inheriting a shop full of trinkets and stuffed dead animals, and sharing a bed with a handsome stranger.' He gave her a lopsided grin.

'You're deluded. What's in the bag?' She sniffed the air animatedly.

'I've brought food. The best fish and chips on Puffin Island. The van only comes once a week.'

Fern inhaled. The tang of salt and vinegar filled the air, cutting through the scent of old books and antique polish. Her stomach let out a tiny, traitorous growl.

'Curry sauce?' she asked, narrowing her eyes.

'A large tub of it.'

She exhaled dramatically. 'Okay. We can be friends again.'

Daniel smirked. 'You drive a hard bargain.' He turned and strolled towards a dusty old suitcase stacked with mismatched crockery, and rummaged through delicate floral-patterned teacups and plates with gold-rimmed edges.

Fern frowned. She stood up and followed him. 'What are you doing now?'

'Getting plates.' He pulled out two slightly yellowed dishes.

She recoiled. 'You can't be serious. I'm not eating off those dusty old things.'

Daniel wiped one against his sleeve. 'There. As good as new.'

'That's not how hygiene works!'

He sighed dramatically. 'Fine. I'll wash them.'

'What's wrong with the ones in the kitchen cupboard?'

'They're in the dishwasher and I forgot to switch it on. These will do.'

As he carried the plates towards the kitchen, a loud *thud* behind her made Fern jump.

She shrieked, leaning back in her chair to see a glass-eyed badger had toppled off a bookshelf. The chair gave a terrible creak just before the back leg snapped, sending her tumbling sideways.

'Whoa...' Daniel moved fast, dropping the bag and trying to catch her, but his knees buckled and the next thing she knew, they were tangled together in a ridiculous heap on the floor, Daniel half-straddling her, his arms braced on either side of her head.

For a moment, neither of them moved.

Their faces were *inches* apart. She could feel the warmth of his breath, smell the faint scent of salt and vinegar clinging to him.

Her heart pounded.

Daniel blinked, his smirk faltering. His dark eyes flickered to her lips for a second before snapping back to hers. 'You seem to be making a habit of falling for me.'

Fern swallowed, suddenly aware of everything – his weight upon her, the tension in his arms, the way his stupidly attractive face was just *there*.

'Get off me,' she whispered, but it lacked conviction.

Daniel didn't immediately move. Instead, his grin slowly returned, this time softer. More dangerous.

'I would,' he murmured, tilting his head slightly. 'But I think you're holding on to me.'

Fern glanced down, and damn it, her hands *were* gripping his shirt, like she had no intention of letting go.

Mortified, she shoved at his chest. 'Move, now. And that chair needs to go.'

'It does now you've broken the leg. Do you know how long that chair has been here?'

'Probably decades, judging by everything else in here.'

He chuckled, finally rolling off her. He held out his hand to help her up and Fern huffed and took it, scrambling to her feet.

'You can let go of my hand now.'

She dropped it immediately.

He was watching her, really watching her, as if something had shifted between them.

Fern swallowed. He gave her a heart-warming smile as he picked up the broken chair and moved it to the back of the shop before replacing it with one from the old dining table pushed up against the shop wall. 'Try not to break this one.'

Fern playfully pushed him towards the kitchen. He was still grinning as he swooped down and picked up the bag of fish and chips from the floor.

'Why don't you make yourself useful and set the table?' he suggested as he moved to unpack the food. He paused, looking back at her. 'Feels like we're a proper married couple, doesn't it?' He winked.

Fern didn't answer, too lost in her own thoughts. It had taken her by surprise how completely at ease she felt in Daniel's company, and she wondered exactly what Daniel Brooks' real story was. She'd come to Puffin Island wanting to get in and out as fast as possible, but he intrigued her. She wanted to know more, even if that meant staying longer than initially planned.

Chapter Nine

The bathroom door was half-open, and Fern could hear Daniel humming off-key in the bedroom, not caring in the slightest about his audience. She sat on the edge of the bathtub, brushing her teeth as he came into the room and leaned towards the mirror, running a hand through his permanently tousled hair.

'This is a bit intimate for a second date, don't you think?' he mused, smirking as he applied toothpaste directly to his tongue, forgoing a brush entirely.

Fern gagged. 'What are you doing?'

He grinned, foamy-mouthed. 'Speed-brushing.'

'That's revolting.'

'Efficiency is never revolting.' He leaned against the sink. 'At least I don't brush my hair for ten minutes like I'm about to meet the Queen.'

She narrowed her eyes, flipping her hair over her shoulder. 'It's called self-care.'

'Oh, sorry, and I suppose me sleeping in yesterday's T-shirt is called…'

'Tragic,' she replied.

'Unbelievable. Second date, and you're already insulting me.'

She shoved past him, their arms brushing against each other as she moved to rinse her toothbrush. She wasn't sure why she felt so weirdly aware of him tonight, why her skin seemed to remember his touch longer than it should, but as she climbed into bed, she felt safer with him lying next to her.

Once he'd climbed in, Fern reached to switch off the lamp on the bedside table. The room sank into darkness, except for the faint glow of moonlight creeping in through the ancient curtains. She lay on her back, facing the ceiling. The flat's eerie stillness made it impossible to ignore the absurdity of their situation. She wasn't supposed to be here, wasn't supposed to be sharing a creaky bed with a man she'd met two days ago, in a flat that felt like a time capsule of someone else's life.

Then, without warning … *touch*.

His fingers grazed hers gently. It was purely accidental, but neither of them moved away.

She swallowed. 'Daniel?'

'Fern?'

'What's your story?' she asked. 'I know you love junk, but why? What's the deal?'

There was a long silence and she thought he wasn't going to answer. Then…

'I lived with my gran from an early age,' he answered. 'She was … everything to me. She raised me after my parents died.'

Fern hadn't expected that. 'I'm sorry to hear about your parents.'

'Both were gone by the time I was ten. My dad got sick. Pancreatic cancer. It was fast, way faster than anyone thought. Three months from diagnosis to funeral. My mum... Jesus, she just couldn't cope. She was gone six months after that. Heart attack. They said it was natural causes but ... it wasn't. I believe it was grief.'

'Daniel, that's so sad. My dad died too, when I was ten,' she shared. It was a tragic experience to have in common. 'Mum passed when I was twenty-two. You were lucky having your gran.'

'I was. She was my dad's mum, and just amazing. We've always been close, and she was always obsessed with car boots.'

'Car boots?'

'Sales,' he said, amused. 'Not actual boots.'

'Go on...'

'Every Sunday morning when I was young, come rain or shine, we'd be at some random field or car park, rummaging through old treasures. She made a game of it, taught me how to spot value in what other people tossed away.' He let out a soft chuckle. 'She said the world forgets things too quickly. That it's our job to remember.'

Fern stared up at the ceiling. She had no idea why that made her chest ache.

'She died a few years back,' he continued. 'Matilda stepped into my life a month later. Remember I said she watched me bidding on the teapot against the posh guy? When I won, she came up to me to say congratulations and that was the start of our friendship. Matilda reminded me of my gran. They had the same spirit. She made sure I was okay when I had no one to look out for me, and she took me in when I had nowhere else to go. Taught me the business. Trusted me with it.'

That's why he didn't want to let it go. Why he couldn't.

Fern turned her head, watching his silhouette in the dark. He lay on his back, staring up, lost in thought.

She found herself whispering, 'I get it now.'

His head shifted slightly. 'Yeah?'

'Yeah.'

A pause.

'That was our first deep and meaningful conversation. If this really *is* our second date, I think you're pretty much in love with me now.'

She burst out laughing. 'Oh, shut up.'

'You are, though.'

She smacked his arm, feeling the warmth of his skin. His chuckle rumbled against the sheets.

'Why don't you go and have a look around the island tomorrow? You need to explore your future home.'

'Ha ha.'

'It's a beautiful place and I'm convinced you'll fall in love with it as much as you have with me.'

She swiped him again. 'Get to sleep!'

But as she turned away, she felt it. That pull towards him, like gravity shifting.

This was going to be a problem.

A big, ridiculous, Daniel-shaped problem.

Chapter Ten

Fern woke to the feeling of an empty bed. She stretched, feeling a little disappointed that Daniel wasn't still there. She reached for her phone and checked the time, and was amazed to see it was already past nine o'clock. She couldn't remember the last time she had slept in this late.

Normally, on a Monday, she would have been up around seven for a run, followed by Pilates, then breakfast at her local juice bar, a little hidden spot in Fulham where she always ordered the same thing: an açai bowl and an oat flat white. Then it would be straight to her laptop to start transcribing an interview or working on a feature for *Sound & Fury*, the music magazine where she had made her name in the industry.

Her phone beeped, and she felt a shiver of excitement as she saw the reminder that had popped up. Two weeks from now, she'd be in London at the hottest gig of the year, standing backstage with exclusive access to the biggest bands on the planet. It was the kind of event she lived for: the rush of the crowd, the electrifying energy, the post-show drinks in VIP lounges where music legends spilled their secrets.

She needed that night. Needed to remind herself who she was, that she wasn't some shopkeeper on a sleepy island but a journalist in demand, with a career people envied. She had worked hard to get where she was. Growing up, she had devoured every issue of *Rolling Stone* and *NME*, sneaking into indie gigs with a fake ID, determined to one day be part of that world. A journalism degree and years of hustling later, she had done it. Now, she spent her life at gigs, had the ears of the industry's biggest names, and had become a name in her own right. The next step in her career was to secure a position of editor, and soon she'd be back in London making it happen, sipping cocktails in some exclusive after-party, far away from dust-covered antiques. Fern swung her legs over the side of the bed and headed for the shower. She knew in time that Daniel would see things her way. The shop wasn't bringing in any revenue, and it was time to face up to the fact that it was at its end.

She padded over to the tiny bathroom, where the shower seemed determined to either scald her or freeze her, but after some careful negotiating with the taps, she managed something lukewarm. Ten minutes later she was wrapped in a threadbare towel staring at her reflection in the mirror. She had survived a second night in the flat, and having someone in her bed for the first time in a long time had felt very comforting. Most of her relationships, if you could call them that, had been built on convenience and little else. Late-night drinks that turned into rushed kisses and tangled limbs, always ending the same way: either she'd kick them out before dawn, or they'd vanish without so much as a goodbye. There was no room for vulnerability, no space for comfort. That was the deal, and she'd never questioned it. But this, sleeping next to someone, feeling their warmth still lingering in the sheets the next morning, felt startlingly different. It unsettled her how much she liked it.

After she said good morning to the moose's head like it was the most natural thing in the world, she followed the aroma of something sizzling in a pan downstairs and stopped in the doorway of the long, narrow kitchen, taking in its assortment of cabinets in varying shades of green, some doors hanging slightly askew, others proudly displaying their mismatched ceramic knobs. A farmhouse sink sat beneath a window, the glass fogged up from the steam from whatever Daniel was cooking. Pots and pans hung from a rack that swayed slightly whenever a breeze caught it. The walls were cluttered with vintage signs advertising long-forgotten brands of tea and biscuits.

The back door stood wide open, leading onto a small, stone-paved yard. Beyond it, rolling green hills tumbled towards the edge of a cliff, where the vast, glistening expanse of the sea stretched endlessly into the horizon. This was the first time she had properly seen the view and it was breathtaking, so much so that Fern found herself walking towards the open doorway, trying to process the fact that she was here, on an island, in a crumbling antique shop, watching a man she barely knew fry bacon and sausage in an ancient-looking pan.

'Wow! Look at that!' she couldn't help but exclaim.

'Morning, sleepyhead,' Daniel greeted her without turning around, flipping a sausage expertly. He was barefoot, his hair messier than usual, wearing another old T-shirt.

'Were you meaning to say that out loud? I know I'm a catch, but—'

Fern rolled her eyes and cut him off. 'I meant the view.'

'It's perfect, isn't it?' he said, turning to look at her properly.

She screwed up her eyes, wondering for a second if he actually meant her. He was definitely flirting, she decided, and she liked it.

'You're making breakfast again?'

'Full English today,' he declared proudly. 'Figured you might need some sustenance before you start plotting your escape back to London.'

She laughed but didn't deny it. Instead, she busied herself laying the table. As she placed the knives and forks down, Daniel turned, eyeing her with mock seriousness.

'This is important,' he said. 'Brown sauce or ketchup?'

'Brown sauce, obviously.'

He let out a dramatic sigh, shaking his head. 'This relationship isn't going to work.'

'Oh, please,' she replied, shaking her head and laughing as she slid into a chair. 'I should be the one reconsidering this whole arrangement. Who puts ketchup on a full English?'

'People with taste.' He grinned, setting down a heaped plate in front of her before taking a seat across from her. 'You don't know what you're missing.'

She simply raised an eyebrow and dug in. As she chewed, she found herself thinking about London, about her sleek, minimalist flat and the constant hum of the city. She should be missing it, shouldn't she? But instead, she felt oddly settled here.

Daniel watched her for a moment before clearing his throat. 'So, I know you're still set on selling the shop…'

She swallowed, glancing up warily. 'That's my plan.'

'Right… But I've been thinking.'

'Definitely dangerous.'

'What if … now, hear me out…what if you don't put it up for sale? Not for a month.'

'Why?'

'Because I think I can make it work. If I can bring in enough sales to keep this place afloat, would you consider keeping it?'

Fern hesitated, studying him. He looked serious, hopeful even, but there was something else in his expression … determination.

'In the past few weeks you've sold one porcelain doll.'

'Give me a chance! Matilda gave me a chance. I want to do this for her. I know how much she loved this place.'

Fern studied him closely. He was deadly serious. 'You really think you can make a difference in a month?' she asked, watching him closely as he tucked into his breakfast, which she had to admit was probably the best breakfast she had ever tasted.

Daniel wasn't like anyone she had ever met before. She thought about the type of men who usually crossed her path, the ones she dated. Their apartments were sleek, they booked tables at exclusive restaurants, ordering expensive bottles of champagne without even glancing at the price. Conversations revolved around stock markets, property investments and the latest tech start-ups they were backing. They were ambitious, successful and utterly predictable … and usually only lasted a couple of dates. Jax Devlin was the exception to the rule. With him, it was something that just happened every time he was in town.

'But then what? You make it work for a month and then…'

He shrugged. 'And then we have another chat.'

Fern couldn't see anything changing enough in a month to make her change her mind. She wanted the property sold and money in the bank.

'Give me a chance,' he pleaded.

It had only been a couple of days, but the more time she spent in his presence, the more she felt herself being drawn to him in a way that both intrigued and terrified her. There was a rawness to him, a kind of natural charm that didn't come from wealth or status but from simply being Daniel. She tried to think of the least snooty boyfriend she had ever had, and even he had owned a Rolex and once argued about a wine pairing he disagreed with at a Michelin-starred restaurant.

She sipped her tea, watching as Daniel smothered his entire plate in ketchup with reckless abandon.

'I know I can do it.' He smiled. 'And, I mean, worst case scenario, you get to watch me fail spectacularly, and you still sell the place.'

'I'll think about it,' she promised.

'You will?'

'I will.'

They carried on eating, but Fern had an important question she needed to ask. Trying to sound uninterested, she dove in. 'So … have you got anyone special in your life?'

He paused and looked up at her. 'Nah. Why, you volunteering?'

'Hardly,' she scoffed. 'I was just wondering what she'd think of us sharing a bed.'

He smirked, taking a sip of his coffee before speaking. 'Well, considering she doesn't exist, I reckon she'd be surprisingly chill about it.'

Fern rolled her eyes. 'You're impossible.'

'No, I'm just saying. If I had a girlfriend, she'd obviously be cool as hell and totally fine with me shacking up with a stranger in my haunted museum of a home. Probably even encourage it.' He grinned. 'That's how I'd know she was the one.'

'Oh, of course. That would be the test.'

'Exactly. But you know, it's a shame you're not volunteering.' He tapped his fork against his plate, pretending to be deep in thought. 'I mean, this time next year, we'll probably be married anyway. Might as well get a head start.'

She gave him an exasperated look. 'I've said it before and I'll say it again, you're deluded.'

'We'll see,' he said, utterly unfazed, going back to his breakfast as if he hadn't just confidently predicted their future together.

Fern shook her head, but she couldn't stop the smile tugging at her lips.

Maybe he was deluded. Or maybe, just maybe, he was onto something.

Chapter Eleven

After breakfast, Fern stood in the doorway of the kitchen, lingering just a moment longer than necessary. Daniel was sitting outside on a worn-out chair, his guitar balanced on his knee, fingers idly strumming a soft melody. His notepad was open on the patio table in front of him, a pen tucked behind his ear. His tousled blond curls fell over his forehead, and the faded grey T-shirt, clinging just right, paired with his Levi's and battered Converse, made him look unfairly good.

When he glanced up and caught her watching, he grinned, an easy, lopsided smile that sent an unexpected flip through her stomach. It had been a long time since that had happened.

'I'm heading out to explore the island. Might as well, since I'm only here for a short time.'

Daniel smiled, strumming another chord. 'That's what you think. Once you see Puffin Island, you'll never leave. There's no place like it.'

'You don't give up, do you?'

'I'm just speaking the truth.'

She watched him for a moment longer before grabbing her bag. His words stuck with her as she stepped outside No. 17 Curiosity Lane. The distant crash of waves and the sharp cries of gulls filled the air, not sounds you hear in the middle of the city. As she set off down Anchor Way the sun was surprisingly warm, casting a golden shimmer across Bluewater Bay. The sea stretched out before her, the waves lazily rolling against the shore. The air smelled of the seaside and something sweet, maybe from a bakery nearby, and she took a seat to savour the view.

Fern had always loved the coast. One of her fondest childhood memories was of a family holiday on the Pembrokeshire coast when she was seven years old. She'd spent hours watching the waves roll onto the shore, mesmerised. There was something deeply calming about the sea. Yet the thought of actually living by it had never crossed her mind. Her parents had been city people through and through, firmly rooted in the hum of urban life. Even as a child, she had been immersed in that world, attending a city school where independence was expected. By the age of eight, she was already navigating the London Underground on her own, hopping onto the tube before switching to a bus, making her way to school with the confidence of someone far beyond her years.

The coast had always been an escape, a fleeting glimpse into another way of life, one she had never considered could be her own. Fern sat on a weathered wooden bench near the bay, staring out at the jetty where the Sea Glass Restaurant sat perched at the end. She'd read about it and its famous glass-bottomed dining experience, where guests could sip wine while watching marine life swim beneath them. On the other side of the bay, the lighthouse stood proudly, its white and red stripes bold against the blue sky. Fern exhaled, letting her thoughts drift back to Daniel's ridiculous proposal. How exactly was he going to make people buy junk? And was she really expected to sit around for a month while he worked his so-called magic before selling the shop? Would this mean staying on the island longer, or could she just leave him to it? She could work remotely, her job allowed it, but she thrived on the energy of the city, with the constant movement, the hum of conversation. Could she really trade that for creaky floorboards and eccentric antiques? She stood, brushing the thought aside for now, and wandered a little further along the bay until she reached a small, inviting hut with a hand-painted sign proclaiming it the Cosy Kettle. The smell of fresh coffee wafted from the hatch.

Fern turned to see a woman with sun-flushed cheeks and a blue headscarf tied over her hair. Her apron was splattered with coffee stains and what looked suspiciously like Nutella. She beamed at Fern, wiping her hands on a tea towel.

'What can I get you?'

'A latte, please.'

'Coming right up. Are you on holiday?'

'Actually, no. I'm Fern. I've … inherited No. 17 Curiosity Lane. Matilda's place. I'm her great-niece.'

The woman blinked, her expression softening instantly. '*Matilda's* shop? Oh wow.' She leaned on the counter, her eyes bright with something close to affection. 'That place is legendary around here. We all wondered what might happen to it. It's wonderful to hear it'll stay in the family.'

Fern didn't have the heart to correct her and share that she was on a mission to get it sold.

'I'm Becca, and this is my little kingdom,' she said, gesturing proudly to the hut. 'The Cosy Kettle. Open all hours. I would have thought I'd have seen you around, visiting Matilda, but I've not seen you before on the island.'

'It's ... complicated. I didn't know she existed until a little over forty-eight hours ago.'

'Gosh! That's a shame, as she was brilliant, but I can guarantee you will love it here just as much as she did. This place gets under your skin.'

'I'm starting to see that,' Fern admitted, taking the warm coffee Becca handed her.

'Well,' Becca said with a smile, 'you've already found the best coffee on the island so you're off to a strong start. If you need anything – a night out, waffles in the morning, a baked potato dropping off at the shop for lunch – just shout.'

'I will, thanks,' Fern replied before settling at one of the little wooden tables. For the first time in ages, she actually felt relaxed. This place had a strange kind of calm, like time didn't rush forward the way it did everywhere else.

'Hello again.'

Fern looked up to see Amelia standing in front of her. She smiled, pulling out a chair and sitting down. 'How's life in No. 17 Curiosity Lane?'

Fern took a slow sip of coffee, then placed the cup on the table. 'Well, it comes with a gorilla named Gerald who watches over the shop; he's very protective of his porcelain kingdom. There's also a moose's head looming over the bed, so each morning I've woken up to the haunting gaze of a woodland beast. Oh, and the best part? It came with a free man.'

Amelia choked on a laugh. 'A free man?'

'Yes. Tall, blond, irritating, humorous. Plays guitar. Thinks he can convince people to buy, and I quote, "junk".'

Amelia grinned. 'Ah, Daniel. And how's that going?'

'He's given me a proposal.'

Amelia's eyebrows shot up. 'Well, that was fast.'

Fern laughed. 'Not that kind of proposal. He wants me to hold off on selling the shop for a month, let him prove he can make it work.'

Amelia leaned back, considering. 'What do you think? Is that an option, or do you really want to get rid of it?'

Fern glanced towards the bay, the glistening water, the peaceful lull of the island. A month. It wasn't that long, was it?

She sighed. 'I think I might be going mad because I'm actually considering it.'

Amelia smiled. 'Ha! Puffin Island has already lured you in.'

'I've got one week's leave to try and sort everything out. I thought I would organise someone to clear the shop then put it up for sale, but now…'

'What if Daniel can make it work?'

'If he was serious about it, why hasn't he made it work before?'

Amelia shrugged. 'Maybe he didn't want to stand on Matilda's toes. He was there for her right up to the very end. It could just be that she was more important to him than actually making money. He's a decent person, fitted straight into this community when he arrived. Matilda met him at an antique fair, and she definitely had a soft spot for him. It was an unlikely friendship, but they really did hit it off. I suppose, thinking about it, he didn't have a chance to try and make it a success until now. After all, it was her shop.'

Fern understood. 'What would you do?'

'I'm biased.' Amelia smiled. 'There is something special about this place and if you have a chance to stay and live on the island, I would say you've won the lottery. Not many places come up for sale here, and with No. 17 Curiosity Lane you get both accommodation and the business. Granted, it may not be to your taste, but you could easily turn it around. If antiques isn't your thing, could you turn it into something else? It's in a prime location. Maybe give it some time, and if you still feel like you want to sell, at least you will know it's the right decision because it wasn't rushed. See what Daniel can do. What do you have to lose?'

Ten minutes later, Fern was making her way back to the shop with Amelia's words still firmly on her mind. What did she have to lose? As she pushed open the door, she was half expecting Daniel to be lounging around somewhere with his usual smirk, but the shop was silent. She dropped her bag onto the counter and shouted out to him but there was no answer. After grabbing a glass of water and her laptop Fern sat down at the desk with only one thing on her mind, something she had been meaning to do since she arrived – digging into Matilda Hartley's past.

Opening her laptop, Fern typed 'Matilda Hartley Puffin Island' into the search bar and hit enter. Immediately, dozens of results surfaced, and she clicked through them, scanning headlines. The usual obituaries, property records and old business listings were there, but then she spotted something more intriguing, a decades-old article from the *Puffin Island Gazette* titled 'A London Musician Trades Her Notes for Nostalgia'.

Fern clicked the link, her heart beating faster as an image loaded at the top of the article, a grainy black-and-white photograph of a young woman standing in front of No. 17 Curiosity Lane. At a guess she was in her early twenties, the same age Fern had been when she first started making a name for herself in music journalism.

The woman in the photograph had sharp cheekbones, unruly waves of dark hair and a gaze that would melt hearts.

She began reading the article.

Matilda Hartley was a promising student, sweeping every award for her compositions at the London School of Music. She was destined for stardom, and her lecturers predicted she would take the music world by storm. But just as all eyes turned to her, Matilda made an unexpected move, trading future concert halls for curiosities. She turned her grandmother's holiday cottage into No. 17 Curiosity Lane in the heart of Puffin Island, where the rhythm of her days is set not by music, but by the quiet intrigue of forgotten treasures.

Fern wondered why Matilda left music behind. If she had been destined for stardom and, it seemed, had the world of her feet, why would she choose to open a shop full of old junk?

Further down the article, a more personal note caught her attention:

Hartley turned her back on the music world under circumstances she prefers to keep private. When pressed, she simply said, 'Sometimes the past must stay buried.'

Scrolling further, Fern found numerous articles highlighting Matilda's extraordinary talent during her years at music school. Even from a young age, Matilda had shown remarkable versatility; not only was she a gifted pianist and singer, but also a budding composer whose original pieces, written during her college years, earned praise from seasoned professionals. Her college performances, both solo and with ensembles, regularly drew large audiences, and often filled local concert halls to capacity. Critics lauded her as a prodigy, frequently noting the emotional depth and technical mastery that set her apart from her peers. She became a regular fixture at regional music competitions, taking home first-place awards and scholarships year after year. Teachers spoke of her as a once-in-a-generation talent, and there was a growing sense among the music community that Matilda was destined for international stages. Fern couldn't find any reason why she had given everything up to open a shop filled with junk. It just didn't make sense to her.

There was still no sign of Daniel. She wanted him to walk through the door so she could ask him whether Matilda had shared anything about her past with him. Surely they must have had some conversations about it? Closing the laptop, she stood and moved through the shop, running her fingers over the oddities Matilda had collected over the years. She was now genuinely intrigued by her great-aunt.

Fern's gaze landed on a small wooden box, its lid slightly ajar. Inside, a pair of wedding rings rested on a velvet cushion, the worn metal inscribed with initials. Next to it was a stack of old books, their pages yellowed with age. She pulled one free, dust rising as she opened it. Further along, she delved into a pile of faded pamphlets, when she noticed an old vinyl record tucked between them. It looked immaculate. The name on the sleeve made her pause. *Nathaniel Loring.* Fern knew Nathaniel Loring's name. He was extremely famous in his day and as a music journalist she was familiar with his work. She studied it; it looked like new. The song title was 'Echoes of the Past'. Fern recognised it as his debut song, the one that had catapulted him into the limelight and ensured every other song he released charted instantly.

Noticing a record player over in the corner, Fern set it up, placed the record on the turntable and carefully lowered the needle. A soft crackle filled the silence, followed by the start of the beautiful song. She hadn't heard it in ages, and it caught her off guard how emotional it made her feel. After the song finished she put the record back in its sleeve. She lifted the lid of her laptop again and for the next hour got lost researching Nathaniel Loring's life. The internet was packed with information about him. There were a series of professional profiles, biographies and news articles. His Wikipedia page showed he was born in 1940. A London Music College graduate, he'd gone on to become one of the most celebrated composers of his generation. She scrolled further. The songs he wrote had been sold to some of the most iconic artists of the sixties, shaping the sound of an era.

He'd made a fortune from his very first composition, a piece that had become globally recognised and re-recorded by countless classically trained artists. His success in the music industry had catapulted him into the realm of multimillionaires. But the most surprising detail was that Nathaniel had spent most of his life in Italy, living in the heart of the musical world, before returning to England just ten years ago. In his early years, Nathaniel had opened a music school in London, which was still thriving and nurturing young talent today. The music she had heard earlier, it wasn't just a song; it was the reflection of a legacy.

Just then, Daniel walked in through the back door, guitar in hand.

Fern smiled and he narrowed his eyes. 'Why are you looking at me like that?'

'Because, Daniel Brooks, I've made a decision,' she said with an exaggerated dramatic flair. 'I'm going to give you a chance.'

Daniel cocked an eyebrow. 'Are you going to suggest moving in permanently? Because if you are, we really need to talk about the bed situation.' He leaned against the door frame, looking more amused than anything. 'You snuck over to my side again this morning. I mean, I don't want to sound presumptuous, but I think that's a little forward. After all, we haven't even made it to date three yet.'

Fern's mouth dropped open. 'Don't be ridiculous.'

Daniel grinned. 'So you were just … *accidentally* making yourself comfortable on my side of the bed? Totally understandable.'

Fern rolled her eyes. 'Be serious for a second!' She walked over to the shelf of dusty knick-knacks and picked up a vase. 'This shop is a goldmine of chaos, but I think we could make it more … functional.'

'Go on…'

She motioned vaguely around at the mismatched furniture, the stuffed badger sitting on top of a bookcase. 'We should put this place in some sort of order, dust the shelves, catalogue everything, and maybe, just maybe, create a social media account to attract some attention.'

Daniel looked at her as though she'd just suggested they open a fire-breathing circus in the back.

'A social media account? For *this*?' He gestured at the

cluttered antique shop, where items were piled upon each other like a mad professor's hoard. 'You keep saying I'm the one who's deluded ... but now you're talking about us selling this as some sort of ... influencer lifestyle?'

Fern grinned mischievously. 'Oh, I'm talking TikTok, Daniel. You could write little songs for all the different items. I'm sure collectors would love that. You could compose music inspired by the 1800s candlesticks or the 1930s toaster. Who knows? People might go crazy for it.'

Daniel took a step back, horror written all over his face. 'You've lost me. I'm no TikTok sensation.' He clutched the guitar strap over his shoulder as though it were a lifeline.

Fern arched an eyebrow, clearly amused. 'Well, if people aren't going to walk through the door, we're going to have to bring the door to them. Let's make it happen. What do you think?'

'You told me it was best I didn't think.'

'You have a month to turn this place around.'

'Why the change of heart?'

'Because it's only a month. Now, fetch the duster and a new logbook.'

He saluted. 'If marriage is on the cards though, you really have to work on your bossiness.'

Fern shook her head in despair but secretly enjoyed the banter between them. 'Right, let's get these dusty old blinds fully open and we need buckets of water. Everything needs a good wash down.'

Chapter Twelve

Daniel strolled back into No. 17 Curiosity Lane from the kitchen, a bucket of water sloshing in one hand and a pile of dusters in the other. But it was the pink rubber gloves stretched up to his elbows that truly completed the picture.

Fern took one look at him and laughed. 'Nice gloves.'

'You can laugh all you want,' he said, placing the dusters on the desk then wiggling his fingers with exaggerated flair. 'These beauties are the only thing standing between me and the unspeakable horrors lurking in this shop.'

'You do realise you're wearing them inside out?'

Daniel glanced down, sighed and began peeling them off to fix them. 'I was going for dramatic effect.'

Fern stood in the middle of the shop, surveying the absolute mayhem around her. Dust motes swirled in the air, the light filtering through the grimy windows in streaks of golden disapproval. Every available surface was crammed with something: precariously stacked books, mismatched porcelain dolls with unsettlingly vacant stares, a collection of tarnished silverware that may or may not have belonged to an aristocrat or a very dedicated magpie. And spiders. So many spiders.

'Right,' she declared, eyeing a cobweb that had taken on the architectural complexity of a small cathedral. 'We are sorting this place out.' She looked up at the shelving unit in front of her. 'There's a spider the size of a teacup in the corner. That's not an ecosystem, that's a horror film waiting to happen. However, he's about to be evicted.' She rolled up her sleeves. 'Along with all his creepy little relatives.'

With that, she grabbed an old broom leaning against the counter and prodded at a particularly cobwebbed bookshelf. A small avalanche of dust cascaded down, followed by a very disgruntled spider. Fern shrieked and stumbled back, swiping at her hair.

Daniel laughed. 'You can't just go attacking them. They have squatters' rights.'

'You're supposed to be helping, not laughing! It's you who wants to keep this place open.'

'You're right.' He saluted. 'Let's make a start.'

That was the moment Fern unknowingly kicked off what she'd later call the 'Great Dust Purge'. Daniel tackled the counter, half-heartedly wiping down surfaces with what may have once been a cloth but had since evolved into an artefact in its own right. Fern, meanwhile, armed herself with a feather duster that had likely not seen action since the Edwardian era.

'This place is a museum of chaos,' she muttered, picking up an ornate clock with an ominous-looking crack down the middle. 'Why do you even have this?'

'Semantics.'

For a while, they lapsed into companionable silence. The bathwater lapped against the sides, and Fern let herself unwind, her muscles loosening after the day's exertion.

Then, on a whim, she asked, 'So, Daniel … what did you do before you ended up here?'

There was a pause that was just a second too long. When he spoke, his voice had lost its usual teasing lilt. 'Bit of this, bit of that.'

Fern frowned. 'Meaning?'

'Meaning,' he exhaled, 'I didn't have a real place or purpose for months before I met Matilda. I was crashing on the sofas of friends and acquaintances, anyone who'd let me stay for a bit. Did odd jobs when I could. Enough to keep going.'

She turned her head towards the door. 'You didn't have your own place or a steady job?'

'Not for a while. There was a time when my possessions would fit in one bag.'

Fern absorbed this in silence. She couldn't imagine it. Not knowing where you'd sleep each night. Living in that state of uncertainty, relying on the kindness or tolerance of others. Her own life was structured, every detail planned. She knew exactly how much she earned and how much went on bills. She had a gym membership, food deliveries every Thursday night, and an exercise class schedule she stuck to religiously. She didn't live in chaos. She lived in order. And yet here was Daniel, this cheeky, sarcastic, infuriatingly charming man who had lived without any of that stability and somehow, he still found a way to laugh.

'That's…' She trailed off, not sure what to say.

'It was what it was,' he said simply. 'Matilda took a chance smelled suspiciously of mothballs, and she was fairly sure there was an entire dust bunny colony residing in her lungs. Needing a bath, she stared at the Victorian mannequin in the bathtub. It had taken her half an hour to work up the courage to move it, mainly because its glassy-eyed stare made her deeply uncomfortable. Once she had dragged the lifeless thing out of the bath and propped it against the wall, she decided the bath was safe for use.

Daniel, naturally, had been no help at all, watching her struggle with obvious amusement.

'You could have helped.'

'I was enjoying the show.'

She shut the bathroom door. 'Privacy is needed.'

With the bath finally hers, Fern turned the taps on full blast, pouring in a generous amount of the vaguely floral-scented bubble bath she had found in the cabinet. It was probably older than she was, but at this point, she'd take anything that didn't smell like antique furniture and despair. The moment she slid into the hot water, a groan of pure relief escaped her lips. Bliss. Absolute, unparalleled bliss.

From the other room, she heard the rustle of Daniel shifting on the bed. 'You alive in there?'

'Barely,' she called back. 'I may never move again,' she said.

He laughed.

'I feel like I've been exhumed.' She stretched out, sinking deeper. 'That shop was disgusting. How did you live in this place before I came along?'

'Low standards,' Daniel said cheerfully. 'And an ability to ignore the horrors of my surroundings. It's a skill.'

Fern rolled her eyes, though he couldn't see her. 'I think you mean laziness.'

'Shut up and help!'

He did, but not before picking up a particularly battered copy and reading aloud. *'The Duke's Forbidden Desire'*. Oh, Fern, you've been holding out on me. You're a secret romance fan, aren't you?'

She snatched it from him, only for another book to slip from the pile and fall open at their feet. *How to Woo a Gentleman in Ten Easy Steps*. She groaned.

Daniel smirked. 'Might be useful.'

'Find me a dustpan.'

By the time they were done, the shop looked marginally better. The dust had been reduced by at least twenty per cent, the spider population had suffered a devastating blow and they'd managed to clear enough space to at least pretend they were running a legitimate business and not an elaborate set for a gothic novel.

Fern collapsed into the not so comfy chair behind the counter. She exhaled, stretching her arms behind her head. 'Well. That was a productive day.'

Daniel leaned against the counter, brushing a smudge of dust from his cheek. 'I think Matilda would be impressed. You did well, city girl. You survived your first real day as an antique shop owner. I think you're going to fit right in.'

Much to her own surprise, she'd enjoyed every second and actually believed him.

Fern had never felt filthier or more exhausted in her life. After a day of scrubbing, dusting and nearly choking on cobwebs, she felt like she'd absorbed a decade's worth of grime. Her hair

Daniel peered over. 'That's the Cursed Clock of Lady Witherington.'

She blinked. 'The what?'

'Legend says it stopped at the exact moment she died.'

'And you just … keep it here? Like a souvenir?'

'People love a bit of macabre history. Besides, it still technically works.' He reached out and tapped it. The clock immediately let out an eerie chime and one of the hands fell off. 'Mostly.'

Fern groaned. 'I'm surrounded by madness.'

A cloud of dust exploded into the air as she lifted a box labelled MISCELLANEOUS MYSTERIES. She coughed and waved her hand. 'What's even in here?'

Daniel shrugged. 'Could be treasure. Could be cursed trinkets. Could be last year's receipts. Life's an adventure.'

Bracing herself, she lifted the lid and immediately recoiled. 'Why is there a stuffed ferret wearing a monocle in here?'

Daniel grinned. 'Oh, that's Lord Nibblesworth. Matilda said he would be very popular with eccentric collectors.'

'I bet he was. Probably haunted their dreams.' She shook her head and shoved the box aside. 'Right. Let's try and make some actual progress before I lose the will to live.'

The hours passed in a blur of sneezes, laughter and Fern's relentless determination to make a dent in the chaos. Daniel, despite his initial reluctance, ended up quite enjoying watching her attempt to battle the forces of entropy.

At one point, she tried to carry a box of vintage books, only for the bottom to give out, sending a cascade of leather-bound novels tumbling to the floor. Daniel clapped slow applause. 'Majestic.'

on me, though. Gave me a roof over my head. Gave me a purpose.'

Fern's fingers traced patterns through the bubbles. 'And now?'

'Now, I have to put up with you, so I'm questioning all my life choices.'

'Charming!'

Silence settled between them again, but this time, it was different. It was charged, somehow. He had let her see something real, something beneath the jokes and the bravado. And she felt... Well, she wasn't sure what she felt.

Then, with a sudden brightness, Daniel broke the mood. 'Tell you what. We've been absolute troupers today. I say we celebrate.'

Fern raised an eyebrow, though, again, he couldn't see it. 'Celebrate how?'

'I'll go and get us a bottle of wine.' His voice was lighter again, teasing. 'Unless, of course, you're too posh for a cheap supermarket special?'

She huffed. 'I'm not posh.'

'I bet you're the kind of girl that has her supermarket shop delivered at the same time every week.'

There was silence.

'Oh my God ... you are!'

'I like efficiency!'

'And you probably have a gym membership.'

'Lots of people have gym memberships! Now go and get the wine.'

He laughed, then pushed a little further. 'You know, this kind of sounds like a date.'

Normally, Fern would have snapped at him to shut up

again. Normally, she would have called him an idiot and dismissed the idea entirely.

But this time … this time, she hesitated.

'See you in the garden,' she said instead, voice light.

There was a pause, then an unmistakable grin in his words. 'It's a date!'

Chapter Thirteen

It was twenty minutes later when Fern stepped out of the bath, wrapping herself in a towel as her phone buzzed on the bedside table, her best friend's name flashing across the screen. Fern smiled as she picked up her phone.

'Hello!' she answered, towel-drying her hair.

'There you are! It's not like you to not check in. I just want to know if you survived your first few days in Antique Purgatory. I thought you'd fallen off the face of the earth.' Ella's voice rang through, bright and full of life. 'I'm assuming you're home now. What are you doing tomorrow night? We're all going to that new wine bar in Soho, super posh, super exclusive.'

Fern tucked the phone between her ear and shoulder as she rummaged through her suitcase. Even though it was just drinks in the garden with Daniel, she wanted to look good. She pulled out a simple but flattering dress and put it on as Ella continued talking.

'Ella, I...' She slipped her feet into her ballet shoes. 'I'm not in London.'

'Where are you then?'

'I'm still here, on Puffin Island, in an antique shop I somehow own, with a man I barely know who insists he's not leaving, and I'—she took a breath—'I might actually be having fun.'

Ella let out a dramatic gasp. 'Fern. Are you being serious? In a place that probably doesn't even have Uber or a decent wine bar? Who even are you?'

'I can confirm there are no Ubers,' she replied, and recounted the horror of her suitcase bumping across the causeway when she arrived.

'It sounds awful!'

'The highlight of my day was dusting a shelf full of porcelain cats.'

'Tell me everything.'

Fern didn't leave out any details. She babbled on about the shop, the flat and, of course, Daniel – his stubbornness, his maddening confidence, the way he somehow made the whole situation seem normal. Then she shared the sleeping arrangement.

'You're sharing a bed? With a stranger?' Ella shrieked so loudly Fern had to pull the phone away from her ear. 'He could be a mass murderer.'

'He's not!' Fern protested. 'And I'm grateful for his company as the bed has a moose head looming over it. I've also built a pillow barricade.'

'This Daniel, does he respect the pillow barricade?'

Fern hesitated. She thought of the moment she'd woken up yesterday morning, tangled in Daniel, his arm draped over her.

'That's irrelevant.' She could sense Ella shaking her head on the other end of the line.

'Fern. This is insane. I don't like the sound of any of this. You're not staying there.'

'I never said I was staying—'

'You need to sell that place. Quickly. Who on earth would want to own a shop full of junk?'

Fern looked around, suddenly seeing it through Ella's eyes. The haphazard furniture, the clutter, the sheer impracticality of it all. She was a music journalist, not an antique dealer. This wasn't her life. Ella was right, she'd just run away with herself, got caught up in the situation somehow.

'Promise me you'll sort it … if not today, then tomorrow.'

'Okay, I promise.'

'Good. And then get yourself home, where you belong.'

After hanging up, Fern mulled over the conversation. Ella had been talking sense. It was a shop full of junk with no income. It wasn't a business and the whole place was in need of repair. She was just thankful it hadn't rained yet, because she was sure the water would leak through the roof and windows. Fern dried her hair, put on some makeup, then sat on the bed, phone in hand. After searching through her emails, she found the email from the local solicitor, Edgar Carmichael, and clicked the link that took her through to his website. She was astonished to see that his office was on Anchor Way. Her fingers hovered for a moment before she booked an appointment for ten a.m. the next day.

She exhaled. It was the right thing to do.

'Done,' she muttered to herself. It was pure due diligence for her to see if she could sell it even with Daniel living and working here. She could make sure he was going to be okay.

She wandered downstairs; everywhere was quiet. The back door was open and as she stepped out into the courtyard she stopped short.

Daniel was there, waiting for her. He had arranged plush cushions on the outside chairs, and the wine was already poured into two mismatched glasses. He'd even scattered lanterns around the courtyard and they glowed softly. He turned at the sound of her footsteps and smiled. 'Took you long enough. I was about to drink both glasses.' Then he really looked at her. His expression shifted, his usual teasing gone. 'You look gorgeous.' The intensity of his gaze caused goosebumps to erupt along her arms.

'Thank you,' she replied, taking the compliment. She sat down and Daniel passed her a glass of wine.

'To us, and No. 17 Curiosity Lane, and the future.'

She swallowed. Her head was telling her to hold on to the firm decision she had made to sell the shop. This wasn't her life, not really. But sitting here, with Daniel and a glass of wine in her hand, wrapped in candlelight, her heart was telling her something different. She glanced at Daniel with his ruffled hair and eyes full of something she wasn't sure she was ready to name, and she found herself wondering: should she listen to her head or her heart?

Chapter Fourteen

Fern swirled the wine in her glass. 'Last week I never would have been able to picture myself drinking wine outside an antique shop that smells like mothballs with a man I barely knew.' She smiled. 'But it's actually not that bad.'

Daniel grinned. 'Correction: it smells like history.' He raised his glass with mock sophistication.

She took a sip, eyeing him. 'Can I ask, how are you actually living right now? If you have no income whatsoever?'

For a moment, something flickered in his eyes, and after a brief silence, he spoke. 'I have a little bit of inheritance … not much…'

Fern could kick herself for asking the question. Why hadn't she realised that it was more than likely he had inherited money?

'But I mainly live for the moment. Take each day as it comes, fly by the seat of my pants. Do I need money to be happy? Absolutely not. I have lost so many people in my life that meant everything to me, and I've realised the biggest life lesson of all – that life is for living, not worrying. Waking up on Puffin Island every morning to that view, and being part of this wonderful community, means more to me than anything else. I just want to be a good person.'

Daniel's views were so different from her own. Of course, she wanted to be a good person, but she also craved routine, a stable job, the security of knowing she didn't have to worry about money. Yet now, for the first time, she found herself questioning, was she happy? Truly happy? How did she actually know?

They both took a sip of wine and looked out at the sea in the distance. 'I think you're right,' said Fern. 'There's definitely something about that view.'

'Isn't there just.' He smiled at her warmly.

'I do think social media will be the way to go to try and put this place on the map. I mean, we could actually set a whole new trend. We need a gimmick. Something different. I honestly think the public will fall in love with you if you make up songs about the different items for sale. What do you think is the most sellable thing in the shop?'

Daniel thought for a moment. 'I've actually no idea. It's all about what catches a particular buyer's eye.'

Fern stood up.

'Where are you going?'

'Wait here.'

Fern walked from the kitchen into No. 17 Curiosity Lane and flicked on the light. She looked around. The shop was now a slightly more organised mess of trinkets, relics and oddities, each with its own questionable charm. If she were to pick something that screamed viral sensation, she needed to think outside the box.

Her eyes landed on a ceramic frog. No. Too predictable. A rusted suit of armour? Too impractical. Then, nestled between a porcelain teapot shaped like Queen Victoria's head and a stuffed ferret wearing a bow tie, she spotted it, the perfect item.

A wooden duck.

It wasn't just any wooden duck. This one had a beady-eyed stare and an expression that hovered between mild disappointment and existential dread. One of its wings had been repaired with what looked like ancient glue, and a faded price tag dangled from its neck.

Perfect.

Snatching it up, she walked back outside to find Daniel looking relaxed with his legs stretched out. He looked up and immediately raised an eyebrow.

'A duck?'

'A wooden duck,' she corrected. 'And not just any wooden duck. This could be the face of our marketing revolution. This could be your chance to shine, to put No. 17 Curiosity Lane on the map.'

'Now I think it's you who's deluded. Who's going to want to buy a duck?'

'There's a whole shop of this junk, so if we can't sell it, we get rid of it.'

'We?' he questioned.

'Yes, we. I like a challenge!'

Daniel smiled then gave the duck a sceptical once-over. 'You're putting an awful lot of faith in an inanimate bird.'

'Let's move into the shop. Grab the wine and your guitar.'

Back inside, Fern perched on the desk. 'We need a tagline before we do this. Something catchy. Something that makes people come back for more.'

Daniel tapped his chin, deep in thought. 'How about "Curiously Curated, Chaotically Celebrated"?'

Fern wrinkled her nose. 'Bit long. Needs to be snappier.'

'What about "One Man, One Guitar, One Bizarre Item at a Time"?'

She considered. 'Better, but…'

'You do know the internet's attention span is about three seconds, right?'

'Exactly! We need a hook! Something like…' She sat up straighter, a lightbulb moment flashing across her face. 'No. 17 Curiosity Lane, where history gets a soundtrack!'

Daniel strummed a dramatic chord. 'You really think people will care about me making up songs about junk?'

'I think people love weird and wonderful things … and you're certainly weird and wonderful.'

He smirked. 'I'll take that as a compliment.'

'Now, serenade the duck.'

'I've done some things in my time, but this…' Daniel gave the wooden bird a dubious look before plucking out a playful melody. He bobbed his head, found a rhythm and then, with an exaggerated flourish, began to sing to the tune of an old-timey sea shanty.

> *'Oh, this ain't just a wooden duck,*
> *It's got that antique, vintage luck!*
> *It's seen some things, it's heard some tales,*
> *From dusty shops to grand estates!*
> *Quack, quack, don't turn your back,*
> *This duck's got charm, that's a fact!*
> *A noble bird, a desk's delight,*
> *Buy it now and sleep at night!'*

Daniel looked horrified as he sung the last word. 'That was absolutely dreadful and didn't make any sense whatsoever!'

Fern clapped. 'I love it! Now, let's film it.'

She whipped out her phone, adjusted the angle, and started recording. 'Welcome to No. 17 Curiosity Lane, where history gets a soundtrack!'

Daniel, grinning, launched into his duck ballad once more, hamming it up with theatrical eyebrow wiggles and a dramatic flourish at the end. He held the duck aloft like a prize-winning trophy.

They reviewed the footage, and Fern cackled. 'It's ridiculous, and it's perfect.'

Daniel peered at the video. 'So now what?'

'Now,' she said, uploading it to the shop's freshly made TikTok account, 'we unleash it on the world and put a price in the title.'

'It's worth pennies!'

'And pennies add up. If we can make more than the porcelain doll, the only thing that has sold in weeks, then we take that as a win.'

Within minutes, the comments began rolling in:

'I don't know why, but I need this duck.'

'What in the Kate Bush fever dream is this??'

'If I buy the duck, do I get a personalised song?'

'What exactly does that mean?' asked Daniel, perplexed until Fern explained.

'A Kate Bush fever dream means it's theatrical, and slightly eccentric. Her music and videos are often dreamy, dramatic and visually striking. The views are going up so quickly!'

Daniel blinked. 'Wait. Are we … trending?'

Fern refreshed the page. 'I think it may take more views than we have right now, but we're definitely setting the trend!'

He stared at her, then at the duck. 'Well. Guess I'd better start tuning up for episode two.' He strummed his guitar, then they clinked their glasses together before Fern began searching for the next item to sell.

Chapter Fifteen

A few hours later Fern and Daniel lay sprawled on the bed, their backs propped up against the pillows, the glow from Fern's phone illuminating their faces in the dimly lit room. No. 17 Curiosity Lane had just made its third sale in less than an hour, and neither of them could quite believe it.

'I mean, we actually sold the duck.' Fern let out a laugh, shaking her head in disbelief.

Daniel grinned, stretching his arms behind his head. 'And a porcelain potty; that's an achievement in itself.'

'Sales are now over forty quid. Isn't social media just the best? Instead of waiting for customers to walk through the door, we're bringing what we have to them.' Fern had immensely enjoyed her evening; in fact, she'd not had this much fun in ages. She turned her phone towards Daniel, displaying the long thread of comments beneath their post. People had been fascinated, entertained and, more importantly, ready to buy.

'I'm still not over the fact someone actually paid money for it.' She tapped her screen, scrolling. 'And look! We've got bids on the set of haunted spoons and the Victorian-era wig stand.'

Daniel smirked. 'Let's be honest, that wig stand is nightmare fuel. I wouldn't keep it in this flat if you paid me.'

Fern arched a brow at him. 'This from the man who sleeps beneath a moose's head?'

He shrugged. 'Me and that moose have an understanding.'

Rolling her eyes, Fern returned her attention to the phone. The thrill of selling eccentric antiques had turned into something of an addiction. She refreshed the page, anticipation buzzing in her veins. Then…

'Oh my God,' she gasped, sitting up so quickly the phone nearly flew from her hands. 'Daniel, it just sold!'

He bolted upright. 'What?'

'The wig stand! Someone just bought it!'

There was a brief, stunned silence before they both erupted into wild laughter. It was ridiculous, absurd, and yet the exhilaration was real. Without thinking, Fern launched herself at Daniel, knocking him back against the pillows as she wrapped her arms around him in pure, unfiltered excitement.

'We did it!' she squealed, her face buried in his shoulder as she hugged him. 'We actually did it! Sales are now at one hundred pounds.'

Daniel's laugh was warm against her ear as he held onto her. 'I take full credit. It was all my excellent salesmanship.'

She pulled back, grinning down at him. 'You take credit? I'm the one who came up with the idea!'

'Yeah, but I'm the one who convinced everyone it had historical charm rather than genuinely terrifying presence.'

Fern let out another laugh, still beaming, still too caught up in the moment. Her eyes flickered over Daniel's face, the teasing glint in his gaze, the way his mouth curled at the corners. Before she could even think, before she could stop herself, she kissed him.

It was quick, instinctual. A press of lips in the heat of the moment. But then she felt it, the solid warmth of him beneath her, the way he inhaled sharply in surprise, and worse – so much worse – she caught the intoxicating scent of his aftershave, which was dark and rich, like cedarwood and spice, and wrapped around her senses, making her stomach flip.

She froze.

'Sorry, I've had too much wine,' she apologised.

He didn't say anything. Their faces were still inches apart, eyes locked. His lips were slightly parted, his breath warm against hers, and she knew, knew, that she should move. Pull away. Laugh it off. But she didn't.

Instead, she felt the way his hands tightened slightly on her waist, how his gaze flickered to her mouth, how something unspoken but heavy crackled between them.

Then … he kissed her back.

It wasn't tentative. It wasn't careful. It was all-consuming. One moment of hesitation, and then a firestorm. His fingers tangled in her hair, his other hand sliding to the small of her back, pulling her against him. Her hands gripped his T-shirt as their lips moved hungrily against each other.

It was a blur of heat and pressure, of shifting bodies and tangled limbs.

Her body pressed closer to his, and he groaned softly against her lips when she ran her hands through his hair.

Somewhere in the back of her mind, a voice reminded her that this was a terrible idea. That she would be selling the shop from underneath him and heading back to London as soon as possible … that this could go horribly, spectacularly wrong. But she didn't want to think about that right at this moment. Not when his lips found the curve of her neck, not when his hands skimmed over her waist, not when every nerve in her body felt electrified by his touch.

'Fern…' Daniel's voice was husky, low, a plea and a promise all in one.

She shivered. 'Yeah?'

His forehead rested against hers as they both tried to catch their breath. 'Tell me this isn't just because we sold a haunted wig stand.'

She let out a laugh, still half-dazed. 'I mean … it was a really big moment for us.'

He chuckled, but his grip on her didn't loosen. If anything, it tightened. 'Be serious.'

She watched him. 'It's not just that.'

His lips brushed against hers again, softer this time, slower. Like he was savouring every second. 'Good,' he murmured.

Fern swallowed, her heart pounding. 'You know this changes everything, right?'

Daniel exhaled, his thumb tracing slow, lazy circles against her hip. 'Yeah. I know.'

Then, just as quickly as it had happened, reality crashed back in.

She was lying on top of Daniel. In his bed. The bed that, only a few days ago, she had sworn was too ridiculous for her to sleep in. They were tangled together in a way that felt so intimate, so natural, and yet entirely inevitable.

She swallowed hard. 'So, uh … what now?'

Daniel smirked. 'I vote we sell more weird antiques.'

She rolled her eyes, but the warmth of his hands on her waist made it hard to be exasperated. 'That's your big takeaway from all this?'

'Well,' he mused, fingers brushing idly over the curve of her back, 'that, and the fact that we're both terrible at pretending we don't want to do this again.'

She swallowed. 'Yeah?'

'Yeah.' He tilted his head, his lips barely brushing hers again. 'Unless you'd rather pretend this never happened?'

She thought about it for all of two seconds before shaking her head. 'Not a chance.'

Daniel grinned. 'Good.' He kissed her again.

Chapter Sixteen

Fern stretched out luxuriously, her body humming with the afterglow of an unforgettable night. The sales, the song and, oh, the sex. She bit her lip, grinning up at the ceiling. Who would have thought that a dusty old antiques shop on a tiny island could lead to a night like that? But as she shifted under the covers, she realised something was missing. Or rather, someone. Daniel wasn't in bed. She sat up and listened. She could hear movement downstairs as she swung her legs over the side of the bed and threw back the curtains. The sun was shining and the view of the sea made her smile even more. As she turned around, she laughed. Daniel's sweatshirt was draped haphazardly over the moose's head mounted on the wall. She tugged on it, then slipped it over the top of her PJ's, inhaling the faint, lingering scent of him as she padded barefoot downstairs.

Walking into No. 17 Curiosity Lane, she was amazed to see it was already open. The blinds had been drawn up and the door was ajar, the fresh morning breeze filtering into the shop. The first thing she noticed was items piled high on the desk, a chaotic assortment of trinkets, plates and things that, if Fern was being completely honest, probably belonged in the bin. Sitting amongst it all, was Daniel, looking entirely too pleased with himself.

She leaned against the door frame, arms crossed over his oversized sweatshirt. 'What are you doing?' she asked.

'Making my fortune!' Daniel declared grandly, tossing his arms wide as if he had just uncovered the lost treasures of the world. 'Now, get yourself up and dressed. We have songs to write, content to upload and items to send to our buyers. I've drafted some songs to go along with these items and listed our sold items in the accounts book. We're aiming to double yesterday's takings today.' He grinned and, before she could protest, he stretched an arm out and pulled her in close. The warmth of him, solid and reassuring, sent a flutter through her chest. He pressed a kiss to the top of her head, lingering just a second longer than necessary. 'I've got a good feeling about today,' he murmured.

Fern stayed nestled against him for a moment longer than she meant to. Last night had been fun, undeniably so. But this morning, reality was creeping back in. There was still the shop, still the uncertainty of what she was going to do with it, and, of course, her solicitor's appointment. She felt a tiny twinge of guilt but told herself it was just an information-gathering exercise.

Shaking off the thought, she turned her attention to the front door, where a bulging bin bag sat ominously on the doorstep. 'What's that?' she asked, pointing towards it.

Daniel barely spared it a glance. 'More antiques. People just leave them outside like this is some kind of magical antique wishing well.'

'It's not a charity shop.'

'You'd be surprised,' he muttered, picking up an old pocket watch and inspecting it as if it held the secrets of the universe.

Fern stepped towards the door and dragged the bag inside, the plastic crinkling under her fingers. It was heavier than she expected, its contents shifting as she wrestled it across the floor. After she untied the knot and opened it, she stared. Inside, nestled in layers of crumpled tissue paper, was a wedding dress. The fabric, though aged, was delicate and intricate, lace cascading down in elegant patterns. The bodice was fitted, the skirt flowing like something out of a fairytale. Fern pulled it fully out of the bag and held it up. Its long train pooled over the shop floor. Pinned to the front of the dress was a note.

'"Find the groom",' she said, reading it aloud. She handed the note to Daniel. 'What do you make of this?'

'This place gets weirder by the second.' He examined the dress in her arms. 'It looks like it's from the 1960s. Expensive, too. But who would leave this here? It looks like it should actually be in a museum.'

'You're telling me someone deliberately left a priceless antique dress on the doorstep? With a cryptic note?'

'Looks that way.' Daniel examined the note. 'Either that or it's a practical joke? If we did find him, then what?'

'Maybe he's a celebrity, or maybe he left someone at the altar. How much do you think it's worth?'

'With the little bit of knowledge I learned from Matilda...'

'You talked about wedding dresses with Matilda?'

'You'd be surprised what we chatted about...' He examined it closely. 'I think this could fetch at least two thousand pounds.'

'No way!' Fern was amazed. 'So it's not the usual kind of junk you'll find in here. Do you think it's a sign?'

'A sign someone no longer wants it?'

She shook her head. 'A sign that this place can actually make money. I think we should investigate. After all, I'm a journalist.'

'A music journalist.'

'What if the groom leads us to another expensive item and then another? It would be like a treasure hunt.' She glanced around, as if expecting a ghost bride to appear and claim it. 'What else are we supposed to do with it?'

'Try it on. If nothing else, you can model it and we can get it on the internet with a song, asking the question of who the groom might be.'

Fern gawped at him. 'Excuse me?'

'It's a brilliant idea. You dress up in it and let's ask social media for clues about the groom.' Daniel held the dress against her. 'I think it'll fit. People get invested in stuff like this.'

Before she could argue, he ushered her behind the wobbly antique privacy screen that was embroidered with exotic birds.

'Just think! You could be the first person to wear that in nearly a century,' joked Daniel.

'That's exactly what I'm afraid of.'

Fern reluctantly took off the sweatshirt and her PJ's and slipped into the dress. The fabric was surprisingly soft, the lace intricate and fragile. It was a perfect fit. Which, frankly, was unnerving.

'Oh no,' she muttered.

'What?' Daniel asked eagerly.

'It actually fits.'

'Excellent. Come out then.'

She hesitated, but there was no escaping this. Taking a deep breath, she stepped out from behind the screen.

Daniel let out a low whistle. 'Bloody hell. You look like you belong in a portrait.'

Fern smoothed her hands over the bodice. 'This is weird, right? Like, actually weird.'

'Oh, absolutely.' He circled her, taking in the details. 'If you suddenly start speaking in riddles and demanding a dowry, I'm running.'

She shot him a look. 'If I start speaking in riddles, you have my permission to burn the dress.'

Daniel chuckled. 'Not a chance. If I sell that dress, the sales for this month would be amazing.' He nodded towards the note. 'So? What do you think it means? "Find the groom"?'

'I don't know. Maybe it's metaphorical.' She struck a dramatic pose. 'Find the groom ... find oneself.'

Daniel considered this. 'Or maybe it's literal, and some poor sod lost his bride a hundred years ago and still haunts Puffin Island, waiting.'

'Or the bride was waiting and the groom didn't turn up.'

Before Daniel could answer, the shop door jingled, and in swept an elderly woman whose presence was as warm as the morning sun spilling through the freshly cleaned windows. She had the kind of face that put people instantly at ease; laughter lines framed her bright blue eyes, and her silver-streaked hair was gathered into a loose bun, secured with a wooden spoon she'd clearly forgotten was there. She wore a cosy knitted cardigan over a floral apron, lightly dusted with flour, as if she'd just stepped away from kneading dough.

'Hello!' she chimed. 'I just thought I'd come and introduce myself. I'm Betty, the owner of The Café on the Coast, and you must be Fern!'

Fern took an instant liking to her. There was something undeniably comforting about Betty's presence, like a grandmother who always had time to listen, and always had a tin of biscuits at the ready.

'Yes, that's me. Matilda's great-niece,' Fern replied, glancing down at herself with a self-conscious chuckle. 'Do forgive my appearance. I'm fully aware I look like a runaway bride.'

Betty's gaze flicked over the billowing vintage wedding gown. But before she could respond, another woman stepped into the shop, her dark curls bouncing as she moved.

'Granny, I told you to wait for me! I'm Clemmie,' she said, turning to Fern with a smile, 'co-owner of The Café on the Coast, and granddaughter to this one,' she said, gesturing ruefully at Betty. 'Amelia told us you were here, so we thought we'd come and say hello. And, like we do with all new arrivals to the island, we've brought cake!'

She held out a well-worn cake tin, and Fern's eyes widened.

'Wow, I wasn't expecting this, thank you!'

'I have to say though…' Clemmie's eyes twinkled mischievously as she took in Fern's attire. 'If we'd known it was your wedding day, we would have made it a wedding cake.'

Fern laughed, shaking her head. 'This dress is a mystery.

We think there's some kind of secret behind it. It was dropped off this morning with a cryptic note.'

Betty and Clemmie exchanged intrigued glances.

'What did it say?' Betty asked, her tone shifting into something more serious.

'I should share with you both that Granny here is the keeper of secrets on this island. She knows everything there is to know about the past, present and even the future,' Clemmie said, a glint in her eye.

Daniel, who had been standing quietly to the side, took the opportunity to lift the lid of the cake tin. 'It said: "Find the groom",' he supplied, his voice slightly muffled as he took in the contents. He grinned, clearly pleased with the discovery. 'Just for the record, lemon drizzle is my absolute favourite.'

Betty, however, had her focus elsewhere. She reached out and ran her fingers over the wedding gown's fabric. 'This is definitely vintage,' she murmured, her expression thoughtful. 'And good material – silk, by the feel of it. This would have cost a fortune in its day.' She studied the stitching, the intricate lace detailing. 'How old do you think it is?'

Daniel, always eager to show his knowledge of antiques, spoke up. 'My guess is early sixties,' he said confidently. 'See the cut of the bodice? And the lace overlay? It's very much in line with the bridal trends of that era. The detailing suggests it wasn't off-the-rack either, this was custom-made.'

Fern glanced at him, impressed. She had to admit, despite his tendency to be exasperating, he really did know some stuff.

She turned back to Betty. 'So, do you recognise this dress?' she asked, tilting her head. 'What do you think it means? I'm all for unravelling a mystery.'

'I've never seen it before but it's exquisite. Do let us know if anything interesting evolves,' said Betty.

Clemmie leaned in. 'She's just being nosey!'

Betty swiped Clemmie before she turned and walked out of the shop. Clemmie followed her, waving above her head. 'Enjoy the cake!'

Chapter Seventeen

Daniel leaned against the counter, phone in hand, reviewing the footage they had just shot for No. 17 Curiosity Lane's social media accounts. The antique wedding dress had been the perfect dramatic centrepiece, draped around Fern as she recited the cryptic note: 'Find the groom'.

With a chuckle, Daniel paused the video. 'Our audience is going to love this. Also, we've had another two sales! I started listing things online while you were still in bed.'

Fern narrowed her eyes. 'Define "things",' she said, stepping behind the screen to change out of the wedding dress.

Daniel grinned. 'Well, we've now sold an Edwardian moustache curler and a Victorian mourning brooch made with someone's actual hair, totalling sixty quid.'

Fern shuddered. 'I don't know what's worse, the moustache curler or the human hair.'

'Personally, I think the taxidermy frog playing a miniature violin will be our next big seller. People love weird things.'

'Ha ha,' Fern shot back from behind the changing screen,

her voice muffled. 'Less commentary, more assistance. I'm stuck.'

'What do you mean you're stuck?'

'I mean, I can't get out of this thing! The zip is stuck. It won't budge.'

Daniel set his phone down and strolled over to the screen. 'All right, hold still. I'll be the dashing hero and rescue you from your fabric prison.'

'Less talking, more unzipping.'

'If you insist!'

Daniel stepped behind the screen, and immediately the space felt smaller, charged. Fern's back was to him, her bare shoulders peeking out where the dress had slipped slightly.

'Can you just ... oh! That's my hair!'

'Oops. Sorry. You're right, it's stuck.'

Daniel focused, tugging slightly at the zip.

'Pull it harder, I'm beginning to overheat in this thing.'

He tugged hard, the zip came undone, and the dress slipped further off her shoulders as she caught it against her chest. She felt her heart beat faster. She glanced over her shoulder and jumped. 'Who was that?'

'Who was what?'

'There was someone in the doorway,' she whispered, eyes wide. 'I didn't see who it was, but they were standing there, watching.'

Daniel turned swiftly, but the entrance to the shop was empty.

'They've gone now. Nothing to worry about.'

'Go and take a look.' She shooed him from behind the screen. 'I need to get changed.'

Two minutes later, she hung up the wedding dress and

hooked it over the door at the back of the shop. 'Do you think someone was checking whether we had the dress?'

He shook his head. 'You're overthinking it. It could have been someone just passing by and you got the jitters because of the cryptic note. This place does wonders for anyone's imagination.'

'I agree, but I have a feeling that this mystery is only just beginning.'

'All we can do is wait and see if any more clues emerge.'

'Or we need to dig deeper.'

'Someone on this island must know something.'

'But if Betty doesn't recognise the dress… You heard what Clemmie said, nothing ever gets past her.'

'Something may have done this time. Let's see if the social media inquiry throws anything up. In the meantime, make me a coffee … wifey!'

'Oh, hilarious!'

'It'll happen one day, you just need to stop fighting it.'

'I've said it before, and I'll say it again…'

'I know … I'm deluded!'

'Milk? One sugar?'

'Perfect.'

Chapter Eighteen

At precisely 9.45 a.m., Fern glanced at her watch and took a deep breath. Her appointment with Edgar Carmichael, the local solicitor, was fast approaching. She hadn't told Daniel where she was going or why, and there was no denying she felt guilty. She knew they had agreed, and she had promised, to give him a month to turn the shop around, yet here she was, slipping out to discuss her options. It wasn't exactly lying, but it wasn't being honest either. The truth was, she needed to know what she was dealing with. The building would need a valuation, and even she could see it was in dire need of repair. There were cracked windowpanes, damp creeping along the skirting boards, the faded sign swinging precariously above the door. It all pointed to a costly headache she wasn't sure she wanted and if she did keep this place, she'd be his landlord by default, responsible for every leaky pipe, every broken window, every late payment. She had no interest in that kind of responsibility.

She looked across at him; he was sitting at the desk,

scrolling through the comments on the social media posts. He caught her eye and gave her a lopsided grin that made the guilt worse, but she pushed it aside. She needed to be practical. This wasn't just about Daniel, it was about her future too.

'Sold!' he announced, his voice full of excitement. 'Gerald the gorilla. We've got another hundred pounds coming our way.'

'Gerald? You sold *Gerald*?'

Daniel's grin faltered as he looked down at the screen again. 'Yeah, well ... Matilda said he's been living rent-free in the wardrobe for years, so...' He leaned back on the chair and rubbed the back of his neck, clearly pleased with the sale, but Fern noticed something else creeping into his expression.

'What's wrong? You suddenly look ... conflicted.'

Daniel let out a soft laugh, shaking his head. 'I feel a little funny. I was excited at first, but now it feels like I'm evicting him. He's part of the family. I mean, the guy's been hanging around this place for goodness knows how long, and here I am, shipping him off for a hundred quid.' He looked over at the old gorilla, now sitting awkwardly in the corner by the door, his glassy eyes staring back at them.

Fern smiled, watching the change in Daniel's demeanour. He was trying to be practical, but the sentimental side of him was undeniable. It was endearing, really. 'You're going to miss him, aren't you?'

'Yeah,' Daniel admitted with a soft chuckle. 'A little. But a sale's a sale.' He glanced at her. 'It's a step in the right direction, isn't it? We're actually doing this, Fern.'

She nodded, feeling the twinge of guilt in the pit of her stomach. 'Yeah, it is,' she agreed. 'I'm nipping out for half an hour. Will you be okay on your own?'

He glanced up. 'Of course. Going somewhere fun?' he asked. 'I thought we could get some more items online.' He picked up his guitar and strummed a note.

Fern hesitated. She didn't want to tell him the real reason for her trip just yet. 'Just a few errands to run and journalist calls to make. I won't be long, and don't you dare touch that lemon drizzle cake whilst I'm gone.' She grabbed her bag and stepped outside on to Anchor Way. She discovered she didn't have to walk far, because Edgar Carmichael's office was next door. Fern would have to time it just right so that Daniel didn't spot her.

A faded sign hanging precariously from a rusty chain swayed over the duck-egg blue door that opened onto the stairwell leading up to Edgar's office. She made sure Daniel couldn't see her open the door, and followed the smell of coffee to the top of the stairs. She knocked and heard the scrape of a chair before the door swung open and she was greeted by a man in his late sixties dressed in a worn but neat suit, with salt-and-pepper hair that curled in an unruly way at the nape of his neck. His pale blue eyes, sharp and discerning, were half hidden behind a pair of wire-rimmed glasses.

'Fern Talbot,' she announced.

'Matilda's great-niece. I've been expecting you. Please come on in. It's lovely to meet you,' replied Edgar.

Fern stepped into the office and smiled, glancing around the room. Shelves sagged under the weight of thick legal volumes and dusty files. The large oak desk was the room's centrepiece, its surface covered with papers, but still meticulously organised. To the left of the desk, a small window allowed slivers of the afternoon light to seep in. She shook his hand and took a seat across from him. 'Thank you for seeing me at such short notice.'

'Not at all,' Edgar said, settling back in his chair. 'She spoke about you on a number of occasions and was especially proud when she read your first article in *Sound and Fury*.'

'She read my article?'

'She did. She wanted to reach out many times, but she was afraid that it might cause complications with the family.'

'I didn't even know she existed.'

'That's what she thought. She was a remarkable woman. Kind-hearted. She had a way of making people feel wanted, at home. She loved that shop. It's a real part of this island.'

Fern smiled despite the lump forming in her throat. 'She certainly left an impression on everyone.'

'That she did. Always had an eye for the unusual. So, what can I do for you?'

Fern hesitated, then took a breath. 'I need to know my options. I've inherited No. 17 Curiosity Lane, but according to the books it's not made any money for a long time … and then there's Daniel.'

Edgar nodded knowingly. 'Ah, Daniel. Yes, I had a feeling this might be the topic you wanted to discuss.'

He pulled a folder from a drawer and opened it, running a finger down the page. 'Now, Matilda was very fond of him. She made arrangements to ensure he wouldn't be left out in the cold. While the shop and property belong to you legally, Daniel has what we call "sitting tenant rights".'

'Meaning?'

'Meaning you can't simply evict him without due cause. He has a right to stay, and he has a legal agreement with Matilda, which complicates things. A property with a sitting tenant may be worth less on the open market because the buyer can't move in immediately or charge market rent.'

Fern exhaled sharply. 'I've not seen anything in writing.'

'I have a copy of their agreement here. Matilda asked me to keep hold of it.' He slid a piece of paper across the desk.

Fern picked it up and looked it over. 'There's no end date on this. How long is this valid for?'

'If you turn to the second page you'll see … it's valid indefinitely.'

Fern raised her eyebrows. 'You're saying Daniel can legally stay for as long as he wants?'

'He can. A private landlord can offer a contractual tenancy that lasts for the tenant's lifetime. It just needs to be clearly stated in the agreement.' He pointed to the place in the document. 'It's carefully drafted to avoid legal loopholes or unintended consequences.'

'Why would Matilda do that?'

'She was very fond of him and knew he had no one left in the world to look out for him, and she wanted to make sure he had a roof over his head.'

Fern was perplexed. Why hadn't Matilda just left Daniel the shop and the business? Then she wouldn't be in this predicament.

'Am I able to just put it up for sale?'

Edgar tilted his head. 'Not easily. If you were to sell, the new owner would have to honour Daniel's tenancy unless he willingly agreed to leave. You could always consider offering him a settlement to vacate, but knowing Daniel, I doubt he'd take it. He's not motivated by money and is very attached to the place.'

'So, I'm stuck with a shop I don't want and a tenant who refuses to leave?'

Edgar smiled kindly. 'I wouldn't say stuck, Miss Talbot. You have options. You could try working with Daniel, see if there's a middle ground. Maybe he could manage the shop for you. Who knows? Perhaps you'll come to see No. 17 Curiosity Lane the way Matilda did.'

'It seems I don't have much choice.'

'There's always a choice,' Edgar said gently. 'But sometimes it's not the one we expect. Is there anything else I can help you with today?'

She hesitated before shaking her head and standing. 'Actually, can I ask you something?'

'Of course.'

'How long have you lived on the island?'

'All my life. Why do you ask?'

'Something out of the ordinary happened this morning. An antique wedding dress was left in a bin bag on the shop's doorstep. There was a note attached, with just three words: *Find the groom.* I'm not sure what to do about it.'

Edgar's brows lifted slightly. 'That is cryptic. If anyone can help you, it's Dorothy. She lives in one of the rainbow cottages on Lighthouse Lane, the bright blue one. She was the island's seamstress for decades, made more wedding dresses than she could count. She's retired, but if she didn't make the dress herself, she might still recognise who did and point you in the right direction.'

'I'll try Dorothy, thank you.'

Fern stepped out of the office, not knowing quite how she felt. The shop wasn't just bricks and mortar; it had a history, a stubborn tenant and now a mystery. The idea of selling it had seemed straightforward, but it was quickly becoming anything but.

Chapter Nineteen

The timing couldn't have been any worse if she'd tried. Daniel had just finished chatting to the postman when Fern walked out of the front door of Edgar's office, and they locked eyes for just a moment before he looked up at the solicitor's sign flapping in the breeze.

Damn. She could feel the guilt written all over her face.

'You've been to see Edgar then?' he said flatly.

Fern hesitated. 'Daniel...'

He bristled. 'You went to him for advice, didn't you? To get me out. You're trying to sell this place.'

Fern exhaled, steeling herself. 'I was just weighing up my options. I thought it was the responsible thing to do.'

'I have a legal tenancy agreement.'

'I know, and I'm sure we are able to work something out.'

His voice rose slightly with frustration and what sounded like a bit of hurt. 'You haven't even given me a month. I thought we had an agreement. But no, you waltz in here, thinking you know best, when really you don't have a clue about this place. What it means to me. What it meant to Matilda.'

'Shall we take this inside?' she suggested gently. 'We don't need to have this conversation for the whole of Puffin Island to hear.'

Daniel stepped inside the shop, leaned against the desk and stared at her. He clearly wasn't going to make this easy for her.

'I'm trying to be practical! Just look at this logically for a second. The shop barely gets customers, Daniel, and even when it does, it's not making enough income to keep it afloat long-term. How can you not see that?'

'Oh, I see plenty,' he shot back. 'I see that you don't want to try. That you'd rather run back to London and leave all this behind because it's messy and unpredictable and doesn't fit into your perfectly organised life.'

'That's not fair,' she protested, though secretly she could see his point.

Daniel exhaled sharply, raking a hand through his hair. 'What about us?' he asked, his voice quieter now. 'What happens to us?'

Fern's stomach tightened. 'Daniel … this … this … is…' She fell silent.

'I want to hear you say it.' His gaze bore into hers, unwavering. 'Was it just a one-night stand after too much wine?'

She hesitated, her throat dry. 'We're adults,' she said finally, though the words sounded hollow even to her own ears.

'So you're saying it was just a bit of fun, to keep you amused, boost your ego, whilst you were here? A way to pass the time of day.'

'No, that's not what I'm saying.'

'It sounds like it to me.'

'I do like you, Daniel, I would hope that goes without saying. And yes, I shouldn't have gone to Edgar behind your back. That was wrong. But you and I ... we're different people, from different worlds.'

He huffed a laugh, but there was no real humour in it. 'Different worlds? Is that how you see it?'

'I like order. I work every hour I can. I play hard with my friends. I even like paying my bills on time. I don't fly by the seat of my pants.'

'Let's get this straight. What you're saying is you regret it happening now because you suddenly realise that I don't drive a flash car, drink cocktails in London bars, have a job that pays a decent salary, and most probably wouldn't fit in with your life and friends.'

'I didn't say that.' This was such an awkward conversation. Why had she complicated things by falling into bed with him? She knew exactly why: because she found him drop-dead gorgeous. He definitely wasn't like her usual type – he was sensitive and shared his feelings – but that was like a breath of fresh air to her.

'You didn't have to.' He shook his head, a mixture of disappointment and disbelief in his eyes. 'You're looking down on me. Judging me by the way I choose to live my life. You think it's beneath you.'

'That's not true.'

'Isn't it? You think I don't work? That I don't try? That just because I don't measure life in how much I can control, it makes me some kind of failure? I live, Fern. I enjoy things as they come. I don't stress about nonsense like bill reminders or whether my dinner plans fit into a Google calendar. I take people as they are. I like them for who they are, not for what they have. Maybe you should try that sometime.'

Fern swallowed. She wanted to argue, to tell him he was wrong, but was he? That's exactly how she had been living her life and, right at this moment, she wasn't proud of it. The silence stretched between them. Then, without another word, Daniel turned and walked away.

'Daniel. Please don't go.'

'I just need some space.'

She watched him walk out the door and down the lane. She couldn't really blame him. After closing the door, she sat down at the desk and glanced towards Gerald, who was leaning against his wardrobe door with a SOLD sign hanging around his neck.

'I think it's safe to say I've messed up, Gerald.' She sighed and wiggled the computer mouse. The screen lit up and a quick glance at the open sales page showed a neat little total in the corner.

£300.

She stared at it, stunned. Daniel had already made three hundred quid today. Maybe she had underestimated him and the shop.

Fern knew she needed to find him and talk to him. She didn't want to let things fester. She had been wrong about the way she had handled this, and though she could be stubborn, and had never been one to apologise easily, this was different. Daniel was different. He was getting under her skin, making her question everything she thought she knew. It only took a second a lock up the shop and turn the sign to CLOSED.

Now, where did someone go on Puffin Island when they needed space? Her guess was the bay.

She wandered down the narrow, winding street, scanning the crowds along the beach. It was busy and as she glanced towards the Cosy Kettle she spotted Amelia talking to Becca.

'Hey, sorry to interrupt, but have you seen Daniel?'

Amelia and Becca exchanged a glance before Amelia answered, 'Yes, just now, but he didn't look happy.'

'That's down to me. I owe him an apology.'

Amelia's expression softened. 'He headed up to the cliff top.' She pointed towards the winding path that disappeared into the sand dunes. 'Hope you can sort it. By the way, I was hoping to catch you today. There's a few of us have drinks at the pub tomorrow night if you fancy it, just a girly thing we do each month.'

'Please do come, Fern!' Becca encouraged.

'That would be great.'

'Fab! We'll be meeting at seven,' said Amelia.

Fern thanked the women before heading towards the clifftop path via the sand dunes, which were covered with wild grass swaying in the breeze. She climbed steadily, the sound of the waves becoming more distant. At the top of the hill, a quaint cottage came into view. It was beautiful and looked straight out of a storybook, with whitewashed walls and a thatched roof. Wildflowers spilled over the garden wall, a riot of colour against the deep green grass.

Then she spotted him. Daniel was sitting on a weathered wooden bench, just near the cottage, looking out to sea.

It wasn't just him that stole her breath away, it was the thousands of puffins dotting the cliffs and wandering in and out of their burrows. She had never seen one before, and now they were everywhere. Their little orange feet, their bright beaks, the way they bobbed and waddled – it was mesmerising. The sheer number of them, nesting and gliding effortlessly over the waves, was unlike anything she had ever seen before. It was a world away from the chaos of London, the deadlines, the constant drive to get ahead. For a moment, she simply stood there, taking it all in.

Daniel must have sensed someone was there as he looked over his shoulder. His expression was unreadable at first, and for a moment, she thought he might turn away. But he didn't. He simply watched as she made her way over and slid onto the bench beside him. For a second neither of them spoke; they listened instead to the distant sound of the waves crashing below, felt the breeze blowing through their hair. She took a deep breath. 'I'm sorry.'

Daniel didn't respond right away, but he didn't move either.

Fern swallowed, summoning the nerve to continue.

'I was wrong about everything. I should have considered how you felt before I barged in, acting like I had it all figured out. The truth is … I've never been in a situation like this before. I've never inherited a shop, or met anyone like you.'

That got his attention. He turned slightly, his eyes locking onto hers. 'What do you mean, "anyone like" me?'

'Someone who genuinely cares about people, community, doing the right thing, and isn't motivated by money.' She gave a shaky laugh and shook her head. 'Which, honestly, scares the hell out of me. I didn't come to Puffin Island expecting anything, or anyone. It was supposed to be a quick visit to get the shop ready for sale, before going straight back to London.'

He raised an eyebrow.

'There's a small part of me that's afraid,' she admitted quietly. 'Afraid of this place, of what it's starting to mean to me, and afraid of you. Because...' She hesitated. 'After speaking with Edgar, I've realised that Matilda left me this place for a reason. I just don't know what that is yet.

'This island is all about people and what they mean to each other. You wouldn't get anyone in the apartment block where I live nipping in with a home-baked lemon drizzle to welcome you. You'd get a grunt of a hello in the lift if you were lucky. I've never really had that in my life. In my industry, people use each other for what they can get out of the relationship. Friendships are superficial.' The thought of Ella popped into her head. Though she'd been a constant in Fern's life since childhood, lately she'd found herself wondering if they were slowly becoming different versions of themselves, shifting in ways neither of them was ready to acknowledge. Ella was still chasing the nights out and cheap thrills, whereas Fern could see a different future for herself, one that was a bit calmer, a bit quieter, and perhaps even had more ... puffins?

'Whatever is going on between us, it's started to matter more to me than I'm ready to admit. I'm not used to anything that even resembles a real relationship.'

Daniel's expression softened.

'This isn't going to sound great,' she went on, 'and I'm not proud of it, but in London everything moves fast, including relationships, if you can even call them that. My focus has always been my career. The men I've been with were ... convenient. The kind who don't ask for commitment. Sometimes I didn't even ask for their names. It was easier that way. Detached. Safe.'

She glanced up, meeting his eyes. 'I've made a habit of keeping my distance from anything real.'

Daniel's voice was low when he finally spoke. 'Isn't that a little sad?' he asked. 'Don't you think you deserve more?'

It was such a simple question, but it struck her like a blow. She looked away, blinking back the tears, pretending to focus on the puffins even though they were a blur. 'I don't know,' she said finally. 'I think, somewhere along the line, I convinced myself that I didn't. That wanting more never worked out and was maybe even selfish. I've always wanted to be an editor, to rise to the top, but the hours, the time and commitment needed, wouldn't leave any space for anyone else, and that's why I learned to keep things light. Flirt, smile, walk away before anyone got too close. That way, no one could hurt me. No expectations, no messy feelings, no heartbreak, and I could focus on making my work a huge success.'

Daniel listened in silence.

'I was good at it,' she continued, laughing softly. 'I became the kind of person who was always in control. Who didn't need anything real. But then I came here, and suddenly everything I thought I knew about myself started shifting.' Her eyes found his again. 'You're not like anyone I've ever met, Daniel. And that terrifies me because I don't know how to be the kind of person who opens up. Who stays. Who tries.'

'You don't have to have it all figured out,' he said gently. 'You just need to be open to change and vulnerability.'

A tear slipped down Fern's cheek before she could stop it and she wiped it away with the back of her hand. 'I really don't want to fall out with you.'

Daniel slid his arm around her shoulders, pulling her in close. She didn't hesitate to lean into him. Wrapped up in his warmth, she felt a million miles away from her life in London.

Her phone buzzed in her pocket. 'Sorry,' she said.

'Go ahead. I don't mind.'

She whipped her phone from her pocket and glanced at the screen. Ella.

'It can wait.'

She knew exactly what the message would say. *When are you coming home? There's another party to attend.*

But Fern wasn't ready to answer that question just yet.

For now, she just wanted to sit here, beside Daniel, wrapped in his arms, savouring the moment and watching the puffins as they surfed the cliff-top breeze.

Chapter Twenty

The door to No. 17 Curiosity Lane swung shut behind them, the tiny bell above it jingling in the quiet afternoon air. Daniel reached for the wooden sign to flip it to OPEN. But before he could, Fern's hand covered his, pressing the sign firmly back to CLOSED.

He raised an eyebrow, amusement dancing in his expression. 'We're closed?'

She stepped in closer, the warmth of her body radiating against his as her fingers grazed his forearm. 'I thought we could spend the afternoon together.'

His smile came quickly but he hesitated and then his expression shifted. He gently took her hands in his. 'Fern, look ... I need to say something before this goes any further.'

She looked up at him.

'I'm not interested in sex just to patch something over or to make either of us feel less alone. That's not what I want, not with you.' He paused. 'I understand that the first time was spontaneous, but I'm looking for more than just sex. I want to build a connection. I don't want to be just a moment of comfort.'

Her smile faltered. 'Are you rejecting me?'

He shook his head. 'No. I'm respecting you and whatever this is, or could be. Let's work this out ... together.'

Fern admired him for being vulnerable, speaking his mind and being honest about how he felt. It made a refreshing change compared to the likes of Jax Devlin, who would expect sex after any gig she attended, with no communication for weeks at a time in between meetings. Daniel was different and she admired that about him.

'Come here,' he said, pulling her in for a hug. 'But just so you know, it's very difficult to do the right thing as you're very fanciable.' He kissed the top of her head. 'Shall I make us a coffee?'

'Sounds like a plan.'

'I think there's even some lemon drizzle left.'

'Now you're talking.'

They walked into the kitchen and Daniel switched on the kettle.

'There's something I haven't mentioned about my visit to Edgar. He gave me a lead on the wedding dress.'

'Really?'

'He suggested we visit the local seamstress. Apparently, she lives in the blue rainbow cottage on Lighthouse Lane. Her name's Dorothy. It's worth a shot. Shall we go and visit?'

'Dorothy! Why didn't I think of her? She was good friends with Matilda. She sat with her right up until the end.'

'Shall we go after work?'

'Sounds like a plan, but what I need now is coffee and cake.'

No. 17 Curiosity Lane

Just after five o'clock, Fern and Daniel walked up Lighthouse Lane towards the row of rainbow cottages, each one distinct in its charm, their gardens overflowing with beautiful vibrant blooms. They walked side by side, Daniel carrying the wedding dress inside the bin bag.

They stopped outside the blue cottage and Fern gave a tiny gasp. 'Can you imagine living here?'

It was a quaint two-storey house with a thatched roof and an oak porch, its beams weathered by time but still strong. Climbing up one side of the porch was a cascade of tumbling roses, their petals a delicate blend of blush pink and cream. The garden was immaculately kept, a riot of colour with lavender and foxgloves swaying gently in the breeze, and a low stone wall enclosing the property. Lanterns hung both sides of the deep-blue door and potted geraniums graced the step.

'It's just beautiful,' she said. 'Straight out of a story book.'

They walked up to the door and Fern pressed the bell. Within moments the door had opened, and Dorothy greeted them with a warm smile. 'Daniel! Lovely to see you. How are you?'

Dorothy was a small woman. Her silver hair was swept into a neat bun, and her sharp blue eyes studied them with quiet curiosity. Wrinkles fanned out from her eyes and mouth, but they only deepened the warmth in her face. She wore a soft lavender cardigan over a floral dress, and Fern could easily picture her sitting at a sewing machine, guiding delicate lace beneath the needle.

'I'm all good. Can I introduce you to Fern?'

Dorothy immediately placed both hands on her chest. 'Fern, from London. Matilda's great-niece.'

'I am and I'm so pleased to meet you. Daniel has just told me you were friends with my great-aunt.'

Just behind Dorothy, there was a man putting on a coat in the hallway. He walked towards the front door and nodded at Fern and Daniel before kissing Dorothy on the cheek. 'I have a train to catch but I'll give you a ring in the next few days,' he said picking up a case and walking towards a taxi that had just pulled up outside.

She nodded, then waved at him. 'My brother,' she shared. 'It was quite a surprise he came to visit. Lives in London. Was out this way on business.'

Fern recognised him instantly. He was the same man who'd come into the shop and played the piano.

'Do come in and have a cup of tea and help me eat some scones I baked this morning.'

'We've just had cake,' replied Fern, 'but a tea would be lovely.'

'Speak for yourself,' announced Daniel. 'I'll help eat your scones.' He grinned. 'Dorothy makes the best scones, but don't tell Betty I said that.'

'Oh, you do tease me,' replied Dorothy giving him a warm smile. 'Now, what can I do for you two? And what do you have in there? It looks heavy.'

'We've come to ask you about something a little unusual that's happened at the shop. The mysterious arrival of a wedding dress.'

Dorothy tilted her head. 'That sounds intriguing.'

They followed her inside. The cottage was as beautiful within as it was without, filled with an air of nostalgia and comfort. The living room was a haven of floral prints and antique furniture, with crocheted doilies placed carefully on the armrests. Shelves lined the walls, stacked with books and photo frames showcasing a lifetime of memories.

Dorothy led them to the conservatory at the back of the cottage. 'Take a seat. I'll be just a moment.'

It wasn't long before she returned with a pot of tea, side plates, butter, jam and a cake tin full of scones. She poured the tea then gestured to the plates and scones. 'Do help yourself,' she said before looking towards the bin bag. 'Now, what is this about a wedding dress?'

Daniel already had a scone on his plate so Fern was the one who began to explain. 'It was left on the shop's doorstep, wrapped in a bin bag. With it was a note that said, "Find the groom". We're trying to figure out who it belonged to, why they'd leave it there and why we would need to find the groom. We think the dress may date back to the sixties and Edgar suggested asking you about it, as you've been the seamstress on Puffin Island for many years. Perhaps it could be one of yours?'

'Let me take a look.'

Fern carefully lifted the dress from the bag. Unfolding it, she lay it across her lap and the arm of the sofa. The moment it was fully displayed, Dorothy inhaled sharply.

'Oh, my.' She reached out and ran a wrinkled hand over the delicate lace. 'This is exquisite work.'

'Could it be one you made?' Daniel asked.

She studied it for a moment before shaking her head. 'No, this isn't my work,' she said. She looked carefully and turned the dress over, her fingers searching until they found the label stitched into the seam.

'But I recognise the label. This was made by a seamstress in Sea's End – Eliza Valentine. She's a marvellous talent.'

'Is she still in Sea's End, do you know?'

'No, Eliza is the same age as me and long retired, but I know her daughters and her grand-daughters followed in her footsteps and they're currently based in London. Eliza lives there too, with her family. Eliza never made two dresses the same – each one was bespoke – and I know she kept a record of every design, so if you can get in touch with her she might be able to give you the name of the buyer.'

Fern's mind raced. Another lead. Another connection.

Dorothy's fingers moved over the fabric with an expert touch. 'The quality of this... Whoever left this dress behind either didn't know its worth or had a very specific reason for getting it into your hands.'

'What do you mean?' Daniel asked.

Dorothy lifted her gaze to meet his. 'All of Eliza's dresses are worth a small fortune. She was very talented.'

'I valued it around two thousand pounds,' volunteered Daniel.

'I beg to differ,' declared Dorothy. 'With the quality of this fabric, the stitching and the vintage, I would triple that estimate.'

Silence settled over the room as Fern and Daniel exchanged a look. Whoever had left this dress behind wasn't simply discarding an old relic.

'What do you think this all means?' asked Daniel.

Dorothy took a sip of tea. 'I think someone doesn't want the past staying in the past. They want you to discover the story behind this dress.'

Fern's pulse quickened. This was no ordinary mystery.

After they finished their tea, they thanked Dorothy for her time, and as soon as they stepped outside, Daniel let out a breath.

'Six grand for a wedding dress. That is unbelievable.'

'Why would you just discard a dress of that value?'

Daniel shrugged. 'Maybe you have more money than sense, or you just don't know its worth.'

'Someone must know something! By the way, did you notice Dorothy's brother was the same man that came into the shop and looked at the piano?'

'I did. She's never mentioned him, and I don't think Matilda ever did either. What is the plan now?'

'We find Eliza Valentine and pay her a visit,' declared Fern.

Chapter Twenty-One

Fern stirred as the scent of freshly brewed coffee reached her, coaxing her into wakefulness. She opened one eye, then the other, squinting against the early morning light filtering through the mismatched bedroom curtains.

'Morning, Sleeping Beauty.' Daniel smiled, approaching with two coffee cups and a folded newspaper under his arm. 'Coffee, just for you.' He handed one of the cups to Fern and placed the newspaper on the bed next to her.

'Why are you always cheerful in the morning?'

'Because every day is for living and sales have gone up overnight. More of Matilda's old treasures have been sold online! No. 17 Curiosity Lane has made seven hundred pounds in sales this week so far.'

'No way!'

'I told you, the internet loves weird stuff.'

Fern stretched, inhaling the aroma of coffee. 'That's actually impressive.'

'I'm listing more today. I've already posted a couple of

videos this morning.' He flipped his phone screen towards her, showing her the growing social media engagement. 'Comments are wild. Listen to this. "This guy belongs on TV!" and "I'd pay good money to watch a full concert of the singing junkman".' He laughed. 'They love me!'

Fern shook her head, grinning. 'So it begins. Next, you'll be hiring a manager, then refusing to get out of bed for less than ten grand. Your ego will be massive.'

'Fame is a heavy burden,' Daniel said dramatically, 'but I'll bear it.'

Fern rolled her eyes and took another sip of coffee. As she leaned back against the pillows, her gaze fell on the newspaper. The bold front-page headline made her pause.

'Final Cadence: Composer Nathaniel Loring Retires on a High Note as Ill-health Takes Hold.'

She placed the coffee mug down on the bedside cabinet and picked up the newspaper.

'That doesn't sound good, does it?'

'One of the world's greats. It's just been all over the radio. Apparently his health is failing rapidly.'

Fern skimmed the article.

Nathaniel Loring, the legendary composer whose melodies defined a generation, is reportedly living out his final months in seclusion. The 85-year-old maestro, best known for his timeless composition 'Echoes of the Past', remains a towering figure in the world of music. Sources close to Loring confirm that his health has deteriorated significantly in recent weeks, and he has now finally admitted the need to retire to his countryside estate in Hampshire.

Loring's impact on the music industry is immeasurable. Rising to fame in the early 1960s with his debut, he became one of the wealthiest composers in history, his music transcending borders and generations. Despite his immense success, Loring never married or had children, instead dedicating his life to his craft. He spent most of his years in Italy, composing masterpieces that cemented his legacy as one of the greats.

In a rare interview a decade ago, Loring stated: 'Music is the love of my life, the only constant, the only truth.'

As he retires from public life, speculation has grown. Will he release a final composition to mark the end of his extraordinary career? Whether he does or not, his music will endure, forever an echo of the past.

Fern let the paper rest in her lap, exhaling slowly.

Daniel nudged her. 'Such a big name. A huge part of music history.'

'I googled him just the other day when I came across his vinyl in the shop.'

'I don't remember logging it into the book.'

'I logged it. I did wonder whether it was an original pressing as it was in such good condition.'

'I wouldn't think so. Quite a lot of vinyls are in good nick, as people tend to look after them. Now, what's the plan for today?'

'Sell more junk, and I'm going to look into Eliza Valentine. Try and see if there's still a shop, a contact number....' She hesitated. 'But there's something else we need to talk about.'

Daniel glanced at her, his expression turning wary. 'That sounds serious.'

'I have to go back to London. I only took a week's annual leave, and I've got a huge interview coming up, at one of the biggest gigs this year. The magazine's arranged backstage passes for the whole team. It's not something I can miss.'

Daniel took a sip of his coffee. 'But you're coming back?' His voice held an edge of something. Hope? Uncertainty?

She hesitated, then said with a smile, 'I can work remotely for a while. I'll be home by the following weekend.'

His reaction was immediate. His eyes widened and a slow grin spread across his face.

'What?' she asked, baffled. 'Why are you looking at me like that? I said I'll be back by the weekend.'

'No,' he corrected, his grin widening. 'You said you'd be "home".' Daniel looked insufferably pleased with himself. 'I knew Puffin Island would get to you.'

She opened her mouth to argue, but nothing came out. Because the truth was, she wasn't sure if it had been a slip of the tongue or if, somehow, without realising it, she was starting to feel exactly that way.

Chapter Twenty-Two

A few hours later, Fern's mouth fell wide open as she raised her eyebrows discreetly at Daniel. She wasn't quite sure what was happening but all of a sudden No. 17 Curiosity Lane was packed. The place had likely never seen such a crowd! Fern leaned against the counter with her arms crossed and watched actual customers peering at trinkets, running fingers over old books and exclaiming over peculiar curiosities.

Daniel nudged her with his elbow. 'What the hell is going on?' he whispered, eyes wide. 'I've never seen so many customers.'

Fern barely had time to shake her head before a group of young women clustered around Daniel, giggling and tossing their hair. One of them, a blonde with oversized sunglasses perched on her head, held up her phone. 'Oh my God, are you the guy from that viral video? The antique shop hottie?'

Daniel blinked. 'The what?'

'Oh, he totally is,' another woman chimed in. 'I saw the

TikTok last night. It's all over Instagram, too. Someone said this shop is a hidden gem but mostly they just made comments about you.'

Daniel turned to Fern in horror. 'What did you do?'

'Me?' she questioned. 'You're the one who uploaded the reels. It's nothing to do with me unless you think I have a secret side hustle making thirst-trap videos of you polishing brass candlesticks?'

Daniel groaned, but the women were undeterred. One held out her phone, already poised for a selfie. 'Do you mind?' she asked, fluttering her lashes.

'Oh, uh, sure?' Daniel said uncertainly, offering his most confused-but-obliging smile as the woman snapped the picture. The other women queued up instantly.

Fern rolled her eyes. 'You do realise this means you're officially an influencer now?' she teased, watching as he awkwardly posed with another admirer. 'Maybe you should start selling merch. "No. 17 Curiosity Lane Hottie" mugs? A calendar?'

'You're not helping. I hate everything about this,' Daniel muttered through gritted teeth as yet another woman cooed over the charming old-time aesthetic of the shop.

Fern smirked. 'Oh, you love it. You're practically glowing. Maybe this is your true calling, charming the ladies while surrounded by musty books and creepy dolls.'

Ignoring her, Daniel turned back to his fans, who were now inspecting the shop's oddities with an almost suspicious enthusiasm. 'So,' he said, clearing his throat, 'any of you actually interested in antiques?'

One woman picked up a rusted pocket watch and turned it over in her palm. 'Ooh, what's this?'

'Victorian, late 1800s,' Daniel said automatically. 'Solid silver.'

She frowned. 'Does it ... do anything?'

'Well, it tells time.'

'Oh, cute,' she replied, putting it back.

Fern coughed to disguise her laughter and turned back to the laptop on the desk. While Daniel continued to navigate his newfound heartthrob status, she utilised her time clicking away, searching for information on Eliza Valentine.

The name had been on her mind since their visit to Dorothy, and there was a plethora of information available online – articles from fashion magazines, archived interviews, newspaper clippings. Eliza Valentine had been a celebrated seamstress in the 1960s, renowned for her breathtaking wedding dresses. She had operated out of a small shop in Sea's End, the coastal town having once been a haven for artists and designers, and her work had been in great demand, worn by socialites, actresses and even royalty. Some of her gowns had won prestigious awards, praised for their exquisite craftsmanship and timeless elegance.

It was all fascinating, but then Fern's eyes caught something else. An image of a shop in London bearing Eliza Valentine's name. Without hesitation, she googled the company to see if it still existed and discovered that Eliza Valentine had moved from Sea's End to London, where she had established a boutique in Mayfair, one of the city's most exclusive shopping districts, known for its luxurious atmosphere and high-end clientele.

Meanwhile, Daniel was valiantly attempting to escape another photo-op, his patience visibly fraying. 'If you aren't interested in antiques, this shop isn't for you,' he protested weakly, trying to edge away from a particularly determined admirer.

'Are you single?' she asked brightly.

Fern bit back a laugh as Daniel spluttered. He turned, throwing her a desperate look.

'You know what?' Fern said sweetly, closing the laptop. 'He is very single. And he just loves long, romantic walks through graveyards where he mutters about historical inaccuracies on headstones.'

Daniel shot Fern a withering glare, but she just grinned, feeling victorious as the woman subtly backed away.

The shop was buzzing with energy, and for the first time, Fern felt a spark of something new; possibility, maybe. She had no idea how long this social media frenzy would last, or if these women would ever buy anything beyond a single vintage postcard. But for now, the shop had come to life. As Fern turned back to the counter, she noticed a man at the back of the shop picking up an old vinyl record – the one by Nathaniel Loring. She continued to watch him as he glanced over it. The man studied it for a while, carefully sliding the record out of its sleeve. He examined the label, his fingers hovering over the grooves before he pulled out his phone and made a quick call. His voice was low, and though she couldn't hear his words, something about him set her on edge. After hanging up, he walked purposefully to the desk. 'How much for this?' he asked, placing the record down.

Fern hesitated. Every instinct told her not to sell it. But her hands moved automatically, ringing it through the till. 'Five pounds.' Then, at the last second, she stopped. 'Actually,' she blurted out, holding on to the vinyl, 'it's not for sale.'

The man frowned. 'But you just—'

'It's from my personal collection,' she said quickly. 'Somehow it got mixed up with the shop stock. I can't part with it.' She placed the vinyl under the counter. 'Sorry. Please do accept my apology.'

His eyes narrowed, clearly irritated, but after a beat, he gave a short nod. 'Fine.'

As he walked out, Fern's heart was beating fast. Whatever was going on, something about this record felt significant. She couldn't put her finger on why, but she was certain it was important.

It was midday when Daniel quickly closed the door, his face pale and strained. 'Throw me the keys!' he shouted, looking completely traumatised. As soon as the lock clicked into place, he turned the sign to CLOSED and leaned against the door, exhaling deeply. 'And breathe,' he muttered, running a hand through his hair. 'Oh my God, what the hell just happened?'

Fern grinned. 'Apart from you nearly giving yourself a heart attack, we've got another £150 in sales.' Her eyes twinkled with mischief as she added, 'I've had another idea.'

Daniel raised an eyebrow, already anticipating trouble. 'Absolutely not. Whatever your idea is, the answer is no.'

'You haven't even heard it yet,' she countered.

'I don't want to hear it.'

Her grin widened. 'So, you're saying you don't want to come to London with me, go to a gig, and'—she swung her laptop in his direction, revealing her plan—'pay a visit to Eliza Valentine in her London shop?'

He sighed. 'Go on then. If I must.'

'I knew you'd say yes! It would mean closing the shop for a couple of days.'

'I think I can live with that.'

She looked out the window to see the same women from earlier taking photos through the window.

'TikTok has a lot to answer for,' Daniel muttered.

'It does, but the fact is it's brought in most of the sales in the last week.'

'Lunch?' he asked.

'Definitely.'

Chapter Twenty-Three

Fern walked down Curiosity Lane, the warm coastal air feeling so different from London's. She looked forward to a night in The Old Ship Inn with Amelia and her friends. As she reached the pub, she paused before stepping inside. The pub looked so cosy, and the laughter and chatter suggested it was busy. Walking through the door, she scanned the room and spotted Amelia waving from a table near the fireplace.

'There you are!' Amelia called, lifting her pint.

Fern made her way over and smiled. 'This place is busy!'

'Quiz night,' Amelia said with a grin. 'Did I forget to mention that bit?'

'You did!' replied Fern.

'Oh, you'll love it,' said Becca, who was already there with a half-empty pint and a bowl of chips. 'We're very supportive. Unless someone gets a question wrong about puffins!'

'Hi, Fern,' said Clemmie, smiling warmly from the other side of the table. 'Welcome to the madness.'

'And this,' Amelia added, gesturing to the one woman Fern

hadn't met yet, 'is Dilly. Artist, resident lighthouse dweller and notorious sore loser.'

Dilly raised a hand in greeting. She had wild curly hair tied up in a scarf, smudges of paint on her hands, and a twinkle in her eye. 'Nice to meet you. Don't worry, I only throw pencils at people if they confuse Monet with Manet.'

'Duly noted,' Fern said, sliding into a seat. 'I have a GCSE in Art and zero quiz skills, so I'm mostly here for moral support and crisps.' She grinned.

'Perfect,' Becca said. 'You'll fit right in.'

'And this is Verity, vet's assistant and now a permanent resident after arriving on a whim because she discovered a postcard sent years ago from Puffin Island.'

'Pleased to meet you,' chimed Verity, as she took the last unoccupied chair.

'And you. That sounds very intriguing.'

'It was, and now I'm here for good.'

They passed Fern a menu and within minutes someone had put a cider in front of her and a plate of onion rings that tasted suspiciously like actual heaven. The quiz sheets were already on the table and the argument about their team name was soon underway.

'Let's Get Quizzical,' Amelia said confidently.

'Too obvious,' replied Clemmie.

'What about "Agatha Quiztie"?' Fern suggested, sipping her drink.

There was a pause.

'That's not bad,' Becca said. 'Very on brand. Murder, mystery and a decent pun.'

'Agatha Quiztie it is,' Amelia declared, scrawling it across the top of their answer sheet. 'Team registration complete. No backing out now.'

'That's Pete,' Amelie said, pointing to a man near the front of the bar. 'Tonight's quizmaster lives in Cliff Top Cottage, counts puffins, is a retired vet and was once a singer in a famous band.'

'Really?' replied Fern. That last bit of information had certainly piqued her interest. Before she could ask any more questions, Pete tapped his microphone.

'Right! Let's get started... Round One is General Knowledge. Remember: no phones, no cheating, and no arguing with the quizmaster unless you've bought me a pint.'

The room erupted in a chorus of good-natured groans and shouts.

Round One began with a mix of easy and obscure questions. Fern surprised herself by getting a question right about capital cities, and even more by knowing who invented the World Wide Web (thanks to a particularly boring ex-boyfriend who worked in IT and explained it at great length during a cinema date).

Dilly was unbeatable on anything artsy, Clemmie nailed the food and drink round with unnerving precision, and Becca got into a passionate disagreement about whether Jaffa Cakes were legally cakes or biscuits.

Amelia, naturally, was the glue holding it all together – half team captain, half chaos coordinator. Since she owned a book shop, all literary questions were hers.

By the halfway point, Fern's cheeks ached from laughing. Someone had bought a round of shots 'for luck', and it was loud and messy and completely joyful at their table.

During the music round, Fern correctly identified three

boybands and an obscure Shania Twain lyric, all to raucous applause from the group.

'You've been holding out on us,' Amelia said, nudging her. 'Secret pop princess.'

'I'm a music journalist, but I also do own an entire collection of *Smash Hits* magazines,' Fern said modestly.

They didn't just do well ... they stormed it. By the final round, Agatha Quiztie was tied for first place with a rival team made up of local fishermen, who had an unsettling knowledge of 1980s soap operas.

The tie-breaker question was about the population of Iceland and the girls huddled together, whispering guesses.

'Three hundred thousand?' Fern said.

'Maybe more,' Clemmie whispered. 'I feel like it's more.'

'We're going with 372,000,' Amelia said confidently.

It was 376,000.

They won.

Their prize? A £25 bar tab and eternal glory.

Amelia raised her glass. 'To Agatha Quiztie. May we reign supreme.'

'And never be asked to spell Czechoslovakia again,' said Dilly.

Fern couldn't stop smiling. She felt a bit buzzed from the cider, a bit giddy from the win, and completely full of something she hadn't felt in ages: belonging.

Around eleven p.m. she stepped outside the pub. It was dark and quiet, the kind of peaceful that only an island could be. As she walked home, she could picture herself doing this again. A monthly quiz night spent catching up with the girls. Laughing too hard over too many chips. Not rushing. Not checking her phone every five seconds.

She looked up and was surprised to see the vivid tapestry of stars. There were so many more than you ever saw in the city.

And in that moment, with the cider still warm in her belly and her cheeks pink from laughter, she thought she could get used to this slower pace of life.

But she wasn't quite ready to admit that out loud.

Not just yet.

Chapter Twenty-Four

Friday morning saw Fern and Daniel in a taxi early and being greeted by the sight of Sea's End's railway station nestled against the backdrop of the rolling hills. The station was full of vintage charm with its platform of worn stone, ivy-covered walls and freshly painted wooden benches. A white sign with hand-painted lettering welcomed travellers to Sea's End Station. As they made their way to the platform, Fern heard a train whistle sounding in the distance, growing louder as it began to approach. They sat on a bench, each with a rucksack on their back, and in the small wheely case at their feet was the wedding dress.

The train pulled into the station with a screech of brakes. After they climbed on board Daniel lifted the small case onto the overhead rack before settling into the seat beside Fern. She noticed the way he looked at the seat numbers, a slow, satisfied smile appearing on his face.

'What are you smiling at?' she asked, tilting her head.

Daniel turned to her. 'Because these are the exact same seats we were in when we first met.'

Fern blinked, caught off guard. 'How do you even remember that?' she asked, impressed – and, if she was honest, touched.

'Because,' he said, leaning slightly towards her so no one could hear, 'I knew you were going to stay in my life for ever, and it was something I wanted to be able to tell the grandkids.'

Her stomach flipped at his words, but she rolled her eyes, determined to keep her cool. 'You are so ridiculous.'

He grinned. 'And yet, here we are.'

She gave him a playful shove, but he leaned forward and pressed a soft kiss to her lips, causing a swarm of fireflies to flutter frantically in her stomach.

Daniel let the moment linger before he added, 'I had an errand to run so I had to get off the train early, but when I arrived back on the island I bumped into Amelia. I had a feeling it was you who was coming to take over the shop, so I told her to look out for you.'

Fern gasped, her head snapping around to face him. '*You* were the one who said I was the sort who drinks overpriced lattes, wears designer coats and will probably see inheriting the shop as a massive inconvenience. That was you? You told her that?'

His grin widened. 'Guilty. But was I lying? I rest my case.'

'Unbelievable!' she exclaimed, though she took it all in good humour.

'Never fear,' he said smoothly, reaching into his rucksack, 'I'm going to make it up to you.'

He pulled out a neatly packed brunch: a basket of fresh

pastries, strawberries, a small jar of Nutella and even a bottle of fizz. The sight of it stole her breath for a moment.

'You did all this?' she asked, surprised.

'Of course I did,' he said with a wink. 'Figured if I was going to spend a train journey with a snooty Londoner, I might as well keep her in good spirits.'

She narrowed her eyes at him. 'Well, I suppose I can forgive you – after a glass of that, at least.'

Daniel expertly popped the bottle open with a quiet hiss. Unfortunately, the cork shot out like a bullet, flying straight down the aisle, only to be expertly caught in mid-air by the conductor just as he was approaching to check their tickets. He blinked at the cork in his hand before slowly shifting his gaze to Daniel, who grinned sheepishly.

'Sorry,' Daniel said.

'You're forgiven if it's all in the name of romance. Tickets, please.'

Once all the food was laid out on the table in front of them, with two plastic cups for the fizz, Daniel showed Fern the empty rucksack.

'What am I looking at? There's nothing in there.'

'Exactly. I forgot to pack my clothes for the night.'

Fern laughed. 'So you remembered the jar of Nutella, but not your clothes?'

'Priorities, Fern!'

'You are something else!'

After a change of trains, it wasn't long before they were due to arrive at Euston Station. Fern was leaning into Daniel's chest, watching out of the window. The landscape had shifted from rolling countryside to the sprawling outskirts of London, the clusters of grey buildings and winding roads growing denser with each passing mile. Normally, this moment would bring a familiar flicker of excitement, a sense of return, of stepping back into the rhythm of home, but Fern didn't feel like that at all.

In the distance, the unmistakable arch of Wembley Stadium loomed against the afternoon sky. Wembley had always been a landmark of significance, a beacon of London life, the place where music's greatest legends had played, and it had always reminded her why she loved what she did, why she chased stories and lived for the pulse of the industry. But now, her thoughts were far from stadiums and interviews, far from the next headline, as her mind drifted to the tiny antiques shop on a sleepy island, where a moose's head watched over a too-small bed, and a man with infuriatingly good hair was making her smile every day.

It was only days ago that she had stepped off a train in the opposite direction, bound for Puffin Island with every intention of closing the shop and leaving it behind. Instead, she had found herself tangled in a life far removed from the polished, predictable world she had built for herself in London. The carriage rattled over a junction, jolting her out of her thoughts. Euston was minutes away now.

'Here we go!' said Daniel, shoving all of the rubbish in a nearby bin. The doors slid open with a mechanical hiss, and a sea of commuters started to spill out on to the platform. The carriage was actually rammed and they stayed seated until most of the commuters had left. Holding hands, they stood up, and Daniel reached up to take the suitcase down off the rack. Instead he did a double-take – their suitcase was no longer there!

'Fern, we have a missing case and a missing wedding dress.'

Her pulse raced. 'That dress is too valuable to lose.' Panicked, she scanned the area. There was another suitcase on the rack but it wasn't theirs. 'Do you think someone has taken it by mistake or on purpose?' They were the only ones left on the train. 'We need to get off. Do we take the case that's left or leave it there?'

'Let's take it to Lost Property. Maybe the person has realised their mistake and taken ours there too.'

'Good idea.'

Daniel lifted the case down and Fern began to wheel it down the aisle. A moment of silence passed between them, punctuated only by the chaos of the station as they stepped onto the platform, and then, as if by divine intervention, Fern's eyes locked onto a woman in a smart blazer, effortlessly wheeling a black case through the station. A very familiar black case.

'There! That woman was sitting by us. That's our suitcase! I'm sure of it! Yes, it has my black tag around the handle. She probably just didn't notice as it's so similar to every other black case.'

The woman, blissfully unaware of her role in this unfolding catastrophe, disappeared down the stairs to the Underground.

'Move!' Fern yanked Daniel's wrist, pulling the other suitcase behind her as they hurtled through the station.

'Can you see her? I've lost her,' said Daniel, scanning the crowd.

'There she is!' But the woman was just a little too far ahead. She breezed through the ticket barriers at Euston with the ease of a seasoned commuter whereas Fern fumbled with her

Oyster card before she and Daniel practically threw themselves onto the escalator.

'Which line?' Daniel gasped as they reached the bottom.

'She's heading towards the Victoria Line! Southbound!'

They sprinted to the platform just as the doors were sliding shut. Fern smacked her palm against the glass. 'NO!'

Daniel groaned. 'We are officially the worst detectives ever.'

'Wait! The suitcase – I use it all the time and have an Apple tracker thrown into the zip compartment.'

'You're kidding me.'

'I kid you not.'

Daniel smacked her lips with a kiss. 'You are a genius!'

Fern whipped out her phone but there wasn't a single bar. 'No service! I'm going to have to go to the top of the escalator again. You wait there.'

Waving her phone in front of her as she attempted to get a signal, she rode the escalator back to the top. As soon as it kicked in she loaded up the app. The woman was still southbound and her train was approaching Oxford Circus. Fern raced back down the escalator.

'Well? Anything?'

'She's heading to Oxford Circus!'

They tumbled onto the platform at Oxford Circus a few minutes later, dodging tourists and office workers alike. Mercifully, there was service on the platform and Fern checked the app again. 'She got off here,' she exclaimed. 'She's up on Regent Street!'

They raced up the escalators to street level, Fern's eyes barely leaving the moving dot on her phone screen. 'She's fast,' Fern wheezed, her heart pounding as they began to follow the woman's path down the famous shopping street.

They turned right at a side street and headed deeper into Mayfair, getting closer to the blinking dot with every laboured step.

Daniel stopped to catch his breath as they reached Bond Street. 'Where is she?' He spun around, trying to locate the woman in the sea of shoppers and tourists.

Fern glanced at her phone, then pointed. 'There! She's getting into a cab!'

Daniel groaned. 'Oh, come on!'

Fern didn't hesitate. She grabbed Daniel's arm and dragged him over to the nearest available taxi. 'Follow that cab!' she gasped. 'I've always wanted to say that!'

The driver, a man who looked like he had absolutely seen it all, gave them a bored glance in the rear-view mirror. 'You serious?'

'Completely,' Daniel confirmed, flashing a credit card. 'There's a very good tip in it for you if you keep up.'

With a resigned sigh, the cabbie flicked on his indicator and plunged them into London traffic.

Fern looked towards Daniel, who looked hot and flustered. 'Welcome to London! I bet you didn't think it was going to be this much fun.'

'Every day with you is a new adventure.'

They followed the cab for several crowded blocks and watched through the window as it pulled up in front of a grand boutique near the border of Hyde Park.

Fern's mouth fell open. 'Can you see what I can see?'

Daniel followed her gaze, then let out a stunned laugh. 'She brought us straight to Eliza Valentine's shop.'

'What the hell?'

Daniel paid the fare and they stepped onto the pavement.

The woman was already through the shop door, still pulling the suitcase behind her.

Fern let out a stunned, breathless laugh. 'Well, that saved us a phone call. Come on, let's go and see what we can find out.'

Chapter Twenty-Five

As soon as Fern and Daniel stepped into the boutique they were hit with the scent of roses and vanilla drifting through the air, mingling with delicate strains of classical music from hidden speakers. The space was a haven of soft lighting and elegance, a stark contrast to the chaotic jumble of antiques they'd left behind at No. 17 Curiosity Lane.

Fern glanced around. Rows of wedding dresses lined the walls, each shimmering beneath the glow of lavish chandeliers. Gossamer layers of lace and tulle cascaded from hangers, their delicate embroidery catching the light, whilst others were displayed on mannequins.

At the heart of the boutique, a velvet chaise longue sat beside a low table bearing crystal flutes of champagne, golden bubbles rising lazily to the surface. The moment they stepped inside, a woman in a sleek black dress and pearl earrings spotted them. Her eyes lit up with practised enthusiasm as she glided towards them, moving with the grace of someone who had spent years guiding nervous brides through the most significant decision of their lives.

'Oh, congratulations!' she gushed, clasping her hands together as she reached them. 'You must be the couple who've just set the date! How exciting!'

Fern froze and Daniel grinned. Fern opened her mouth to correct the mistake, but Daniel spoke first, leaving her staring at him.

'That's us,' he said smoothly, throwing an arm casually around Fern's shoulder. 'We couldn't resist coming in to take a look, could we, babe?'

She glared. Did he actually just call her 'babe'? He was enjoying this far too much. She could hear the amusement in his voice, feel the smug grin radiating from him as she turned back towards the woman. 'Actually—'

'We haven't told many people yet,' Daniel interrupted smoothly, squeezing her shoulder as if to silence any protest. 'You know how it is. Best to keep things low-key until all the plans are finalised.'

The sales assistant practically beamed. 'Oh, of course! You must be over the moon. And what a perfect time to start looking for the dress.' She gestured grandly to the beautiful gowns. 'I can already tell, you'll be an absolute vision.'

Fern's pulse quickened. This was spiralling out of control. She opened her mouth to correct the misunderstanding, and this time she was faster than Daniel. 'Actually, I'm so sorry,' she interjected quickly, stepping slightly out of his grip. 'My...' She hesitated, struggling to find the right word. What exactly was Daniel to her?

Daniel raised an eyebrow, clearly amused, waiting for her answer.

'Friend,' she finally settled on. 'My friend here is just having a joke with you. I can only apologise.'

The boutique assistant still looked perplexed, and, to be fair, Fern couldn't blame her.

'We're not here about a wedding dress,' she continued, then faltered. 'Well … that's not strictly true. But not one of yours. Actually, that's not strictly true either.' This was going well.

The woman's confusion deepened.

Fern tried again. 'A woman just walked in here. I think she accidentally took our suitcase off the train. The strange thing is, we were heading here, too.'

As if on cue, the woman in question emerged from a door at the back of the boutique.

'That's her,' Fern said, relieved.

The assistant moved towards the woman, engaging her in a hushed conversation before both returned to Fern and Daniel. The woman glanced at the suitcase in their possession and her expression shifted.

'Oh dear, I think you may be right,' she said, looking genuinely apologetic. 'That does look like my case. All black cases look so similar, don't they? I'm terribly sorry, I took yours by mistake. I've just carried it upstairs. Let me go and get it.'

She turned to the assistant with a warm smile. 'Do get them both a glass of something fizzy, would you?'

A moment later, Daniel looked like he was having the best time, sitting on a plush velvet couch with one hand holding a glass of fizz and the other placed on Fern's knee. 'Friends, now, are we?' he leaned in and whispered.

'You need to behave yourself. Are you incapable of being serious for five minutes?'

He took a slow sip of his champagne, eyes twinkling. 'Not when it's this much fun.'

It wasn't long before the woman bustled back in, this time wheeling the case behind her. Her cheeks were flushed, and she offered a sheepish smile.

'I'm so sorry about that,' she said. 'Totally my fault.'

'That's okay,' replied Fern. 'The bizarre thing is we were actually going to give the boutique a call tomorrow as we were hoping you might be able to help us with something,' she said, choosing her words carefully. 'We're looking for Eliza Valentine.'

The woman blinked in surprise, then let out a small laugh. 'Well, you've come to the right place. I'm Eliza Valentine.'

Fern hesitated. That didn't make sense. The woman before them couldn't be her, or at least, not the Eliza Valentine they were looking for.

'I think there must be a mistake,' Fern said, shaking her head slightly. 'The woman we're looking for would possibly be in her eighties. She used to make wedding dresses in the town of Sea's End, on the Northumberland coast.'

Understanding flickered across the woman's face, and she smiled warmly. 'Ah. Then I think you must be looking for my grandmother. Eliza Valentine is a name that's been passed down in my family, and I've followed in her footsteps professionally. She taught me everything I know.'

'Wow,' Fern murmured. 'Would you mind if we asked you a few questions about her?'

The younger Eliza tilted her head, curious now. 'Of course, but … may I ask why you're looking for her?'

Fern reached down, unzipped the case and carefully unfolded the wedding dress. The fabric spilled over her arms, and Eliza and the shop assistant gasped in unison as they gazed at it.

'Oh,' Eliza breathed, stepping closer. Her hands hovered just above the delicate lace. 'It's exquisite.'

'We were wondering if this was one of your grandmother's. There's a label that pointed us in her direction, and I know it's a long shot, but we wanted to try and find out who it belonged to … if that's at all possible?'

Eliza's fingers finally brushed against the fabric, trailing over the fine stitching. 'This craftsmanship … it's stunning. It looks like something she would have made, but I'd have to take a closer look to be sure.'

'We'd really appreciate any insight you can offer,' Fern said, before adding, 'Especially because of the way it came into our possession.'

Eliza looked up. 'What do you mean?'

'It was left outside the antique shop that I own,' she explained. 'Inside a bin bag.'

Eliza gasped. 'You're joking.'

'Wish I was.'

'Someone just … abandoned this?'

'Pretty much,' Daniel chimed in.

'This dress is a masterpiece. Why would anyone do that?'

'That's what we're trying to figure out. There was a note with it,' shared Fern.

'A note?'

Fern reached into her coat pocket and retrieved the small slip of paper. She unfolded it carefully and held it out.

'"Find the groom",' Eliza read aloud. She looked at them both. 'And you think my grandmother might know something about it?'

'Like I said, it's a long shot, but hopefully,' Fern admitted. 'Or maybe she could at least help us trace who the bride was. If she can remember anything about the dress it would be so helpful, but we do appreciate she must have made so many dresses in her time.'

'Thousands,' replied Eliza. 'But I do know one thing about my grandmother, and that's that she never made the same dress twice. Every single one was an original, as she worked with each bride to design the dress of their dreams.' Eliza's expression grew thoughtful. 'Actually, there's a simple way to find answers. Each dress was numbered.'

'Numbered?' queried Fern.

'Numbered and logged. Every one of them.'

Fern's eyes grew wide in anticipation. Could it be that simple?

Eliza carefully turned up the hem on the dress to reveal a tiny square label bearing the numbers 64. 24.12. She read the numbers out loud, then smiled. 'This was one of my grandmother's earliest pieces ... a Christmas Eve wedding.'

'How do you know that?' asked Fern.

'The first number is the dress's sequence. This was the sixty-fourth gown she ever made. The second two numbers are the day and month of the wedding. It generally makes it easier to find the bride's information quickly, but as this is one of her earlier designs it's unfortunately not logged onto the computer.'

'Will it be logged anywhere?'

'Yes, in one of the old ledger books, but they aren't kept here. Are you going to be in London long?'

'We're heading home on Sunday afternoon,' replied Fern.

'The first logs are still kept by my grandmother, but I

suspect she'd remember this dress if she saw it. She has a remarkable memory for detail and still remembers most of the gowns she's ever made.'

Fern looked at Daniel. She couldn't quite believe their luck. It was possible they were about to discover who the dress was actually made for. 'Would it be possible to meet Eliza?'

The younger Eliza gave the dress another appreciative glance. 'I'm sure that would be okay, but I'll check with her first. Would you mind if I took a few pictures of it? So I can show her?'

Fern nodded. 'Of course. Thank you.'

Eliza fetched her phone and snapped several careful shots from different angles. When she was finished, she said, 'This is quite the mystery you've found yourselves in.'

'It might turn out to be nothing, but…' Fern trailed off, exchanging another glance with Daniel.

'But you're invested now,' Eliza finished, smiling knowingly. 'I have to admit I'm intrigued too.'

Fern carefully placed the dress back in the case and zipped it up.

'Can I take a contact number? I'll let you know as soon as I've spoken with my grandmother.'

'Yes, of course,' Fern said sincerely. 'We really appreciate this.'

Eliza gave a small nod. 'Something tells me you two won't be letting this go until you get to the bottom of it. Can I ask, where is this antique shop?'

'It's No. 17 Curiosity Lane on Puffin Island.'

Eliza nodded. 'Let's see what we can do.'

Fern finished her drink and stood up. 'Thanks again.'

They left the boutique, wheeling the case – the right one this time – behind them.

'I honestly think we're about to find out who this dress belonged to,' Fern enthused.

'I think you're right, but I do have a question…'

'Which is?'

'Are you sure you don't want to look for a wedding dress whilst you're here? Because you do know it will happen one day. You'll be begging me to marry you.'

Fern rolled her eyes, but she couldn't help the smile tugging at the corner of her lips.

Chapter Twenty-Six

Fern and Daniel boarded the tube at Green Park Station, weaving their way through the steady stream of commuters and tourists. The Piccadilly Line train arrived with its familiar metallic screech, and they stepped aboard, settling into a corner of the carriage as the train rattled and hummed beneath London's sprawling streets. At Earl's Court they switched platforms and hopped onto the District Line.

The carriage was wider, the seats newer and less scuffed from years of city life, and the air carried the mingled scent of coffee and sweat, the signature perfume of London's Underground. Eight minutes after their journey began, they emerged at Fulham Broadway, stepping out into the sunshine.

They navigated the busy high street, passing an assortment of artisan bakeries, slick wine bars and the occasional independent boutique nestled between glassy new developments. Turning off the main road, they reached Fern's apartment block, a stark steel-and-glass building that loomed sharp against the soft sky. It was the very definition of contemporary urban living: angular, unapologetically sleek and utterly devoid of the warm, weathered charm that clung to the coastal cottages on Puffin Island.

The block's façade was a grid of floor-to-ceiling windows, each reflecting the London skyline and the shifting clouds. The lobby was polished and pristine, minimalist, all cool marble and brushed metal.

The lift doors slid shut and Fern pressed the button for her floor.

Daniel raised an eyebrow, watching the numbers glow. 'The penthouse,' he remarked, his voice light with surprise.

Fern tilted her head, offering him a playful, almost conspiratorial smile. 'Only the best.' She grinned as the lift began its smooth, silent ascent.

'Here we are,' Fern said as she pushed open the door to her apartment a few moments later, stepping aside so Daniel could follow her in. She caught the way his eyes swept over the place, knowing exactly what he was going to say.

'Do you actually live here?' he asked, eyebrows raised as he wandered further inside. 'Because, honestly, there's more personality in a dentist's waiting room.'

Fern let out a dry laugh as she slid her keys into the dish on the otherwise bare console table. 'I don't like clutter.'

Daniel grinned. 'Says the woman who's just inherited an antique shop. Bit of a plot twist, that one.'

She pulled off her jacket and draped it over the back of a chair, the weight of his words sinking in more than she expected. She'd always been proud of this flat, the clean lines, the calm, the order. It was her safe little bubble, her grown-up badge of honour. But standing here now, with Daniel's familiar, easy energy filling the room, the place suddenly felt … dull. Cold, even.

The home at No. 17 Curiosity Lane was the complete opposite – mismatched, a bit battered around the edges, and cluttered with the ghosts of someone else's life. But after the initial shock of the place, she had found she loved waking up there. It all felt warm and cosy in a weird kind of way. Lived in. Real.

She glanced over at Daniel, who was now poking around her bookshelf, no doubt judging the alphabetised spines.

'I hate to admit it…' she said, surprising even herself. 'But it does feel a bit … empty.'

He looked back at her, one eyebrow raised, playful as ever. 'Careful, you'll ruin your reputation. Next thing you know, you'll be leaving mugs out and buying scatter cushions with actual colours.'

She nudged him gently as she passed. 'Let's not get carried away.'

But deep down, she couldn't help thinking: maybe a little mess or chaos wasn't the worst thing in the world.

'You must have at least a dodgy candle?' he said, running a hand over the spotless kitchen counter before his eyes landed on a single potted plant sitting by the window. 'Wait. Is that … a plant?'

'That's Leonard,' Fern said matter-of-factly.

Daniel raised an eyebrow. 'You named your plant Leonard?'

'He seemed like a Leonard,' she replied with a small shrug.

Shaking his head with an amused grin, Daniel wandered over to her fridge and pulled it open. 'All right, let's see what culinary delights—' He stopped short, then laughed. 'Fern. There is nothing in here but wine and a tub of butter.'

'Essentials,' she said defensively. 'I'm about to add Chinese takeaway to the mix. Are you hungry?'

Daniel leaned against the counter as she handed him her phone with a menu on the screen from her favourite takeaway. After a few minutes of scrolling, they both pointed at the same dish at the exact same time.

'Sweet and sour chicken?' Daniel asked, looking mildly impressed.

'It's the only correct choice,' Fern confirmed. 'Looks like you have decent taste after all.'

Twenty minutes later, they were curled up on Fern's spotless grey sofa, the coffee table transformed into a makeshift dining space covered in cartons of noodles, sticky ribs, and enough prawn crackers to feed a small army. The scent of soy sauce and sweet chilli hung in the air as Fern balanced her laptop on her knees, scrolling through her notes for tonight's interview.

Daniel sat with chopsticks in hand at the other end of the sofa, twirling them between his fingers. She could feel his gaze flicking from her screen to her face, his curiosity impossible to ignore.

'You actually prepare for the interviews?' he asked, leaning in a little closer. 'I thought you just waltzed in, flashed that smile and asked whatever popped into your head.'

Fern crunched a prawn cracker, smirked and pointed a finger towards the shelf. 'Contrary to popular belief, I do take my job seriously. See those?'

Daniel followed her gesture to the neatly stacked pile of music magazines, arranged – like everything else in her apartment – in perfect order, spines aligned, not a corner bent. He reached across, swiping the top few copies off the pile then flipping through them.

Page after page, her name stared back at him in bold print, alongside glossy photographs of gigs, album reviews and exclusive interviews with bands that had filled stadiums and topped charts. His fingers paused on a double-page spread, the photo catching his attention before the headline did.

'Lust Theory,' he read aloud, angling the page so she could see, even though she didn't need to look. She knew the photo by heart. 'You've been hanging out with the big boys, then. Look at you, standing there next to Jax Devlin, looking like a proper rock chick.'

That photo had been taken on a night that was burned into her memory for all the wrong reasons. It was when the whirlwind had properly started. She could still see it: the dim, smoky glow of the club, the crowd pressed tight around the stage, the bass so loud it thumped in her chest like a second heartbeat. Jax Devlin had owned the room the moment he swaggered onto the stage, leather jacket clinging to his frame like it was stitched onto his skin, dark hair falling perfectly messy over his eyes.

Those eyes … that's what got her. He'd locked onto her from the second the spotlight hit him, holding her gaze between every song, like the rest of the crowd didn't exist. It wasn't entirely the fame, or even the music, that pulled her in. It was that feeling. That laser focus. Like, for that night, she wasn't invisible. She was *the* girl.

After the gig, the band had swept her along like she was part of the furniture for drinks in some exclusive, hidden-away bar, the kind of place where you didn't ask for the menu, the staff just knew what you wanted. Jax's arm had been around her waist by the second drink. By the fourth, he'd had her laughing like they'd known each other for years.

The night ended in his hotel room, if you could even call it that. It was more like a penthouse playground. Floor-to-ceiling windows overlooking London's skyline, a grand piano casually perched in the corner like some oversized prop, and a sunken spa tub that seemed more suited to a music video than real life.

Champagne, the expensive kind, the kind she'd never even looked at the price of, let alone bought, flowed like water and so did the compliments.

You're different, he'd told her. *You're not like the others. You're clever, sharp, funny. Not like the clingy ones. Not like the ones who just want to be seen on my arm.*

For a while, she'd believed him, and for a while, it had suited her. The thrill of it all. The backstage passes, the free drinks, the whispers when people recognised him and, by default, her. The sex, wild and unfiltered, with Jax always knowing the right thing to say, the right way to touch, like he was reading her mind.

The longer the game went on, the clearer the rules became. Whenever he was in London, the phone would ping. One text – sometimes with just a hotel name and room number – and Fern would go, every single time. No questions, no expectations. Just her, at his beck and call. When he wasn't in London? She knew the drill. There was always another girl. Different cities, different names. The same tired story.

At first, she'd told herself it didn't matter. She wasn't in it for love, after all. She was having fun, wasn't she? She was living the life people dreamed about, dipping her toes into a world of fast cars, private parties, gated mansions with driveways longer than most streets. There were nights spent in his sprawling house, lying by the indoor pool under fake stars printed across the ceiling, drifting off to the sound of him strumming on an acoustic guitar, whispering lyrics she later realised weren't even about her.

But ultimately she'd been coming to realise that the price of admission had been steeper than she'd initially expected. The longer she stayed, the more she saw behind the curtain. The drinks were never just drinks. The late nights bled into early mornings, fuelled by things that came in neat little bags. The women weren't just 'fans' and, sooner or later, they stopped pretending they didn't know about her. She was just another notch on the bedpost. Another face, another night. Yet still, every time his name flashed on her phone, she'd answered. Like clockwork. Like a fool.

Fern caught herself glancing sideways at Daniel. God, he was worlds apart from Jax. No leather jackets, no smoke and mirrors, no penthouse views or afterparties that stretched until sunrise. Just him. Easy, honest, no hidden agenda. Pure, in a way that felt rare. He was naturally funny and made her laugh without trying, never using charm like a weapon, the way Jax had done.

In fact, the more she thought about it, the harder it was to find a single fault with him. She'd been searching, too, because old habits die hard. But so far, Daniel was uncomplicated. The kind of man you could rely on, and she always felt safe in his company.

'Earth to Fern,' Daniel's voice cut through her thoughts, light and teasing. He nudged her foot with his. 'You've gone all quiet on me. What's going on in that head of yours?'

She blinked, shaking her head, covering the slip with a small laugh. 'Just thinking...'

For the first time in a long time, she wasn't chasing the high. She wasn't waiting for the text, or the next fix of attention. She was here. With him. That was enough.

Just as she reached for another prawn cracker, her phone buzzed twice on the coffee table, the screen lighting up with two new messages.

The first was from Ella.

> **ELLA**
> Are you home? Are we going to the gig together?

The second, almost perfectly timed, was from Jax Devlin.

> **JAX**
> Strap yourself in. I'm in town.

Her stomach did a little flip, though not the kind it used to when his name flashed on her screen. The old Fern would have felt that spark of adrenalin, the quick rush of excitement that came with the promise of his attention. Tonight, she didn't feel any of those things. All she felt was flat.

She already knew Jax was in town and headlining the same gig she was meant to be covering after interviewing the band. She'd pencilled it into her diary weeks ago. But the prospect of the backstage passes, the free drinks and schmoozing, wasn't what she wanted tonight. She'd rather stay right here where the air smelled of soy sauce and sweet chilli, and the only soundtrack was the soft murmur of the TV in the background and the occasional rustle of Daniel shifting beside her. She'd rather finish the food, curl up under a blanket and pick a film to watch with him, feet tangled, conversation easy, no makeup, no pretence.

She realised Daniel was talking but she hadn't been listening.

'Have you checked?' he repeated, nodding towards her phone. 'More items sold today from our No. 17 Curiosity Lane.'

When she turned to face him, he was wearing that crooked, boyish smile of his.

'What are you smiling at?' he teased. 'You didn't think we could actually make money, did you?'

Fern bit her lip before the smile she hadn't realised had bloomed stretched wider. It wasn't the sales, or the growing list of customers, or the fact that their little second-hand treasure trove was starting to turn a real profit that had her grinning. It was one word. One small, casual, off-the-cuff word that had slipped so naturally out of his mouth.

Our.

She hadn't expected it to land the way it did, but it wrapped itself around her heart like the softest, warmest blanket.

Chapter Twenty-Seven

Fern closed her laptop with a satisfied snap, the last of her interview questions finally polished, and leaned back against the sofa, stretching her arms over her head. Beside her, Daniel was already stacking the empty Chinese food cartons into a neat pile.

'Full?' she asked, raising an eyebrow as she watched him lean back and rub his stomach.

'Stuffed,' he groaned. 'If I eat another bite, you'll have to roll me to this gig.'

She chuckled, pushing herself upright and brushing a stray piece of rice from her top. It was already half-past seven; if they didn't start getting ready now, they'd be the ones standing behind the velvet rope with the hopefuls, rather than breezing through the side door like the slightly jaded professionals they were supposed to be.

'I need to quickly change. Bathroom is that way if you need it,' she said before wandering into the bedroom and opening the small wardrobe where her work-life and social-life outfits awkwardly coexisted. Black jeans were always a safe option, paired with a vintage band tee and her leather jacket; professional enough for an interview, casual enough for blending in with the crowd afterwards.

Daniel appeared at the bedroom door. Fern was changed and now holding up a shiny laminated card dangling from a lanyard. 'Your golden ticket. Backstage pass. Don't lose it, or security will throw you out faster than you can say VIP.'

Daniel flipped the pass over in his hands, clearly trying to play it cool but failing miserably. His smile stretched wider. 'So this is legit?' he asked. 'I'm going to be backstage, like, properly backstage? With the band and everything?'

Fern smirked, reaching past him to grab her bag. 'Yes, properly backstage. Try not to faint when you meet them, yeah? I don't think they do autographs for unconscious fans. Are you ready? You're about to meet Ella.'

'Ella?'

'Best friend and work colleague in crime. Known her since primary school and been inseparable since. We work at the same magazine and live in the same apartment block.'

'That sounds like a hell of a friendship.'

'It is.'

They headed towards the lift just as Ella stepped out of her apartment. 'There you are!' Ella called, swiping her dark hair out of her face with one hand and waving her phone around with the other. 'I thought Puffin Island had kidnapped you. Is that shop up for sale yet? We need you home, woman!'

Fern shot her a sharp, warning look, the kind only best friends could decode in a split second. One that said: Not. Now.

Ella's mouth twitched, her eyes flicking between Fern and Daniel with quick curiosity.

'This is Daniel,' Fern said, clearing her throat. 'He worked with Matilda at the shop.'

Ella's eyebrows shot up, but to her credit, she recovered fast, extending her hand towards Daniel. 'Hi, it's lovely to meet you.'

Daniel shook her hand, his grin relaxed but curious. 'Nice to meet you. So, you're the best friend trying to lure Fern back to London?'

'Guilty,' Ella said brightly. 'I'm not even subtle about it.'

The three of them left the building and climbed into a cab, the ride across the city threading them through the pulsing streets of London. The closer they got to the venue, the more the crowd swelled on the pavements, and with the window down the buzz was unmistakable, electric.

Daniel gazed out at the queue that snaked around the block. The crowd was full of people in ripped jeans and leather jackets, fishnet tights, heavy eyeliner, denim vests patched with band logos … in short, the unofficial uniform of gig-goers who knew the lyrics before the first note hit the air.

'I can't believe we don't have to queue with them,' he said, eyes wide, as the cab pulled right up to the side entrance.

'Perks of the job,' Fern said, flashing him a smile as she paid the cabbie and took the receipt.

A security guard barely glanced at her pass before unclipping the velvet rope, letting them through the side gate where the low murmur of voices shifted to the thumping bass of the soundcheck echoing through the walls. Fern noticed Daniel's head whip back to look at the crowd one last time, as if he still couldn't quite believe they were skipping the whole cramped queueing experience.

Just as they rounded the corner towards the artists' entrance, the wave of confidence Fern had been riding stalled in her chest. There, by the loading bay doors, was Jax Devlin. He was leaning against the wall, Sharpie in hand, signing autographs for a cluster of fans who hung on his every word. His signature leather jacket was slung across his shoulders, dark hair a deliberate mess, smile cocky and easy, with every girl looking up at him in the hope that he would invite them backstage. And right before her eyes he flashed his signature wink at a pair of girls in front of him, their voices climbing higher in a chorus of giddy squeals. Fern felt the sharp pang of familiarity.

Jax's head turned and his gaze swept the crowd before landing on her. He had the audacity to give her the same wink; slow, deliberate and very much loaded. Fern's heart was thudding against her chest as they passed through the last line of security and slipped into the safety of the building, the fans' cheers fading behind them.

'We need to go this way,' said Fern, leading them down a corridor.

Ella slipped off in the opposite direction after noticing their colleagues from the magazine, telling Fern she'd see them after the interview.

Fidgeting with his backstage pass like a kid unwrapping a Christmas present, Daniel walked at Fern's side. His grin was impossible to miss, as if he still couldn't quite believe where he was going. 'I can't believe this is your life,' he murmured, turning the laminated pass over in his hands. 'I'm about to see

Atlas Midnight live and go backstage. Then I get to see Lust Theory. It's surreal.'

As they made their way to the lift, the excitement wrapped itself tighter around her chest, but not for the reasons it once did. There was a time when nights like these would have had her heart racing – for the gig, for the music, for the thrill of being in the same orbit as the likes of Jax Devlin. But she knew now that spark had been extinguished. In fact, as she thought about it, she actually shuddered at the idea. Why had she felt so little about herself to even entertain him?

The roar of the crowd grew louder as they moved deeper backstage, the energy pulsing through the concrete walls. They weaved through crew members, sound engineers and artists in various stages of pre-show rituals. As they reached one of the backstage lounges, the door swung open to reveal none other than Atlas Midnight, the band that had soundtracked half of her teenage years. The lead singer, Cole Maddox, looked up from tuning his guitar and grinned. 'Fern! Been too long.'

Fern beamed and greeted them all like old friends. 'Boys, this is Daniel. He's sitting in on the interview tonight,' she added, waving him over. 'Be nice. He's a fan.'

The band made room for him on the battered old sofa, and as Fern pulled out her phone and began to record the interview, she caught the glint in Daniel's eye as he listened, completely starstruck. When the last question was asked and photographs were taken, the band excused themselves to warm up. Fern and Daniel found themselves at the side of the stage, soaking up the electric atmosphere.

Daniel leaned in close, his voice warm against her ear. 'This is just amazing! Thank you!'

Fern smiled. 'You're welcome! I'm just off to use the bathroom. I'll be five minutes, don't move!'

As she weaved her way through the backstage corridors, her phone buzzed again in her pocket, but before she could even glance at it, a figure stepped from the shadows, blocking her path.

Jax Devlin.

Before she could react, he pulled her in, lips crashing against hers without a second thought. The scent of leather, cigarettes and that familiar intoxicating aftershave hit her all at once.

'There you are,' he murmured against her mouth. 'Where the hell have you been? You normally come and see me in my dressing room.'

She stepped back, flustered but trying to mask it. 'Sorry, busy tonight. Work. Life. You know, the usual.'

But Jax wasn't letting her off that easily. His hand curled around her waist, eyes scanning her face. 'I've missed you, baby. Thought you'd done a runner on me. You've been quiet.'

Fern's pulse was racing for all the wrong reasons. She tried to step back but Jax only tightened his grip. He flicked his cigarette to the floor and crushed it under his boot. 'I've been hearing rumours about you.'

'Which are?'

'You haven't gone and shacked up with some loser who owns an antique shop, have you?' He smirked.

Fern froze. 'How do you know about the shop?'

Jax's grin widened. 'Ella's been keeping me up to date. Your mate's got loose lips when there's wine involved.'

Her stomach flipped. 'When have you had wine with Ella?'

Jax leaned in again, voice low and mocking. 'Whenever you're not free.'

Fern's stomach churned. Surely not. She didn't even want to think about it.

'Whatever happened to standards?'

Fern couldn't quite believe he had the nerve to talk about standards. She wrestled herself free and took a step back, the anger bubbling just beneath her skin. 'Grow up, Jax.'

'Don't be like that. You know we have good sex every time I'm in town and tonight won't be any different. You'll be there waiting in the hotel room as normal. You know you can't resist me.'

The arrogance made Fern's skin crawl. What did she ever see in him? She was about to walk away but he wasn't done. Another kiss landed on her lips, but this time she pulled away, wiping her mouth with the back of her hand.

A voice crackled over the radio, calling him to his dressing room.

Jax winked, cocky as ever. 'Same hotel as last time. Same room. See you after, baby, and I hope you're wearing my favourite underwear.'

Shaking, she watched him swaggering down the corridor like he owned the world.

Thankful he was gone, Fern turned around, only to stop dead in her tracks.

Daniel stood there, eyes dark, jaw clenched. It was written all over his face that he'd heard every word of her conversation with Jax.

Her stomach sank.

'Daniel…'

'You're sleeping with both him and me, and you didn't think to tell me?'

The words stuck in her throat, lost somewhere between regret and explanation.

Before she had time to explain, Daniel had walked away and disappeared into the crowd. She tried to follow him, shouting his name, but as weaved through the masses of fans he disappeared without trace.

Damn Jax Devlin.

Chapter Twenty-Eight

Fern had never known a stadium could feel so suffocating. One moment she'd been caught up in the electric buzz of Wembley – the flashing lights, the earth-shaking bass, the endless sea of fans waving their phones in the air like fireflies – and the next, all she could think about was Daniel, or rather the absence of him.

She'd scoured the wings of the stage, the back corridors, even the grimy side entrance where the band vans unloaded, but he was nowhere. He'd disappeared.

Her phone was practically useless, signal bars flickering on and off like a bad relationship. When her calls did connect, Daniel's phone went straight to voicemail. She must've hit redial a hundred times, each time her heart beating faster hoping he would pick up. He was gone and she couldn't blame him.

She hated herself for hurting him. How did she ever think Jax was a good idea?

Her mind went into overdrive. Would Daniel go back to her apartment? Or would he head straight to the station, desperate to put as much distance between them as a train would allow? The logical thing would be to make her way home, but Fern checked and found that the last train from Euston heading north left in a couple of hours. It was a gamble, but she decided to go to the station.

Fern jumped on the tube and slumped into a seat, her reflection wobbling in the opposite window as the train jerked to life. Even if she found Daniel, she didn't know whether he would listen to her, but she had to try.

Jax crept into her mind. All it had been with him was proximity, validation and convenience. She'd convinced herself it was enough, but it wasn't. *He* wasn't good enough for her.

Daniel was of a different calibre. With Daniel, she knew she could be herself – sarcasm, flaws, bad hair days, all of it. No airs needed, no carefully curated version of herself for Instagram. Just Fern. Messy, chaotic, stubborn Fern.

The train screeched to a halt at Baker Street, and the surge of people boarding pushed her further into her seat. Feeling tearful, she stared out of the window, watching the dark of the underground tunnels flash by. The thought of Daniel wandering through Wembley alone and upset made her stomach twist. She wanted to turn back the clock. She wanted to un-meet Jax.

By the time she reached Euston station, her mind was a jumbled mess of apologies and half-formed speeches. She practically bolted through the barriers, scanning every face she passed, hoping and praying that Daniel would be there. But the station was mostly empty, just a few stragglers and the occasional lost tourist dragging a suitcase behind them. She checked the departure board, but the train wasn't due for another hour.

She sank onto a bench and waited. The minutes ticked by painfully slowly, her thoughts still spinning in circles. She played out every scenario in her mind, him walking through the station and pretending not to see her, him not coming at all... But underneath the panic, the guilt, the regret, there was clarity. For the first time in a long time, she understood what she wanted. Not Jax. Not fleeting flings or convenient distractions. She wanted to get to know Daniel better. A man who treated her like she mattered and not just another girl in a long – *long* – line of pretty faces.

She ran through the things she'd say if he gave her the chance. How meeting him had been like a breath of fresh air. How he made her laugh, how gorgeous he was and how Jax had never been anything more than a lesson. All she wanted to do was make it right. But the minutes stretched out, and her hope was stretched thin. The station emptied, the last train announcement echoing through the concourse like a countdown she wasn't ready for.

She stood up, paced, scanned the arrivals and departures, clutching her phone like it was a lifeline. No texts. No missed calls. No Daniel.

There was only one thing for it. She'd make her way back to her apartment.

As she headed for the tube her phoned beeped with a text from Jax.

JAX

> Where are you?

It wasn't the text she wanted to receive.

Fern briefly closed her eyes before deleting their message chain and blocking his number.

Chapter Twenty-Nine

As Fern turned the key in the lock and pushed open the door, her phone buzzed sharply in her coat pocket, breaking the silence. Her heart raced, hoping it was Daniel, but when she looked at the screen she saw Ella's name.

She hesitated. Her thumb hovered over the green answer button, but instead she let the call ring out. She didn't want to explain what had happened, especially knowing Ella would be at the after-party, high on free drinks and music-world gossip, and no doubt with Jax. She slipped off her boots and coat, and switched on the kettle.

She'd half-hoped – probably foolishly – that maybe Daniel would've been here. She flopped down on the sofa, pulling her knees to her chest. All she could think about was the look on his face backstage, the hurt, the confusion.

There was a soft knock on the front door and she raced to peer through the spy hole. And there he was. Daniel. Fern flung open the door.

'Hi,' he said, voice low, soft, but steady.

'Oh thank God. Daniel, I'm so sorry.' She opened the door wide and stood aside. 'Where did you go? Come and sit down.'

'I needed to clear my head. That … wasn't exactly something I expected to hear tonight.' He sat on the edge of the settee. 'I'm not judging you, but I was expecting a little bit of honesty at least. I didn't think you were in a relationship with anyone else when … I thought … I hoped there was something for us.'

'I know.' She wrapped her arms around herself, her voice cracking slightly. 'I owe you an apology and the truth.' She paused as she sat down next to him, trying to gather her tangle of thoughts into something that sounded halfway coherent.

'Jax is something I'm not proud of and it's not a relationship.'

'I saw you kissing.'

Fern shook her head. 'No. He kissed me, yes, but I pulled away.' She could see that Daniel didn't look convinced.

She carried on. 'It wasn't anything, what he and I had. Just something convenient whenever he was in town.'

'I wouldn't have you down as someone who hooks up for convenience's sake.'

'It's hard to explain.'

'You don't have to.'

'I do because I know I've hurt your feelings, and I should have mentioned it before we went tonight.'

'Why didn't you?'

'Embarrassment about my own choices. I've never been the best at picking the right people,' she admitted. 'When I met Jax, I was at rock bottom. I was so tired of feeling like I wasn't enough for anyone. When he came along he made me feel seen. But I wasn't blind. I knew he was sleeping with other women. It wasn't a relationship. It was ... I don't even know what it was. I just wanted to feel something. Wanted to feel important, even if it was only for a moment. The stupid part is, most of the time it only made me feel worse.'

The confession hung between them, leaving Fern feeling raw and exposed.

'My self-esteem's been at an all-time low for a long time,' she went on. 'Every guy ... it's like I've had a neon sign flashing "walk all over me" on my forehead. They'd cheat. Or lie. Or treat me like I was disposable. Jax was the same. I was just too wrapped up in the thrill of his being a rock star to admit it to myself. Being with you ... it made me see things in a new and unexpected light.'

Daniel's expression softened, but there was still a flicker of something sad in his eyes.

'You shouldn't have let anyone treat you like that,' he said quietly. 'You're worth so much more than that.'

Fern had never heard those words before, not like this. Not like it was the most obvious truth in the world.

'Maybe I didn't believe I was,' she replied.

For a time, Daniel said nothing. Then he said something that surprised her. 'I've always felt like I wasn't enough. With the women I've dated before ... it was always the same. They'd want me to be someone I wasn't. More driven. More ambitious. The kind of man who had a five-year plan pinned to the fridge. But I'm not that guy. I don't need a mapped-out future. I just want ... someone who likes me as I am. Who doesn't want to fix me or nudge me into a different shape. Who lets me be me. The second you walked on to the train I noticed you. There was something about you that was different and I so badly wanted to talk to you and hoped you would sit next to me. But tonight... Well, it's made me realise we live in separate worlds, and maybe all the thoughts and possibilities that have been whirling around in my brain are just some sort of fiction. Something that can never be real.'

'What are those thoughts?'

Daniel let out a soft, almost self-conscious laugh as he rubbed the back of his neck. 'That you'd fall in love with Puffin Island,' he said, voice low but honest. 'With the place, the calm, the sea air ... and me. That you'd walk into the antique shop and feel like it was meant to be yours as much as mine. That we'd take it over together, the pair of us. I know it sounds daft. Like some postcard life I made up in my head. But I wanted it, Fern. And I wanted you to want it, too.' He shook his head, reality settling in his eyes. 'But you're not that girl, are you?' His voice wasn't bitter, just accepting. 'You've built this life here – the interviews, the gigs, the backstage passes and big names. You've got your world, and I've got mine. And they couldn't be more different. I love the coast, Puffin Island, the community, the way they're all just one big family. I couldn't even imagine going about my day, walking through the streets, with no one acknowledging anyone. I like people, good people, and life on the island.'

Fern stared down at her hands, her fingers twisting together. She'd always thought she knew what she wanted; the rush of city living, the excitement of concerts and gigs, the lights of London, the late nights clinking glasses with strangers, being wrapped up in the world of chart-toppers and fame-chasers like Jax Devlin. The thrill of being in the room, being on the list. Yet, sitting here, listening to Daniel, she wasn't so sure anymore.

He was steady, kind and genuine. A man who didn't need fixing, who didn't wear a mask, who wasn't playing a game.

Her voice cracked slightly when she finally spoke.

'I don't know what I want,' she admitted. 'I thought I did. I thought I was chasing the right things: the parties, the so-called glamour. But lately … I don't know. I think I've been so used to arseholes like Jax, to the chase and the drama, that I convinced myself that was what I deserved.' She glanced at him, seeing the way his eyes softened. 'Of course, I thought you were handsome and funny, and I was drawn straight to you when I saw you on the train. I didn't think I would ever see you again and then I walked into No. 17 Curiosity Lane and… I'm sorry, Daniel…'

'What are you sorry for?'

'I suppose I didn't think about the bigger picture or think about your feelings. I just jumped into bed with you … literally … but…'

'But?'

'I know I have feelings for you.' Her gaze was unwavering as she looked into his eyes. 'That's not the problem. The problem is: how do we know it's something real? Could I really just up and leave this life? Walk away from everything I've built, everything I've known, and start again…' Her voice trailed off, the answer to the question scaring her even more than the thought.

Daniel didn't rush to fill the silence. He just reached out, his hand brushing over hers.

'It's scary because it matters,' he said simply. 'I'm not asking you to decide now. I'm not asking you to change your life overnight. I just wanted you to know how I felt. That you aren't like anyone I've met before. I can't deny that tonight hurt. I didn't like seeing you kiss someone else ... I was jealous.'

'I'm sorry again. I promise you that that part of my life is over. But life is never that simple, is it?'

'It's not.' He smiled, brushing his thumb against her knuckles. 'But it could be simple.'

For the first time in a long time, the idea of simple didn't sound boring to Fern. 'One day at a time?' she said.

Daniel nodded. 'One day at a time.'

Chapter Thirty

Fern woke up in her own bed, her head nestled against the curve of Daniel's shoulder, his arm slung lazily around her waist. For a blissful moment, she didn't move. The usual city sounds of car horns, the distant hum of life in London drifted in from the window, and for once it all felt peaceful. Last night they had climbed into bed after their heart-to-heart and cuddled each other until they fell asleep.

Daniel stirred beside her and murmured, 'You know what's weird? Waking up and not seeing a moose hanging over our heads.'

Fern laughed.

'You London types are all about minimalist chic.'

She lifted her head and gave him a mock serious look. 'I'll have you know, I've got plenty of quirks. I'm very partial to a velvet throw pillow, and I have a Leonard, don't forget…'

'Ah, the plant fighting for survival,' Daniel teased, propping himself up on one elbow.

They lay there a little longer, the sheets tangled around their legs, neither in a rush to move. London might have been awake and buzzing, but inside her apartment, time slowed down, cocooning them in the soft bubble of morning-after happiness.

'So,' Daniel said after a while, his fingers tracing idle circles on her bare shoulder, 'what does a big-shot music journalist actually do with her weekends? When she's not busy interviewing superstars and breaking hearts, that is.'

Fern tilted her head thoughtfully. 'You're assuming I don't spend every Saturday in the British Museum.'

'You don't?'

'More often it's brunch. Too much coffee. A painfully overpriced pastry. Wandering around markets pretending I'm cultured when I'm really just buying cheese. Or the odd rooftop bar with Ella.'

He smiled, brushing his lips softly against her temple. 'You make it sound like it's all so perfect.'

'Then there's the housework.'

'Which must take all of ten minutes...' teased Daniel.

She turned onto her side to face him properly. 'Most weekends are spent wishing I had someone to share it with – the real stuff, the boring stuff. Coffee?' she asked, and he nodded. 'I'll be back in five.'

After handing a mug to Daniel she slipped back under the covers. 'I suppose we must try and get up soon,' she said, taking a sip of her own coffee. She reached for her phone, which had been charging on the nightstand, and the screen lit up with a scatter of notifications, including the inevitable slew of messages from Ella.

ELLA

> You missed the BEST after-party!

> Jax was in prime form. You should've seen it. The whole band partied hard!

Attached was a photo of Ella, glowing with her signature after-party sparkle, standing sandwiched between the band members. Jax's arm hung casually around her waist, fingers resting far too comfortably on her hip.

For a flicker of a second, she wondered if Ella had slept with him. Before she could dwell on it, her phone buzzed again with a text from a number she didn't recognise.

Reading it, Fern flapped her hand at Daniel. 'We have a message from Eliza Valentine! She has a lead on the wedding dress and has invited us over for brunch! It's a Hampstead postcode.'

'Where's that?'

She passed her phone to him so he could read the message. 'One of London's greenest, most enviable corners. The kind of place where houses come with manicured gardens, sweeping staircases and family portraits older than the street itself.'

'Wow!' replied Daniel as he read the message and passed the phone back to Fern.

'Looks like we've got a brunch date. Are we ready to find out who the mysterious groom is?'

'I have to say I'm intrigued about the bride, too! It could be something or nothing.'

'Either way, we can make a decision to sell the dress, now we have some idea of its worth. That money could help spruce up the shop. Maybe even replace the windows and the front door.'

But Fern's mind had already drifted, her attention snagged by a different notification lighting up her screen, an email from Edgar Carmichael, Puffin Island's solicitor. She skimmed the subject line.

Offer Received: No. 17 Curiosity Lane.

The email was short and to the point: a client of Edgar's, someone private but serious, had made an offer for the shop including all its contents. A very generous one. The kind of figure that needed careful consideration. She glanced sideways at Daniel, who was drinking his coffee with a blissful smile on his face.

Could she really sell it? This offer wasn't just a passing daydream or a 'what if the right buyer came along?' scenario. It was a hefty six-figure sum. This was real and the pros were easy. Money in the bank, and she wouldn't even have the headache of getting rid of any of the stuff. But the cons ... they came with faces. One in particular, and he was lying right next to her. Edgar hadn't mentioned Daniel in the email. She didn't think he could persuade him to leave. Or maybe she could, if the price was right?

Fern sighed, staring at the screen. The temptation was so strong but the question that was really playing on her mind was: was financial freedom worth the risk of hurting Daniel and destroying their relationship?

Daniel's voice cut through her thoughts. 'We'd best shower and make ourselves presentable for brunch.'

'We'd best,' she replied, taking a swig of coffee.

'We're going to crack this case ... it's all about teamwork.'

Fern watched as he jumped out of bed and straight into the shower, but all she could think about was Edgar's client's offer, which seemed way too generous for the old, rundown antique shop.

Chapter Thirty-One

Fern and Daniel hopped off the tube at Hampstead. The streets here were quieter than the usual city chaos. Just quiet roads, leafy trees swaying like they had all the time in the world, and houses that gave off serious old-money energy. They followed Google Maps up one immaculate street after another, passing homes that seemed like they'd stepped straight out of a magazine shoot. As they rounded a corner, the address on her phone matched up with a house. Fern slowed to a stop. 'This is it.'

'Blooming hell,' Daniel muttered, pulling his sunglasses down like it might help him process the view.

It wasn't just a house, it was a mansion. The kind of place that had probably seen more champagne corks pop than most wedding venues. The gates alone looked like they belonged outside a palace.

The house behind the gates was beautiful – grand, old-school, with cream stone walls, wide bay windows and a perfectly mowed front lawn.

'This place feels like it should come with a butler and at least one family ghost,' murmured Fern.

'This place is worth millions. Imagine living somewhere like this.' Daniel pointed to the intercom.

Fern pressed the button and they waited.

The intercom crackled. 'Good morning! How can I help you?'

'It's Fern and Daniel, we're here about the wedding dress.'

'Come on in.'

The gates creaked and then swung open. As they walked up to the front door, Fern turned to Daniel. 'Why is it I'm suddenly feeling nervous?'

The front door opened and they were greeted by the Eliza they'd met the day before. 'Do come in. It's lovely to see you both again.'

'What a beautiful home you have.'

'Thank you.'

Inside, the place was just as impressive. The high-ceilinged hallway led them through to a sitting room bathed in the mid-morning light. Floor-to-ceiling windows framed an immaculate garden that seemed to stretch on for ever, the manicured hedges sculpted into perfect shapes, and a stone fountain trickling in the centre like something out of a Jane Austen adaptation.

A long table near the window had been laid out for brunch, a spread that could've fed an army, with freshly baked pastries, glistening bowls of fruit, thick wedges of sourdough and pots of jam that looked almost too pretty to open.

Eliza, reached for the teapot. 'Tea?' she offered.

'That would be lovely, both with milk and one sugar,' said Fern.

'Coming right up, take a seat.'

They sat down on the sofa but before Eliza could finish pouring the tea a voice echoed from down the hallway.

'Don't start without me!'

A smiley elderly woman appeared at the doorway. She was small, maybe no more than five feet, but her presence filled the room. Her hair, a perfect crown of soft silver waves, was swept back with a velvet headband, and she wore a tailored lilac jacket paired with an elegant string of pearls that hinted at a lifetime of impeccable style. Tucked firmly under her arm was a large, leather-bound book, worn at the edges and with what looked like scraps of fabric and old photographs peeking out from between the pages.

'Let me introduce you to my grandmother,' the younger Eliza said. 'This is the original Eliza Valentine, known as Zaza. Seamstress to the stars and the woman who made your recently acquired wedding dress.' She put the china cups and saucers down on the table and took the leather bound book from her grandmother. 'The name Zaza comes from me, because I couldn't say "Grandma" when I was a small child. The name stuck.' She shrugged.

Fern stood up and stretched out her hand to Zaza. 'It's lovely to meet you.'

'Pleased to meet you,' Zaza said, offering a genuine smile and a handshake.

'This is Daniel, and I'm Fern.'

Zaza's sharp blue eyes sparkled as she nodded towards Daniel. She carried herself with the quiet elegance of a woman who had lived a life draped in silk and stitched with stories. 'I believe you've been asking about one of my very early wedding dresses,' she said, easing herself down into a velvet armchair opposite them.

Fern sat too, perching on the edge of the sofa as the whole tale spilled out, and added that she hoped that Zaza might just hold the missing thread to its history.

Zaza listened intently. 'This is all very curious indeed,' she said, pulling the well-loved leather book towards her. 'Where did you say this antique shop was?'

'Puffin Island,' Fern replied.

Immediately, Zaza's face lit up with a fond, wistful expression. 'Ah, Puffin Island. One of my favourite places in all the world,' she said. 'And I've travelled to many, including Paris, Milan and New York, crafting dresses for the famous, the fortunate … and, on occasion, for dear friends.'

'It was Dorothy, the seamstress from Puffin Island, who suggested we look you up,' Fern added. 'She thought you might be able to help.'

At the mention of the name, Zaza's smile deepened. 'Dorothy,' she repeated, her voice lined with nostalgia. 'We were once friends. Rivals, too, in the way only two ambitious young women can be, but always friends. We met at sewing college in Newcastle, fresh from school and both dreaming bigger than the world seemed ready to allow. Back then, we had nothing but a battered set of dressmaking shears and more ideas than fabric. We'd haunt the local market stalls on weekends, browsing lace we couldn't possibly afford, sketching gowns on scraps of paper and spinning stories about the women who'd one day wear them.'

Daniel and Fern sat spellbound as Zaza continued, her voice soft but animated. 'We were thick as thieves, always sneaking out of class to chase boys along the Quayside or get lost in the music halls. But when it came to dressmaking, Dorothy was a natural. With her eye for detail she could spot a crooked seam at a glance. She was the one who taught me the importance of hand-finishing, the kind of craftsmanship that speaks without needing labels or price tags.'

Zaza had a look of pride on her face. 'When college ended, we both struggled to get a foothold. Neither of us had wealthy families or connections, but we had talent and determination. It was Dorothy who helped me get my first real break. She lived on Puffin Island and helped me secure a tiny shop along the coast in the nearby town, Sea's End. Just a single window display and a sewing table in the back, but to me it felt like the world. Dorothy sourced fabrics for me in those early days, as she knew all the hidden corners of every market from Berwick to Newcastle. She even helped stitch the final hem on my first commissioned wedding dress. We celebrated that night with a bottle of cheap fizz on the beach, sitting on the sand in our best coats, pretending we'd made it.' Zaza paused. 'She always believed in me, more than I did, sometimes. I owe her a great deal, and not just for the shop or the fabric. She reminded me that the best dresses aren't stitched from silk or lace, but from the stories of the women who wear them.'

Fern felt emotional. They were lovely words.

Zaza gently patted the leather-bound book on the table. 'I may still have the original sketch for that gown in here,' she said. 'And of course, the name of the bride.'

Fern and Daniel exchanged a glance.

Zaza's gaze softened as she looked back at Fern. 'Let's see if we can solve your mystery, shall we?'

Fern had the undeniable feeling that whatever the story, this was only the beginning.

Chapter Thirty-Two

'What was the number stitched inside the dress?' asked Zaza.

'64. 24.12,' stated Fern.

Zaza opened the book. The pages were filled with elegant sketches, swatches of fabric pinned in the corners, and looping handwriting that belonged to another era entirely.

Fern leaned in, barely able to contain her curiosity, while Daniel settled back, watching Zaza with quiet fascination. The drawing that emerged first made Fern give a tiny gasp. 'That's the one.'

The sketch included all the tiny details, and Eliza's initials – a curling EV – were signed neatly in the corner like a painter signing a masterpiece.

'The sixty-fourth dress I made,' Zaza began, her voice soft but laced with unmistakable pride. 'I remember every stitch, every fitting, like it was yesterday. It was made for a Christmas Eve wedding, planned to take place at the church on Puffin Island. There's something quite magical about a winter wedding, don't you think? The snow falling, candlelight flickering, the scent of pine and mulled wine in the air. When this order came through, I was still working from my little shop in Sea's End. It was the most elaborate gown I'd been asked to make at that point, with ivory silk tulle, hand-sewn pearl detailing and lace imported from France. It took me close to eight weeks, working through the nights by lamplight, hands pricked raw from all the hand-beading.'

Fern could practically see the scene in her mind's eye, a younger Eliza hunched over the gown in a cold little seaside shop, driven by both passion and the pressure of making her mark.

Daniel let out a low whistle. 'That must've been some endeavour.'

'Oh, it was,' Zaza replied with a soft chuckle. 'The bride wanted it to look like she'd stepped straight out of a fairytale and, I dare say, the dress did. I remember the final fitting. The way her eyes lit up when she saw herself in the mirror. She looked utterly enchanted.'

Fern couldn't hold the question in any longer. 'So ... can you tell us who the bride was?'

Eliza lifted the page slightly, revealing a name written in the flowing, unmistakable script of the past.

'Matilda Hartley.'

Fern's eyes widened as she stared around them all. 'Matilda Hartley?' she repeated, her voice catching in the back of her throat. 'That's my great-aunt.'

Zaza's eyes widened. 'She's your great-aunt?'

Fern nodded. 'Which makes all this very strange. I don't think the wedding ever happened,' she said, looking to Daniel for confirmation, as he was the one who knew Matilda.

But it was Zaza who gave a nod. 'Dorothy did share that with me. I never knew the reason why but—' She stopped mid-sentence.

'But?' Fern questioned.

'It's not for me to keep rumours alive.'

'Please, can you tell us what you know? We don't even know where to go from here.'

Zaza still looked a little uneasy. 'Soon after the wedding was called off, Matilda's family disowned her. The majority of people thought that it was her fault and that maybe she'd had an affair.'

'You knew her at the time. Is that what you think?' asked Fern.

'I don't like to make assumptions without facts, and it really wasn't any of my business to ask.'

'I know what I'm thinking,' cut in Daniel.

'Go on,' urged Fern.

'Where has this wedding dress been hiding until now? Why does someone want us to discover this information, and what are they expecting us to do with it?'

'I've just been thinking the same,' added Fern. 'Have you got any details of the groom?' she asked Zaza.

'I don't even need to look his name up. The groom was Nathaniel Loring.'

Fern's mouth dropped open so suddenly it felt like her jaw had unhinged. 'Nathaniel Loring? As in Nathaniel Loring the composer?'

Zaza offered a slow nod of the head. 'The very one.'

Daniel sat back against the plush sofa, running a hand through his hair. 'You've got to be kidding me,' he murmured.

Fern's mind spun. Nathaniel Loring, the world-renowned

composer whose music still echoed from grand pianos in every concert hall, the man whose name had graced album covers and symphony programmes, had been engaged to her great-aunt? She was flabbergasted and still trying to process the revelation. 'This is quite unbelievable. Do you know any more details? Can you remember any conversations from when you fitted the dress? I appreciate it's a very long time ago.'

'I can remember that she and Nathaniel originally met at a London music school, but it was a summer on Puffin Island that cemented their relationship. Nathaniel stayed on the island, and Matilda was helping out in the local guest house. They fell in love like characters from a novel, so quickly and completely it swept them both off their feet.' Zaza reached for her teacup and took a slow sip. 'But Nathaniel came from a world of acclaim, opportunity and temptation. On the day of the wedding, it was all over.'

Fern swallowed hard, feeling an ache deep in her chest for her great-aunt. 'She must have been devastated.'

'She was,' Zaza said softly. 'She lived her life quietly, gracefully, but afterwards always alone.'

'That's so sad. How did she end up owning a junk shop?' asked Fern.

'I've no idea,' replied Zaza.

Fern's thoughts were tumbling over in her mind. 'I'm not sure where to go with this. Is this just the end of the story? We've found out who the groom is, but what are we meant to do with that information?' She looked over at Daniel, who shrugged.

'Newspaper articles are suggesting that Nathaniel has removed himself from the limelight and is in ill health,' he volunteered.

ELLA

> I need to tell you something. I've been sleeping with Jax for a while. I didn't mean for it to happen, and I feel awful. I know I overstepped. I shouldn't have, I really shouldn't, but you know what he's like ... he's hard to resist. I'm so, so sorry. We're together and I hope you can forgive me. x

How could Ella do that? She was meant to be Fern's best friend. They'd been through everything together – dodgy boyfriends, flatmate disasters, wine-fuelled meltdowns. Now this? She didn't even feel sad exactly, just ... gobsmacked. A bit ragey. But mostly hurt. Properly hurt. Because Ella knew what she was doing. The betrayal would've been easier to endure if it had come from a stranger. But from Ella? Her *best friend*? That was the twist of the knife.

And the worst part? It wasn't even the first time she'd pulled something like this. As soon as she'd read the text, Fern's mind had flicked back to London, years ago, to the night they'd sat side by side in that sticky little dive bar in Soho, both a few glasses of cheap wine deep, scribbling ideas for freelance pitches on napkins like two underpaid geniuses about to change the world. Fern had told her about a column idea, a music feature on unsigned London artists, a spotlight series for the magazine circuit. Ella had smiled, nodded and toasted to the future of music journalism.

A week later, Ella's byline appeared in *Echo Beat Weekly* under a headline that read *The Fresh Faces of London's Music Scene*. She'd stolen Fern's idea. She'd secured a regular gig with the magazine, and the substantial salary that came with it.

Fern had forgiven her back then. Or, at least, told herself she had. She'd chosen the friendship over the fallout. But now,

Chapter Thirty-Three

Fern stood in the shop, pretending to rearrange a tray of vintage brooches for the tenth time, even though her head wasn't in it. She could feel Daniel watching her while dusting an old radio that probably hadn't worked since the seventies.

She knew he'd clocked her mood the second they'd had breakfast. 'All right, out with it,' he finally insisted. 'You've been quiet for the last hour.'

Fern glanced over at him, forcing a half-smile. 'I'm fine.'

Daniel raised an eyebrow. 'You're about as fine as that lamp with the wobbly base. When a woman says she's fine, that's code for not fine.'

She let out a soft laugh. She hadn't told him about the email from Edgar Carmichael she'd received in London, or about the text from Ella that had popped up on her phone in the middle of the night while Daniel snored softly beside her. She'd read it twice. Then a third time, hoping the words might rearrange themselves into something less disappointing.

No. 17 Curiosity Lane

'Yes.' Fern looked towards Zaza. 'Do you think there's more to this story, or did someone just want me to know that my great-aunt was once going to marry a famous composer?'

'I would say someone is trying to tell you something, and my guess is it's about why the wedding didn't actually happen,' she replied. 'It seems to me there was more to the story, and it could possibly be coming out now because whoever gave you the dress knows Nathaniel is in ill health. Maybe he's the only one who knows the answers.'

'Looks like this mystery isn't over. My guess is, we're only just scraping the surface,' replied Fern.

given this new betrayal, she was looking at things differently. Maybe it had always been more about convenience than closeness with Ella? After all, they'd worked the same gigs, lived in the same apartment block, moved in the same circles. It had been easy. But now? Now it just felt like another nail in the coffin of Fern's former life.

Daniel interrupted her thoughts. 'So?' he prompted, tilting his head and waiting for her to open up.

She swallowed, then gave him the easiest lie she could muster up, part of which was true.

'I've just been thinking about Matilda and Nathaniel. Surely Dorothy is going to know something, and possibly Betty? Maybe I should have a chat with them both.'

Daniel didn't look convinced that that was all that was on her mind, but he nodded slowly. 'Okay, good idea.'

When he turned away, she glanced at the clock. Edgar would be in his office very soon and she really wanted to chat with him about his email and the offer from the mystery buyer.

A few minutes later, while Daniel was chatting to an elderly couple who were trying to decide between two slightly rusted oil lamps, Fern took her chance. She grabbed her bag. 'Back in a bit,' she called lightly, waving over her shoulder. The second the shop door swung shut behind her, she slipped next door and climbed the stairs to Edgar's office. She knocked and waited.

'Fern,' Edgar said, holding his door open. 'I thought you might pop in today.'

'I was intrigued by your email,' she said as she slid into the worn leather chair across from his desk. 'You have a potential buyer for the shop? But how? It's not up for sale.'

Edgar slid across the desk a single sheet of paper that outlined the details of the offer.

Fern's eyes scanned the numbers first.' She let out a low whistle. 'Eight hundred grand from an anonymous buyer for the shop and its contents. It feels too good to be true.' She had no idea how much the shop and the contents were worth, but Fern had to assume that this offer was way over the odds, given how rundown the place was. Her heart raced. 'Surely this is some sort of joke?'

'No, it's a genuine offer.' Edgar adjusted his glasses, folding his hands neatly on the polished oak desk. 'You couldn't ask for more than a cash buyer with no conditions. But they want an answer by close of business on Friday, a week from now.'

Fern raised her eyebrows. 'Is this the normal practice?'

Edgar hesitated, the pause stretching just long enough to confirm her suspicion. 'No, not really,' he admitted. 'It's a little … unorthodox, I'll grant you that. But given the figure on the table, it's also remarkably generous. If your heart's set on walking away from the shop, Fern, this is the solution. Simple and clean.'

'What about Daniel?'

'Talk to him. With this amount of money, maybe you could pay him a lump sum.'

She leaned back slightly, letting her gaze settle back on the proposal. The offer was solid, and it was more than enough to pay Daniel a lump sum, to make sure he'd be comfortable and able to find a new flat, maybe even more than that … but he wasn't the kind of person to be bought; he wasn't motivated by money. As for the rest? She could take it and run. Go back to London, back to the life she'd pressed pause on the day she'd stepped into No. 17 Curiosity Lane. She could avoid the headache of clearing the place out or trying to sell it on the open market. It was the smart choice. The practical one.

But then an uninvited image slid into her mind: Daniel behind the counter that morning, coffee in hand, flashing her that soft, familiar smile he always saved for the moments he thought she wasn't paying attention. Could she really do that to him? Cut the thread so abruptly, hand him his share and walk away like it hadn't mattered – like *he* hadn't mattered? She knew it would mean she'd probably never see him again, and did she really want that? She cleared her throat and looked at Edgar. 'I'll have a think about it.'

Edgar nodded solemnly. 'As I said, the offer expires on Friday,' he reminded her, his tone gentle but firm.

'Can I ask you something else? About Matilda and Nathaniel Loring.'

If Edgar was surprised, he didn't show it. His expression remained composed, his eyes steady.

'I've discovered that the wedding dress belonged to Matilda,' Fern explained. 'And yesterday I met the designer, Eliza Valentine.'

Edgar smiled; a genuine, wistful smile, touched with fondness. 'Eliza Valentine. Now there's a name I haven't heard in a while. A remarkable woman. Charismatic, sharp as a tack and wickedly funny. Once upon a time, we ran in the same circles. I haven't seen her in many years.'

'What happened between Matilda and Nathaniel?'

Edgar's smile faded, replaced by something closer to professional distance. 'There were … whispers,' he said carefully. 'But my line of work teaches you to value facts, not gossip. The truth is, no one really knew. They were meant to have a Christmas Eve wedding and everything was set, right down to the last detail. But the ceremony was called off that morning.'

Fern let the information settle. 'Why do you think someone wanted me to "find the groom"?' she asked quietly. 'I now know it was Nathaniel Loring, but is that it? Am I supposed to just leave it there?'

Edgar tilted his head, thoughtful. 'It feels like someone doesn't want the past to stay in the past. What are you thinking of doing about it?'

'I'm not actually sure.' Standing, she reached across the desk to shake his hand. 'I'll be back in touch once I've had a think.' As she left his office, Fern found she didn't want to go back to the shop. Not yet. She needed to calm her thoughts, especially around Daniel, who could read her moods so easily.

As she walked she thought about Nathaniel. She'd spent enough time chasing interviews to know how hard it was to get face time with a musician of his status. She wondered if it was worth picking up the phone and calling his management to ask for one last interview about his career. Would her connection with the magazine be enough? Fern knew it was the only way to get close enough to him to ask about Matilda, but if he didn't want to talk about it, he would probably have her removed.

Five minutes later, she found herself outside The Café on the Coast. Amelia was sitting outside enjoying breakfast and she looked up and smiled when she saw Fern walking through the gate.

'You look like you've got the weight of the world on your shoulders,' Amelia said. 'Want to join me?'

Fern managed a faint smile. 'I have got a bit of a dilemma ... thank you, that would be good.' She pulled out the chair opposite Amelia, her gaze drifting to the chalkboard menu. Her stomach gave a loud, undeniable grumble.

'I think I need a second breakfast. A big one.'

Clemmie appeared at the side of the table, pad and pen already in hand. 'How are you? Any news on the wedding dress? We all love a good mystery!' she chirped.

'Actually, yes. I do have news.'

That caught both Clemmie's and Amelia's attention. Clemmie immediately pulled up a chair. 'What have you found out?' she asked.

'Dorothy knew who the designer was,' Fern began, 'and Daniel and I went to London to meet her. She invited us to her home, which, honestly, was something out of a magazine.'

'And? Who's the designer?' Amelia leaned in.

'Eliza Valentine.'

Clemmie's eyes widened. 'Not *the* Eliza Valentine? The designer who dressed celebrities and royalty back in the sixties and seventies?'

'The very same,' Fern confirmed. 'She's logged every dress she's ever made, and according to her records, the wedding dress belonged to my great-aunt Matilda.'

Amelia and Clemmie exchanged looks, their expressions now brimming with excitement.

'Who was the groom?' Clemmie asked, practically bouncing in her seat.

'Nathaniel Loring.'

'The composer?' Amelia questioned.

Fern nodded. 'That's him.'

'You're kidding!' Clemmie breathed. 'But I thought Matilda was single?'

'She was.' Fern shook her head slowly. 'The wedding was

planned for Christmas Eve, right here on Puffin Island, but it was called off that very morning.'

'Why was it cancelled?' Amelia asked.

'That's what I don't know. I was hoping someone on the island might.'

Amelia and Clemmie answered in unison. 'Betty!'

They laughed, but there was a gleam in their eyes.

'My granny knows *everything*,' Clemmie said with a grin, glancing over her shoulder at the counter where Betty was chatting with a customer. The moment Betty finished ringing up the bill, Clemmie waved her over. 'Granny!'

Betty bustled over, her face lighting up as she saw Fern. 'How are you?'

'All good, thank you. That lemon drizzle cake you dropped off? Incredible.'

Betty nodded her head proudly, then looked between the three women. 'I take it there's more to this chat than cake?'

'Fern needs a little island intel,' Clemmie said. 'We thought you might be able to help.'

Betty arched a brow. 'Intel on what?'

'The wedding dress,' Fern said. 'It belonged to my great-aunt Matilda.'

Betty's expression shifted. 'Ah … did it? No one ever got to see the dress as it was the wedding that never was,' she said almost wistfully.

'You remember it?' asked Clemmie.

'I was a guest,' Betty said with a nod. 'It was Christmas Eve and the snow was falling… The island looked like something on a postcard. It was all so romantic … until it wasn't.'

'Aunt Matilda was really set to marry Nathaniel Loring?' Fern asked.

'She was.'

'What happened?' asked Clemmie. 'Why didn't they go through with it? Surely you must know.'

Betty shook her head slowly. 'No one knew for sure, though there were rumours, of course.'

'What kind of rumours?' Fern pressed, remembering what Eliza had hinted at.

'That Matilda might've had a fling,' Betty said reluctantly. 'But she was so head over heels for Nathaniel, I never quite believed it.'

'Did they ever see each other again?' Fern asked.

'Not as far as I know,' Betty replied. 'I was actually thinking of them only this morning. There's another article about Nathaniel in today's newspaper.'

Betty reached over to a nearby table and grabbed the folded newspaper. She smoothed it out and tapped the front page. The headline read: *Famed Composer Nathaniel Loring Admitted To Private Clinic Amid Health Concerns – Estate to Be Left to Agent Alistair Montgomery.*

Below was a photograph of Loring in a wheelchair, looking frail and shielded from the camera flashes by sunglasses and a scarf. The article went on to detail his wealth, all of it to be left to his lifelong agent and friend, Alistair Montgomery.

'I've never heard of Alistair Montgomery, which is surprising given the line of work I'm in.'

'From what I know, he wasn't an agent to the stars, only to Nathaniel Loring. He dedicated his life to him,' Betty offered.

Fern was already on her phone, googling Alistair Montgomery. She began reading aloud. 'They met at the London School of Music, became best friends and graduated together. That means he would have known my great-aunt Matilda, too.'

'Yes, he knew Matilda. The three of them were thick as thieves and inseparable until the wedding day, when the friendship collapsed. Alistair took Nathaniel's side and never spoke to Matilda again,' shared Betty.

Fern googled his picture and scrolled through the images. Wide-eyed, she looked up. 'I know him. I saw him twice last week – once in the shop and then again leaving Dorothy's.'

'Yes, Nathaniel Loring's agent is Dorothy's brother,' Betty confirmed.

Fern was amazed. 'I'm not sure what to think.'

'There's only two men alive who know the truth of why that wedding didn't take place,' declared Betty, 'Alistair and Nathaniel. And according to the news, soon there may only be one.'

Chapter Thirty-Four

After Clemmie had written down Fern's order, she and Betty disappeared back inside the café.

Amelia sipped her coffee. 'The plot thickens. Did he mention who he was when he visited the shop?'

Fern shook her head. 'He asked about an item and I can't quite remember...' She racked her brain. 'A music box,' she finally said. 'He wanted to know if the shop had any music boxes.'

'Does it?' asked Amelia.

'No, but why didn't he tell me who he was? He even sat down and played Matilda's piano. I'm wondering if he would talk to me about what happened, especially if he knew Matilda too.'

'You could try, but if he didn't speak to Matilda after that Christmas Eve, my guess is you probably won't get the truth, just the narrative they want to spin.'

'You're probably right,' agreed Fern. 'But someone wants

me to uncover something … and on top of that I've got another dilemma.'

'You know what they say about a problem shared…' Amelia prompted.

Fern exhaled and looked at Amelia. 'This stays between us.' She barely knew Amelia but there was something about her that told Fern she could trust her.

'Of course.'

'There's been an offer on the shop from an anonymous buyer, which includes both the shop and the contents.'

'Wow. That's amazing … isn't it?'

'I'm not sure. I would have to persuade Daniel it was a good idea, or sell him with the shop, so to speak, but it would mean I could just walk away, go back to London and my normality. There would be no more worry about what to do with the place and there'd be money in my pocket. For once, quite a lot of it.'

'Sounds tempting,' Amelia said carefully. 'But you don't seem excited.'

Fern's food arrived at the table, and as she picked up her knife and fork she admitted, 'I haven't told Daniel yet, and I'm feeling very guilty about it.'

'What does he want to happen?'

'We agreed I would give him a month to show that the shop could generate an income. He loves that place and doesn't want me to sell. It's his job and his home, but he can't afford to buy it from me. I have until Friday to make a decision, then the offer is off the table.'

'That is intriguing.'

'Whoever the buyer is they're offering over the odds.'

Amelia gave her a look. 'How do you feel about Daniel? I can see you're torn.'

'I wasn't expecting to get tangled up in any sort of relationship, but I do like him … really like him,' Fern admitted.

'There's a "but" coming…'

'Not a "but" as such. Oh, I don't know. He's so … chill and I'm the complete opposite. I plan everything. I write lists for my lists. He probably decides what to eat ten seconds before cooking it.'

Amelia chuckled knowingly. 'Opposites attract for a reason. It can work, if you let it.'

Fern smiled a little. 'He's easy to be around, which is very new for me. With Daniel, everything is calm, enjoyable, but is that enough?'

'What do you mean?'

'I'm ambitious, and he's happy to try and sell a few antiques that are mainly not worth anything. Why an antique shop out of all the things Matilda could have left me?'

'Maybe because it came with Daniel.'

Fern smiled.

'That smile says a lot.'

'Feeling like this after such a short time is very new to me.'

'Maybe he's the one.'

Fern felt herself blushing. 'Stop it!'

Amelia leaned back. 'Just saying. What I'm gathering is the only thing keeping you from taking the money and running is Daniel.'

'That's not entirely true. I can't deny that I'm starting to question a few things … no, a lot of things actually, like living in London, my job, all of it. It used to mean everything. Now I'm not so sure.'

'Apart from the shop, has something else happened?'

Fern nodded. 'My best friend has just admitted to sleeping with the guy I was kind of seeing before I arrived here, and now I'm beginning to question if we were friends just because of our shared history. Since I've been here – and before that, if I'm being truly honest with myself – the friendship has felt like it's becoming more … surface-level.'

'How do you feel about the guy?'

'I don't.'

'What about the friend?'

'I think the word friend is probably questionable now.'

'Which is very understandable. And the job?"

'I enjoy it, but based on my last interview and the gig … I think I'm outgrowing it. I always wanted to work up to being an editor, but maybe that's not the path for me. Could I go freelance? Definitely. I've made a name for myself and have lots of contacts. But I keep thinking there's a reason Matilda left me this shop. Could I make it work? Maybe. But the thought of stability and a decent salary – what I have now – is difficult to give up for the unknown.'

'It's a tough one,' Amelia admitted. 'Maybe it's not about picking the easiest route, maybe it's about choosing the one that feels like it matters more. I've seen the shop's following on social media – it's growing by the day, and the number of people I've had wandering into The Story Shop in the last few days asking where to find No. 17 Curiosity Lane has been fairly substantial.'

'We've had so much fun setting that up. Daniel is getting

rid of stuff that's been in there for years.' She hesitated. 'I didn't expect the shop to matter to me. But it does.'

'Then trust that feeling.'

'I also don't want to be foolish. Selling the shop to the anonymous buyer would put money in my bank account that would set me up for life.' Fern finally took a bite of toast. 'I think I just needed to say it all out loud.'

Amelia smiled. 'And now that you have?'

Fern looked up. 'I'm still confused. But maybe slightly less.'

'Progress,' Amelia said with a grin. 'Take that as a win.'

Chapter Thirty-Five

As soon as Fern finished eating she headed back to the shop. Just as she was about to step through the doorway, she stopped and hovered. She couldn't resist watching Daniel without him knowing. He was kneeling on the rug in the centre of the shop, a vintage magic set laid out in front of him. A small boy was sitting opposite him, eyes wide, mouth slightly open in amazement, the boy's mum standing beside the two of them.

Daniel held up a small red ball in his palm. 'Okay, now. Watch carefully. This ball … is a very cheeky little thing.' He wiggled his eyebrows dramatically. 'You put him here,' he closed his hand, 'and say the magic words… Pickle-pie penguin pants!'

The boy burst out laughing. 'They're not magic words!'

'Ah,' Daniel said, very serious, 'but that's where you're wrong. You see, this particular ball has very sophisticated taste. If you say boring old "abracadabra" he just ignores you. But pickle-pie penguin pants? That's his language.'

Daniel made the sound of a fanfare and opened his hand to reveal it was empty. The boy gasped. 'Where'd it go?!'

Daniel then tapped the boy's ear and reached behind it with two fingers. 'He said he liked you, so he's moving in.' He produced the ball like it had grown there.

The boy couldn't believe his eyes. 'Mum, please can I have the magic set?'

'How much?' she asked Daniel.

'Ten pounds and I'll even teach him one trick that's one hundred per cent guaranteed to impress at birthday parties.' Daniel winked at the kid. 'You, my friend, are about to become a wizard.'

Once they'd left, magic set under one arm, Fern stepped into the shop. 'Pickle-pie penguin pants?'

Daniel didn't miss a beat. 'Patented. Don't steal it!'

She grinned, tossing her bag on the counter. 'You want a coffee?'

'Always.'

She headed for the back room, filled the kettle, and flicked it on. Her phone beeped with an incoming email.

Subject: Job Offer. Senior Editor Maternity Cover Opportunity

Hey Fern,

Just a quick one. Jules is going on maternity leave, and we'd love for you to step in as acting senior editor for the next six months. It's office-based, starting in two weeks, with a solid bump in pay and a chance to really make your mark.

This is the position you've been waiting for. I know the answer will of course be yes. Let's arrange a Zoom call.

Tom

She stared at the screen. Senior editor. Tom was right, this was an opportunity she had been waiting for, and even though it might be temporary, it was another step up the ladder. She made the coffee and returned to the shop, handing Daniel his mug with a little clink.

'You were lovely with that little boy.'

'Thank you. That kid reminded me of me at that age. I bought my very first magic set from a car boot. My audience was mostly my gran and a very confused Jack Russell.'

Fern smiled, then perched on the desk opposite him. 'Can I ask you something?'

Daniel arched a brow. 'You don't want me to teach you magic, do you?'

'I think my magician days are well and truly over.' Though she wished she could magic up a solution to all of her current dilemmas.

'Go on then, ask away.'

Fern took a deep breath. 'Say someone came along and offered to buy the shop. Like, for way more than it's worth. Enough to give us both a decent payout. What would you say?'

He put his mug down. 'Hypothetically?'

She nodded.

'I'd say they were either bonkers or they know something we don't.'

Her phone buzzed but she ignored it.

'It's not hypothetical,' she said quietly. 'I've received an offer for the shop and all of its contents. A big one. Way over what I reckon this place is worth. I have to decide by next Friday.'

Daniel's smile vanished. 'What? But the shop isn't up for sale. Did you put it up for sale?'

'No, I didn't. The offer came through yesterday via Edgar, but the buyer wants to remain anonymous.'

He sat back. 'Why didn't you say something sooner?'

'I had a meeting with Edgar this morning, to gather all the facts, and now I'm telling you. What do you think?'

'I think it's very weird.'

'I know.'

'You have no inkling who the buyer is? Edgar gave no clues?'

She shook her head. 'Nothing.'

Daniel rubbed a hand across his face. 'That's not a normal offer, Fern. That's not someone who loves crockery and first editions. That's someone who wants this place for their own reason, but why? Is this shop built on a goldmine?'

'Not that I'm aware of.' She stared at him.

He stood up and started pacing like he always did when his brain kicked into gear. 'What if it's connected to the note that came with the dress? Matilda never married Nathaniel Loring. Why? Something happened, something she never told anyone … or perhaps maybe she did. After all, someone very much alive planted that wedding dress.'

'It can't be anyone on the island because Betty said no one knows what happened, and Clemmie and Amelia were adamant that if there was something to know, she would be the one to know it.'

'Do we think there's something in this shop that might give us a clue? Maybe Matilda hid something. Or someone else did and now they're trying to cover it up for whatever reason.'

Fern looked around the shop. 'You think someone's trying to buy the secret?'

'I think someone's trying to bury it.'

'Surely we're just reading too much into this?' Her pulse was racing. 'The offer, the timeline, it all feels like pressure, but there's more. Betty showed me the newspaper this morning. Nathaniel Loring has checked into a private clinic as his health is deteriorating further, but the headline was all about his agent, Alistair Montgomery, who happens to be not only Nathaniel's best friend, but also Dorothy's brother and Nathaniel Loring's sole beneficiary.'

Surprise was written all over Daniel's face.

Fern carried on. 'He also went to the London Music School and was best friends with Matilda, but never spoke to her again after that Christmas Eve. Whatever went on, he took Nathaniel's side and has stayed there ever since.'

'Which has paid him well, if he's to receive everything from Nathaniel Loring's estate. This is all very interesting. Alistair must know the reason why the wedding didn't take place. Why else would he cut Matilda off if they were all friends?' Daniel looked at her with a serious expression on his face. 'Ask yourself why someone wants to pay over the odds for a dusty old shop ... and why they want to stay anonymous. Let's pull up the inventory. Maybe something we logged stands out. Maybe we missed something.'

Fern flipped the lid on her laptop and turned it between then. Fern's inbox was still open from when she had checked her emails early that morning, and it had updated to show the email from Tom. Daniel's eyes were fixed on the words 'Job Offer'.

Daniel turned to her. 'Were you going to tell me, or just sell the shop with me as a going concern, and scuttle back to London?'

'No one is scuttling back to London. It only just landed whilst I was making the coffee and I've not had time to think about it.'

'Do you want the job?'

'It's a massive opportunity to prove myself in the industry, and it will open lots of doors for me. The salary is also a big leap compared to what I'm on now, and living in London is not cheap.'

'It sounds like you've already made up your mind. Is this all about money?'

'Of course that helps. I can't pay the bills on thin air, even though I'm beginning to think that it's possible, if this place is anything to go by.' Fern noticed the atmosphere had suddenly tensed. 'Have you ever had a proper salary?' The words left her mouth before she could stop them. She hadn't meant to sound critical, she was simply trying to grasp how difficult it must be, living without the certainty of a steady income. Then she noticed the sadness in his eyes.

'I didn't always fly by the seat of my pants,' he said. 'I used to have...' He shook his head, like he hated even thinking about it. 'I had a proper job. An office job. Salary, pension, the whole nine-to-five thing. I also had a little flat not far from here. Nothing fancy, but it was mine.

'When my grandmother passed away, everything changed.'

Daniel scrubbed a hand over his face. 'After that ... I couldn't do it anymore. I'd sit at my desk, staring at the screen, and it all felt pointless. Reports, emails, meetings about nothing. Everyone I'd ever loved was gone.' He let out a shaky breath. 'It was hard losing my grandmother. We were so close.'

Fern's chest hurt just listening.

'I really tried at first to show up and get myself into work. I smiled. Told everyone I was fine. But inside I was just empty. It's hard to explain really.' He paused. 'Eventually I stopped showing up. Lost the flat. Burned through what little savings I had, trying to keep it together, and by the time I lifted my head up again, it was all gone. The job, the normal life, everything.' Daniel gave a lopsided smile that broke her heart. 'Somewhere in that mess, I just … made a choice. If everything can be ripped away in a second, what's the point in chasing stability? What's the point in worrying about tomorrow? Fly by the seat of your pants. Roll the dice. Live life like every day might be the last. Because sometimes … it is.'

Fern swallowed. 'Daniel,' she said, leaning and touching his hand. 'I'm so sorry.'

'I know it's stupid,' he said. 'I know it's reckless and selfish and exhausting sometimes. I know it makes me a shit bet for someone like you. Someone who's smart and ambitious and actually has a future lined up.' His voice cracked on the last words. 'You should take that job, Fern. Go to London. Kick ass. Forget about some guy who makes no money and thinks an antiques shop that doesn't actually sell any of its antiques is a good way to spend his time.'

'Don't say that.'

'Why? It's true.'

'Stop it,' Fern said sharply, taking his hand. 'You're not a shit bet. You made a lot of money this week and you're one of the best people I've ever met.'

Daniel stared at her. 'But somehow that's not enough,' he said in a low voice.

'You're kind,' Fern said, her voice shaking, 'funny and brave even when you're scared. You … you didn't give up. Even when it would have been easier.'

Tears began to slide down Daniel's cheeks now, and he didn't wipe them away.

'You make everything feel alive,' Fern whispered. 'That includes me.'

'I feel like I let my gran down.'

Fern stood up and wrapped her arms around him. 'You haven't. She would be really proud of the person you've become.'

He buried his face in her shoulder, clutching her like she was the only solid thing left in the world. For a long time, she just held him.

'This is the first real thing I've felt in a long time. I'm not used to connecting with anyone. I'm falling for you, and I just don't know what to do about that,' he murmured. 'And I'm scared.'

'Me too,' she admitted. 'Maybe that's how we know this is real.'

The old clock on the wall ticked steadily in the background and the laptop screen behind them went dark. Daniel pulled away slowly, and really looked at her. 'If you stay…' he said. 'If you stay, I'll try. I'll try to be better. I'll try to—'

'Hey,' she cut him off. 'I'm not asking you to be anything but you.'

He gave a shaky nod.

Fern brushed her thumbs across his cheeks, wiping away the tears.

'I haven't made any decisions yet,' she said. 'But whatever I choose … it's not just about money. Or a job or London. It's about what matters,' she said simply. 'And *you* matter.' She leaned in and kissed him softly. The offer on the shop was tempting, but whatever happened next, she wasn't ready to say goodbye to Daniel. As she hugged him again, all she could think was: maybe this wasn't about finding the safest path in life but about finding the people who made the risk worth it. Daniel was worth it.

Chapter Thirty-Six

'We've got until Friday to find out who the anonymous buyer is and what they're after,' Daniel said, sipping his coffee as he paced the scuffed wooden floor behind the counter. His boots made a dull thud with every step. 'I think our first stop has to be Alistair Montgomery. Not only did he go to college with them both, he's Nathaniel Loring's agent.'

'What about Dorothy?'

Daniel shook his head. 'We don't know if she'll tip him off that we're sniffing around. After all, they're blood.'

Fern nodded, her pulse ticking faster. 'I think you're right, but I've just remembered this.' She crouched under the counter and pulled out the vinyl she'd stashed days ago, the Nathaniel Loring record she hadn't been able to let go of.

'I had a man try to buy this,' she said, laying it carefully on the counter between them. 'But my gut told me not to let it go so I said it wasn't for sale.'

Daniel took the record from her hand. 'You think this is what they're after?'

'Maybe. It's the only thing in the shop that has something to do with him. Why would Matilda have this if he didn't marry her?' Fern's heart began to race. 'What if it was a business decision?'

'What do you mean by that?'

'What if this vinyl is worth something?'

'It's not going to be worth the sum of money that the anonymous buyer is wanting for this place.'

Fern heard what Daniel was saying but something about the record felt important.

'Let's find out,' Fern said. 'That can't be too difficult.'

Daniel rummaged through the drawers until he found an old brass-handled magnifying glass and one of Matilda's battered collector's guides, *Vinyl Worth Collecting: Rare First Pressings*. He turned the record over carefully. There, on the back of the sleeve, almost hidden in the fine print, was a small code: **SBR001**.

'South Bank Records. First release,' Daniel muttered. He flipped it over and carefully eased the disc from its sleeve.

Fern watched closely as he tilted the vinyl under the light then peered through the magnifying glass. 'No warping. Just a couple of surface scuffs. Pretty damn clean,' he said before flipping to the page in the book on Nathaniel Loring. 'All right, let's see what we've got.' He squinted at the fine print.

'First pressing, near mint condition,' he read aloud. 'Verifiable provenance, £45,000 to £75,000. Higher at auction.'

Fern's pulse quickened. 'It *is* worth something then?'

'But not the cost of this building,' Daniel said, his voice a little flat.

'It's still a hell of a lot of money. Check the dead wax,' Fern said, her voice tight.

Daniel leaned in closer with a magnifying glass, turning the vinyl carefully in his hands. He inspected the matrix numbers near the centre label: **SBR001-A1** and **SBR001-B1**.

'First pressing, both sides,' he confirmed.

But Fern's attention was fixed elsewhere. She looked at the inscription on the record's label, the tiny script etched there. It was faint, almost indecipherable unless you were looking for it, but she knew it was there. She bent closer to the label and read aloud, 'M, For everything I owe you, N.'

Daniel frowned. 'What does that mean? It sounds like a transaction.'

'Not a gift,' Fern murmured, running her fingers over the words. 'Maybe a payment or a debt. Maybe it was something to do with why the wedding was called off?'

Daniel stared at her, his brow furrowing. 'Possibly. But it still doesn't explain *why* the wedding was called off.'

'That is the question. We need to keep this safe.'

'There's a safe at the back of the shop until we decide what we are doing with it.'

After the vinyl was locked safely away, Daniel asked, 'What are you thinking is our next move?'

'I know you said start with Alistair, but I'm thinking we pay Dorothy another visit instead, and we tell her it's Matilda's dress and that we know she went to college with her brother, but we don't say anything about the vinyl.'

Daniel nodded. 'If you give me two minutes, I know of a vinyl expert. I can give him a ring and arrange an appointment, let him take a look.'

'Sounds like a plan.'

Ten minutes later they were sitting opposite Dorothy in her conservatory, a steaming pot of tea on the table in front of them.

'We have news about the dress,' Fern began. 'We met with Eliza Valentine and she spoke so fondly of you, even shared how you helped her secure her very first shop in Sea's End.'

'She was a lovely friend and went on to be a huge success.'

'The wedding dress belonged to Matilda, and we discovered the groom she was set to marry was Nathaniel Loring. We also discovered that they both went to college with your brother, and that Alistair is Loring's agent.'

Dorothy nodded.

'How well did you know Matilda?' asked Fern.

'I know you were close when I first met Matilda,' added Daniel.

'We only became close in recent years,' she said slowly. 'In fact, I would say we became very good friends. But not back then. No, we weren't friends at all back then.'

'Back when she almost married Nathaniel?' questioned Fern.

'Yes. It's true, Matilda went to music college with Alistair and Nathaniel. They were all a few years older than me.' She paused. 'At that age, even a couple of years feels like an enormous gap, and so we ran in different circles, had different interests. The residents on the island were exactly like they are now, a supportive, friendly community where everyone knows everyone. But then there was the wedding that wasn't, and there was … a divide. A need to take sides.'

Fern leaned in, sensing they were close to something important. 'Sides?' she prompted gently.

Dorothy hesitated, the conflict evident in her face. She

clearly didn't relish dredging up history. But finally she said, 'Alistair was family. Blood ties meant loyalty. Or at least, that's what I believed back then. I was a lot younger than what you are now, and I was influenced, didn't see things clearly. It wasn't Matilda's doing, it was about what happened between her and Nathaniel and Alistair.' Dorothy's voice softened, weighted by regret. 'You see, after all that time ... after the fallout ... I realise now, none of us really knew the whole story.'

Fern and Daniel stayed quiet, not daring to interrupt.

'Christmas Eve,' Dorothy continued. 'That's when it happened. The wedding was all set. The entire island was excited. It was going to be the event of the season. Everyone was gathered at the church, and we waited for the bride and groom to arrive. Both were already an hour late. When Alistair arrived, he walked to the front of the church and made an announcement. The wedding was off. Just like that. No explanation, no details. Shock rippled through everyone. I stayed in the church for a while after, then I went home, and when I got there, Alistair and Nathaniel were pacing the kitchen. I could sense their anxiety and Nathaniel looked broken. I remember asking what had happened, why the wedding had been called off. Alistair quite clearly stated that Matilda wasn't who we thought she was, that there had been an infidelity. He didn't give details, but he made it clear he expected loyalty to him and to Nathaniel. He told me – actually no, he demanded – that we stand together as a family, as Nathaniel was his best friend.'

'Did you believe him?' Fern asked gently.

Dorothy's shoulders slumped. 'I did. I was young. Impressionable. He was my brother, why would he need to lie?

I thought I was doing the right thing. I told myself that if Matilda had wronged Nathaniel, she didn't deserve our loyalty.'

'But now?' Daniel asked.

Dorothy's eyes glistened. 'Now I know better. I missed out on decades of friendship with Matilda because of a lie. Or at least, a misunderstanding that festered into something uglier.'

Fern sat back, stunned. 'You didn't speak to Matilda for decades?'

Dorothy nodded miserably. 'Not a word. We lived our lives side by side on this island, never bridging the gap. Until around five years ago.'

'What changed?' Daniel asked.

Dorothy smiled, a soft, bittersweet expression. 'It was chance, really. Matilda had been unwell that winter. We had an early frost, and the cobbles in the village square were slick with ice. I saw her slip and fall, hard. She hit her head, she was dazed, and I rushed over without thinking.' She paused, her voice trembling. 'I helped her back to her house, got her into bed. She soon began to burn with a fever. The doctor was unavailable as he was over at the hospital on the mainland and the causeway was closed. No one could get on and off the island until the tide turned. I stayed the night, worried she might slip into pneumonia. I made her some broth, changed her damp clothes, sat up reading to her when she was too restless to sleep.' Dorothy gave a soft laugh. 'Somewhere in those long hours, something shifted. All those years of resentment, of suspicion, just melted away. We talked. Really talked, mainly about the old days, about Matilda's hurt, and I believed her when she shared how devastated she had been after the wedding fell apart. She loved Nathaniel with her whole heart.'

Fern was spellbound. 'Did Matilda ever say if the allegations were true?'

Dorothy nodded. 'Matilda was never unfaithful. She was a good, honest woman. She never betrayed Nathaniel. I believed her and I was so disappointed in myself for allowing my brother to cut her dead for all those years.'

There was a long moment of silence except for the ticking clock on the mantel.

Finally, Fern leaned forward. 'If she wasn't unfaithful, what other possible reason could there be that they didn't marry?'

'Was it Nathaniel that was unfaithful?' Daniel suggested.

'But Alistair stayed by Nathaniel's side. If he was friends with both of them, wouldn't he have chosen Matilda's side?' Fern queried.

Dorothy's smile faltered, just a little. 'Alistair had just started working for Nathaniel when everything went wrong that Christmas Eve, and it was soon after that that Nathaniel became an overnight success. Alistair knew that taking Matilda's side was never going to pay his wage; he took care of everything, contracts, deals, appearances, tours.'

'We saw in the newspaper that Alistair will inherit Nathaniel's wealth,' said Daniel.

'Yes. Nathaniel's health has been declining for some time now. He's actually just been moved from the private clinic back home so he can be taken care of by a team of nurses in his final weeks … possibly days.'

'You were such a huge help caring for Matilda at the end,' cut in Daniel. 'I will be forever grateful for that.'

'You're very welcome. She was getting a little muddled but

one thing she never got muddled about was how much she loved her shop.'

'Had she always lived on the island?' asked Fern, wanting to know everything about her great-aunt.

'No, Matilda grew up in London, but holidayed here as a child and a teenager, as her grandmother was a resident. Matilda's account of things was that they grew up in a home where music wasn't just encouraged, it was the heartbeat of their world. Her mother was a classically trained violinist, her father an amateur jazz pianist, and from the moment she could reach the keys, Matilda's world was wrapped in sound. As you know, she trained in London, with dreams of becoming a composer and concert pianist. Her future was bright until...'

'Until?'

'He came along.'

'Who? Nathaniel?'

Dorothy nodded.

'When the wedding was called off, her family disowned her.'

'Why would they do that?' asked Fern, noticing that Dorothy looked torn.

'Alistair described her as fragile.'

'What does that mean?'

'I'm not exactly sure, but on that Christmas Eve he claimed she was delusional, unstable, and her family agreed, which was why they disowned her.'

'Did you think that?' asked Daniel. 'Because I have to say, to me, she was one of the most down-to-earth, rational and yet interesting people I've ever met.'

'No, I didn't think that, but Nathaniel had become close to her parents and they chose to believe him for whatever reason.

On that Christmas Eve, Matilda stayed on the island with her grandmother while her parents and her sister travelled back to London. I believe that was the last time she ever saw them.'

'That is terrible,' said Fern. 'It seems Matilda lost everything that day.'

'She also stepped away from her music career that day. Her grandmother, Florence, owned a rundown holiday cottage, and in her school and college holidays, Matilda had helped to clean in between guests. When Florence passed away, the cottage was left to Matilda. At first, the junk shop wasn't part of the plan. Matilda started helping an elderly islander clear out a lifetime of possessions, and in doing so, found solace in the clutter, every forgotten object telling a story, and every chipped teacup and worn record sleeve carrying a past that was uniquely its own. Slowly, she began to collect, to mend and then to sell. She turned the holiday cottage into No. 17 Curiosity Lane, which gave her two things she desperately needed: a living and a sanctuary.'

'And now she's gone, and we've been left with the mystery of what really happened back then on that Christmas Eve. I'd give anything to have a few minutes to ask her some questions,' Fern mused.

Dorothy looked thoughtful for a moment. 'You know, there *was* something she was muttering just before she passed away. It was something about how the truth lies in the old music box.'

'What truth?'

'I have no clue,' admitted Dorothy. 'I asked her the same thing, but she just said the same words over and over again.'

Ten minutes later they were opening the door to No. 17 Curiosity Lane.

'What do you make of all that?' asked Daniel.

'"The truth lies in the music box",' murmured Fern. 'It seems a strange thing to say, but it definitely meant something, especially as Alistair Montgomery came into the shop and specifically asked about an old music box.'

Daniel stood still and stared at her. 'You're right. Like I said before, I don't ever remember seeing a music box, but let's double-check. The inventory is on your laptop.'

Fern opened up her laptop. There were hundreds of items now logged but thankfully they'd managed to put everything in a sort of order. 'M for Music.' He ran his finger down all the items but there was no music box. 'Nothing,' he said, looking over his shoulder at Fern.

'Well, maybe Matilda stashed it somewhere. Or maybe it was never in here in the first place and she meant something else. A figurative truth, perhaps? Or maybe it has something to do with the vinyl?'

He shrugged.

'Let's have another look around.'

They set to work. Fern rechecked the back shelves while Daniel crouched to peer beneath cabinets and lifted up antique tea cosies. They combed through jewellery boxes, decorative tins and old chests. Daniel even opened a Victorian sewing table, only to find nothing more than a lonely thimble and a faded thread spool.

'Maybe it's hidden inside something?' Fern asked, rummaging through a trunk of faded velvet hats. 'Like … disguised.'

'Like a Trojan music box,' Daniel mused, poking at the bottom of a carved wooden owl. 'Anything's possible.'

Two hours passed with the only interruptions being the occasional clatter of a dropped knick-knack or a sneeze because of the dust. They worked in tandem, Fern's brows furrowed in concentration, Daniel's hair dusted with cobwebs, both too stubborn to give up.

'No music box,' Fern said finally, collapsing onto the chair. 'We're missing something. We must be.' She glanced at the piano and immediately lifted the lid. 'Throw me that torch.'

Shining a light inside, she said, 'No, nothing, just another spider minding its own business.'

Daniel perched on the edge of the desk. 'It's not here.'

'It's got to be. Matilda brought it up to Dorothy, and Alistair was asking after it. That's not a coincidence. Where could it be hidden?' Fern's mid was working overtime. 'I've got it!' She flapped her hand at Daniel. 'Come on!' She bounded up the stairs, skipping the fourth step, straight into the bedroom, and stood looking up at the moose's head. She pointed.

'Are you trying to tell me that Maurice is hiding a music box?'

'Who would ever look inside the moose's head?'

'No one,' replied Daniel, taking off his shoes before stepping onto the bed. He unhooked the moose's head from the wall as Fern screamed and ran to the doorway, pointing at the huge spider that had dropped onto the duvet.

'One spider, no music box,' stated Daniel, hooking it back on the wall.

'I really thought I had it then,' admitted Fern, sounding a little defeated as they walked back down the stairs.

'Not that this is helpful to the music box situation, but the antique vinyl expert is coming in tomorrow to take a look at Nathaniel Loring's record, to give a true valuation.'

'At least then we'll know what we're dealing with. What if we're thinking too literally?' Fern said. 'Maybe the truth isn't about the box itself, but something inside it, a letter or a key. Maybe even a confession. Oh, I don't know, I'm feeling muddled myself now!'

'I think there's definitely something here, and whoever the anonymous buyer is they know exactly what they're looking for.'

'Someone could have already taken the music box, for all we know. Have you ever sold one?'

Daniel shook his head. 'Not to my knowledge.'

'The thought of someone knowing something we don't, makes me uncomfortable.'

'Let's see what the vinyl guy says tomorrow and who knows? Maybe we'll find the music box when we least expect it. Maybe it's hiding in plain sight.'

'Maybe it is,' Fern said as she sat behind the desk and pulled out her phone and began to scroll. Tap. Swipe. Notifications. Then she froze.

Daniel caught the change in her face. 'What is it?'

She didn't speak, just turned the phone towards him.

ENTERTAINMENT WEEKLY EXCLUSIVE: Rock Star Jax Devlin OFF THE MARKET. Confirmed Relationship with Socialite and Music Journalist Ella Byrne

Beneath the headline was a photo of Jax, impossibly smug, and Ella, beaming like she'd won the lottery.

Fern couldn't quite believe what she was seeing. Ella had admitted to sleeping with him, but this was public, something he'd never wanted when he was dating her, when it was all about secrecy and not letting the paparazzi get wind of any type of relationship. 'Ella,' she said quietly. 'My best friend and my ex.'

Daniel raised his eyebrow. 'That's a little bit awkward.'

Fern swallowed. 'Isn't it just.'

In that second Fern had forgotten all about the mystery of the music box. Ella hadn't bothered to call to let her know the story was coming out or even tried to have a conversation with her since the text. She wasn't sure what to do but she knew she had been betrayed. Ella was meant to be her best friend, but it seemed she had no consideration for Fern's feelings whatsoever, and that hurt.

Chapter Thirty-Seven

Fern and Daniel were propped up against mismatched pillows, the duvet tucked around them like a badly folded burrito. 'Do you think Alistair and Nathaniel are dodgy?' asked Fern.

Daniel turned his head slowly to look at her. 'Dodgy?' he repeated, amusement curling at the edges of his voice. 'As in, running some kind of underground vinyl smuggling ring?'

She rolled her eyes. 'No, I mean, spreading rumours. What if everything we heard about great-aunt Matilda and Nathaniel was wrong? What if they made sure everyone thought she didn't marry him because she was unfaithful and had to back out, when really it was him who did something awful?'

Daniel considered that. 'Wouldn't Matilda have told her side of the story? Why would she have kept quiet?'

'Maybe she couldn't. It's just – the more I think about it, the more it doesn't add up. He's the only one left who really knows the truth.'

'Well, him and Alistair.'

'Exactly.'

Daniel raised a brow. 'Okay, but even if Nathaniel does know, how are we supposed to get the truth out of him? He's reclusive and sick, if the papers are right.'

Fern hesitated, then said, 'We could break into his estate.'

Daniel leaned back against the headboard and burst out laughing. 'Okay, definitely too much true crime TV for you. What exactly are we looking for? Do you think he even gives Matilda a second thought? I doubt it. It was years ago.'

'We do have his property. Technically. We could use that as a way in.'

'Technically,' Daniel said. 'If the inscription is anything to go by it's Matilda's record. Which makes it yours, and if it is worth thousands, or maybe more, we're not handing it over to some frail famous composer who may not live for much longer.'

'We don't have to give it to him,' she said quickly. 'Just use it to open a conversation. It might be our only chance to ask what really happened between them.'

Daniel looked at her like she'd grown a second head. 'You want to walk into the home of a dying man and interrogate him about a seventy-year-old love triangle?'

'When you say it like that, it sounds weird.'

Daniel was quiet. Finally, he said, 'What are you doing about the promotion?'

She exhaled, knowing they needed to have this conversation sooner rather than later. 'I've got a Zoom with Tom in the morning to talk through the details.'

He turned his head towards her again. 'Are you going to take it? It sounds like it would be a good step for your career.'

Fern hesitated. 'I want to talk it through first.' She stared up at the ceiling. 'I've been thinking about Ella.'

'How are you going to handle that situation?'

'It's something I'm not looking forward to. She's on the team I'd be managing. We haven't even had a conversation about what's happening with her and Jax. All she did was text me to say she'd slept with him. I would have expected a little more from her … at the very least a proper conversation.'

'It is a little disappointing if you've been friends for a long time.'

'It is, and I'm going to be honest with you, it's making me feel uncomfortable about continuing to work with her. I know I should be professional and separate business from personal, but I could never trust her again with anything and I would be her boss, and I'm not sure I even want to see her at the moment. It's making me think twice about accepting the position.'

Daniel was quiet for a moment. 'So the only reason you wouldn't take the job … is because you'd have to work with Ella?'

'I didn't say that.'

'You kind of did.'

She sat up slightly, the duvet slipping down to her waist. 'It's more complicated than that.'

'Is it?'

Fern looked at him, heart pounding a little harder now. 'She's been my best friend for years and now she's dating my ex-boyfriend, and I'm not sure I want to deal with any of it. That's betrayal territory.'

'What about me?'

'What do you mean, what about me?'

Daniel's voice dropped. 'I thought maybe you'd think about staying. For me. For us. Not because it would feel awkward working with her. You haven't even considered staying for all this.'

She blinked, caught off guard. 'Daniel…'

He sat up straight and ran his hands through his already messy hair. 'You know what? Never mind. You're right. It has only been a few weeks. What was I thinking? That you'd just fall in love and decide to throw your London life away for me?'

'People do do that,' she said, but even as she said it, her voice faltered.

'They do in movies,' he muttered. 'Not in real life, it seems. But if someone makes you feel uncomfortable at work, well, that's a different matter.'

The air between them was suddenly colder. Fern reached for the duvet again, tugging it back over her like a shield.

'I don't know what's real anymore,' she admitted. 'Ella was supposed to be one of my constants and now I feel like I don't even know her. I feel like I'm being pulled in two completely different directions. My old life. This new one. You. The shop.'

Daniel stood and crossed the room to the window, his eyes now fixed on the moon as he spoke. 'You mentioned selling the shop.'

'I said *if* I sell it, then at least I could make sure you have enough money to buy your own place, maybe with a decent central heating system, windows that don't rattle in the wind and a shower that doesn't sound like a dying goose.' She was trying to lighten the tension in the room, but it didn't work.

'I don't want a flat,' he said, turning sharply. 'I want the shop. *This* shop. Matilda's shop. It's starting to work. People are buying the antiques. Using social media has been successful. We're building something.'

'Do you think I'm tearing it down?'

'No.' His voice softened. 'But if you sell it to that anonymous buyer then yes, you kind of are. They know something we don't, and you're settling for greed over the truth.'

The silence this time was more final.

When Daniel climbed back into bed, he lay stiffly on his side, facing away from her. She mirrored him, her stomach twisting in knots. What was she doing? How could she possibly make a life decision based on a couple of weeks? That wasn't how responsible people made choices. That was the stuff of fairytales, of meet-cutes and sweeping declarations. Not of real, messy people who had tangled loyalties and rent to pay.

She thought of Ella. Of the giggles and prosecco-fuelled late nights, of all the times she'd said, 'You're my person,' and meant it. But now? How was their friendship even going to work?

Fern glanced over her shoulder at Daniel's back. His breathing was slow and steady, but she knew he wasn't asleep. She closed her eyes and felt more alone than she had in a long, long time.

Chapter Thirty-Eight

Fern woke to the smell of toast and the faint clinking of crockery drifting up from downstairs. For a moment, she didn't move. The duvet was twisted around her legs, her neck ached from sleeping too stiffly on one side, and she felt that uneasy, dull ache in the pit of her stomach after last night's disagreement.

She could hear the sound of plates clattering and the hiss of the kettle reaching a boil. She sat up slowly, then shuffled to the bathroom, splashed cold water on her face and pulled on a cardigan over her pyjamas. She checked her phone: 8.32 a.m. Only half an hour until her Zoom with Tom at nine.

Downstairs, the shop was bathed in golden morning light, the dust motes dancing like it was all part of some magical antique diorama. On the counter was a plate of toast, butter already melting into the slices, and next to it a mug of tea with just the right amount of milk.

Daniel looked up from where he was pulling on his coat by the door. 'Morning,' he said, not quite meeting her eyes.

'Morning,' Fern replied.

'I made tea,' he said. 'And toast.'

'I see that. Thanks.'

Grabbing the keys, he said, 'I'm going to nip to Beachcomber Bakery. Pick up some bits for lunch.'

'Oh. Okay.'

He hesitated for a moment. 'You've got your call soon, right?'

'Yeah. In twenty minutes.'

'Good luck.'

'Thanks.'

The bell over the door jangled as it closed behind him, leaving the faint scent of his aftershave behind. She knew he was disappearing to give her space and privacy while she took the call, and she was grateful for his tact.

After sitting down behind the desk, she took a sip of the tea. It was exactly how she liked it, which made the frostiness between them feel even worse. The tension from the night before hadn't vanished with sleep.

At 8.59 a.m., she logged on to the Zoom call on her laptop and took a deep breath. She ran a hand through her hair to tame the worst of the bedhead and waited for Tom to let her into the virtual meeting.

Soon Tom's familiar face filled the screen, cheerful, boyish and framed by the brick wall of the office's creative nook.

'Fern! There she is! The soon-to-be queen of culture!'

She smiled. 'Hi, Tom.'

'God, you look so ... windswept island chic. I love it. Is that real daylight? Do you even have electricity over there?'

'Ha-ha. Yes. Just about.'

He leaned in closer to the screen. 'Right, I'll get straight to it. As you know, Jules is off on maternity leave. Rumour is she won't be coming back, but let's not jump the gun. So, here's what I'm offering: acting senior editor title, twenty per cent salary increase, remote flexibility two days a week once you're back, and a team of five journalists, including Ella.'

Fern nodded slowly. 'Wow.'

'It's a huge step up, Fern. You'd be brilliant. This could open so many future doors, and if Jules doesn't return you will have all the skills to apply for the permanent position. I've got the contract drafted. All you need to do is sign it.'

Before Fern could respond, there was a burst of laughter in the background. Then the sound of music – something bubbly and early-2000s pop-esque.

Tom glanced over his shoulder. 'Sorry. Bit of a party happening in the office kitchen.'

'It's only nine a.m. Have I missed someone's birthday?'

'Ella got engaged! Jax proposed last night. Champagne and chaos this morning.'

Fern froze. 'Jax?' It had been barely a week since he'd tried to sleep with her.

Tom nodded, distracted by something offscreen. 'Yup. It's all very romantic. Rooftop bar, the works. Anyway, I'd better dash, I know you're going to accept it, you'll be mad not to. We just need the contract signed. I can send it by email today.'

The call ended, and Fern was left staring at the blank screen, her own stunned reflection blinking back at her.

The man who had once told her he was too complicated to get serious was now engaged to Ella, her best friend. The person who'd made every birthday special. The one who knew every weird food combo she liked, who had been there through her heartbreaks, who promised, only months ago, that *they* were the unbreakable ones ... and she hadn't even bothered to tell Fern she was engaged to her ex. Not a text, not a phone call, not a single word. This was a whole new level of disloyalty and betrayal.

Fern closed her laptop and picked up her tea again. She tried to feel anger, but all she could summon was a dense, aching emptiness. Her mind was reeling and her gut was telling her there was no way this was a new relationship, because what sane person would get engaged in what seemed like mere hours? They had to have been sleeping together while Fern was also sleeping with Jax.

Her phone pinged with a new email from Edgar Carmichael.

Subject: Offer Expiry Reminder

Dear Fern,

As discussed, the formal offer to purchase No. 17 Curiosity Lane will remain valid until Friday at 5 p.m. After that time, the buyer will pursue alternate opportunities.

Please let us know your decision by close of business.

Regards,
Edgar

Fern stared at the screen, feeling under pressure. Everything was getting on top of her: the decision about the shop, the job offer, the truth about Ella. Each thread of her life seemed to be pulling tighter around her. She tried to imagine staying on Puffin Island, turning down the job she had been working towards for the whole of her career. What would it be like to keep the shop, renovate it, breathe life back into it?

She could already picture the constant smile on Daniel's face. Next, she pictured her London apartment. The independence and control she had carved out all on her own. She was close to tears and briefly closed her eyes. Her best friend had betrayed her. Her ex had moved on and she was stuck halfway between a life she wasn't sure she wanted anymore and a new one she hadn't dared to believe in until now. When she opened her eyes, she looked around the shop again and realised how much it was beginning to mean to her.

Chapter Thirty-Nine

By the time Daniel returned, the tea was cold, the toast untouched, and Fern was pacing. He stepped into the shop, waving a carrier bag like it was a white flag. 'I've got us a mushroom and leek tart,' he said, offering a tentative smile. 'And a custard twist each.'

Fern looked up, nodded. 'Thanks, that's lovely.'

'Are you okay?'

Before she could answer the shop bell jingled again and a tall, wiry man stepped inside, wearing a sharply tailored overcoat the colour of oxblood. His silver hair was slicked back with a precise side parting, and round, gold-rimmed glasses were perched on his aquiline nose. A leather satchel hung at his side, polished to a high sheen. He looked like someone who'd walked straight out of a black-and-white film.

'Daniel, Fern?' he said, looking between them.

Fern blinked. 'Yes?'

'Reginald Hayworth. Vinyl antiquarian. We spoke on the phone, Daniel.'

'Thank you for coming.' Daniel extended a hand. 'This is Fern. The vinyl technically belongs to her.'

Hayworth gave a polite nod, then looked around the shop with a connoisseur's eye, taking in every item.

'Well then,' he said. 'Shall we have a look at it?'

Fern disappeared to the safe, leaving Daniel with Hayworth. When she returned, a velvet cushion had been laid on the desk and Hayworth was drawing a pair of fine gloves from his satchel and slipping them on with theatrical precision. Fern placed the vinyl on the cushion. Hayworth leaned in, eyes narrowing behind his spectacles.

Daniel crossed his arms, watching like a hawk. Fern stood beside him, heart racing, suddenly aware that if Hayworth confirmed this was the original as they thought, it could change everything.

Hayworth picked up the record. 'Nathaniel Loring,' he murmured, taking a look at the serial number. He carefully slid the disc out of its sleeve and turned it towards the light, his breath catching slightly. 'The first … what a rare find.' He pointed to the label. He'd spotted the inscription. '"M, For everything I owe you, N." This looks like it was a personal gift. Do you know who M is?' asked Hayworth.

'My great-aunt, Matilda Hartley. Do you think it's worth something?'

'Indeed…' Hayworth's voice faded and they watched as he carefully set the record onto a portable player that he'd taken out of his case. The needle dropped, and a rich, haunting melody filled the room: piano, and the unmistakable timbre of Nathaniel Loring's voice singing over the top.

Fern felt emotional. The song completely moved her, it was beautiful.

Hayworth didn't speak until the song ended.

'This,' he said solemnly, 'is a treasure. Beyond monetary value, truly. But if we must speak numbers...' He placed the record back in its sleeve then turned to them, removing his gloves. 'I would estimate this record at seventy-five thousand pounds. Possibly more at auction.'

'This is unbelievable,' murmured Fern.

'I would advise you not to advertise you have this until you decide what you want to do with it – and, for heaven's sake, insure it immediately. Pieces like this attract attention. The kind you don't want.'

Fern managed to nod. 'Of course. Thank you. That's ... wow!'

'I'll email you a formal valuation,' Hayworth added, returning the record player to his case. 'Now, if you'll excuse me, I have a seminar in Glasgow this evening.'

They saw him out, the bell tinkling as he disappeared into the street like a time traveller vanishing back into his era.

Back inside, Daniel let out a breath and ran a hand through his hair. 'That's a hell of a lot of money.'

Fern cradled the record like it might vanish into dust if she moved too quickly. Together, they walked to the small safe tucked in the storage alcove behind the curtain. Daniel knelt and turned the dial, unlocking the heavy door.

Fern reached for the velvet pouch they'd set aside that cushioned the record, but as Daniel leaned in to place the record inside, he paused.

'What's that?' he said.

She crouched beside him. 'What?'

He was peering at the back of the safe. 'There's ... a seam.' He reached in, tapping gently at the metal. 'It's not flush.'

Together, they examined the back panel more closely. Though it was almost imperceptible, they could just see a thin indentation along the edges, an outline that suggested the panel wasn't fixed.

'Is it a false back?' Fern whispered.

Daniel pressed on it, then tugged gently. With a soft click, the back panel slid open like a drawer.

Inside was a small box, ornately carved, the wood dark with age. The brass inlays curled like ivy around the edges and there was a tiny keyhole on one side. The top bore a faded floral motif and a name etched in elegant script.

Matilda

Fern stared.

Daniel slowly lifted it out. 'Is this...?'

'The music box,' Fern whispered. 'The one Matilda mumbled about to Dorothy. "The music box holds all the secrets."'

They stared at it in silence.

Daniel reached for the lid.

'Wait,' Fern said. 'Shouldn't we...?'

But he had already lifted it.

There was no music, no tinkling melody, no movement from any little mechanism. The inside was padded with velvet, and nestled at the bottom was a sheaf of papers.

Fern carefully lifted them out. The paper crackled faintly in her hands and her pulse raced. The ink had faded to a soft sepia, but the contents were unmistakable: bars of music, hand-drawn with care, the notes flowing in elegant curves. A composition.

At the top, in Matilda's looping handwriting, was the inscription:

M.H. / London / 1963

Daniel looked at it. 'Matilda must have written this.'

'Yes, and judging by the date ... would that be the time she was at music school?'

Daniel nodded. 'What are we going to do with this?'

There were no other words on the paper, no explanation. Just a melody, frozen in ink, waiting to be played.

Chapter Forty

The manuscript sat between them on the desk. Untouched.

'Right,' Daniel said, exhaling. 'Only one problem.'

'What?' Fern asked.

'I can't read sheet music.'

Fern blinked. 'Wait, what? I thought you played guitar.'

'I do. By ear,' he said. 'Which is very different from being able to read something that looks like this.'

He gestured to the dense tangle of black notes, clefs and rests. 'What about you? You're a music journalist, surely you've picked up something about notes during your career?'

Fern looked sheepish. 'I played flute in Year Eight. Badly. I mostly faked it.'

Daniel scratched the back of his neck. 'We need help. I've got an idea.'

Five minutes later, they were hunched over Fern's phone, the manuscript propped up against a book, and a beginner piano app open on the screen. Fern lifted the lid then patted the stool beside her. 'Ready, Mozart?' Fern grinned.

Daniel gave her a wary look. 'This is going to be painful.'

'Pain builds character.'

He sat beside her as the app chirped cheerfully, 'Welcome to Piano Pals! Let's learn middle C!'

Fern winced. 'This is so humiliating.'

'Shh,' Daniel said, mock serious. 'We're artists.'

They spent the first fifteen minutes trying to locate the notes on the keys, laughing every time they hit the wrong one and the app offered passive-aggressive encouragements like '*Almost there!*' or '*Oops! Try again, you brave musical warrior!*'

Fern pointed at the sheet. 'Okay, so if this is C, then this must be…'

'F?'

'No, E.'

'Are you sure?'

'Absolutely not.'

They tried again.

It was awkward and slow, more like codebreaking than music-making. Fern played the left-hand notes while Daniel tried to fumble through the melody line, but nothing sounded like a real song.

'This is hopeless,' Fern groaned, stretching her back and shaking her hands.

Daniel cracked his knuckles. 'One more go…'

'Stubborn, aren't you?'

'Determined. Besides, I think I'm starting to get a feel for it now.'

It wasn't perfect, but his guitarist's ear was picking up the intervals. He could predict where the melody wanted to go, and as they leaned into it, the rhythm began to fall into place. Slowly, the awkward clunks turned into hesitant chords, then repeating phrases, then something almost beautiful.

After nearly an hour, it happened. Daniel struck a sequence of notes, and Fern, reading ahead on the manuscript, followed with a soft chord. It rang out, clear and unmistakable.

Fern grabbed Daniel's arm as his fingers hovered above the keys. 'What?' he said.

She turned slowly to look at him. 'That's it.'

'What is?'

She lifted her finger, pointing to the progression. 'That's the chorus from "Echoes of the Past". The vinyl. Nathaniel Loring's song. It's the same melody.'

Daniel's eyes widened. 'Are you sure?'

'Positive, listen.' She played it again.

They looked down at the manuscript together, seeing the same chorus repeated in Matilda's fluid notation.

'You're right. But I don't understand. This is Nathaniel's song; he made millions from it.' Then her heart began to pound. 'What if … what if *Matilda* was actually the one who wrote this?'

Daniel leaned back slightly, staring at the piano keys. 'What are you saying? That he stole it? She may have just given it to him.'

'I don't know.' Fern looked at the paper again. 'What did she mean, "the truth is in the music box"? He may have claimed it was his and went on to become world famous on the back of Matilda. That would have been downright hurtful.'

'Maybe she found out just before the wedding,' Daniel added. 'Nathaniel stole it and it made him famous. Or we could just be clutching at straws.'

'What about the inscription on the record? It said he "owed" her.'

Daniel exhaled. 'He could have owed her anything.'

They stayed like that, side by side on the piano stool, for a long time.

Daniel finally took a sideward glance at her. 'What do we do with this?'

Fern didn't answer right away. She picked up the manuscript, careful not to crease it. 'I think we need to dig deeper.'

Daniel nodded. 'Then we start with the one person who might know.'

Fern looked at him.

'Alistair,' said Daniel.

Fern nodded. 'Or even Nathaniel himself, if we can get close to him.'

Chapter Forty-One

They stood in front of the safe, the manuscript in Fern's hand. 'Let's put it in there.'

'What about the music box?' asked Daniel.

'Just leave it on the desk for now. The manuscript is the valuable bit, and it's locked away.' Fern turned the key in the safe and double-checked it was locked.

'Are we really going to do this?'

She nodded. 'We're going to attempt to see Alistair, and who knows … we might even get to meet Nathaniel.'

'So that we're clear, the plan is to lie to Dorothy to get his number?'

'We're going to … reframe the truth,' Fern corrected. 'But we're not telling her about the manuscript. Not yet.'

'Because…?'

'Because Alistair is her brother,' she said. 'And if we're right, there could be a chance *he* was the one who stole the song that made Nathaniel's career.'

They exchanged a glance.

'Are you thinking what I'm thinking?' asked Fern.

'I'm thinking that he's probably the anonymous buyer trying to get the shop as they think the original manuscript is hidden here somewhere. But if Alistair and Nathaniel are behind the offer to buy the shop, then why plant the wedding dress? Why lead us down the Matilda-and-Nathaniel rabbit hole in the first place? Because surely they wouldn't want us to find the original manuscript.'

'That's the part that doesn't make sense,' Fern added. 'If he wanted us to sell quietly, why draw attention to the past?'

'Which would suggest someone else planted the dress,' Daniel said. 'Someone who wanted us to find the connection.'

'But who?' Fern asked. 'Who would have known about Matilda's past and wanted us to know, too?' she continued.

Daniel shrugged. 'You're the sleuth.'

'Yeah, but even I know this is starting to feel like a game of Cluedo.'

'Next we'll be accusing Colonel Mustard.'

'With the candlestick.'

'In the conservatory.'

They both laughed as they locked up the shop and walked up Lighthouse Lane towards Dorothy's cottage.

Dorothy answered her door with a large tabby cat slung over one arm and a teacup in the other hand. 'Hello! Back again so soon? What can I do for you two?'

'We found an item of interest in the shop – a Loring vinyl – and we've had it valued.'

Dorothy's eyes glinted with interest, and she ushered them in. The cat, whose name they learned was Gregory, trotted ahead of them and leapt up on to the windowsill.

As they sat down, Fern said, 'It's an original and we were wondering about the back story – how it ended up in the shop. We obviously think that Nathaniel must have given it to Matilda, but were they even together when his first record came out?'

'His first record was released after they broke up, if I can remember correctly,' said Dorothy.

Fern looked towards Daniel and deliberately didn't mention the inscription. 'Nathaniel isn't well, so we were thinking, maybe it could be displayed in a music museum? A piece of history to honour his legacy.'

Daniel picked up the thread smoothly. 'We heard there's talk of a music exhibition at the Loring School of Music? Or maybe the British Library might be interested?'

Dorothy smiled. 'That's … thoughtful of you.'

'We were hoping you might give us Alistair's number, so we could talk to him about it.'

'Of course.' She stood and went to a drawer, rummaging until she pulled out a sticky note and a pen and wrote the number down. 'Here you go.'

Fern took the note. 'Thank you.'

'Do let me know how you get on.'

As they stepped back out into the street, Daniel whistled under his breath. 'That was easy enough. But do we really think Alistair or Nathaniel is the anonymous buyer of the shop?'

Fern shook her head. 'More and more, I think it's likely to be Alistair trying to protect Nathaniel's reputation. He's the one who came into the shop asking for the music box, after all. If it gets out that Nathaniel stole a song from Matilda, and it's proven, Alistair could possibly lose the promised fortune when

Nathaniel dies.'

Daniel nodded. 'As Matilda's only surviving relative, it would potentially come to you.'

'Let's not run ahead of ourselves.'

'It's him, I know it is. He's trying to buy the shop and bury the past so it won't surface anytime soon.'

'But someone else knew,' Fern said. 'Someone who wanted us to stop him. They left the wedding dress and pointed us in the right direction. Any guesses as to who that could have been?'

'Not yet,' he replied as they reached the shop. 'He'll deny it, you know.'

Fern looked at him.

'Alistair,' Daniel said. 'He'll say he had no idea. That it was all a coincidence. That Matilda never wrote that song.'

'But we have proof.'

'We have a manuscript in her writing, yes, but they could have written it together.'

'We have the record with the inscription.'

'I doubt it would hold up, especially against a man with money, lawyers and a good reputation.'

Fern didn't answer.

As they crossed the road, Daniel touched her shoulder. 'Maybe it's not about proving anything. Maybe it's just about knowing the truth.'

'I'll call Alistair this afternoon,' she said. 'We'll set up a meeting.'

Daniel squeezed her hand. 'We'll do it together.'

She smiled. 'I like the sound of that. Do you fancy a walk? I feel like stretching my legs.'

'I do.'

They made their way towards Blue Water Bay. 'We've had a right couple of days of it, haven't we?' said Daniel.

'Understatement of the century,' Fern replied.

Daniel pointed ahead. 'If we walk past the lighthouse and round by the harbour, there's another cove just past the puffin cliffs.'

She tilted her head. 'There's another bay?'

'Castaway Cove,' he said. 'And if you keep walking the whole way round the island, you end up at Cockle Bay Cove.'

'You're just making these up now.'

'I swear I'm not. This island's basically the Netflix of secret beaches. Endless options, but a terrible signal.'

She laughed. 'It's the island that just keeps giving.'

The path curved gently upwards, and as they reached the top of the last dune, the view opened up like a scene change in a movie. Below them, a wide sweep of beach gleamed in the lunchtime sun. The sea sparkled, waves tumbling on to the sand. A few dogs were tearing around in the shallows, and nearby, a couple walked slowly.

Daniel reached for her hand. She glanced at him and felt a flutter in her stomach as she let him take it.

They walked on, hand in hand, down the old wooden steps to the sand, continuing until there was no one else in sight.

'The tourists never seem to find this little slice of the island; they tend to stick to Bluewater Bay. Funnily enough, I used to come here with my mum and dad on holiday. They loved this place,' Daniel mused. 'We'd bring flasks of soup in the winter, Dad would pack cheese and pickle sandwiches in the summer, and Mum always had a novel she'd never get around to reading.'

Fern glanced at him. His expression was fond but distant, like he could still see them on the sand somewhere ahead.

'You must miss them.'

'I do. It's a strange feeling thinking you have no one else in the world.'

'I get that feeling too. That sudden, hollow space where family used to be.'

There was a pause. The waves rustled against the shore like they were listening in.

'But I have good memories,' she added softly. 'Seaside ones, too. Mum always insisted on packing an entire picnic, even though we'd end up buying chips. Dad used to carry one of those awful windbreaks and swear it was the last time. It's funny the things that stay with you.'

Daniel smiled. 'Yeah. Those bits matter. When I met Matilda at the auction and she said she lived on Puffin Island, I took that as a sign. It may sound daft, but I actually feel close to my parents by being here. This place is just full of good memories. Matilda was really good for me. In the grand scheme of things, it was an unlikely friendship, but it worked. She was so full of knowledge and very humorous. She used to tell me that the shop would hold my destiny. I was never quite sure what she meant by that, but then I met you.' He nudged her arm playfully. 'You barged into my life with your big city bags and your questions, and your oat milk requests,' he said with a grin.

'I've never requested oat milk.'

'Give it time. The point is, I remembered how to laugh again. You made the shop feel alive. You made *me* feel alive.'

She couldn't look away from him.

'God knows we've had our moments, but you've brought

colour back into my world. I'm not deluded, I know we've not known each other long, but it just feels right, you being here.'

They sat down on a rock and when he looked at her Fern didn't need to think twice about it; she leaned in and pressed a soft kiss to his mouth. 'It feels right being here to me too. Do you honestly get the feeling we've been set up?'

He grinned. 'I bet Matilda is up there now, looking down on us, thinking her plan worked.'

'She brought us both to the shop, and then to each other.'

'Maybe she just knew we would be a good match. Come on,' he said, grabbing her hand and pulling her up and running towards the sea.

'Don't pull us in – we have shoes on!'

Daniel kicked his off and Fern followed suit, and within seconds they were chasing each other through the shallows, soaked to their calves and breathless with laughter. Fern hadn't had so much fun in ages. Eventually, they collapsed onto the warm sand and Daniel pulled her close.

'I know this probably feels like a holiday to you,' he said, catching his breath, 'a beautiful blip before you go back to London.'

Fern opened her mouth to respond, but he held up a hand.

'I get it. I do. You've got this whole life there. A career, friends … well, maybe not Ella anymore,' he added with a grimace, 'but still.'

She nodded slowly.

'I'm not asking you to give all that up,' Daniel said. 'But I'm asking you not to sell the shop. Not yet, because I want to see if I can raise the money. Be a proper adult. Take responsibility. Go to the bank, see what kind of loan I can get. The revenue's rising. I've started tracking it properly. People are coming in more. They love the social media posts.'

Fern's heart twisted at his enthusiasm.

'I just feel that place is a part of me.'

'Maybe a part of us.' Fern stared up at the sky, trying to catch her breath in a different way now. The clouds drifted lazily overhead, and seagulls called to each other across the cliffs. 'Do you know what I feel like right now?'

Daniel grinned. 'We don't want to get arrested; it is a public beach, after all.'

She swiped him playfully. 'Not that! I feel like an ice cream!'

They made their way up to the Cosy Kettle, where Becca greeted them and served two towering cones: mint choc chip for Fern, and vanilla with raspberry ripple for Daniel. They sat on the sea wall, feet swinging like kids, as she pulled out her phone and the sticky note that Dorothy had written Alistair's number down on. 'Shall I ring and see if he can see us?'

Daniel nodded. 'Go for it.'

Fern handed him her ice cream. 'Here goes.' She dialled the number and to her surprise, he answered almost immediately.

'Alistair, hi, it's Fern Talbot, owner of No. 17 Curiosity Lane on Puffin Island.' Fern put the call on speaker so Daniel could hear it. Thankfully there was no one else around. 'I got your number off Dorothy because I've discovered something in the shop that I think might be of interest to you. Daniel and I are going to be in London later this week, and I wondered if you might have time to meet?' That was a little white lie, but Fern didn't want it to appear they were only coming to London to see him.

There was a pause. 'Oh? What do you think may be of interest?'

She glanced at Daniel, then replied, 'We found an old vinyl and believe it might be one of Nathaniel Loring's earliest recordings. Maybe his first. We thought you would know.'

Alistair was quiet for so long Fern thought the call might've dropped.

Then finally, he said, 'That's quite a find.'

'It's probably nothing,' Fern said quickly. 'But we thought, since you're Loring's agent, you might be able to help us verify it.'

She left out the part about the record being valued at seventy-five thousand pounds, and the fact that they'd discovered the music box and the manuscript inside it. She figured those were details best kept in her pocket for now. She just needed a foot in the door to try to get a face-to-face conversation with him.

Alistair cleared his throat. 'Yes. Yes, of course. When were you thinking?'

'Thursday, late morning?'

'I have a meeting until noon, but I can make myself free at one-thirty. Bring the record. I'd be very curious to see it.'

'I thought you might.'

Fern ended the call before he could say anything else. 'We're in.'

'This is going to be interesting.'

'Isn't it just.'

'We do have to think about this carefully. We can't just

accuse someone of stealing a song when it might not actually be the case.'

'I agree with you, but we can gauge his reaction if we get a chance to bring it up. It's no coincidence he asked about the music box when he visited the shop. He knew where that manuscript was hidden.'

After they finished their ice cream, they walked back through the village hand in hand.

When they reached the shop, Daniel dropped her hand and pointed towards the door. It was ajar.

'I thought we'd locked it.'

'We did.'

Slowly, Daniel kicked it open. They both froze.

'We've been burgled,' Fern exclaimed.

The shop was a disaster. Drawers open. Books thrown to the floor. The glass cabinet by the till had been smashed, shards glinting like ice.

Fern walked towards the desk. 'This is unbelievable, it's the middle of the day. Who would do this? Someone must have seen something.'

'Someone was looking for that music box.'

'Don't be daft,' she said, but when she looked to the desk where she had left it, she couldn't see it. She checked the floor and all around. 'It's gone.'

'They knew exactly what they were looking for. We need to check the safe.'

Fern's heart pounded. 'Surely they couldn't get into the safe.'

Daniel sprinted to it, Fern close behind, but the safe door was thankfully still locked, untouched.

No. 17 Curiosity Lane

'Thank God they didn't find the manuscript or take the vinyl,' Daniel exclaimed.

'Just look at this place.' Fern sat down on the chair. 'Do you think it was Alistair and Nathaniel?' she asked.

Daniel looked at her. 'I can't see people of that stature organising petty crime.'

'It depends how high the stakes are. Someone's playing a very dangerous game.'

'We'd better call the police before we tidy up.'

Chapter Forty-Two

Fern had barely slept. The image of the ransacked shop was firmly on her mind. She stared out of the bedroom window, mug of tea in hand, watching as grey clouds gathered over Puffin Island. Downstairs, she could hear Daniel on the phone, his voice clipped and purposeful.

'That was the police again. They're sending someone out this morning,' he said as he stood next to Fern, who was pulling on a hoodie over her pyjamas. 'Local detective's name is Smith. Should be here within the hour.'

'Did you tell them what was taken?'

'I said the only thing that we can see was taken is the antique music box. I didn't mention the manuscript.'

Fern nodded. 'We'll have to. Eventually.'

The front doorbell jingled at exactly 9.47 a.m. and a stocky man in a windbreaker stepped in, flashing a badge.

'Detective Smith. You reported a break-in?'

Daniel stepped forward. 'Yeah, uh, it happened yesterday afternoon. We went for a walk and reported it straightaway when we returned and found the shop turned over, but they couldn't send anyone over until this morning because of the tide.'

'You found it like this?' Smith asked, taking a slow look around. 'And you're sure nothing else is gone?'

'Yes,' Fern said. 'We've just done an inventory and the music box is the only thing missing. It was sitting right there, on the desk.'

Smith pulled out a small notepad. 'Can you describe it? Was it valuable?'

Daniel described the music box. 'I'm not sure how valuable it is.'

'Are you the antique dealer?'

'Yes.'

'But you don't know how much it was worth?' he quizzed.

'It only came into our possession yesterday. I hadn't had time to value it yet.'

'It sounds like someone knew its value. I'll need a proper statement from both of you. Might take a little while.'

He sat down at the desk, and pulled out an iPad from his bag. 'They make us use these things these days,' he said. He put it aside. 'I still prefer pad and pen. Let me take some details.'

After all personal details were taken, he asked, 'This music box … any particular reason it's important?'

Fern looked at Daniel, then took a breath. 'Yes. There was something inside it. Something that changes everything.'

Smith raised his eyebrows. 'Go on.'

Fern leaned her elbows on the counter. 'We found a handwritten composition. Old, delicate, signed "Matilda Hartley", and dated when she was still at university.'

'And?'

'It's the exact melody of Nathaniel Loring's "Echoes of the Past",' she said. 'Down to the phrasing, key changes ... everything.'

Smith looked perplexed. 'I'm not quite sure what you're trying to tell me here.'

'Do you know who Nathaniel Loring is?' asked Fern.

'Who doesn't know who he is?'

'I think Nathaniel stole my great-aunt Matilda's composition.'

'How would he do that? Do you have proof?'

'They went to college together and were in a relationship.'

Daniel stepped in. 'We think he used Matilda's melody as the foundation of the piece that made his career.'

Fern added. 'We didn't know they were in a relationship until recently, but something happened on their wedding day, and they called it off.'

Smith leaned back. 'Do you think that was what the break-in was about? Someone looking for the manuscript?'

'We do,' Fern said. 'That song is his most famous work. It built his reputation. His fortune. If he didn't write it ... he wouldn't want that information getting out.'

'What does Matilda Hartley say about this?'

'She recently passed away.'

That got Smith's attention. 'I see. You're talking copyright infringement. Fraud. Possibly even theft of intellectual property if you can prove intent.'

'We can't, not yet,' Fern admitted. 'But this manuscript is dated and in her handwriting. We found it hidden in a false back of the safe inside the music box. That has to mean something. We've read that Nathaniel Loring's health is deteriorating and his agent, Alistair Montgomery, will inherit everything. I ... we ... think he's behind the break-in.' Fern knew how far-fetched it all sounded.

The detective scratched his chin. 'It sounds like something off a TV show to me.' He gave a chuckle. 'It's my job to find evidence, not to assume, but a famous musician and agent breaking into a curiosity shop would be quite a story.'

'I know how it sounds,' admitted Fern.

'Let me be honest with you, cases like this are difficult. He's a public figure. Ill health, high profile ... and dead artists, no matter how crooked, are a hard sell for scandal.'

'He's not dead yet,' Fern said sharply. 'He's just hiding behind people like Alistair Montgomery.'

Smith narrowed his eyes.

'I've also received an above-market offer for the shop from an anonymous buyer who wants the building and everything in it. We think it's Montgomery, and that he plans to get rid of evidence before Loring dies so he will inherit his fortune.'

Smith paused in his note-taking. 'Have you still got this manuscript? Can I see it?'

After the detective took a photo of the manuscript, he scribbled a few more notes then closed his notebook. 'I'll open a case as you've given me enough to work with. But I won't lie, without hard evidence, and with how delicate Nathaniel Loring's condition is, this could hit a wall.'

Fern nodded. 'We understand.'

The shop was quiet again after the detective left. Daniel put the kettle on while Fern sat quietly at the desk, thinking hard.

'That went ... okay,' he said, offering her a biscuit. 'Didn't think I'd be accusing a national treasure of theft over my morning tea, but here we are.'

She managed a smile. 'He's not a national treasure if the music wasn't his.'

Daniel sat beside her. 'We'll find a way to prove it, but we also have to consider that it may have been a gift.'

'I don't think it was, because if so, then why steal the music box? Someone is looking for something. It's not a coincidence.'

'Thank God we still have the manuscript then. Seriously, Fern – you coming here, this place, all this, I want to help you finish what she started.'

Fern rested her head against his shoulder. 'It's about finding the truth. If Matilda did write that composition, which I think she did, it would explain why Nathaniel wrote that he "owed" her in the inscription.'

'Maybe she knew he was using her music, and it was a goodwill gesture?'

'I doubt it. There's something deeper happening … and whoever sent us the wedding dress with the cryptic note wants us to find out what it is.'

They sat like that for a moment.

'I'm determined to uncover the truth,' said Fern.

Daniel looked at her. '*We* are determined to uncover the truth.'

'Teamwork,' she said, grabbing her laptop and flinging it open. 'I need to look into something.' Her fingers were already tapping. 'If Nathaniel gave interviews, maybe he mentioned when and where he composed "Echoes of the Past". Maybe he slipped up and there's a quote or something.'

'Look at you with your journalist's instinct. I bet that's the reason Matilda gave the shop to you; you're like a dog with a bone.' Daniel peered over her shoulder as she pulled up a string of archived interviews.

'Here,' she exclaimed, scrolling through a newspaper scan and then reading aloud, 'The melody came to me in a dream when I was on holiday a year after I left college. One of those flashes of inspiration.'

Daniel snorted. 'Right.'

Fern narrowed her eyes. 'Matilda wrote it when she was at college.' She was still tapping away. 'He and Matilda were born in the same year, which would mean they would be in the same year at college. I think he took it and erased her from the song's story.'

Fern opened up another tab, and began reading another article, this time from a televised interview years later. Nathaniel sat at a grand piano, the host gushing, *'Tell us about the inspiration behind "Echoes of the Past", your first big hit.'*

'Oh, it's a funny story. It came to me in a dream and when I woke up I couldn't get the melody out of my head.

'We have until Friday to figure this out. Let's see what happens when we visit Alistair on Thursday.'

Daniel sat opposite Fern as she printed out the Loring quotes. 'What if we talked to someone who knew her back then?' he said. 'A professor, or an old classmate? Someone who might've heard her play the song before Nathaniel made it big.'

Fern's eyes lit up. 'That's brilliant. Maybe the music department has records. Or ... or recordings of the recitals!' she said, printing out the last of the interviews and taking out a plastic wallet from the desk. She stuck a label on the front and marked it *Operation Truth*.

'I can't wait to come face to face with Alistair. He can't deny he asked about a music box.'

'You think he'll tell us why?'

'No. But I want to see his face when he realises we're on to them.'

Daniel nodded. 'I think we're close to something.'

Fern looked around the shop. 'Can you imagine if we exposed the biggest music scandal ever? What a way to start the new job.' She realised what she had said the second the words had left her lips, and immediately tried to backtrack. 'I didn't mean anything by that. It's just…'

'I know. Ultimately, it's your choice, but I don't have to like the thought of you going back anytime soon.'

'I know.' Deep down, neither did she. She knew this promotion would help financially, but the thought of not seeing Daniel every day was firmly on her mind.

Chapter Forty-Three

The news of the break-in spread through Puffin Island like seagulls on chips. By mid-morning, half the village seemed to have heard, but it was Betty who was first through the door, holding a foil-wrapped parcel in her hand.

'I heard what happened! You poor dears,' she said, thrusting the parcel into Fern's hands. 'Sausage rolls. Still warm. You can't solve mysteries or fix broken locks on an empty stomach.'

'Betty, you didn't have to—'

'Nonsense.'

Moments later, Amelia popped in, her cardigan flapping as she rushed through the door. 'I've just heard! Is everyone okay?'

'We're both fine. We were out to lunch when it happened,' said Fern.

'I've brought the number of a locksmith.'

Fern was about to respond when the door jingled again. This time, Dilly walked in, holding the hands of identical twins. 'I heard about the break-in, and I wanted to offer help, if there's anything I can do?'

Fern blinked at the sudden influx of warmth and goodwill. 'Thank you, all of you. I don't even know what to say.'

Daniel appeared from the back with a tray of tea things and a slightly overwhelmed expression. 'I thought we were being burgled again with all the noise.'

Amelia smiled. 'Just your neighbours descending to make sure you're okay.'

Even Dorothy wandered in not long after, with a plastic bag full of scones.

'I just thought you might need a pick-me-up,' she said, eyes soft behind her spectacles.

Fern accepted them with a smile but suddenly felt her guard go up. A ridiculous thought had just flashed through her mind – was it possible Dorothy knew more than she let on? She had become close to Matilda only in the last few years; was that a conscious decision? An attempt to get close to try to find out about the manuscript to protect Alistair's inheritance? She tried to shake the suspicion away, told herself that was ridiculous, but there was still a tiny niggle in the back of her mind.

While the shop buzzed with a comforting energy, Fern linked her arm through Daniel's and found herself smiling.

'What are you smiling at?' he murmured.

'This. People looking out for each other.'

'It's called community – and Puffin Island has the best.'

'I can see that,' she replied, leaning her head against his shoulder.

After everyone had left, Daniel popped out to pick up some more milk. Fern was still riding the wave of warmth from the community as she pulled out her phone to check No. 17 Curiosity Lane's social media accounts. Daniel had been doing an incredible job as the singing antique dealer, and sales had been rising. She moved on to her own personal social media and gave a tiny gasp.

A photo of Ella. In a white dress.

The man beside her Jax Devlin.

Married.

At Gretna Green.

Fern couldn't believe what she was seeing. They had got engaged barely two days before and now this. She read the caption.

A small, romantic ceremony, just the two of us.

There were gold bands on their fingers, a kiss under the wooden arch. The photos were all soft lighting and whimsical filters. Surely this had to be some sort of joke, but not according to thousands of comments underneath the post.

Fern stared. This was her best friend … or had been. She couldn't stop her eyes blurring with tears. She hadn't expected the deceit of it all. Hearing the door open she looked up to see Clemmie walking through it, waving a bunch of flowers. 'I thought these would cheer you up…'

She took one look at Fern and stopped in her tracks. 'Fern? Oh, being burgled is such a horrible thing to happen.'

Fern placed her phone on the desk, and covered her face with both hands. A sob escaped before she could stop it.

'What can I do?' Clemmie asked kindly.

'It's not even about the burglary,' Fern said, looking up. 'It's Ella. My so-called best friend has been sleeping with my ex, and I don't mean just recently. I mean more than likely *while* we were still together. I'd bet anything on it.' She took a shaky breath. 'Barely a week ago he was trying to get me back into bed and now … now they're married. *Married*. She didn't even tell me.'

'That doesn't sound like a friend. I'm so sorry this is happening to you.'

'No doubt it will be plastered all over the newspapers tomorrow. I feel so humiliated.'

'Why would it be plastered over the newspapers?'

'My ex is Jax Devlin.'

Clemmie's mouth dropped open in shock and Fern would have laughed if she wasn't so busy crying. 'I wasn't expecting that.'

'They got married at Gretna Green. White dress. Daisies in her hair.'

'That's not good.'

'I don't care about Jax, but I always thought Ella was my person. We were meant to be each other's family and now I feel like I don't even know her at all. I feel such a fool.'

'You are not a fool.'

'In the past, we'd even had chats about our wedding days. How we'd be there for each other. I feel blindsided. How long has this even been going on? I'd expect it from him but not her.'

'It must hurt. I don't think anything I could say now would make it any better. When are you going back to London?'

'I'd taken some leave, but I'm expected back in the office on Monday, and to complicate things further I've just been offered a short-term promotion. Editor is a job I've always wanted … but Ella would be in the team I manage. I'm not sure how I feel about seeing her again. I don't want to face her or hear what she has to say.'

'It doesn't sound ideal. Do you have to go back? What about this place?'

'I've got to admit, I'm enjoying being here. All this – though not the burglary, obviously – it's been great, and spending time with Daniel and getting to know him is just...' She smiled.

'He's a very good catch,' Clemmie acknowledged.

'I know, he makes me smile every day and that was something Jax never did. All he ever did was make me anxious and confused. Whenever he was gigging all I could think about was how many groupies would end up in his bed, but I never imagined it would be my best friend.'

'I would say you've had a lucky escape, probably from both of them.'

'I'm beginning to think you may be right.' She sighed. 'I've worked so hard for that job, but if I don't take it...'

'You won't lose anything, you'll just build a better future. Look what you have here. Does it have to stay an antique shop? It's a fabulous location, and you could start your own magazine, become your own boss. You have choices, and one huge win for choosing Puffin Island is that you don't have London prices. You could get a fresh start with a great community, a slower pace of life, and friends that aren't going to sleep with your boyfriend.'

Fern smiled. 'That's good to hear.'

'It will all work its way out.'

'If I don't go back to London—'

'Aha!' Clemmie cut in. 'So you're thinking about staying?'

'It's on my mind,' Fern admitted. 'But how can I make a life decision having spent so little time here? I also worry Daniel thinks I'd only be staying because of Ella, that avoiding her makes this the easy option.'

'Maybe it's just the change you need. And what's the worst that can happen? If you decide to stay and you don't like it here, you can always go back to London. There's nothing stopping you keeping your place in the city for six months, then seeing how you feel. Can you work remotely? Go freelance. There are always options.'

Fern mulled over what Clemmie had just said. It all made sense. It was just that taking the leap was terrifying her. She was torn.

'Talk it over with Daniel.'

'I will.'

'And for what it's worth, we would love to add you to our little community.'

Fern glanced around the shop, at the tea mugs that were still warm, the gift-wrapped sausage rolls, the lingering scent of scones. Puffin Island had reached out with both hands today. She just had to take hold.

Outside, the sea breeze rattled the shop sign. Fern wasn't going anywhere just yet. She had a lot of thinking to do.

Chapter Forty-Four

The vinyl was on the desk in front of Fern and Daniel. 'I don't think we should risk taking the original with us. Shall I take some photographs instead?' suggested Fern.

'Smart. Yes, let's take some photos. We don't want anything to happen to it, and I don't trust him.'

'Me neither.'

Fern took the photos and locked the vinyl back in the safe. 'Let's go and catch that train.'

The train to London rattled through the countryside. Fern sat beside Daniel, half watching the hedgerows blur past, half mentally preparing herself to sit across from Alistair, smile politely and pretend she hadn't spent the past week convinced he was hiding some deeply unsavoury secrets.

Daniel had bought coffee and almond croissants from the trolley, and they sat quietly, sharing breakfast.

When they pulled into Euston, Fern felt the shift immediately, London was so much noisier than Puffin Island. The platform was busy with people hurrying about their business and Fern stood and watched it all for a moment.

'You okay?'

'Yes, just thinking.'

They stepped off the train together, and as they headed through the station she heard a chorus of camera clicks, and people yelling.

'It must be someone famous,' she said to Daniel. She glanced over at the jostling press pack and that's when she saw them.

Ella and Jax.

Jax carried his signature leather coat slung over one shoulder, and despite the lack of sun was wearing sunglasses. His arm was wrapped around Ella, who was dressed in head-to-toe cream knitwear, large sunglasses, and a scarf arranged like she was about to pose for a *Vogue* winter editorial even though it was the middle of summer.

The paparazzi's cameras flashed as they jostled and shouted things like 'Over here, Jax!' and 'Ella! Give us a smile!' Enjoying the attention, she turned towards the nearest camera, pushed her sunglasses down her nose in a playful, practised way and beamed.

Daniel noticed Fern's tightened grip on his arm before she did.

'Breathe,' he said softly.

'I'm okay,' she murmured, though she wasn't convinced.

They hadn't seen her yet. It wasn't until Jax said something and turned his head slightly. And then, there it was, a flash of recognition. He whispered something in Ella's ear and she visibly tightened her hold on Jax's arm. Ella glanced at Fern and then just as quickly looked away. No wave, not even a smile. She just turned her face back to the cameras, like Fern had never existed.

Ella, her best friend since school, the person who used to finish her sentences and knew every stupid in-joke, had blanked her. Had she really changed that much? Or had Fern never really known her at all? The thought lodged somewhere between anger and heartbreak, and for the first time Fern wasn't sure which hurt more.

The newly married couple walked off in a flurry of flashing bulbs, laughter and chatter. Fern just watched them. Before Daniel could say anything, she turned towards him. 'Have you ever suddenly realised someone wasn't who you thought they were, and maybe never really was?'

He nodded. 'I'm so sorry. That must have been awful for you, but at least you've seen the truth,' he said gently, taking her hand.

'Come on, let's get out of here and see what Alistair has to say.'

Daniel nodded. 'Let's go meet the man who might've stolen a legacy.'

Chapter Forty-Five

The taxi curved up through the quiet, tree-lined streets of Hampstead, far from the city's noise and chaos. Fern looked out of the window, watching the houses get bigger and further apart. Walled-in worlds with private driveways and iron gates and names instead of numbers. The driver made a sharp turn off the main road and onto a narrow gravel track that curved through woodland. After about half a mile, the trees opened up, and the car came slowly to a stop before a set of wrought-iron gates flanked by towering stone pillars.

'Is this it?' Daniel asked, peering out of the window.

Fern checked the address. 'Yeah. That's it.'

After they climbed out of the taxi, they walked towards the gates and announced their arrival via the intercom. The gates creaked open and they stepped through.

The driveway was long and snaked through meticulously kept grounds, the manicured lawns rolling out on either side of Fern and Daniel. Ahead, the house was four storeys of pale stone, with a terrace and tall windows.

'How the other half live,' Daniel murmured.

'I still prefer our place. I bet they don't have a moose's head hanging over the bed.' Fern gave him a lopsided grin.

'Our?' Daniel had picked up on her choice of word. 'I like that.' He smiled, holding her gaze as they carried on walking. Up ahead a black Jaguar was parked beside a stone fountain, water trickling peacefully over carved cherubs. A low, rhythmic thumping drew their eyes skyward where they could see a sleek black helicopter was descending at the back of the house.

Daniel stepped beside her, watching. 'You thinking what I'm thinking?'

'Alistair arriving in style after whatever meetings he had.'

They climbed the wide stone steps towards the massive double doors. Before they could knock, the left door swung open silently. A butler stood there in a dark suit. 'Fern and Daniel,' the man said, as though he were announcing royalty. 'Please come in. Alistair is expecting you.'

The entrance hall of Nathaniel's house was absurdly elegant. Sunlight streamed in through stained-glass windows, pooling across the polished wooden floor. A grand piano sat casually in one corner, and framed sheet music lined the walls, some pristine, some crumpled and scribbled on in bursts of inspiration.

They followed the butler into a living room that somehow managed to outdo the entrance hall. There was another grand piano and floor to-ceiling windows, which showcased immaculate gardens and the helicopter they had just seen arriving.

Alistair was walking across the lawn and it wasn't long before he stepped into the living room. 'Fern,' he said smoothly, flashing a smile. 'Daniel. Welcome.' He was dressed casually in navy chinos, a soft grey jumper and loafers. He propped his cane against the wall before taking a seat opposite them.

'Thanks for seeing us,' Fern said. 'What a beautiful home this is.'

'Now,' Alistair said lightly. 'Tell me why you're here. A vinyl, was it?'

Fern pulled a plastic sleeve from her bag. Inside were high-resolution photographs of the record, label, sleeve and serial number. She slid them across the table. 'We didn't think it was wise to bring the original,' she said, watching Alistair closely.

He adjusted his glasses, leaned forward and took his time studying the images. 'Well,' he said finally, 'the serial number certainly suggests this is the first pressing of Nathaniel's debut track…'

Before Alistair could continue there was the sound of slow tapping approaching from the hallway.

The door opened, and in stepped Nathaniel Loring.

Fern and Daniel turned in his direction. Even now, clearly very frail and unwell, the man had presence. He was tall and elegant, with white hair combed back and skin that had once glowed under stage lights but now looked paper-thin. He leaned on a carved walking stick, his movements careful.

'Who have we here?' he asked, looking towards Alistair.

Fern noticed Alistair looked uncomfortable.

'Nathaniel,' Alistair said, rising a little too quickly. 'These are antique dealers, and they've found something rather special.'

Fern took her chance to expand on Alistair's all-too-brief

introduction. 'Mr. Loring. I'm Fern and I own No. 17 Curiosity Lane on Puffin Island. I'm Matilda Hartley's great-niece.'

The effect was instant. Nathaniel froze. His eyes locked on hers, then flicked to Alistair. 'Matilda?' he repeated quietly, almost to himself.

'We found a vinyl in the shop,' Fern continued. 'What seems to be your very first pressing, according to the serial number. We couldn't help but look into your past and were shocked to find that you, Matilda and Alistair here all went to college together.' She looked towards Alistair, who had paled, before turning back to Nathaniel. 'Can you tell me about her? Did you gift the vinyl to her?'

Glancing at Alistair, Nathaniel crossed the room and lowered himself into a nearby armchair. Fern noticed his hands were trembling slightly as he set the cane aside.

'As you said, we went to college together,' he said. 'Matilda was … clever. Bright. Musical. Wild. I gave her that record as a thank-you for her friendship. That's all there was to it. She was one of the first to hear it. I always wondered if she'd kept it.'

Fern tilted her head. 'Did you not stay in touch?'

Nathaniel looked at Alistair again. His expression darkened slightly. 'No, I'm afraid we lost contact.'

Fern said, 'She passed away very recently.'

A beat passed.

'I'm sorry to hear that,' Nathaniel said. 'Matilda was unforgettable.'

'Yes, there is certainly someone who doesn't want us to forget her,' added Fern, watching him closely.

Nathaniel turned to Alistair. There was a flicker of something on his face – displeasure, maybe, or suspicion.

'Is that so?'

Fern took her chance. 'A wedding dress turned up at the shop with a cryptic note.'

Nathaniel's brow lifted. 'A note?'

She nodded. 'It said, "Find the groom".'

Alistair shifted uncomfortably.

'It was my great-aunt's dress,' Fern continued. 'Matilda's. We confirmed it with the designer, Eliza Valentine. She keeps records.'

Daniel stepped in, voice casual but steady. 'Which means, by process of elimination ... you're the groom we're looking for, Mr Loring.'

'We were hoping you could help us understand why someone would want us to find you now,' Fern said, her tone light but her words landing with precision.

Nathaniel remained silent, his expression unreadable.

'We appreciate this is personal,' Daniel said, attempting to soften the edges, 'but we've been told the wedding was called off on Christmas Eve morning.'

'That's enough,' Alistair cut in, sitting forward sharply. 'You can't just come in here asking these kinds of questions.'

'You invited us,' Fern pointed out, holding her own. 'Since Matilda passed, weird things have been happening. The dress, the note ... and now we've had a break-in.'

Alistair gave a short, incredulous laugh. 'What are you implying?'

'That someone's still digging around in her life,' Fern said. 'Someone who wants the past made present.'

Nathaniel's eyes darkened.

'The record you gave Matilda,' she continued, 'had a message engraved on it, saying: *I owe you everything.* What did that mean?'

Still no answer.

'Why did you leave her?' she asked, quiet but direct. 'What happened that fateful morning? Did she find out something? Something you were hiding? Everyone we've spoken to doesn't believe the claim that she was unfaithful.'

Alistair stood abruptly. 'Okay, that's enough. I'm not letting this turn into some kind of interrogation.'

Fern didn't move, her gaze locked on Nathaniel. 'Why didn't you marry her?'

'That record wasn't just sentimental, was it? You felt guilty. Because she didn't cheat, did she? That was just the story that you put out,' Daniel pressed.

Fern stepped in again. 'Did you steal her composition?'

That was it. Alistair's face flushed, and he jabbed a hand towards the door. 'Please leave. Now.'

Fern and Daniel stood slowly. No big dramatic exit, no shouting match. As they walked out, Fern could feel there was more. They weren't finished with this conversation. Not even close.

'What do you make of that?" asked Daniel once they were outside and heading back up the drive.

'Guilty as hell.'

'I agree.'

Chapter Forty-Six

Fern and Daniel were the only ones in their train carriage as they travelled back to Sea's End.

'I really think we're onto something,' claimed Fern.

'I bet he thought no one would ever find out, but he must have been living on edge all these years, wondering if Matilda would out him, or if she ever told anyone.'

'My gut feeling is telling me we're right and he did steal the piece.'

'It must have been a right dig in the heart for Matilda, watching him rise to fame on her music. There's no way she would have been able to find the money to fight his legal team,' added Daniel.

'We have the manuscript, but it still doesn't prove anything. So the question is, what are we going to do about it? How long will Nathaniel live if he's in ill health? He didn't look the best, and, like Matilda, we also don't have the money if a legal case evolves.'

'I have a little bit of my inheritance left. I would use that for Matilda.'

'Oh, Daniel, that warms my heart, but I wouldn't ask you to do that and I'm sure Matilda wouldn't want that either. That's your money.'

'I'd do it for her.'

She smiled at him. 'You are just amazing.' She linked her arm through his and rested her head on his shoulder.

'I still think Alistair is the anonymous buyer,' said Daniel after a moment.

'Absolutely. Or could Nathaniel and Alistair be in it together? Nathaniel needs to protect his legacy and image whilst Alistair wants his fortune when Nathaniel passes away. If they buy the shop, they might have discovered the manuscript.'

'I think he'll be scared of what we might do next.' Daniel leaned back in his seat, his gaze settling on her. 'And we still don't know who planted the wedding dress, or what they know.'

A few hours later they reached Sea's End. As they walked back towards the shop, Daniel asked, 'What's the plan?'

'Open a bottle of wine. It's been a long day and tomorrow we need to go and see Edgar and tell him that we're not selling to the so-called anonymous buyer.'

'Do you think we'll need a solicitor?'

'I'm not sure, but we definitely need more concrete evidence to hand over to the police.'

Daniel was quiet for a second.

'What is it?' asked Fern, opening the door and placing her bag on the desk.

'There's something else I just remembered – the shed out back. It's where Matilda used to store a lot of her personal things: old photos, tapes, even some of her old equipment. There could be something in there.'

Fern's pulsed raced. 'You didn't think to mention this sooner?'

Daniel looked sheepish. 'I forgot.' He gestured towards the back of the shop. 'Come on, let's take a look.'

They stepped outside the back door and headed down to the weathered shed at the bottom of the garden, partially hidden behind overgrown ivy. The door creaked open and Fern followed Daniel inside. The light was dim, casting long shadows over the piles of old trunks and forgotten crates that littered the space.

'Help me with this,' Daniel said, lifting a crate off a stack of boxes. It was heavy, but they managed to pull it free. Inside, they found old photos. 'Look at this, a very young Matilda sitting at a piano.'

Fern pulled out an old film projector. It was covered in dust, but it was still in surprisingly good condition. Next to it were several boxes containing reels of film, all unlabelled. 'What do you think these are?'

Daniel's eyes lit up as he pulled a few more reels out of a crate. 'There's only one way to find out; we'll have to take a look.'

They spent the next few hours sorting through the crates, sifting through old letters, photographs and more reels of film. Each one seemed to tell a different story, a snapshot of a life once lived in vibrant detail. The further they dug, the more they felt like they were uncovering a hidden world, one that had been sealed away for years.

Finally, Daniel found something that made his heart skip a beat. He pulled out a reel labelled simply 'Matilda Puffin Island 1963'.

'This is the earliest one we have. Let's have a look at it,' said Fern.

They rushed back inside the shop, bringing the projector with them. Fern carefully threaded the reel, her fingers trembling slightly as she set it into the machine. They plugged the projector in and it stuttered to life with a whirr. Fern sat on a chair while Daniel fiddled with the old machine. There was light and movement, then the wheel began to turn and an image appeared on the wall before them.

Matilda looked young and radiant, running barefoot across the sand at what appeared to be Blue Water Bay. Her hair streamed behind her and she wore a white linen dress that clung to her knees in the wind. Behind her were the cliffs filled with puffins. There was no sound, just the soft mechanical clicking of the projector. They watched in silence as Matilda twirled once, laughing, before a young man ran into frame. He was tall, dark-haired, with a shy smile.

'Is that him?'

'That's Nathaniel,' Fern confirmed.

The reel jumped and jittered. Even in fuzzy black-and-white, there was no mistaking the two young people were in love. They chased each other playfully along the shore, and then Matilda grabbed Nathaniel's hand and pulled him towards the camera. For a moment, he looked directly into the lens.

Then: a cut.

New footage began. They were indoors now. Matilda was wearing the same dress but with her hair now pinned back. She sat at a dark upright piano. The camera wobbled slightly before zooming in slowly.

The film caught Matilda's hands moving with precision across the keys. The camera zoomed in again, shakier now. Resting on the piano was a sheet of paper covered with scribbles, and a pencil. Matilda paused mid-chord, reached for the pencil and added a couple of bars to the staff.

'She's writing music,' observed Fern.

'She looks like she's upset,' added Daniel.

Tears had started trickling down Matilda's face and when she stopped for a moment Nathaniel walked into the frame and hugged her before she carried on.

'She *is* upset,' confirmed Fern. 'Why is she crying?'

Daniel shrugged. 'I've no idea. Maybe the music is emotional and she's feeling it?'

Matilda added more notes and the camera zoomed in on her name, written in looping, elegant script.

Fern gave a tiny gasp. 'That's the composition we have. It's exactly the same as the one in the safe. She definitely wrote it and composed the music, not Nathaniel.'

Daniel stared at her. 'Is this proof enough?'

'Surely it is.'

Onscreen, Matilda carried on playing then scribbling. The film ended and the screen faded to white.

Fern turned to Daniel. 'We have to show this to someone.'

He nodded.
'I think this could possibly change everything.'

Chapter Forty-Seven

The first thing Fern became aware of was the warmth of Daniel's body curved against hers, their legs tangled beneath the covers. His arm was draped across her waist, his hand resting just below the curve of her ribs.

She shifted slightly, and Daniel stirred behind her, his breath warm against her neck.

'Morning,' he murmured, still half-asleep.

Fern turned to face him. His hair was a mess, his eyes closed but smiling.

'Hi,' she whispered.

His fingers skimmed her cheek. 'You okay?'

She nodded, her hand covering his. 'More than okay.'

He leaned in and kissed her.

'I'll have more of that, thank you.'

He kissed her again as his hand slid through her hair then down her spine. She moved closer to him. 'This isn't a bad way to wake up in the morning.'

She was happy. This was worlds away from anything she'd

ever had with Jax ... which had been all adrenalin and no connection, like riding a rollercoaster you couldn't quite get off. She thought of Ella, who still hadn't called, hadn't texted and hadn't bothered to explain. It was like their friendship, all the years of sleepovers and secrets and loyalty, had just evaporated. If Fern was honest, she didn't even want the explanation anymore, she had bigger issues to deal with and time was ticking. Her leave was coming to an end and she was due back in the office – not a thought she was relishing.

'Can we just stay here, like this, for ever?' she murmured, snuggling into Daniel.

'Sounds good to me, but why are you getting all maudlin on me?'

'I don't know ... when things seem too good to be true, they usually are, but you seem to be the exception to the rule.' She knew someone like Daniel was worth hanging on to, and her feelings were intensifying. Laying her head on his chest, she traced small circles with her fingertip across his skin.

Daniel spoke first, his voice quiet. 'Last night being together was ... different.'

She smiled, remembering. He'd barely got under the duvet before she pressed up against him, her hands winding around his waist, pulling him impossibly closer. He groaned as he kissed her, his hands sliding down to her hips, fingers pressing into the fabric of her PJs, desperate to feel the warmth of her skin beneath. Her legs wrapped around his waist, anchoring him to her as his lips left a scorching trail along her jaw and down her neck. She had shivered, her pulse racing as his tongue began to explore every part of her body, whilst his fingers tangled in the hem of her top as he pushed it up.

A small moan had escaped her as she arched into him, letting herself melt into the intoxicating sensation of his touch.

Now she tilted her chin to look up at him. 'Different how?'

He glanced down at her with a soft smile. 'Like something we're both going to remember for the rest of our lives.'

This connection was real; she felt it and so did he.

'Just as I predicted, you've fallen for me,' Daniel teased, grinning at her with that signature lopsided smile that made her heart flip in the most ridiculous way.

Fern rolled her eyes and gave his bare chest a playful swipe. 'Maybe.'

He caught her hand before she could pull it away, pressing a kiss to her knuckles. 'There's no maybe about it. Good job the feeling's mutual then.'

She smiled. 'That's good to know.'

They sank back into silence, wrapped in each other's arms, legs tangled under the duvet, the rest of the world feeling miles away. The minutes passed and all they could hear was the sound of the gulls outside.

'Do you know what day it is?'

'Friday,' he said, brushing her hair back from her face.

'Yes, but it's also the last day of the month. Time to do the accounts and see how many millions we've made…'

'Don't joke,' he said, feigning seriousness. 'This place is on the up.'

She smirked. 'I know. And so we're going to pay Edgar a visit and tell him that we will *not* be accepting any offers from any mysterious, anonymous buyers today, despite the deadline.'

Daniel grinned, pleased. 'And?'

Fern's smile faltered just slightly. She knew what he meant. *And what about you, Fern?*

Her annual leave was ending. Technically, she was supposed to be back in London next week. Back behind her desk at *Sound & Fury*, back to the inbox chaos, the editorial meetings, the playlist reviews, the after parties and, of course, Ella. She stared at the ceiling for a moment, feeling his fingers travel lightly over her skin. Did she really want to go back to her old life? To the job that once felt like everything but now felt a little hollow? To the flat that had been home for a long time but would now seem empty if she was living in it on her own?

She glanced at Daniel, at the faint stubble on his jaw, the warmth in his eyes. All this had come out of nowhere and yet she trusted him more than people she'd known for years. Somehow, without trying, he made her feel seen, steady and safe. Then there was the shop, this odd, creaky little treasure trove that had begun to feel like home in a way her city flat never had.

'I don't know if I want to go back,' she admitted quietly. 'To any of it. I don't think I can manage without seeing you most days.'

Daniel smiled but didn't say anything. He just held her a little tighter.

An hour later Daniel was sat in front of the computer. The Excel worksheet, usually as empty as the till, was full of numbers. Glorious, profit-shaped numbers. He scrolled down, eyes scanning the list of items they'd sold.

Across the room, Fern was elbow-deep in packing paper, wrapping a ceramic teapot shaped like a badger. She stuck a mailing label on the box then reached for the next item.

Looking pleased with himself, Daniel let out a low whistle. 'You aren't going to believe this.'

Fern didn't look up. 'Nothing would surprise me. Go on.'

He swivelled dramatically in the chair, scooped up his guitar and gave it a theatrical strum.

'Ladies and gentlemen,' he said before playing a bouncy tune, pausing every few bars to think of a rhyme, pulling exaggeratedly pained faces as he fished for words.

'Oh we've sold the porcelain llama…'

(He grimaced like he wasn't sure how that had happened.)

'And the haunted garden gnome…'

(He raised his eyebrows and mouthed, 'Seriously?')

'A wig from 1940…'

(He pointed at his own hair and mimed confusion.)

'And a toucan made of chrome…'

Fern laughed.

'Three thousand quid, I tell ya, We're practically a bank!
'The till is full of glory, The ledger's in the green…'

(He glanced at the screen and gave it a thumbs-up.)

'We might just pay the heating bill.
'What a novel little dream!'

'Three grand? Are you serious? This place has made three grand in a month?'

'Absolutely serious.'

'Bloody hell!' She joined him at the computer. 'I actually can't believe it, especially since you hadn't sold anything for months before I arrived.'

'I'll be able to take a wage at this rate.'

'Don't go getting ahead of yourself,' she teased. 'But that balance sheet is starting to look healthy. We'll soon need to be sourcing more antiques to sell.'

'That's the best part, looking for treasures! I told you to give me a month and I'd make this place work, and I did it.'

'You sure did.'

He balanced his guitar against the desk and pulled her towards him. Wrapping his arms around her waist, he kissed her. 'I knew we could turn it around. Teamwork is what it's all about.'

'Teamwork,' she repeated, pressing a soft kiss to his lips. 'Are we ready to go and see Edgar? And then we probably need to think about updating Detective Smith with our findings.'

After they locked up the shop, they made their way next door and up the stairs. As they approached Edgar's office they saw the door was slightly ajar and could hear voices drifting out, low and tense.

Fern stopped in her tracks and placed her hand on Daniel's arm.

'They're going to uncover the truth,' a woman said. Fern recognised the voice; it was Dorothy.

Fern's heart raced and her eyes widened as she looked at Daniel and brought a finger up to her lips.

'I think they're getting close now. This is going to end in a right scandal.'

'What do we do?' came Edgar's voice, muffled but urgent.

Fern turned to Daniel, her voice a whisper when she spoke. 'They're in on it. Dorothy, Edgar, this whole time...'

'We don't know that for sure,' he mouthed back.

'I *do*. I can feel it.'

Before Daniel could stop her, Fern had pushed the door open and stormed into the room.

Startled, Dorothy turned in her chair and Edgar looked up sharply.

'You?' Fern said, voice shaking with fury. 'You're part of this? Trying to cover up the fact that Nathaniel somehow stole my great-aunt's composition that gave him the most affluent life ever.'

Edgar stood up. 'Fern—'

'You're working with Alistair and Nathaniel. You're covering it all up. Even acting as his solicitor to try and buy the shop so they can find and destroy the evidence.'

'Fern, that's not—'

'We heard you!' Her voice cracked. 'You said we're getting close and it's going to end in scandal. I think we should call the police,' she said as she turned towards Daniel. 'Let them investigate exactly what is going on here.'

Dorothy stood up, holding out her hands in a calming gesture. 'It's not what you think.'

'You said we'd uncover the truth. That's what this is about, isn't it? You're all protecting Nathaniel Loring. Protecting the lie. He stole great-aunt Matilda's composition. I thought you were her friend, but I suppose blood will always be thicker than water. You'll always have Alistair's back, even though you know what he did was wrong.'

Daniel placed a hand on her back, grounding her. 'Do you want to hear them out, or do we go straight to the station?'

Edgar cut in before Fern could answer. 'You're wrong about us.' His voice was quiet but firm. 'We're not the enemy, Fern. Far from it. We've been waiting for you.'

Chapter Forty-Eight

Edgar's words hung in the air.
Fern was trying to absorb what she'd just heard. 'What do you mean?' she asked, her eyes darting between him and Dorothy.

'I'm not acting on behalf of Nathaniel Loring or Alistair,' Edgar replied. He gestured towards the two spare chairs across from his desk. 'Please sit.'

Fern and Daniel exchanged a glance before taking a seat. Edgar looked at Dorothy, then gave a solemn nod.

'I'm the anonymous buyer,' Dorothy declared softly, taking Fern and Daniel by surprise.

'You?' said Fern.

Daniel sat up straighter. 'Why would you want the shop?'

'Because she's helping Alistair and Nathaniel,' chipped in Fern.

'Not because I'm helping Alistair, but because I'm helping Matilda. She was my friend … and whilst I'm confessing, I'm also the one who left the wedding dress outside your shop.'

Fern blew out a breath. 'You left the wedding dress? What is going on here?'

'Matilda gave it to me,' Dorothy replied. 'She knew its worth, but she also knew its story. She never parted with it, though she'd kept it hidden away in my sewing room for the last few years. It upset her to look at it, but she couldn't bear to let go of it either. All she ever wanted was a family, a husband who would love her unconditionally.'

'But why drop it off outside the shop? Why now? Did Nathaniel really steal her song? And if you knew, why buy the shop? Were you trying to cover it up for them?' Fern fired off the questions in rapid succession, her tone sharp and accusing.

Dorothy looked at Fern, tears brimming in her eyes. 'He did steal the song, and I was helping Matilda because I promised her I would.'

'You promised her what?' Daniel asked. His voice was measured, not confrontational.

Dorothy drew in a shaky breath. 'You remember, Daniel, that I was with her the night before she passed away?'

He nodded slowly.

'She was fading fast, but her mind was sharp. She asked me to listen. She said she couldn't leave this world without telling someone the truth.'

Fern leaned forward, her heart pounding. 'The truth about the song?'

'Yes,' Dorothy whispered. 'About how Nathaniel stole "Echoes of the Past". He signed a record deal behind her back, passing it off as his own, and he kept her silent by taking something even more precious than her music.'

Daniel raised an eyebrow. 'What do you mean?'

Dorothy looked directly at Fern now. Her voice broke. 'Matilda and Nathaniel had a child. At university. A baby boy.'

Fern gasped. 'A child? They had a baby together?'

'Yes.'

Fern turned to Daniel. 'Did you know? Did Matilda ever say anything to you?'

He shook his head. 'No. This is the first I'm hearing about this.'

'No one knew,' Dorothy said. 'I was shocked when she told me. Only two other people knew the truth at the time.'

'Who?' Fern asked.

'Nathaniel and Alistair. They were both there the night the baby was born, and what I'm going to share with you isn't going to be very favourable towards my brother or Nathaniel.'

Fern's eyes narrowed. 'Why would you tell us something that doesn't put then in a good light?'

Dorothy held her gaze. 'Because Matilda and I trusted each other. We came a long way together at the end.' Her voice faltered. 'I now have no illusions about who Alistair really is. Just because we share blood doesn't mean I'm blind to his faults or even like him.'

'What is he, exactly?' asked Daniel.

'A man who has always put himself first,' Dorothy said bitterly. 'Even in his twenties, he had this knack for charming people just long enough to get what he wanted. He nearly got our family business repossessed once, trying to "flip" it for a quick profit. Lied to our parents' faces about it. He's clever, calculating, but heartless when it comes to consequences.' She exhaled shakily and continued. 'Matilda told me Nathaniel and Alistair were the only ones there when she gave birth.'

Dorothy closed her eyes briefly, and Fern had a horrible feeling in the pit of her stomach that whatever Dorothy was going to say next could be deeply upsetting. 'The baby didn't cry, so Nathaniel took the child in his arms and stepped out of the room. A moment later he returned without the baby. He told her it was stillborn. Their son was gone.'

Fern felt stricken. 'Matilda's baby was stillborn?'

Dorothy now looked visibly upset and Edgar reached across and squeezed his friend's hand. 'No, the baby wasn't stillborn.'

'So what happened to him?'

Dorothy took a deep breath before continuing. 'Nathaniel and Alistair arranged for an adoption. I doubt it was legal. Matilda had no idea what they'd done, believing what they'd told her – that the baby had died.'

Fern hadn't known her great-aunt Matilda, but she felt for her. How could anyone be so cruel? This was heartbreaking to hear.

'How did she find out the truth?' asked Daniel.

'I don't know; I didn't ask, and she didn't tell me. She was sharing so much that night…' Dorothy said. 'Anyway, she somehow discovered the truth that the baby had survived, and it was a boy. But by the time Matilda finally tracked him down, which was only a few years ago … she discovered he had passed away many years ago. She never got to tell him she was his mother.'

Fern shook her head in disbelief. It was one tragedy after another. What gave Nathaniel and Alistair the right to do this to her great-aunt?

'Alistair and Nathaniel do not know I know, that we'—

Dorothy gestured between herself and Edgar—'know.' She dabbed her eyes with a tissue. 'I just wish we had been friends at the time. I could have helped her track the baby down sooner. Matilda was never looking for revenge, she just wanted the truth to be known. Nathaniel didn't just take her music, he took her son and her future, and my brother helped him do it. I gave you the dress because Matilda wanted someone to find the truth after she was gone, and she thought you might be the one person able to discover it and put the record straight.'

Fern looked at her, incredulous. 'But if you knew all this, why not just tell me? Or tell Daniel? Why give me the dress?'

'It was my way of coming clean without betraying my brother directly in words. If I confronted Alistair and Nathaniel, or told the story, I feared no one would believe me, that they would pass it off as me being deluded. I know they would have found a way to destroy me. Giving you the dress allowed the evidence to start speaking for itself. If the truth came from someone outside the inner circle, he wouldn't see it coming, and with your journalistic background, you had more of a chance of discovering everything than I did. That was the only way I could see to help expose the truth about Matilda's stolen legacy.'

Fern sat in silence, her mind racing. The threads were tangled, but they were slowly coming together.

'Why would Nathaniel get rid of his own baby?' Fern asked. 'Why didn't he want to keep the baby, be a family? After all, he was ready to marry Matilda. They got engaged when they were at music college and were meant to marry the Christmas after they graduated. He loved her, didn't he?'

Dorothy looked at her with sadness. 'No, Fern, I don't

believe he did,' she said gently. 'He was in love with her talent. Matilda had the spark. She was the talented one and he knew it. That's why he took the song, along with her notebook filled with all of her ideas. He used it to map out his career.'

'His songs were *all* Matilda's songs?'

'Every last one of them. She only discovered he'd signed a record deal the morning of the wedding. Alistair went to visit her and told her that the wedding was off and that Nathaniel had no more need of her.'

'But the baby?'

'He didn't want a baby. He wanted fame more than anything, and he thought being a father would tie him down, limit his image, distract from the brilliance he was ready to claim as his own. And marriage?' Dorothy gave a hollow laugh. 'Matilda was sadly just a pawn in his game.'

'Why pretend he wanted to marry her?'

'Because he's a cruel man and strung her along to the very last second. He didn't want her finding out about his record deal until it was signed.'

Fern shook her head in disbelief. 'Still. Why didn't Matilda fight him? Why not blow the whole thing wide open?'

'Because she was still grieving. The baby was born in the February of their last year of college, ten months before the wedding. After Nathaniel called the wedding off, they planted rumours about Matilda being unstable, unfaithful. If she had gone public, if she'd tried to accuse him of stealing her songs, she would've been painted as a bitter woman trying to bring down a rising star.'

'And the song?'

'She confronted him privately,' Dorothy said. 'He couldn't deny it as they both knew the truth.'

'All this just for fame?' Fern couldn't believe what she was hearing.

'"Echoes of the Past" was written by Matilda about the child she lost. She never got over it. As a cruel and mocking gesture he sent her the first pressing, told her it would be worth something one day.'

'What sort of monster is he? This is just heartbreaking.'

'As Nathaniel made more money and built his own legal team it quickly became impossible for Matilda to expose the truth.'

'But we could expose the truth.' Fern looked at Daniel. 'We have the evidence.'

'We have,' confirmed Daniel. 'Not only have we discovered Matilda's original manuscript, but we've also uncovered a film of her at the piano composing it.'

Dorothy looked towards Edgar and smiled. 'Thank God. We knew it was there somewhere, but didn't know where to start looking. That's why I put in an offer on the shop, to buy time to protect any evidence, just in case Alistair and Nathaniel had thought of that – my guess is that the burglary was not a coincidence – and to nudge you two into searching the shop for clues.'

'Did Matilda give you any more details about her son?' asked Daniel.

Dorothy shook her head. 'No. There's only two men who will have those details.'

Just then, Dorothy's phone buzzed, and she rummaged in her bag. When she found it and looked at the screen, the colour drained from her face.

'It's Alistair,' she said, answering hesitantly. The call didn't take long and as soon as she hung up, she filled them in.

'Nathaniel Loring's health has deteriorated further. The doctors have given him a week, maybe less.'

Daniel exhaled hard. 'Time is running out. What do you want to do about this?'

'Is it right to confront a dying man?' Fern was battling with her conscience. 'Or do we let things lie?'

'It might be your only chance, especially if you want the truth about the baby and to discover the identity of Matilda's son. I can't see Alistair ever divulging that information, as he will want to keep all of Nathaniel's money,' said Dorothy.

Fern was thinking fast. 'I'm going to give it a go. I want him to take accountability for what he did to Matilda. I'm going to go back and see him again. I've got to give it one last try.'

'And if he won't, or can't, see you?' Edgar asked.

'Then I'll tell Alistair I have the original manuscript and the fact that I'm the new editor of *Sound & Fury*. This story will go global if he doesn't come clean. I'll tell the world that Matilda wrote all the songs that spanned Nathaniel's career, and his wealth and success don't actually belong to him. This will be the biggest music scandal of the decade, and I'll make sure the whole world knows he was a fraud.'

'Where are the manuscript and the tape?' asked Edgar.

'In the safe along with the vinyl, which has had a huge valuation.'

'When are you going to go?' asked Dorothy.

'As time is ticking, there's no time like the present. Back to London we go.'

'Come on, I'll be right by your side.' Daniel took her hand as they stood up.

'Do we even know if he's at home?' asked Fern, looking towards Dorothy.

'Yes, he is,' replied Dorothy, standing up and giving Fern a hug.

'Thank you for looking out for great-aunt Matilda.'

'It's what friends do.'

'Good luck,' said Edgar as they left his office.

Chapter Forty-Nine

A few hours later they arrived back at Euston and jumped into a cab. It wasn't long before the taxi pulled up outside the wrought-iron gates of the Loring estate, where Fern and Daniel were met with a chaotic scene. A crowd of reporters had gathered along the perimeter, TV crews with shoulder-mounted cameras jostling for position.

Fern leaned forward, peering through the window as the car slowed. As they climbed out, a woman in a red blazer stood front and centre before a camera, speaking urgently into a microphone. 'With reports that the great Nathaniel Loring's life is drawing to a close,' she said, her voice tense with drama, 'the world waits to see if the musical legend will leave behind any final compositions. His most celebrated work, "Echoes of the Past", has defined a generation...' Her voice trailed off as Fern and Daniel walked towards the gates, which were closed tight.

Fern pressed the intercom. A sharp buzz followed, then silence. She pressed it again, longer this time.

Nothing.

'No one's answering,' Daniel said quietly, glancing over his shoulder at the cameras now trained on them. 'I'm not surprised. They're probably fed up with the reporters pressing it to try and get an interview.' She pulled out her phone and scrolled to Alistair's number. She exhaled as she hit call.

He picked up on the third ring. 'This is not the time,' Alistair snapped, not bothering with a greeting.

'Actually, it's exactly the time,' Fern replied, her voice low and firm. 'We know about the stolen song...'

'Not this again—'

'And the child.' Fern interrupted. 'If you don't let us in, we'll tell them.' She glanced behind her at the sea of microphones and flashing lights. 'Everything.'

There was a second of silence. Then a sharp mechanical click.

The gates creaked open.

Daniel looked at her. 'We're in.'

'I can't quite believe it.'

Side by side, they stepped through the gates, the noise of the press fading behind them, swallowed by the gravel crunching beneath their shoes as they followed the sweeping curve of the path towards the house. Once again, the front door opened before they could knock. Alistair stood there, his face stern, his mouth drawn in a tight, disapproving line. His eyes, cold and sharp, flicked from Fern to Daniel. He stepped aside. 'Come in,' he muttered, though there wasn't a hint of welcome in his voice. He led them through to the sitting room and shut the door with a quiet finality.

Before he could speak, Fern did. 'I understand this is a bad time,' she began, 'but we want to see Nathaniel.'

'Do you really think that is possible or what he needs right now?'

'I'm not here to distress him,' Fern said. 'I just want to speak to him. Just a conversation.'

'You can speak to *me*,' he snapped. 'About whatever ludicrous stories you've managed to concoct.'

'They're not stories,' Fern replied firmly. 'And you know it. We have the original manuscript. We have the tape showing Matilda composing the piece. We have dates, and handwriting comparisons. We know what he did to Matilda. We know what you did to make Nathaniel as rich and as famous as possible. How could you tell a woman who had just given birth that her baby had died?' She stared at Alistair with contempt. 'You hoped the secret would stay buried, but it didn't.'

Alistair paled, but his tone remained sharp. 'You don't understand the consequences of this.'

'I understand them perfectly. I also understand that if Nathaniel dies without setting the record straight, the fallout will land squarely on you,' Fern stated clearly. 'Because you're the one who manipulated everything to protect his legacy and your own interests. If this story breaks, you'll be the face of a fraudulent musical scandal. The man who let a genius's work go uncredited, who helped cover up the truth about a child, and stood to inherit the fortune of a dying composer that was built on a lie.'

Alistair's voice dropped to a hiss. 'Do you think blackmail will get you what you want?'

'I'm not blackmailing you,' Fern said. 'But I am a journalist, and from Monday the editor of the most established music magazine in the UK. It won't take me long to write and circulate this story, which I can guarantee will hit the world news by midday on Monday. You can try me if you don't believe me. I'm giving you a choice, Alistair. Let me speak to him, now, so we can give him the chance to tell the truth himself. Or we walk back down that drive and I'll write an exclusive.'

He stared at her, every muscle in his face taut with fury.

'What exactly do you want from him?' he spat. 'Money? We can give you money just to go away and leave him, us, in peace.'

'I don't want your money. I just want the truth.'

'And then what?'

'That depends on what he says,' Fern replied. 'But I'm not walking away from this. Not now.'

For a long moment, Alistair looked at her and Fern could see the fear in his eyes. He was losing control. He knew it and she knew it, and she wasn't going to let this go. He was scared of Nathaniel saying something unscripted. Something dangerous. Something … honest.

He drew a slow breath, but the fight in him was faltering.

'I'll see if he's awake,' he said curtly, and left the room.

Daniel moved to Fern's side. 'Oh my God, you were brilliant. Do you really think he'll let us see him?'

'He doesn't have a choice anymore,' she whispered. 'Not if he wants to keep even a shred of Nathaniel's legacy intact.'

Chapter Fifty

Two minutes later, Alistair returned to the sitting room. 'He will see you.'

Immediately, they both stood up.

'Just Fern,' he said firmly. 'You can wait there.'

Fern and Daniel exchanged a glance before Daniel said it was fine and motioned for her to go ahead. Fern reluctantly left Daniel in the sitting room and followed Alistair down a hallway that led to an outside door. They crossed a small stone courtyard then entered another building. Alistair paused outside a large oak door. 'He's very weak,' Alistair muttered, avoiding her eyes. 'Do not stress him out or expect too much.'

Fern didn't reply. The man on the other side of that door had taken everything from her great-aunt, but he might also hold the key to making it right.

Alistair opened the door and stepped inside. Fern followed him in.

The room was dim, the blinds drawn, with a narrow strip of daylight slicing through a small gap. Everything was clean and clinical, almost austere in its minimalism. A double bed stood in the centre, flanked by simple bedside tables, one of which held a glass and a jug of water. In the corner, a small basin was mounted to the wall, and a single chair – currently occupied by a nurse – sat beside the bed. The space resembled a private hospital room more than a bedroom. There were no signs of grandeur now – no awards, no shelves of records or framed photos – just a frail-looking man propped up on too many pillows.

Nathaniel Loring looked nothing like the glossy PR photos that still floated around the internet. His skin was pale and drawn, his eyes dull with exhaustion. He looked … small. Like the last few days had drained the life out of him.

As soon as Fern entered, he turned his head slowly and gave the nurse a faint wave of his hand.

'You can go,' his voice rasped. 'It's all right.'

Alistair stayed where he was.

'You, too. Go,' Nathaniel ordered, firmer this time.

Alistair looked like he was going to argue, but thought better of it. He followed the nurse out, the door clicking shut behind them. Fern stepped closer to the bed, pulled out the chair and sat.

Nathaniel studied her. Really looked at her. It was unnerving. A long silence stretched between them.

Then he said, 'What do you think you know?'

'That "Echoes of the Past" was written by Matilda,' Fern replied. 'She didn't get any credit. You stole her song and her fortune.'

His gaze drifted to the ceiling.

'You covered your tracks well,' she continued. 'But we have the original manuscript. And footage of her composing it. Did you ever love her, or did you only love what she could give you?'

He didn't answer right away. His head rolled slightly to the side, his eyelids heavy – with fatigue or lack of interest? Fern couldn't tell.

'I loved what she gave me,' he finally said. 'The music. The passion. The promise of something bigger than myself. That was enough for a while.'

Fern felt her stomach twist. 'You left her at the altar. Spread a lie about an affair. You even told her your baby had died at birth.'

Nathaniel's lips twitched into something like a smirk. 'The baby was inconvenient. A burden I didn't ask for. Fame doesn't wait around for people with baggage.'

Fern stared at him, disgusted. 'So you lied. Let her grieve her own child while you – what? Counted your money and collected awards?'

He exhaled a dry, shallow laugh. 'You think I got where I did by playing nice?'

'No,' she said coldly, 'I think you got where you did by stepping on the heart of the only person who ever truly believed in you.'

Nathaniel didn't argue. He looked almost bored now. But then, with a small twitch of his fingers, he reached to adjust the blanket across his chest. His hand trembled.

'She found out,' he murmured, eyes fixed on a spot just beyond her. 'About the baby. A few years ago. Did one of those DNA kits and registered herself. I don't know why. Curiosity, maybe. Guilt. But somehow, it brought up her son.'

'How do you know?'

'She showed up. Knocked on my door, said she wanted to

know everything. I told her. Gave her the details. Not that it mattered by then.'

'Why not?'

'He was already dead,' Nathaniel said flatly. 'Died from an illness. I don't remember. I didn't dig too deep.'

Fern closed her eyes. The tragedy of it all was suffocating. 'Is that the only time you saw her after breaking her heart on what was meant to be your wedding day?'

'Yes.' A harsh, rattling cough wracked through him then. His chest heaved. He fumbled weakly at the bedside, and hit the call button.

Moments later, the nurse appeared. 'Time to let him rest,' she said gently to Fern.

Fern stood, but paused at the door, hand on the frame. She looked back at the dying man, the one who'd ruined so many lives without an ounce of remorse. 'At least give me his name,' she said. 'The boy. What was his name?'

Nathaniel didn't lift his head, but his lips moved.

'William Brooks.'

Fern nodded once, swallowing the tight knot in her throat. She left without another word. The door shut behind her.

As she walked back to the sitting room, her stomach twisted with a sharp, nauseating churn at the thought of what both men had done to her great-aunt.

'We're ready to go,' she said, looking at Daniel, who stood and crossed the room towards her without a word, reaching for her hand. She took it without hesitation, then she turned and fixed Alistair with a hard, unflinching stare. 'What you did…' she said, her voice low but shaking with fury. 'You should be ashamed of yourself.'

Alistair didn't speak, just silently followed them into the front hall and closed the door behind them.

Fern and Daniel didn't speak again until they were through the iron gate, past the waiting journalists, and into the quiet of the side street beyond.

'What the hell happened in there?' he asked.

Fern shook her head slowly. 'He's a man without a soul, no remorse, obsessed with money, with being adored. He used Matilda for her talent, her love, and when she became inconvenient, he tossed her aside like she was nothing.' She exhaled. 'I can't begin to imagine what she went through. Losing the man she thought loved her. Her songs stolen. Believing her baby died at birth … only to find out years later he'd lived. She ran a DNA match and found him but then learned he'd already passed away. It's all just … heartbreaking.'

Daniel glanced over at her, the concern in his face growing. 'Did he give you anything? A name?'

Fern nodded. 'I asked for it. I just thought … maybe I could visit the grave. Let her know, somehow, that someone cared enough to remember him.'

Daniel's grip on her hand tightened.

'What was his name?' he asked.

'William Brooks.'

Daniel stopped walking.

'Say that again,' he urged.

She turned to face him, confused. 'William Brooks.'

Daniel's face went white. His mouth opened, but no sound came at first. Then, barely louder than a breath: 'That's my father's name.'

Chapter Fifty-One

The train clattered along the tracks, heading north, the sea flashing in and out between clumps of windswept trees and scrappy hedgerows. Fern sat across from Daniel, who hadn't said much since she had shared the name of Matilda's child. She didn't push him. 'This is us,' he said suddenly, standing up just as the train began to slow.

'This isn't our stop.'

'I know. Come on.' He didn't explain or even smile. Just added, 'Trust me.'

The platform was tiny, the station one of those blink-and-you'll-miss-it stops. There wasn't even a station building, just a shelter with a bench. Beyond that, a quiet lane wound towards the coast. They walked in silence along the lane for about fifteen minutes until he turned down a narrow track. At the end of it, nestled between two hills, was a house.

Fern stopped in her tracks. 'Oh … my … God. Look at that.'

The house looked like something out of a countryside romance film. Cream-coloured stone walls, ivy climbing all over, pale blue shutters, a front porch with a swing seat gently moving in the breeze, and a roof made of weathered slate tiles. The garden was wild but beautiful, lavender bushes, tall grasses, and daisies sprouting between the flagstones of the path.

'Okay, what is this place?' she asked.

Daniel looked towards the house before meeting her gaze. 'My family home, and now my home.'

Fern stared at him. 'This is yours? And you're living at the antique shop?'

He gave a small, sheepish shrug. 'Yes, I couldn't face it.'

'Daniel ... it's stunning.'

He took her hand. 'I might need you to hold me up.'

'I'm here for you,' she reassured as they headed towards the door.

The inside of the house was somehow even better. Not fancy or grand, just ... warm. The hallway with scuffed wooden floors and a slightly lopsided coat rack showed the house had been lived in. Had been loved. Photos lined the hallway walls, images of holidays, birthdays, and one of a very serious-looking Daniel in a school blazer and a mullet haircut that should've been illegal. Fern pointed then chuckled softly.

'Don't laugh. It was the fashion!'

'Was it though?' She gently nudged his arm.

They moved into the sitting room, where time felt like it had paused. Cushions were slightly squashed on the sofa. A stack of books sat haphazardly on a side table. A teacup had been left on the windowsill as though someone had meant to come back for it but forgotten. The fireplace was grand and a bit dusty, with a painting of a lighthouse hanging above it.

Fern turned slowly on the spot. 'This place feels ... alive. Like your parents just popped out to get milk.'

Daniel gave a half-laugh. 'I lived here with my grandmother after they passed away, but I know what you mean. That's why I couldn't deal with it. It felt like if I came back, everyone would really be gone.' He paused. 'I do know my father knew he was adopted, but it didn't seem to affect him in any way. He had a happy life, and my grandmother was just the best mum to him, but now... Knowing he was the son of Nathaniel Loring? I'm not sure how he would have reacted to that.'

'I can relate to your father.' Fern wanted to say something that might help, or at least make him feel less alone, and this felt like the right moment to share something she'd never really talked about. 'I've never told anyone this,' she said, 'but ... I'm adopted, too.'

Daniel looked up, surprise flickering across his face. 'Really, how do you feel about that?'

'It's not something I've consciously hidden from people in my life, it's just... I never felt like I needed to linger on it or talk about it. My childhood was amazing. I had the kind of parents who were always in my corner, no matter what. School play? They were always in the front row. Big dreams? They backed every single one. They made everything feel possible. They sat me down at an early age to tell me about my origins, but it didn't change a thing. It just made me feel all the more special, the fact that they had chosen me and they loved me. I don't feel the need to look for my birth parents, and I'm not angry at them or curious about them. I've never felt like anything was missing from my life.'

She looked at Daniel now, really looked at him. 'I'm only

telling you this because maybe your dad felt like that too. Maybe he didn't feel like something was missing, because he was happy, because he had a good life. That's something to hold on to.'

'Thank you,' he said quietly, 'for telling me.'

He pointed to the door in front of him. 'This is my dad's study. Let's see what we can find,' he said, his tone upbeat, as though he knew they both needed the reset after such an emotional confession.

It was everything you'd expect from a proper old-school study. Walnut desk, deep armchair, bookshelves bursting at the seams, and one of those globes that opened up to reveal drinks inside. There was a fire grate and a threadbare rug, and even a little brass telescope pointing out the window.

'This room hasn't been touched since his passing. I can remember he basically lived in here,' Daniel said. 'He often joked that this was where he came to think, but what he meant was to avoid doing the washing-up.'

Fern smiled. 'Wise man.'

Daniel walked over to the desk and rested his hand on it. 'Before she passed away, Grandma told me that there was a box in the desk. Full of my dad's personal stuff.'

He started pulling open the drawers. The first two had the usual desk junk: paperclips, old pens, about four different types of envelopes. The third was locked. Daniel scanned the bookshelves, then suddenly reached up and took a small brass key from a small plate on one of the shelves. He unlocked the drawer. Inside was a wooden box. Daniel didn't open it right away. He just stared at it.

'I knew this was here, but I couldn't bring myself to...' he began before trailing into a contemplative silence.

Fern gently placed a hand on his shoulder. 'You don't have to open it now, if you're not ready,' she said. 'We can do whatever you want. It's your call.'

'Now Nathaniel has said the name William Brooks, I need to know. Because my gut feeling is telling me it's him, that my dad was Matilda's son. I've got so many things spinning around in my mind. Matilda said that shop was my destiny – at our very first meeting. Did she know then who I was? Is that why she took me in and looked out for me? She never told me, if she did know.'

'I think she could have known who you were, but we may never know for sure.'

'I think I need to know,' he said. 'Especially after today. If there's anything in this box about who he really was, where he came from, I want to see it.'

Fern nodded. 'Okay. Then I'm right here with you.'

He sat down at the desk, took a breath and lifted the lid.

Chapter Fifty-Two

Inside were just a few things: a folded-up baby blanket – soft, pale blue and worn thin with time – and an envelope addressed to 'William' in tidy, looping handwriting.

Daniel hesitated, fingers hovering over the letter. 'He opened it,' he murmured, taking the contents out of the envelope. There was a letter and another sealed envelope inside. The words were written in blue ink that had faded slightly, but were still perfectly legible.

My darling William,

We've talked about this before, I know. Many times. I remember each conversation so clearly; me asking if you were ever curious, and you, always so sure, saying, 'I've got everything I need, Mum.'

You never wanted to go looking, and I respected that. But I also made a promise to myself, just in case one day, after I was gone or you were just ready to know more, you'd have the information at your fingertips. So, if you've opened this letter, that day might have come.

I've enclosed a sealed envelope. This is for you to open when you are ready. As you know, your biological mother died during childbirth and I was never told your father's name, but there are two people who may hold the key to that mystery.

I need to preface this by saying that nothing will ever change the love your father and I shared for you every single day.

It's not a straightforward story, I'm afraid. The adoption wasn't done through the usual channels, but I swear to you, we never did anything with bad intentions. We loved you from the moment we saw you.

Your father and I were given a call one evening by someone we knew: Alistair Montgomery. You met him once when you were little, though I doubt you remember. He was a distant cousin on my mother's side, though we hadn't stayed close over the years. He and his friend, Nathaniel Loring, came to us in confidence.

They said a tragedy had happened. A young woman had died giving birth, and there was no one else; no family, no next of kin. They wanted the baby to go to someone who would raise him with love, in safety and privacy. They said they trusted me. That it had to stay quiet, that the child's legacy was going to possibly be complicated. We didn't go through the system. No paperwork. Just a private arrangement.

I think back now and wonder, Why me? Why not someone else? I think they believed I wouldn't ask too many questions and, for better or worse, I didn't. I saw you, and I couldn't imagine a life without you in it.

I know we have talked about you registering your DNA on different sites in the future to track down your biological father but I can share with you, your mother's name was Matilda Hartley.

You were – you are – my greatest joy. Nothing could ever change that.

With all my love,
Mum (Mabel)

By the time Daniel finished reading, his hands were visibly shaking.

'So that's how Alistair and Nathaniel managed to pass this off, by saying Matilda had died during childbirth. It's just lie after lie,' murmured Fern.

'So my grandmother told my father that his biological mum had passed away, and he went looking for his real father through a DNA website…'

'Which, we know, is how Matilda found out about him,' Fern finished.

'This is all so sad.'

Daniel looked down at the other envelope, then met Fern's gaze before he opened it.

Inside was a short note and a composition.

They also gave me this piece of music and said it was written by your mother, and that maybe, one day, you'd want to know who she was through her music. I remember holding it in my hands for the first time, thinking it was heartbreakingly beautiful when I played it on the piano. It's definitely in a class of its own.

Daniel looked at the title: 'Waiting for His Arrival: A New Chapter, for My Baby Boy'. He sat there in silence, the letter from Mabel still in his hand, the composition laying on the desk in front of them. Close to tears, Fern picked up the manuscript.

'Matilda wrote a song for her unborn baby … your father,' Fern said softly. 'Then she wrote "Echoes of the Past" when she thought she'd lost him.'

Daniel nodded. His eyes teemed with tears and he couldn't speak.

Fern glanced at the letter again. 'There's something I don't understand,' she added. 'Why would Alistair and Nathaniel give the composition to your grandmother? Does that mean … maybe, deep down, they felt conflicted? Guilty, even? Like they knew what they'd done was too awful to wipe Matilda away completely?'

Daniel let out a long breath. 'It's the only thing that makes sense. Maybe this was their twisted version of a conscience. A parting gift. Like they were trying to hang on to some shred of decency.

'I'm going to learn to play this,' he said, placing it carefully back in the envelope before pulling her in for a hug. They stayed wrapped up in each other's arms for a long while, neither of them wanting to move.

Finally, Fern pulled away slowly. 'Let's go home.'

'Home?' he quizzed.

'Our home. No. 17 Curiosity Lane.'

Chapter Fifty-Three

Fern stirred first, leaning across to switch off the alarm blaring from her phone. She stretched lazily, one leg tangled around Daniel's, her cheek resting against the soft cotton of his T-shirt. His arm was still tucked around her, heavy and warm, holding her close. She saw that his eyes were still shut, and smiled.

'You're awake,' she teased, prodding him a little.

'I am now,' he whispered, snuggling in tighter. 'But I don't want to move just yet.'

She kissed the top of his head. 'You stay there. I'll go and make you a coffee. You've made me one pretty much every single morning since I arrived here. It's time I returned the favour.'

'Wonders will never cease.'

She grinned, kissed his cheek and wriggled free from the duvet. Padding downstairs in one of his oversized T-shirts and her socks, she clicked on the kettle and, yawning, scooped generous spoons of instant coffee into their mismatched mugs. As she reached for the milk, there was a soft thud at the front door. When she went to check, she found the morning newspaper lying on the mat. She scooped it up and carried it upstairs along with the coffees.

Daniel sat up in bed, hair all tousled and wild. With a grateful grunt he reached for the mug she handed him, and she climbed back into the warm cocoon of the duvet beside him.

'Paper's here,' she said, tossing it onto his lap. 'I can't believe you still read the news the old-fashioned way.'

'My dad had a newspaper delivered every morning. Some things should never change.'

He unfolded it lazily, then stared. 'Look,' he murmured, nudging Fern.

'Mind the coffee!'

He nodded towards the headline that screamed back at them both in bold black letters.

Music Genius Nathaniel Loring Dies at 85

A glossy photo of Loring in his prime sat beneath it, the familiar one where he was all slick hair and smug charm, fingers splayed dramatically across piano keys.

'Well,' she said quietly, 'he's gone.'

Daniel let out a slow breath and set the paper on the bed beside him. For a moment, neither of them spoke.

Then Fern looked at him, her voice soft but sure. 'What do you want to do with all the information we've discovered?'

Daniel turned to face her, still very quiet. She tucked her legs beneath her and held the coffee between her hands.

'We can't do anything about Nathaniel's life now,' she said gently. 'But Alistair … he played a huge part in it all. He helped cover it all up.' She reached for the newspaper again, tapping Nathaniel's photo.

'He's your grandfather, and Matilda was your grandmother. She wrote those songs, so that inheritance, all of it, should have been your father's, and by rights it should now be yours.'

Daniel ran a hand through his hair, then let it drop, rubbing the back of his neck. 'God. It's so much. A week ago I was just a singing antique salesman with a weird obsession for moose heads and stuffed gorillas.'

Fern laughed. 'And now?'

'Now I'm apparently the grandson of one of the greatest songwriters the world never got to know, and the grandson of one of the most famous musicians, who is about to be exposed as a fraud.'

He leaned back against the headboard, warming his hands on the coffee mug. 'I don't want the money,' he said. 'That's not what this is about. It's not about some inheritance.'

'I know,' Fern said softly. 'It's about the truth.'

'Exactly.' He looked over at her. 'Matilda deserves her name back. Her music. Her story.'

They sat for a long moment, just letting it all sink in.

Fern finally said, 'Whatever you decide, I'm with you. We'll do this together.'

He reached for her hand, tangled their fingers. 'Then maybe it's time the world found out who Matilda Hartley really was, and the lie that was Nathaniel Loring.'

'You know what I can't quite believe?'

'What's that?'

'Considering your bloodline, you're rubbish at reading music.'

He laughed. 'That's something I intend to put right.' He smiled that slow, honest smile she was beginning to fall completely in love with.

Epilogue

Twelve months had flown by since the truth finally came out, and when it did, it was like a tidal wave. The story had exploded across national headlines and spilled over into the global spotlight. Puffin Island had gone from sleepy seaside haven to the centre of a media whirlwind, and No. 17 Curiosity Lane was now officially world famous. Music lovers, journalists and antique hunters all came in droves to see the little shop that had changed music history.

Everything was different now. Nathaniel Loring, once hailed as a national treasure, had been stripped of his glory and exposed for the fraud he truly was. Meanwhile, Matilda Hartley, whose voice had been silenced for so long, was finally being celebrated. Even though she was no longer here to see it, the world had caught up. Matilda had become an icon in her own right, her name etched into the heart of music history where it had always belonged.

No. 17 Curiosity Lane had undergone a transformation. The once tired old antique shop now boasted sparkling new windows, a fresh coat of paint and a deep green wooden door with a brand-new sign swinging gently above it. Fern had transformed right alongside it. She'd stayed in her old job just long enough to write the article, the one that finally exposed the truth about Nathaniel Loring and the slippery dealings of his agent Alistair Montgomery. It made headlines around the world, ruffled all the right feathers and gave Fern exactly the closure she needed. After that, she handed in her notice. Journalism had served its purpose for her.

Now, she worked alongside Daniel in No. 17 Curiosity Lane, buying and selling antiques, dusting off forgotten treasures, learning the difference between a chamber pot and a vase (the hard way) and arguing over where to display a particularly questionable stuffed ferret. Life was slower and sweeter. For the first time in ages, Fern wasn't chasing a story. She was part of one.

Tonight, the doors of the shop were wide open, and the entire community had turned out for a party like no other. Fairy lights had been strung from one side of the street to the other and glowed like fireflies as laughter echoed in the air. Fern, in a bright floral dress and white trainers, stood proudly in the doorway, Daniel's hand tucked firmly in hers.

'Everyone!' she shouted over the buzz of excitement. 'Shush now, we're nearly at number one!'

People giggled and hushed each other. Glasses of prosecco were passed around. Clemmie and Betty had laid out a full street buffet, with sausage rolls, fairy cakes, mini quiches and jelly in plastic cups. Amelia and Dilly were weaving through the crowd, handing out cups of fizz and lemonade.

Edgar and Dorothy stood beside Fern and Daniel, beaming. 'I wish Matilda was here to see this,' said Dorothy.

'She never missed a good party. She'll be smiling down on us.' Edgar looked up at the sky and Fern could have sworn she saw a tear in his eye.

'I have to ask, something that's been on my mind. Why did Matilda call this place No.17 Curiosity Lane? Fern asked.

'Because when she first put the shop together, she filled it with curiosities, antiques, oddities, little treasures she couldn't resist. And then there's the location: the building backs onto a quiet, unnamed alley that reminded her of the hidden places she used to slip away to after her fall from the music world, little pockets full of silence, stories and second chances. The "17" came from the practice room she'd spent hours in as a student – Room 17 – the place where she still remembered what it felt like to believe in beginnings,' replied Edgar.

Just then from the speaker in the doorway, the live chart show was blasting. The DJ's voice rang out: 'At number two this week, after a phenomenal climb, it's Lust Theory with "Marriage Breakdown".'

Fern grinned and leaned over to Daniel. 'Looks like Jax is going to have to settle for silver and a divorce.'

Daniel chuckled, brushing a kiss against her temple.

'Which means,' the DJ continued, 'your brand-new number one … it's Daniel Brooks with "A New Chapter", written by Matilda Hartley! I think we all must know the story behind this song. Congratulations to Daniel on his debut number one and don't miss the show next Thursday when he joins us live in the studio.'

The crowd erupted and applause and cheers broke out up and down the street. 'Huge congratulations to Daniel, number one in the charts! This is for Matilda, too!' Fern shouted. 'Her story. Her legacy. Her music!'

Tears filled her eyes, and Daniel's too. They weren't just celebrating a song. They were celebrating a woman who had been silenced and stolen from, and now finally, the world knew the truth.

Over the past year, the Nathaniel Loring scandal had become one of the biggest ever to hit the music industry. Loring's money and assets had been frozen during the lengthy investigation, and Alistair had disappeared from public life.

Despite the chaos, Daniel had made a decision. 'If anything ever comes from this, if we do get any of Nathaniel's inheritance,' he had told Fern, months earlier, 'I want to build something good from it. Something Matilda would be proud of.'

They'd agreed to open a music school in Matilda Hartley's name, right here on Puffin Island.

For the past six months, Daniel had thrown himself into learning the piano, often spending hours in the back room of the shop. He'd never imagined himself performing publicly, but then a record label had approached him with a dream offer, to release one of Matilda's songs, and he chose the one she had written for his father.

He sang it simply, just his voice and the piano, and something about it had captured hearts around the world.

'I'm actually at number one,' he exclaimed, picking up Fern and spinning her around. 'We need champagne!'

The song began to play over the speakers, and the crowd went quiet.

Fern looked up at him. 'I'm so proud of you.'

Daniel blinked back tears. 'Thank you. I'm proud of you, too.'

After the final notes faded, the applause came again, louder this time, and the celebrations carried on. 'Just before I get the champagne, I have one last surprise for you. Wait here.'

She left Daniel wondering where she was disappearing to. He burst into laughter when she returned – holding Gerald the Gorilla. 'I couldn't let him go. He's worth more than a hundred quid, he's family!' she claimed, sitting him in a nearby chair.

Daniel grinned, pulling her into his arms. They stood in the doorway of No. 17 Curiosity Lane, the little shop that had once held so many secrets, and now so much promise, and they watched the people they loved celebrating not just them but everything they'd uncovered, everything they'd reclaimed, everything they'd rebuilt.

There was Amelia from The Story Shop, waving a homemade banner with one hand and holding a glass of fizz in the other, shouting something joyful and completely unintelligible. Becca from the Cosy Kettle was dancing with a cupcake in each hand, while Clemmie and Betty from The Café on the Coast had taken it one step further, linking arms and waltzing in the middle of the street. Betty's apron was flapping in the breeze and Clemmie was laughing so hard she nearly dropped her wine.

Dilly from the lighthouse had brought sparklers and was trying to light them despite the sea breeze, while veterinary wizard Verity had tears in her eyes and her arms around Sam, her partner and the chef genius behind the Sea Glass Restaurant, who was already planning a celebratory tasting menu in Daniel's honour.

And of course, Puffin-loving Pete, in his usual knitted jumper and an expression of quiet pride, stood off to the side with a beer in hand and a camera slung round his neck, ready to capture the moment for posterity.

Fern looked at them all, this warm, wonderful group of people she hadn't known just a year ago, and now couldn't imagine life without. They weren't just neighbours. They were her people.

'This…' Fern whispered, resting her head against his shoulder, 'this feels like forever.'

He kissed the top of her head. 'That's because it is.'

The sign above them swung gently in the breeze, catching the golden glow of the fairy lights strung across the street. Children danced on the cobbles, neighbours toasted with prosecco, and Gerald the Gorilla was now wearing a party hat and being fussed over like royalty.

Together, Fern and Daniel had turned heartbreak into hope, secrets into truth and music into something magical once more. A new chapter had truly begun, not just for the shop, or the island, or the story of a song that had been stolen, but for them and their future.

From the very first time she'd stepped through the creaky old door of No. 17 Curiosity Lane, Fern realised, she had known in her heart: this was exactly where she was meant to be.

Acknowledgments

Dear Readers,

This book was inspired by my fascination with antique shops. I can never walk past an antique shop without going in, and my ramshackle cottage is crammed with treasures from the past, each one carrying its own little piece of history.

There's a long list of wonderful folk I need to thank, and since *No. 17 Curiosity Lane* is inspired by my love of antiques, I thought I'd liken each of them to a little item you might find tucked away on a dusty old shelf in an old curiosity shop…

First, to Charlotte Ledger, the captain of the One More Chapter ship and my boss – you're the sturdy old compass that always points me in the right direction and the skilled hand who turns my stories into books.

To Laura McCallen, my wonderful editor – you're the magnifying glass of the shop, spotting the tiniest details others might miss and making everything shine that little bit brighter.

To Helen Williams, who so brilliantly oversees everything to get the book published – you're the gleaming shop bell above the door, ensuring everything runs smoothly and welcoming each new story safely into the world.

To Tony Russell, my eagle-eyed copy editor, is the polished pocket watch that always keeps me running on time and makes sure the words tick just right.

To my four children, Emily, Jack, Ruby and Tilly – you are the most precious family heirlooms, unique and irreplaceable.

To my dogs, Nellie and Cooper – my faithful companions, like the scruffy but much-loved teddy bears every antique shop secretly hides.

To my best friend Anita Redfern – the trusted key that always unlocks the right door.

To my good friend Julie Wetherill – the well-worn armchair, a place of comfort and laughter I can always fall into.

And finally, to all the wonderful readers, librarians, bloggers and bookshops – you are the treasure hunters, the ones who pick up each story, dust it off, and give it a new life. Without you, these shelves would be empty.

If you enjoyed *No. 17 Curiosity Lane* and loved Fern and Daniel's story, do let me know! Nothing makes me happier than hearing which characters and tales have stayed with you.

Warmest wishes,

Christie x

DON'T MISS MORE UNFORGETTABLE ROMANCES FROM PUFFIN ISLAND

Is there anything more tempting than a good book?

When travel writer Jack Hartwell arrives on Puffin Island amidst a terrible storm, he stumbles into The Story Shop, the island's quaint bookshop.

Seeking refuge, he finds himself immersed in Amelia Brown's enchanting world of books, puffins, and an eccentric group of book club regulars. So when the enigmatic Amelia challenges Jack to read a mysterious novel *The Temptation Bucket List* – and to complete its challenges with her – he can't resist.

With Jack's time on Puffin Island ticking away, the stakes rise. The final item on the list? To share a secret no one else knows…

AVAILABLE IN PAPERBACK, EBOOK AND AUDIO!

Can a cake change your life?

Clemmie Rose's great-great-grandmother's beloved clementine torte is her ticket to the prestigious Royal Baking Competition. A win could put Puffin Island's charming Café on the Coast on the map, land Clemmie her very own cookbook deal, and secure her a coveted invitation to a royal garden party.

But when she discovers the competition is being hosted aboard the Royal Yacht by none other than her ex, Oliver Lockwood, the stakes – and the soufflés –suddenly rise, and Clemmie's bid for the Golden Whisk trophy is at risk of collapsing like an underbaked sponge.

When a decades-old secret is thrown into the mix, she'll need more than the perfect recipe to keep her dreams from crumbling.

AVAILABLE IN PAPERBACK, EBOOK AND AUDIO!

ONE MORE CHAPTER

One More Chapter is an award-winning global division of HarperCollins.

Subscribe to our newsletter to get our latest eBook deals and stay up to date with all our new releases!

signup.harpercollins.co.uk/
join/signup-omc

Meet the team at
www.onemorechapter.com

Follow us!

@onemorechapterhc

Do you write unputdownable fiction?
We love to hear from new voices.
Find out how to submit your novel at
www.onemorechapter.com/submissions

The author and One More Chapter would like to thank everyone who contributed to the publication of this story...

Analytics
Imogen Wolstencroft

Audio
Fionnuala Barrett
Ciara Briggs

Design
Lucy Bennett
Fiona Greenway
Liane Payne
Dean Russell

Digital Sales
Laura Daley
Lydia Grainge
Hannah Lismore

eCommerce
Laura Carpenter
Madeline ODonovan
Charlotte Stevens
Christina Storey
Rachel Ward

Editorial
Rosie Best
Kara Daniel
Catherine Jackson
Charlotte Ledger
Laura McCallen
Jennie Rothwell
Tony Russell
Sofia Salazar Studer
Helen Williams

Harper360
Emily Gerbner
Ariana Juarez
Jean Marie Kelly
emma sullivan
Sophia Wilhelm

International Sales
Ruth Burrow
Bethan Moore
Colleen Simpson

Inventory
Sarah Callaghan
Kirsty Norman

Marketing & Publicity
Chloe Cummings
Grace Edwards
Katie Sadler

Operations
Melissa Okusanya

Production
Denis Manson
Simon Moore
Francesca Tuzzeo

Rights
Ashton Mucha
Alisah Saghir
Zoe Shine
Aisling Smyth

Trade Marketing
Ben Hurd
Eleanor Slater

The HarperCollins Contracts Team

The HarperCollins Distribution Team

The HarperCollins Finance & Royalties Team

The HarperCollins Legal Team

The HarperCollins Technology Team

UK Sales
Isabel Coburn
Jay Cochrane
Leah Woods

And every other essential link in the chain from delivery drivers to booksellers to librarians and beyond!